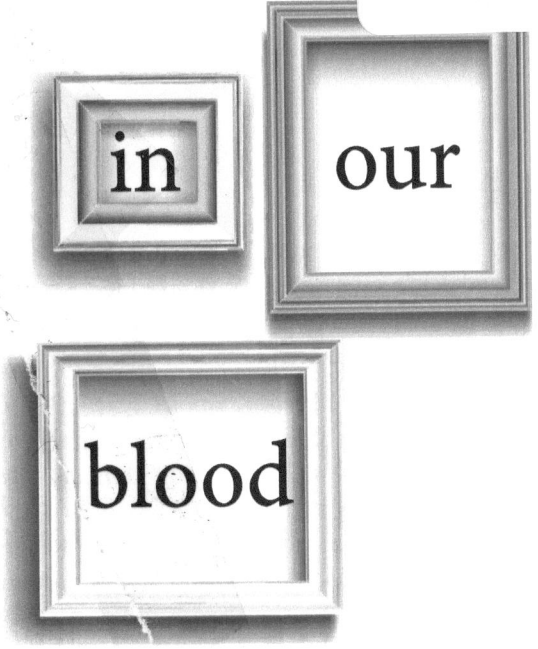

in our

blood

Kellyn Liston

Published by Mirror K Books
Cover and Interior Page Design: James Knake

mirror K books

Sarasota, Florida

ISBN: 979-8-9945544-1-8

Library of Congress: 2026901611

Printed: January 2026

For JJ — you've always been my why

For MH — thank you for waiting

And for all survivors — you are seen and heard and believed

In loving memory of my mom,
Reverend Kathie Iris Kuhn
October 14, 1947 - September 23, 2022
The original badass

PART ONE
Prior

Words are tangible things
Changing molecules
Charging the air
Spinning around heads
Lighting on skin
Settling onto shoulders
Burrowing into brains
Words have power
Like the mightiest sword
Like the gentlest breeze
Like cotton candy on tongues
Like acid in ears
Words have energy
Lifting our spirits
Renewing our faith
Slicing our psyches
Marring our souls
Words are indelible
And hearts are delicate
Let them be caresses, not scalpels

Chapter One — 1996 — Kimberly

"What's that supposed to mean, Sabrina?" Kimberly pressed the sticky pay phone receiver to her ear, bringing a menthol cigarette to her lips, and flicking ashes onto the sidewalk. She'd decided before making the call that this was her last shot. Requesting to stay in her sister's luxurious home was a big ask. Even bigger than Sabrina could know. If she said no, Kimberly was out of options.

"Just what I said, Kimberly. I don't appreciate you assuming we can support you and your child."

Kimberly's Converse-clad foot rested on the wheel of her daughter's stroller, slowly rocking it back and forth. "But that's not what I—"

"Bottom line, Grey and I are unable to have you stay here."

"Unable or unwilling?"

Sabrina sighed. "Did you talk to Jesse and Taylor?" Kimberly's lack of response gave Sabrina her answer. "That's what I thought. Listen. You're nearly thirty years old. Don't you think it's time you got your shit together? If not for you, at least for Julie? Look, Kim. Maybe if you're left to figure it out on your own rather than getting bailed out every time you reverse-charge a phone call, you might start to grow up a little."

"But that's not—you don't actually—what gave you that impression about me? Let me guess . . . Mom."

The silence on the other end of the line was palpable.

The last conversation between Kimberly and her mother had been ugly. It had left Kimberly wondering why she'd ever gotten back in touch with her family after so many years. Now she realized it had been a colossally bad idea.

"Sabrina, she lies. Whatever she told you, she's lying. I never asked her for a thing! You know this—it's just what she does!"

"Kim, I just can't welcome any drama into my life right now. Things are really good for me. It just wouldn't work. You're smart—you'll figure it all out."

"Brie, you don't unders—," she began and heard the buzz of a dial tone.

Kimberly's hand shook as she took the last hit, threw the butt to the ground, and smeared it out with the toe of her sneaker. Tears pooled in her eyes, one slipping loose and sliding down her weary face, where it rested in the corner of her mouth, salty. She muttered a sad, quiet 'okay' as she hung the receiver back on its paint-chipped cradle.

She closed her eyes and leaned her forehead against the metal box that held the phone. The smell of cheap Chinese food and vehicle exhaust permeated the air. Impatient drivers honked as the stoplights changed from red to green. A car radio blared a hip hop ballad "See you at the crossroads—you won't be lonely."

I'll always be lonely. None of them get me. Not even my own sister.

Wiping her runny nose with a tattered cuff of her gray sweatshirt, she adjusted the baby blankets around her sleeping daughter, tugging her tiny knit cap down to cover the tops of her ears. She pushed the stroller down the sidewalk to the convenience store, carefully maneuvering it over the threshold of the door. The air inside smelled of all-day roller-cooked hotdogs. At the back of the store, she opened a cooler door and lifted out a six-pack of beer.

Pocketing the few coins returned from the cashier, Kimberly made her way home, passing the pay phone, where underneath lay the pieces of her broken heart.

She arrived at the rundown brick building that housed four small apartments. The maintenance man sat in an old, brown resin chair in front of his door.

Whispering "Hi, Mr. García," Kimberly motioned to the sleeping baby. He smiled and winked at her, raising a finger to his lips. She picked up the stroller by the front bar and back handle, and carried it up the rusty iron stairs to her unit. Unlocking the front door, she rolled Julie into the tiny room they shared and quietly pulled the bedroom door closed behind her. She removed a can and placed the rest of the six-pack in the fridge, careful to step around a peeling corner of the warped vinyl flooring.

She took a long look around the living room. She saw the old rust and black plaid sofa she'd tried to make presentable by covering it with a blanket, the matching chair that was now draped with a beach towel to conceal holes and stains, the upside-down milk crates serving as tables that she'd lifted from behind the convenience store, the letters on top of a milk crate threatening eviction for late rent, and the one from her primary care physician requesting she make an appointment to discuss treatment.

Kimberly popped the top of the can in her hand, savoring that first foamy, cold sip, and opened the front door. She sat cross-legged on the concrete walk leaning her tired back against the door and lit a cigarette, taking a long draw. She sipped the beer. She could do this. It wouldn't be hard. Early in her life, Kimberly had believed she could do anything she set her mind to. Although it had been a long time coming, she'd definitely set her mind this time. She knew this was it. The best decision she'd ever made. Her family would no longer be ashamed of her. Everyone would soon forget about her. She'd finally be able to rest. To not feel so full of anxiety and fear every moment of her life. Failure and guilt and shame . . . all of that would go away. A grim smile creased her face and she closed her eyes.

Chapter Two — 1996 — Sabrina

Sabrina hung up the phone and sighed. She felt like an ogre. A sad, frustrated ogre. She had agreed with her mother to show Kimberly supposed 'tough love,' but now she was questioning why she'd ever gone along with her mother on anything. Sabrina wanted to reach out through the phone and hug her sister. To hold her close and tell her everything was going to be okay, the way Kimberly used to with her when they were small. But to do so would have caused a brand new rift between Sabrina and her mother, and she was just unable to go there.

Unable or unwilling?

"Both," Sabrina mumbled.

"What's that?" Grey asked. Standing at the bar cart facing floor-to-ceiling windows, his dark, wavy hair sprinkled with silver reflecting in the glass, he made their apéritifs—dirty gin martini for her, single malt scotch for him. From the 30th floor of The Floribbean Tower, the bay spread out before them in all its dazzling splendor. He turned to his wife, who was curled into the corner of the white sectional, her raven hair a striking contrast.

"Just thinking out loud," she said.

Grey crossed the room. Before he handed her the icy cocktail, he met her eyes and raised his eyebrows in a question. She shook her head no.

"Negative again," she said, reaching up to take the glass. Grey lifted her chin with his thumb and forefinger, then smoothed her black, silky bangs away from her forehead.

"It'll happen, honey. When it's meant to." She nodded quietly in agreement. "Let's move outside for sunset tonight."

They settled onto matching chaise lounges and soaked in the warm evening sun. "You were on the phone when I came home. Sounded like your sister? What drama has she gotten mixed up in this time? Or was she just calling with her hand out?"

Sabrina leveled her eyes at him. His unappreciated comment necessitated a breath before she spoke.

"I know I agreed with my mom that we wouldn't enable her, but she's barely been back in our lives. That conversation just now was really hard. I feel like a demon. I don't know that she deserves that, Grey. And what about little Jules? My heart just breaks. Isn't there something we could do? Maybe we can help them anonymously or something? I don't know . . . " she trailed off, lost in thought.

"I have to agree with your mom this time, Brie. Every time she gets in a jam, usually due to her own poor choices, someone in your family takes care of her."

"Well, that's what family does. Besides, we don't even know that for sure. It's just what Mom's been saying."

"If it's true, it's not doing her any favors. Just like rewarding an animal who misbehaves, they simply continue in their unsavory habits."

"I'm sorry, did you just compare my sister to an animal?" Sabrina said, her eyes flashing.

Grey sighed. "No, Sabrina, it's just an analogy. All I am saying is that you made the right decision."

"Then why do I feel so lousy?" She took a soothing sip of her cocktail, feeling the warmth spread through her belly. *Someday I'll feel life growing in there instead.* "Enough about me. How was your day? Were you able to lock down the Clifton contract?"

Grey Hanover was an entertainment attorney. He and his partner, Charlotte Richardson, formed their boutique firm soon after graduating from University of Miami School of Law. The most recent feather in their cap was being retained by the rapper turned mogul, Jimmy Clifton, aka C-Note. He and his entourage recently moved from Dallas to Miami, where he'd been referred to the Richardson Hanover firm.

Grey took a sip of amber liquid, his ice-blue eyes on the setting sun. "Almost. Just a few more wrinkles to iron out and we'll officially be C-Note's Miami representation. Quite a victory for us. How was your day? Anything new at the gym?"

Sabrina was co-owner of an exclusive Pilates gym, walking

distance from their condo in downtown Miami. Charlotte had been one of Sabrina's earliest clients and they'd become fast friends. Knowing Grey's taste in women ran toward slender brunettes, Charlotte invited Sabrina to a cocktail party celebrating the opening of the firm. She'd introduced Grey to Sabrina and let nature take its course. Two years later, they'd asked her to be maid of honor in their intimate wedding.

"Not really. Same clients, different day. Sorry, but I just can't shake this guilt, Grey. I really feel like we need to help Kimberly."

Grey set his drink on a small glass table between the chairs and reached for her hand, brushing her fingers with his thumb. "Brie, I know your heart and I know you want to help her, but the best way to do that right now is to leave her alone. Let her figure it out. You've always told me she is the strongest person you know. Give her a chance to prove that to herself and everybody else."

"I guess you're right. She is strong, but her pattern has been to disappear when life gets hard. If things don't improve for her soon, I may need to defy my family and step in. I'm afraid of what she might do this time. She was always there for me growing up, Grey. It just feels wrong to do nothing."

Grey squeezed her hand and let it go. "From everything you've told me about her, I think she'll surprise everyone."

Chapter Three — 1973 — Kimberly

Jesse rolled his eyes and crossed his freckled, dusty-haired arms over his chest, scowling.

"Mom, why do we have to take her? She's a baby and a brat and no fun. C'mon! You said me and Kim could go spend our allowance at the Stop 'N' Go. You didn't say we had to take Brie. It's not fair!" Jesse kicked the baseboard by the back door for added emphasis.

"Young man, that's enough sass out of you. Would you like me to withhold your allowance for the next two weeks? And before you ask, no, that does not mean you don't have to do your chores. In fact, I may dream up some fun additions to your list, if you keep it up. Just maintain that attitude, big guy, and you'll see. Try me," Marjorie said. She raised one eyebrow and, with hands firmly on her hips, locked eyes with Jesse. Her eyes did this crazy-fast back and forth flicking motion when she was angry. It was unnerving. Kimberly had no idea how Jesse could plant his feet firmly in a stand-off with Mom with her eyes doing that thing. Kimberly always had to look away so she didn't get dizzy. Or giggle. That would have been a huge mistake.

As always, because he was only ten, Jesse caved first. He dropped his arms to his sides, and, with a sigh, said, "Fine. We'll take her. But if she has to go potty I am *not* handling that."

Marjorie stooped down to three-year-old Sabrina's eye level and asked, "Brie, do you have to go potty before you go with the bigger kids to the store?" Sabrina shook her head and reached out for her mommy's hand.

"You go with me, Mommy?"

"No, not this time. Mommy has to start dinner. You hold onto Jesse and Kimberly's hands and don't let go, okay?" She pulled Sabrina's dark, smooth hair up into a high ponytail and fastened it with an elastic band with purple plastic knocker balls on the ends.

Kimberly was not liking any part of this. She and Jesse never got to do things by themselves anymore. They always had to include 'the baby' every time. *If you're going out to the swing set, take the baby. If you guys are using Play-Doh, let the baby play.* And so on and so on. It was a total bummer. Brie was little and didn't understand the jokes they told, couldn't keep up with them when they raced each other, she couldn't even read yet! And what if they found something really cool on the way to the store like a bottle on the side of the road? They wouldn't be able to smash it because they had 'the baby.' This was no fun *at all*.

"Mom, I don't think Brie had her nap today, did she?" Kimberly offered.

Marjorie looked down at her seven-year-old daughter and said, "You let me worry about that, missy. Take the baby to the store or you two won't be going again this summer."

The three Stevens children set off on the four block trip to the small strip of stores along 62nd Avenue. Kimberly was already thinking that she may not want to get the giant Sweet Tarts again. Last time she got them, she wound up with a jillion tiny cuts on her tongue from the sour, sugary discs. Maybe she would get Now'N'Laters. The watermelon and apple flavors were the best. Hopefully, she would have enough allowance left over to get a couple of Tootsie Rolls or maybe a Blow Pop.

The late August morning was hot and muggy, heat rising in shimmery waves from the pavement, causing Kimberly's curls to stick to her neck. Flies and mosquitoes buzzed near their sweaty heads as they walked hand in hand along the gutter, tall weeds tickling their shins, making them itch. Flat, fuzzy hitchhikers from the weeds attached themselves to the cuffs of Kimberly's socks. She would need to remember to pull those off before putting the socks in the hamper or she would hear it from Mom.

Being the oldest, Jesse walked protectively along the street side, looking into the gutter for anything cool or interesting. So far, nothing but trash and pop tops from aluminum cans. Last summer, he and Kimberly had collected hundreds of pop tops on their way to and from the store and made super long chains that they decorated their room with, pretending it was Christmas. Mom freaked out and told them to take those dirty things down and throw them away. What were they crazy to bring those filthy things in the house? So, no more pop tops this year.

"I has to go potty."

"Brie, no. Mom already asked you and you said you didn't have to go."

"But I has to go now," Sabrina whined, swiping at tiny gnats around her face. Jesse and Kimberly looked at each other and rolled their eyes. Great. They *knew* this was going to happen. Now what? They were still about a block and a half from the store and the only place around was an overgrown lot to their left and a busy street to their right.

"Okay, listen, I'll take her into the weeds right there and I'll stand over her to block while she pees," said Kimberly.

"I don't gotta tinkle," said Sabrina.

"Ugh, dangit, Brie, really?" Jesse said. "It just figures. Shoot. What are we supposed to do about this?"

"Oh my gosh, I don't know," Kimberly said, looking for a place to take her sister. "Can you hold it till we get to the store, Brie?"

"Nooo, I gotta gooo . . ."

"Aw, man, this kinda crap always happens," Jesse said.

Kimberly giggled. "You said crap!"

"Yeah, very funny, moron. Maybe one of us can carry her and we'll run the rest of the way to the store. She can use the bathroom there."

"You mean you can carry her. She's way too heavy for me."

"Fine, jeez, you don't have to whine about it."

"I'm not whining!"

"Just shut up. I'll pick her up, but you have to keep up with me, okay?"

"Fine! I will!"

Jesse let Sabrina wrap her arms around his neck and he lifted her up onto his narrow hip. He lost his balance slightly and staggered a couple of steps into the street.

Kimberly hollered, "Car! Look out!" A car horn blared and all of them screamed.

Jesse jumped back into the grass, panting. "Sheesh, that was close. Come on, let's go!" They broke into a run for the store.

Chapter Four — 1996 — Kimberly

A car horn blared, jolting Kimberly awake. She groaned, her stiff legs and neck creaking. She had fallen asleep on the walk in front of her apartment. The setting sun allowed a chill to creep in on the February evening.

"Oh, shit, what time is it?"

Kimberly scrambled to her feet and threw open the front door to the muffled sound of Julie crying in her stroller in the bedroom.

"Oh, peanut, Mommy is so sorry. Here, come here, sweetheart. Shhhh, shhhh . . . " She scooped Julie out of the stroller and pulled her close. "Let's get you in the bath, sweet pea."Kimberly bathed Julie, combed out her sweet-smelling blonde ringlets, and changed her into fuzzy, feetie pajamas. She fed her bologna a American cheese cut up into bite sizes with some raisins for dessert. Refilling Julie's sippy cup with tap water, Kimberly lay her down in the playpen in their shared bedroom.

Hush a bye, don't you cry

Go to sleep, my little baby

When you wake you shall have

All the pretty little ponies . . .

"Mommy loves you, Jules. To Jupiter and back," she whispered to the sleeping little girl. She counted the number of Pull-Ups and diapers left beside her bed. Maybe enough for one more week.

Kimberly opened the top drawer of her cardboard mini-dresser, digging under socks and underwear, to locate her spiral notebook and pen. She took it to the living room, stopping at the fridge for another beer. Opening the drawer next to the fridge, she removed a roll of black electrical tape and a pair of scissors.

Taking the supplies with her to the living room, she set them down on the makeshift table. She knelt in front of the couch, feeling underneath for the strong metal box she knew was there. Unlocking it with a small key she kept on her keychain, she lifted out the item on top. It was a tin box that used to hold stationery from another lifetime ago, when Kimberly actually cared about corresponding with people.

She began to remove items one by one: Julie's hospital bracelet and birth announcement introducing Juliana Susanne Stevens. An envelope marked "Julie's first haircut," containing a baby-fine lock of blonde hair. Medals awarded to Petty Officer Second Class Aviation Life Support Technician Kimberly M. Stevens. Assorted photos and letters.

As she removed a stainless steel ball chain from the box, Kimberly wrapped the dangling ID tags in her fist to silence the tinkling. She smiled at a tender memory of finding a different set of dog tags inside that box the day it became hers many years ago.

At the bottom corner, in a small, deep red velvet box, sat the emerald and diamond ring that she'd never envisioned removing from her left hand. She gingerly lifted it out of the box and slipped it onto her ring finger. Even in the dim light of the crummy apartment, the two-carat oval cut emerald gave off sparkling fractals. Six tiny diamond baguettes on each side of the center stone twinkled, not wanting to be overlooked. She sighed. Another lifetime ago indeed.

She cut off a tiny piece of electrical tape and removed the small key from her keychain. Lifting the velvet insert out of the jewelry box, she carefully used her fingertips to tape the key to the underside. She smiled. Someday, Julie would figure it out. And then she would understand. Everything would be set in motion tomorrow. She prayed she would have the courage to go through with it.

Chapter Five — 1974 — Kimberly

The sun peeking through the gap under the Holly Hobby curtains in her bedroom window is what awoke Kimberly. But what made her sit straight up and break into a big, goofy grin was that it was Saturday. And it was her birthday. Eight years old today! She grabbed her covers tightly in her fists and held them up under her chin, squirming with excitement. This was the one day of the year she felt special. And this year was going to be even more special. Darci across the street had a birthday tomorrow, so her mom and Kimberly's mom had arranged a block party for all of the neighborhood kids today right out in the street and the Stevens' front yard.

Water balloons and a Slip 'n' Slide, hot dogs and Doritos, cake and ice cream, and everybody on the street was invited. Even that stupid Landon kid at the end of the block. That's okay, Kimberly didn't even have to pay him one bit of attention. Stupid boy.

Kimberly's feet barely hit the floor as she ran down the hall to the kitchen. Jesse stood in front of the open refrigerator door peering inside. Kimberly nudged underneath him to reach the milk.

"Wait your turn, idjit fidget," said Jesse, rubbing the sleep out of his eyes, his sandy hair sticking up at points all over his head.

"Hurry up, butthole." Kimberly backed up against the sink counter, arms crossed, foot tapping impatiently. Nothing was going to tick her off today. Not even that jerk-face brother of hers. Marjorie called out from the room Kimberly shared with Sabrina.

"Kimberly Marie, get in here!" *She heard me!* Kimberly's heart sped up and blood rushed to her ears. She felt her tummy roll as she walked back down the hall to her room, anticipating the spanking.

"Yes, ma'am?" She entered the room to see Marjorie standing in the center of the rug holding her nearly life-sized, stuffed Raggedy Ann doll in front of her body like an accusation. Her grandmother had the doll specially made for her last Christmas. It was as tall as Kimberly and had a real dress and apron and black shoes and white socks you could take off and put back on. Kimberly loved that doll.

"What happened here?" Marjorie asked. Kimberly stood stock still, not knowing what to expect, her heart pounding.

"What do you mean?"

"I *mean* . . . look at your doll. Do you see something amiss, young lady?" Marjorie held the doll out, away from her body, with both hands. Kimberly leaned in a little bit and squinted her eyes dramatically. She scanned the doll quickly, head to toe. She wasn't sure what her mother was talking about, until . . . gasp! . . . she saw it. One of the special glass button eyes was missing. A big blank spot existed where the eye no longer did. Raggedy Ann looked like an incomplete Mr. Potato Head.

"Oh my gosh, Mom, where did the eye go?" Kimberly asked.

"Well, if I knew that, missy, I wouldn't be in here asking you, now would I? Your grandmother had this doll custom made for you. This is an *expensive* doll. I cannot easily replace these glass buttons." Kimberly's pounding heart sank into her stomach.

"But, Mom, I am always so careful with her. I promise it wasn't me!"

"Sure, Kimberly. Get started combing this room for that button so I can sew it back on. You will not leave this room until it's found, do you understand me?" Marjorie said, her eyes twitching and flicking.

"Yes, ma'am." Kimberly ran to her bed, frantically flipping covers and pillows all over the place. It had to be here somewhere. Raggedy Ann spent every day in the middle of her nubby, white chenille bedspread resting up against the pillows with pink cases. The doll only came off the bed to sit in Kimberly's baby rocking chair at night while she slept, because Mom said she was too special and expensive a doll to sleep with. Kimberly was always so very careful with her. Where could the stupid eye be? She could not believe this was happening to her. Not today of all days!

Kimberly slowed down and took a breath. She would need to make a plan if she was going to find one loose button in that room full of toys and books and stuffed animals. She decided to start in the furthest corner on her side of the room and work her way along each of the walls, looking under the beds and the toy box, even under the dresser. It had to be here!

She had searched about a quarter of the room when her belly

started to growl. She hadn't had breakfast yet. But she knew Mom was serious. Mom was always serious. Visions of the last spanking she received flashed through her mind. If she didn't find that button, she definitely wasn't leaving her room. She backed out from under her bed, brushed dust bunnies off of her shirt and kept looking.

About an hour later, Jesse came into the room wearing a t-shirt, his bathing suit, and flip-flops. He had a beach towel around his neck and sunglasses on.

"Hey, Charlie and I are gonna go help Dad set up the pool and the Slip'N'Slide. Hurry up so you can help. It's your dang birthday, not mine," Jesse said. Kimberly looked up with desperation in her eyes.

"I can't find it! I have looked everywhere and I can't find it anywhere and it doesn't make any sense because I never take her out of the room and I never play with her 'cept really gentle and I don't even sleep with her! I can't find it and Mom won't let me leave the room until I do!" Kimberly was hiccuping and gasping between words.

"Wait, what? What's missing?" Jesse asked.

"Raggedy Ann's *eye!*"

Jesse paused for a second. He took off the towel and sunglasses, lay them on the bed, and got down on his hands and knees.

It wasn't long before their dad came in the house hollering.

"Jesse! I thought you were coming out to help set up. Where are you?" Jack said.

"In here! Kim and Brie's room. We're looking for the stupid eye from her dumb doll and Mom says she can't leave the room until she finds it."

"What? Oh for Pete's sake. Marjorie, what's going on?"

Their mom and dad bickered in the kitchen, part of it reaching their ears: *Are you serious? . . . birthday!* And . . . *will never learn to take care of her things unless,* and . . . *be consistent with punishment or it's completely ineffective,* and . . . *let me do this my way—I don't interfere with Jesse* and . . . *good things are earned not just given . . . doesn't deserve . . .*

Jack appeared in the doorway to the room. "Come on, Jesse, I need your help outside. Kimberly will find the button. Darci's parents are already outside and the other kids will be showing up soon. Kim, keep looking, you'll find it."

Jesse looked at Kimberly. Her lower lip quivered. He patted her on the shoulder. "You got this, Kimmy. We'll see you outside in a few minutes." He and her dad disappeared from view in the hallway. Putting her face into her hands, Kimberly quietly cried. She lay down on the floor and curled into a ball. She knew she was never going to find that glass button. Mom never, ever backed down from a punishment. She was going to miss her own party. And nobody had even wished her a happy birthday.

***

The evening was quiet in the Stevens house. The family had enjoyed the block party—neighborhood parents all sitting together in lawn chairs and sunglasses, kids playing and screaming and getting soaked with water games until it was time to pack everything up around dinner time. All of the kids except the birthday girl, who stayed in her bed, inconsolable, and Marjorie, who sat on the sofa in the living room, crocheting an afghan, looking at the festivities through the picture window. She'd instructed Jack to excuse Kimberly with a 'bad tummy,' should anyone ask.

While washing dinner dishes, Marjorie explained in a low voice that she knew she'd made the right decision. That Kimberly had definitely learned her lesson in taking care of her things this time. That she would be damned if she was going to raise an ungrateful brat. And that if she was remorseful tomorrow, Marjorie would give Kimberly her birthday packages. Jack listened without comment, dried the dinner plates, and sipped Crown Royal on ice.

With the last of the dishes put away and the kitchen floor swept, Marjorie stepped outside to take their black Labrador retriever, Spooky, out to do his business in the back yard while she smoked a cigarette. Donning a Playtex rubber glove and pulling a paper sack from her pocket, she screwed up her nose and bent down to scoop up the pile he'd left. And there, sticking out of the still warm mass, was a formerly shiny, black glass button.

Chapter Six — 1979 — The Family

Jack and Marjorie always wanted to take their family on a real vacation. Somewhere like Disney World, or a cabin in the mountains, or a little cottage on the beach. They even considered a cross country road trip in an RV to the Grand Canyon, visiting various national parks along the way. But every year, money was tight, and Jack had only two weeks of paid vacation from his position as a district manager for Eckerd Drug.

So, twice a year, they loaded up the station wagon with their three-room tent, a Coleman stove and lantern, coolers full of food and beverages, and Spooky. Together they headed to Fort DeSoto Park, just a short thirty minutes down the road from their new home in Clearwater, to go camping for a week. Days were spent on the beach and playground, or in rented kayaks tooling around in the bay. Marjorie spent most of her time preparing meals and keeping the campsite sufficiently tidy. While the kids were off on adventures with Jack, she would get lost in a paperback and a refreshing cocktail on a hammock, one eye peeled for their return. After dinner dishes were done, some nights they would gather in the middle room of the tent to play games of cards or Yahtzee.

Some of the same local families came to Fort DeSoto every year and the Stevens family would make a point to gather with them around each other's campfires at night. Jack had a beautiful baritone singing voice and fiddled a bit on the acoustic guitar, which was always a treat, since he only played around campfires and Christmas trees these days. Folks would sing along, providing makeshift drum beats on laps and logs. There never seemed to be a shortage of beer and soda with coolers constantly stocked. As the nights got later, and the hard liquor would emerge, it wouldn't take long for Jack's fingers to get sore from playing, for his smile to fade. And for him allow the salty barbs from his wife to trigger him as only she could. Marjorie usually knew better than to engage him during these moments. Usually.

Except when Marjorie had a bit of a heavy hand pouring her afternoon cocktail, glass of dinner wine, or night cap, and the filters fell away. And those nights didn't end so well.

Three nights into an eight-night stay during the kids' spring break, the campfire was popping and beginning to dwindle at the Stevens site. It was thirteen-year-old Kimberly's first attempt at building a fire without help and had burned successfully for a couple of hours. She sat close, stoking the embers with a heavy branch.

The night was a fairly cool fifty-eight degrees. The kids were huddled in hooded sweatshirts, their hands and faces sticky from gooey s'mores. Two other local families had joined them for music and conversation and were beginning to pack up chairs and go back to their campsites for the night. Jack had just finished playing "Joy to the World" by Three Dog Night, let go of the neck of the guitar, and began flexing the muscles in his left hand. The old guitar callouses he had as a younger man no longer dotted his fingertips. He was a middle-aged, white collar businessman with a family of five and more debt than income. Marjorie had been needling him a week about buying a new car. Although present in body in front of the fire, he was somewhere up in his head. He tossed a shot of Crown Royal from a flask down his throat, and lifted his Miller Lite longneck from the ground by his camp chair, wiping the sandy bottom of the bottle on his jeans. Flicking his Zippo and clinked it shut, he squinted against the cigarette smoke curling into his eyes. Marjorie leaned toward him, and in a slurry stage whisper said, "Maybe stick to the softer stuff, tiger."

As soon as the words left her mouth, she regretted them. A shadow crossed Jack's face as he lowered his head and looked at the ground for a long moment. The other parents mumbled something about blanket-wrapped kids being sleepy and morning coming earlier while you're camping and thanks for everything, as they headed into the darkness. Without hesitation, Jesse picked up a pail and shovel and began quickly filling it with sand to douse the fire, while Kimberly and Sabrina dipped pails in coolers of melted ice, the fire hissing in protest with every fling of water at its base.

Jack said to Jesse, "Take your sisters into the tent," then wrapped his sore hand around Marjorie's wrist and quietly through a clenched jaw, said, "Car."

The kids looked at each other as their parents moved to the front seat of the car, the only place that offered any kind of privacy in the campground. Jesse motioned toward the tent and the girls followed him inside. Kimberly grabbed her brother's transistor radio, spinning the dial to try to pull up a local rock radio station for background noise. While their parents' argument was muffled from inside the closed car, the kids heard much of what was said, not for the first time, not for the last.

"Since when did you become the booze police, Marjie? Have I said a word to you about how the level of your gin bottle dwindles faster each day we're here? Not to mention the wine bottles piling up in the garbage." Marjorie reddened as if she'd been smacked in the face.

"Jack! You know that's not entirely true. Why are you picking on me? I was only trying to—"

"Stop. You have no right to say one word to me about what I do or do not drink. I am a grown man. I work my ass off every single day so that you don't have to."

"Don't have to work? What do you think taking care of a house and three children is, exactly, a vacation?"

"I drive a very old car and do my own maintenance. I haven't bought a new suit in ten years. I pay for your manicures and pedicures and shopping trips to department stores that we cannot afford. I pay for your lunches with the ladies from the Junior League because somewhere in your deluded brain you think you're married to a wealthy man. Or, should I say, you *wish* you were. What was his name? Chip? That guy you throw in my face *every single chance you get* because you turned him down for me. And he's, what . . . a millionaire living on Davis Islands now, right? But you were gonna support me in my dream to be a professional musician. The job at Eckerd's was just 'temporary' until we could pay off the car, and then it was the credit cards, and then a bigger house. And what do I get for all of this? A woman who keeps up her precious appearances while not giving a good goddamn about me or our children. Do you even know them at all?"

"Well, I *never*! Jack, this is getting way out of hand, I—"

"I asked you a question. Do you even know them? Do you bother with anything they care about?"

"I could ask you the same thing. You spend every goddamn day at that office and on 'business trips' to God knows where, and when you're home you're buried in a beer and a ballgame!"

Jack's face darkened. "What exactly are you accusing me of, woman? *Don't* start with me. You've taken away my dreams. You've ruined our relationship. I will not stand for you accusing me of something illicit and I will *not* let you tell me I don't know my own kids. They are my entire life!"

"Jack, please!" She choked. "You're all I'll ever have. You made a promise!"

Inside the musty tent, Kimberly hummed a little too loudly along to the radio, her face twisted in a faux smile. She sat next to the sleeping bag containing a curled-up Sabrina, scratching her back and playing with her long dark hair, soothing them both. Jesse sat on his sleeping bag, chin resting on drawn up knees, one hand drawing imaginary circles over and over on the nylon fabric.

Kimberly rubbed her nose and eyes, sleepy. When Sabrina's breathing turned to soft snoring, she whispered, "I don't think either of them know us, to be honest. I started my period last week. I had to go next door to Laura's house and ask her how to use tampons. Mom wasn't around. She never is. I would never dream of going to her with anything anyway. She's so self-focused that somehow *my* period would wind up being stories about *her* period. She's clueless." She rolled her eyes.

"Yeah, I know what you mean. They don't know a thing about me, either." Jesse sighed, closing his eyes, tracing circle after circle.

Chapter Seven — 1976 — Jesse

Finally, Jesse thought, as his dad's car approached the entrance to Camp Winona. At thirteen, he was old enough to attend the overnight teen camp week during summer break between 7th and 8th grade. One whole week without bratty little sisters and *Jess, walk the dog,* and *Jess, take out the trash,* and *Jesse, I meant NOW*! Ugh, he was sick to death of every single person he was related to. He seriously could not wait to have seven whole days and nights of freedom!

Charlie and his older brother had been coming to this YMCA camp for years. Jesse had begged his parents to let him go, too, from the time he was ten, but they always said the same thing: he wasn't ready for sleep-away camp because they knew exactly what would happen. He would be there one night and then start crying to come home and they would waste all that money and have to drive all that way to go pick him up again and money doesn't grow on trees and wait until you are at least 13 and show us you can be responsible and not cry like a baby whenever you're away from us for more than a few hours, and blah, blah, blah.

One time. One time and they always threw it in his face. One time, he was made to sleep over at his grandparents' house in Tampa when his mom and dad had a wedding anniversary night at the fabled and luxurious Don CeSar hotel on St. Pete Beach. Kimberly and Sabrina had lucked out—one of them stayed with their dad's sister, Aunt Donna, and the other one with their *nice* grandparents in St Pete. His mom's parents had always scared the crap out of him. They were kind of hoity-toity, upper crust, status-symbol-loving, not very nice, non-hugging old people. Everything in their house was perfect without a speck of dust in sight. It even smelled like old people. He was so afraid to touch anything, to sit anywhere, to relax or let his guard down even slightly.

Every time his grandmother spoke to him, he pictured that green witch in the *Wizard of Oz,* how she kind of leaned in and said, "Hmmm?"

after every question. Like, "So, Jesse, what kinds of things do your parents do on the weekends, hmmm?" or, "Jesse, what do you do for fun at your other grandparents' house, hmmm?" It freaked him out. He would just shrug, afraid to say anything, knowing whatever he said would be taken the wrong way and it would start a huge fight when she went back to his mom with, "By the way, Jesse mentioned that . . . " So, he just shut the hell up when he was around her.

Anyway, he claimed he was tired after dinner (the less time he had to interact with them, the better), and went to the guest room to change into his pajamas and get into bed. The sun hadn't even gone down yet. His grandmother came in after he was under the covers. She sat on the side of the bed, holding a glass of red wine, instantly making him feel uneasy. She began to tell him stories about how horrible his mother was as a young girl, giving example after example of the petulant and ungrateful behavior Marjorie displayed on so many occasions, and how she sincerely hoped Jesse would never behave that way because no punishment, no matter how severe, ever seemed to work with his mother. Jesse was a little nauseous by the time she was through, and terrified that she was going to invent some bad thing he had done during the night and come back into the room and beat the crap out of him or tell his parents and then they would beat the crap out of him when he got home.

So, he cried.

And he asked if he could go home.

No, he begged and pleaded and said he had a horrible stomach ache and it was probably appendicitis or cancer or something and he just needed to go home and please call the hotel and tell his parents to please come pick him up. He cried so hard for so long, that his grandfather, who wasn't even his *real* grandfather, was pushed completely over the edge because he couldn't enjoy his cocktail and his Tsaikovsky records, and Jesse overheard him dial information and get the number to the Don CeSar, locate his parents' room, and order them to leave right now and come pick up this ill-mannered child this instant or so help him, God . . .

So, Jesse was not allowed to go to sleep away camp until he turned 13. Which had happened in March. And now it was June. And now they were pulling onto the sandy dirt road under the wooden ranch gate that read Camp Winona with a big C on the left side gate and a big W on the right. Jesse was so excited he thought the butterflies in his stomach might come flying right out of his mouth. Jack put his cigarette out in the ashtray and glanced down at his son.

"Jess, are you ready for this?"

"Yep, Dad. I really am. I can't wait. It's gonna be so much fun! Swimming and sailing and archery and doing arts and crafts and all that stuff, and I'm pretty sure I'll get to bunk with Charlie."

His dad smiled and said, "Okay, slugger, cool. It sounds great. But I want you to promise me one thing, okay? No matter what, no matter how badly you might want to, I do not want to get a phone call in the middle of the night with you crying to come home, you get me? You're a young man now, not a little boy. You need to buck up. Whatever bad stuff you're feeling, swallow it. Stuff it inside. Because nobody wants to deal with a whiny little sissy boy, you hear? So, be tough, be a man, and stay here until we come back to get you next weekend. Have I made myself clear?"

Jesse looked down at his hands in his lap. "Yes, sir," he muttered.

"Good. Let's go get you checked in."

***

Jesse shed no tears as his dad said goodbye, got back in the station wagon, and drove away. He headed to his assigned cabin feeling nervous and excited all at once. After his eyes adjusted to the dim interior of the cabin, he looked around at the other boys choosing their bunks and getting settled. He scoured several bunk beds for Charlie, but he didn't see him anywhere. Timidly, he carried his duffel bag to the back of the room and chose an upper bunk at the end of the long line. It didn't look like anyone had claimed the lower bunk yet, so he thought he would save it for Charlie. He wondered what was taking him so long to get there.

Jesse climbed up the ladder at the back of the bed carrying the duffel with him, and found the thin, gray and white striped mattress to be clean. A scratchy, dark gray blanket sat folded at the foot of the bed. His mom had packed some sheets for him, so he pulled these out and threw them to the middle of the bed. The trick was going to be how to make it while he was in the middle of it. It wasn't going to be as neat as he made his bed at home, but oh well. It was camp! Who cared? His mom wasn't there to correct his bed-making abilities.

As he was getting the corners tucked in, a tough-looking boy with brown feathered hair down to his shoulders, wearing a black AC/DC t-shirt and cut-off jean shorts, plopped his bag on the lower bunk. Jesse felt his heart speed up a little bit. He wanted to tell this boy he was saving the bed for Charlie, but . . . gulp . . . never mind. He guessed it didn't matter all that much. Besides, he wasn't trying to get his butt kicked his first hour at camp.

The boy jerked his head in Jesse's direction.

"Name's Max. What's yours?"

"Uh, Jesse."

"Where you from?"

"Clearwater. What about you?"

"Daytona. You like music?"

"Sure, of course. Doesn't everybody?"

"Not everybody likes *good* music. Whadda you listen to?"

Jesse thought about this for a minute. He tried to picture his dad's record collection. He didn't have any albums of his own yet. A stereo was another thing that he was told he had to wait for until he was older. Fingers crossed he would get one for Christmas.

"Um . . . Doobie Brothers, Eagles, Three Dog Night . . . "

"Ugh, NO, man! What are you, forty? Here's where it's at—AC/DC, Led Zeppelin, Aerosmith, Black Sabbath—that's the shit right there. I'm gonna go see *all* those bands with my big brother next year. It's gonna be the best ever!"

"Wow, that's awesome, Max."

"What was your name again?"
"Jesse."

"Right. Jesse. You eat yet? We can go over to the dining hall soon for lunch. Food here is pretty shitty but it'll fill you up."

"Okay, cool." Jesse couldn't believe it. He wasn't even one hour into camp and he had already made a new friend. Probably the coolest kid here, too. He hurried to finish making his bunk, tossed the duffel on the floor, and jumped down. He was ready to get this camp adventure started. And he'd forgotten all about Charlie.

***

As it turned out, Charlie was assigned to another cabin entirely, so Jesse didn't get to see much of him during the week. They waved to each other during meals at the dining hall and passed one another on their way to various activities.

Mostly, Jesse spent every waking hour tagging along with Max. It seemed there was nothing this kid couldn't do. He was good at everything—archery, volleyball, badminton, sailing. For the week-long arts and crafts project, the boys chose woodshop. Max made a perfect birdhouse with a shingled roof and three different sized openings with perches. Jesse made a pretty crooked key rack. Morning, noon, and night, the duo were inseparable. They ate, swam, hiked, and played frisbee together. Max was constantly singing rock songs, randomly jamming on air guitar. Jesse made mental notes of the songs Max sang so he could listen to them on the radio when he got back home. Maybe if he saved his allowance for a few weeks, Mom would take him to the record store so he could buy his first album. Of course, it would have to be AC/DC's *High Voltage*. It's all Max ever talked about. Hopefully, Jesse's dad would let him use the stereo. He would have to prove he was mature enough to take care of his dad's expensive things.

At night in their bunks after lights out, they would whisper to each other about their favorite things—mostly food, tv shows, and, of course, music. Jesse told Max how his mom and dad wouldn't let him have a stereo yet. Not even a record player. One night, Jesse was complaining about how strict his mom was when Max interrupted him.

"Don't talk that way about your mom, man."

"You don't even know, man, she's the worst!"

"No, seriously, Jesse. *You* don't know. You're lucky to have a mom and a dad. I don't."

"Wait, what? What happened?"

Max spoke so quietly, Jesse had to lean over the side of the bunk to better hear him. He lay still and quiet, listening intently to his new friend.

"My mom died when I was five. Cancer. It was awful. She got really sick and it made her so weak. I remember trying to hug her at the end and she was just skin and bones. Scrawny. My dad started drinking after that. Like every day. One day, like a couple years after Mom died, we found out Dad had stopped going to work and was hanging out in this bar every day. We found out because first the power got shut off, then some cops came and said they had to put a lock on the door. We were being evicted. It's a shitty little house, but it's all we had. My oldest brother Danny ran down to the bar, but Dad wasn't there. He asked the bartender but he hadn't seen Dad all day. Turns out he was in jail for writing checks for cash at the 7Eleven and didn't have any money in the bank to cover it. They picked him up when we were at school. Danny was twenty and had a good job, so the cops let me and Mike stay with him. Told us to call the landlord and work it out. The next day, my brother pawned his cherry '57 Chevy. The lights came back on and we stayed in the house. That was six years ago. Danny never got the car back. And we never saw Dad again. Danny told Dad not to come back until he had cleaned up his act. Told him to go to a hospital and dry out. It was only supposed to be like a month or something. A few months later, more cops came to the house. Said they found Dad in an empty parking lot by the Speedway. He'd been beaten up pretty bad. The cops thought maybe he owed some bad people money. We'll never know for sure if it was the beating or the booze that killed him that night. So, as lousy as your folks may seem to you, at least you've got 'em."

Jesse remained quiet as Max's voice faded; the soft snoring of the other boys in the cabin filling the silence. He let his arm drop down into the open space between the bunks and wiggled his fingers. He wasn't sure Max would even be able to see it in the dark. After a moment, he felt Max's hand grab his, tentatively at first, then he laced his fingers through Jesse's. Jesse felt the rhythm of his heart speed up. He knew his hand was getting sweaty. Probably shaking, too. But he held on, sending a heart full of comfort through his fingers to his friend.

Jesse fell asleep wishing camp never had to end.

At the end of the week, all of the parents showed up to pick up their sunburned, smelly, exhausted campers. There were so many hugs, and kids shouting over each other to tell their parents about the most fantastic things they had done during the week. Arts and crafts projects were proudly shown before being loaded into the trunks of cars. Max's brother, Mike, was eighteen and had already come to pick up Max and gone. They were heading to Daytona Beach for the day. So, the goodbye between the boys had been brief. They exchanged addresses and phone numbers and handshakes and promised to keep in touch. Maybe they would even see each other at camp again next year.

It was getting close to lunch time when Jesse finally saw his dad's station wagon pull up. When the car came to a stop near the cabin, Jesse hoisted his duffel bag and scuffled his feet across the sandy ground over to his waiting dad. His heart felt heavy as his dad took the bag from him and tossed it into the back of the station wagon. He held up the key rack without enthusiasm for his dad to see, then tossed it in with the bag. Accepting his dad's arm around his shoulders in a brief hug, he climbed into the passenger seat. Jesse took one last look at the cabin as they pulled away to begin the long drive home. His entire body felt weary all of a sudden. He was so filled with grief, it was as if someone had died. He looked out the window at the scenery speeding by.

"Hey, slugger, why the long face?" his dad asked.

Jesse shrugged, rubbing his eyes with fists. "Just tired, I guess," he said. He leaned his head against the window. He knew he may never get a chance to see his friend again. A part of him felt a little broken inside. He understood now why they called it a crush.

Chapter Eight — 1996 — Kimberly

Kimberly put out her cigarette and went back inside the apartment, plopping back down on the lumpy couch. After a long swallow of beer, she picked up the notebook and pen. She sat cross-legged on the couch, bracing the notebook on her right leg. Taking a deep breath, she began to write.

All of my life, you've been there for me. I've trusted you with everything for as long as I can remember. If you ever sat in judgment over me or my decisions, you never said so. Any time I came to you for advice or a favor, you never said no. For these reasons, I love and appreciate you more than you will ever know. I'm going to ask one more favor from you, and this one is the biggest yet. You'll be receiving a phone call soon from a 904 area code — please take the call. This is extremely important. I love you.~~Kim

After rereading the letter, Kimberly ripped the sheet out of the spiral binding, carefully pulling away the fringed edge. Folding the letter into thirds, she closed her eyes, and pressed the letter to her lips. Kissing it, she whispered 'I love you.' She placed the letter into an envelope, addressed the front, added a stamp, and placed it on the makeshift table, mentally noting to mail it first thing in the morning.

Kimberly flipped up the two latches on the lockbox and tried to open it. Satisfied that it was indeed locked, she reset the latches and set it on the sofa, placing the smaller tin on top. Then she began a new note:

Jess: I'm broken. Nobody can fix me this time. Not even you. Don't waste your time trying to find me. I need to do this my way. It's the best thing for everyone concerned. It all ends today. Trust me, there's no other way. These boxes contain everything of any importance to me. They are for Julie's eyes only. I mean it. Julie only. Please give them to her when she turns 18. Hopefully, everything will make sense to her then. I know you'll honor my wishes and you'll know what to do. You always did. Thank you for everything. All my love always. ~~Kimmy

She tore the note out of the notebook and lay it on top of the boxes. She wrote another note, placed it in an envelope, which she marked 'Sabrina', and set it under Jesse's note. It'd been an emotional day. She drained her beer and leaned back against the sofa. One more letter to write, the one most difficult. Soon, she told herself. This will all be over soon.

Chapter Nine — 2012 — Julie

The sparkler blazed from the center of the round cake, fizzing down the stem as the family sang. When they cheered "Make a wish!" Julie leaned low toward the flickering light. The sparkler had been positioned to dot the i, highlighting the blue icing message that read "Happy 18th, Julie!" She closed her eyes. Her wish had always been the same. Every birthday for as long as she could remember.

Please let me see you again.

Julie's eyes slowly opened. "Now what? I can't blow this thing out!" she said, grinning. Julie's aunt Sabrina swooped in to plop the sparkler into a cup of water.

"Don't tell your wish or it won't come true!" Sabrina said, as she licked chocolate frosting from her fingertips.

"I won't, Aunt Brie." *I never do.*

"Come on, let's cut that cake," Uncle Grey said. He lifted it from the table and handed it to Sabrina, who walked into the kitchen. Julie looked around the large dining room of her aunt and uncle's high-rise condo. The fragrance of fluffy pink and white Esperanza roses in a cut crystal vase mingled with the aroma of the homemade cake. She recalled so many happy gatherings in this space, the place she'd called home for nearly sixteen years. Today was no different, as friends and family members milled about in the living room and onto the terrace, sipping cocktails, laughing. Only one person was missing. Julie chided herself for allowing her mind to go there, always threatening to ruin her good time.

Julie's friends handed her an oversized card. She side-eyed the girls while sliding her finger under the flap of the envelope. Inside was a pop-up card of girls surrounded by surf and sand saying 'Happy Birthday, Beach!' Her present was a gift card for a full day at a spa. Julie opened her arms for a group hug.

"We'll be here at nine o'clock tomorrow morning to scoop you up for a beach day. Be ready," the girls said, as they made their way out the double front doors to the hallway, good wishes and thanks flowing. Julie closed the door and smiled, grateful.

Hearing a little whistle, Julie looked up to see Uncle Jesse at the sliding door to the terrace, motioning for her to join him. She crossed the room, her white cotton maxi dress swishing over sparkly silver sandals. Her long, light brown curls were swept up into a messy bun, large silver hoop earrings brushed her shoulders as she walked across the rug.

Affording them privacy, her family moved into the study on the far end of the condo. Grey turned down the stereo on his way to join them. Only Sabrina remained close by in the living room, tucked into the corner of the white sectional sofa.

Out on the terrace, the setting sun warmed Julie's skin, blanketing Biscayne Bay in sparkling diamonds on the tips of the waves. Squinting her blue-green eyes, she reached a spot near her uncle in the shade.

"What's up?" she asked.

Jesse reached under his chair and brought out two boxes. One was a steel lockbox with a heavy black handle on the lid. The other was a small square aluminum tin, the opening sealed all the way around by black electrical tape. He put them on the end table between their chairs and gently placed his hand on her knee, his smile solemn.

"A long time ago, I was instructed to wait to give these to you until your eighteenth birthday. I was furious at the time, and to be honest, I'm still pissed off. But I made peace with it. I also made a promise that I would never look inside. These are for you, not me, not anyone else. So, I'll leave you alone and let you process all of this. We love you, Jules. We'll be right inside if you need us."

Julie hesitated. Her breath caught in her throat. She knew immediately who these were from.

Time stood still as she peeled back the heavy black tape and lifted the lid off of the stationery tin. The first item inside was an envelope with "My sweet Juliana Susanne" written in loopy script. Julie took the envelope out of the tin and replaced the lid, not going any further until she saw what the envelope contained. Her hands felt clammy and blood rushed to her ears. All ambient sound went quiet. She felt the thump of her heart, her breathing shallow. Taking a sip of water, she slid open the envelope flap, hands trembling.

Julie removed the letter and unfolded it. A small sound escaped her throat.

Hello, my darling baby girl. Since you are reading this letter, and I know Uncle Jesse well enough to believe he honored my wishes, I'm going to say HAPPY 18th BIRTHDAY, BEAUTIFUL!! I sure wish I was with you celebrate the woman you have become. The first thing I want you to know is that I am so very sorry. Sorry for the pain I know I have caused you. Sorry that I missed out on most of your life. You may have a hard time believing this, but I had no other choice. My decision was the hardest one I'd ever had to make. It was the only way I knew for you to have the best life possible. The only thing I can hope for in this moment is that you can find some way to forgive me.

Oh, Mom, Julie thought, *I forgave you a very long time ago.*

Chapter Ten — 1961 — Marjorie

Marjorie frequently said that all she ever wanted to be was a mother. In truth, all she ever wanted was someone to love her unconditionally.

Sadly, she was raised in a meritocracy. Love was doled out as a reward for good behavior, and taken away just as quickly in a hiss of shame and humiliation. Beatings were frequently the primary discipline, but the true punishment was indifference from the frigid heart of her mother.

When at the age of seven, sexual abuse at the hand of the new man of the house began, she screwed up all her courage and tried to seek refuge and protection, only to be called a liar, a manipulator, a bad girl. How dare she try to ruin the one thing that made her mother happy? Certainly she was simply jealous at the loss of what little time and attention had been meted out to her in the early years. And so his fingers continued to violate the private parts of her as his liquor-soaked breath permeated her nostrils. To this day, she cannot smell bourbon without retching.

As she grew older, abuse became the norm, woven into the fabric of the household, as regular as breathing, yet she found the most painful thing to be the lack of attention. When the belt struck her bottom, the palm stung her jaw, the spittle-laden screaming sprayed her face, at least then she knew she existed. She was an actual person with breath and skin and blood with bruises and salty, sticky cheeks to prove it.

But the indifference—well, that was a pain so deep, it hurt in her bones. To be ghosted, brushed away as a nonentity, deliberately ignored, robbed the girl of all sense of self. She didn't matter. She understood completely that she was simply unworthy.

It came as no surprise, then, that the moment she was paid some attention, she latched onto it with all of her might, like a lifeline thrown to a drowning sailor.

***

Marjorie and Charles became engaged before they even graduated from high school. Try as he might during their brief courtship, Marjorie would not be persuaded to be one of those naughty girls who 'went all the way' before marriage. After all, her mother raised her to be a good girl. She and her siblings attended Catholic school, Mass twice a week, and confession on Saturday mornings. Their family donated clothing to the needy, wrote checks to Catholic Charities a couple of times a year, and voted conservatively.

They met at a bonfire on the beach after the Jesuit Tigers slaughtered the Tampa Catholic Colts in football on a warm, humid Friday night. The drubbing came as no surprise, as brand new TC barely had a full varsity football squad. It was also the first co-ed Catholic school in the bay area. Marjorie transferred to TC at the beginning of her sophomore year from the all-girl Academy of the Holy Names. The new campus was close enough for Marjorie to walk to and from school each day. Having been to all-girls schools all of her life, the co-ed campus was quite a culture shock. Seeing boys everywhere she looked was just so weird! Until she realized that they were seeing her, too. Not just seeing her, but actually gawking at her. Marjorie paid little attention to the changes in her body, where at fifteen she'd begun to have curves in previously straight and flat places. Prior to the school year, she'd had the inconvenience of replacing all of her school uniforms, as buttons and zippers would no longer close. The attention she received every day from most of the thirty-four boys in her class was surprising and confusing. Just for being herself, people were noticing her!

Someone else noticed her new, womanly body, too. Her stepfather. And her mother noticed him noticing. And that was the end of that. Marjorie said nothing when the announcement was made to the entire family after church one autumn Sunday that he would be moving out of the house into a nearby apartment. She said nothing, eyes downcast, when her mother cornered her in the laundry room and demanded to know how long she'd been using her body to seduce him. Clearly, she didn't remember her young daughter coming to her, begging her to make it stop. She said nothing as her face and head were repeatedly smacked in an attempt to draw out answers, only raised her forearms to shield the blows. She said nothing as her wrist was gripped and she was jerked in front of her mother to receive a swift kick in the behind, and told to go to her room and get used to it because she was only going to be seeing those four walls for the foreseeable future. She didn't even allow herself to shed any tears. What was the point? As she overheard her mother consoling her younger twin brothers in their grief over their newly fatherless home, Marjorie lowered the shade of her bedroom window and crawled into bed. There would be no supper tonight. But there would also be no visitors. She sighed, closed her eyes, and smiled.

***

"Mother?" Marjorie called through the kitchen screen door. It was 8:00 pm on Saturday night and the kitchen was still lit up. "Mother, are you here?" She stepped into the room, practically floating on air. "I have enormous news!"

Her mother emerged carrying a basket of folded laundry, her hair held back by a bandana scarf.

"It's unnecessary to raise your voice, child, I'm right here. What is it?"

"Mother! Look!" Marjorie thrust out her left hand, fingers wiggling, and sporting a half carat diamond solitaire that sparkled like the young girl's eyes. "Can you believe it?"

Her mother set the basket of laundry on the floor, and took Marjorie's hand in her own to get a better look at the ring. She smiled her Mona Lisa smile—closed mouth, no teeth, the smile never reaching her eyes.

"Well, will you look at that. Chip asked you to marry him. Awfully soon, don't you think?" She narrowed her eyes at Marjorie. "Do you have something you need to tell me?" She eyed Marjorie's belly.

"Oh my goodness, no! Lots of couples get engaged before graduation and we've been going steady all year. Besides, I'm not that kind of girl." She pulled her hand out of her mother's and held it up toward the light, turning the ring this way and that, watching the diamond twinkle. "Oh, Mother, I am so happy!"

"A bit disappointing he didn't come and ask for my blessing. Hmph. Have you set a date yet?"

"No, not yet. He only just asked me an hour ago. We'll need some time to take a look and see what venues are available and when. I mean, for the reception, of course."

"Of course. Naturally, for the ceremony, you'll be married at Christ the King by Father O'Hara."

"Uh, I don't know, Mother. His family belongs to Sacred Heart. I'm pretty sure they'll want us to be married there. Plus, the photos of us on the steps in front of that gorgeous cathedral will be amazing! I've always dreamed of being a bride on those steps," Marjorie said, her eyes lost in the vision.

Her mother bent down to retrieve the laundry basket. She placed it on her hip and met Marjorie's eyes.

"And this wedding will be paid for by whom? Since your stepfather moved out, there isn't any extra money lying around."

Marjorie felt her heart sink a little. While she never expected an opulent wedding fit for a princess, she did always picture herself in a beautiful gown with a chapel length train and a glorious veil, carrying a stunning bouquet that was as fragrant as it was vibrant. She'd dreamed of being surrounded by many happy guests with love flowing from all of them to the bride and groom, and a party that went on into the night celebrating their marriage, and their guests sending the happy couple off on their honeymoon with applause and congratulations. From the sounds of it, Marjorie might be relegated to having her confirmation dress altered and carrying daisies picked from the neighbor's yard.

Never mind. None of that mattered. As long as she was with Chip, she would be happy with however the ceremony and reception turned out. She was not going to let anything put a damper on her mood tonight.

"I don't know, Mother, and I'm not going to worry about it tonight. I'll be in my room if you—"

"Not so fast, young lady. There are dinner dishes to be done," her mother said, gesturing toward the sink.

"But why didn't Billy and Bobby do them? I wasn't even here for dinner!"

"'*I wasn't even here for dinner,*'" her mother mocked nasally. She approached slowly, her gaze never wavering. "I'm not sure I heard you correctly, Marjorie."

"Yes, ma'am," Marjorie said, as she headed to the sink. She carefully slid off the diamond ring she'd only been wearing for an hour and slipped it into the pocket of her shorts. Heaven forbid anything happen to it! She began to fill the sink with hot water and dish soap, and heard her mother leaving the kitchen behind her.

Oh my dear God, please deliver me from this house . . .

***

Tuesday evening, Marjorie was sitting on the living room sofa in front of the open windows, enjoying the evening breeze and pairing socks from the laundry—Billy's had red stripes, Bobby's had blue, thank goodness or she never would have been able to tell them apart—when she heard her mother coming up the walk, humming happily to herself. Marjorie was pleasantly taken aback. She planted a smile on her face, anticipating her mother's arrival through the door.

"Hello, Mother! Looks like you had a nice evening at the American Legion."

Her mother smiled and said, "Yes, it was very nice, thank you. I've been seeing someone there for a few weeks now. You might be interested to know he's very successful and he's *very* single with no children. He was married to his military career. Just retired three years ago. He's picking me up here tomorrow night for dinner. I would like for you and your brothers to make yourselves scarce, is that clear?"

"Yes, of course. That's great news! What time is he picking you up?"

"We agreed on six o'clock. You can pick your brothers up from baseball practice and take them to get a burger. Surely you have some babysitting money saved?"

"Yes ma'am. I'll take care of it." Few things made Marjorie happier than the thought of her mother being with a new man. This new relationship had the potential to resolve so much unhappiness and grief in the house. Marjorie's biological father died during World War II and she'd never known him. The boys' father, the monster, had moved out a couple of years ago. Her mother had been bitter and angry ever since. But everyone deserved the chance to be happy. And just maybe that happiness would filter down to everyone else in the house. One could only hope. Marjorie would make sure she did everything in her power to help this new relationship happen.

A month later on a warm spring afternoon, Marjorie was lost in thought as she walked home from school. She delighted in the sparkle of her engagement ring in the bright sunlight. Although Marjorie could not wait to become Mrs. Charles Carter, Jr., and move out of her mother's home, they'd agreed to wait until after his freshman year of school at Boston College. He wanted to be acclimated and settled before he moved his young bride up to Massachusetts. At the suggestion of her future mother-in-law, Marjorie planned to attend finishing school after graduation. All she wanted was for Chip to be proud to have Marjorie on his arm. She wanted to provide him with a warm home and to be a perfect lady at all of the dinners and functions they would surely attend in New England. Chip would be majoring in business and finance and planned to apply to Harvard Business School for his MBA following undergrad. Marjorie practically tingled just thinking about it!

As she rounded the corner of her street, she saw a familiar car pulled up to the curb in front of her mother's house, with the passenger doors and trunk opened. A feeling of dread lay in the pit of her stomach as she approached the house. She could hear the raised voices of her mother and former stepfather as she got closer. Marjorie stopped walking and took in a deep breath. As she passed the eight-foot tall hedgerow of viburnum along their driveway, she took in what was happening. She turned to her left to look at the car and saw Bobby and Billy in the back seat with tear-stained faces. Wheeling around to her right, she saw her mother pointing furiously into the face of the monster.

"I will see you in court, you son of a bitch, and then I'll see you in jail!"

"Oh, shut up, woman. I have dirt on you a mile wide. Good fucking luck," he said.

He pushed past Marjorie and tossed the boys' bags into the trunk, slamming it closed. Marjorie smelled the familiar stench of stale booze as he moved by her.

"I'll send for the rest of their things and they'd better be packed and ready to go." Then he gestured at Marjorie. "If you get hard up for cash, you can always peddle this little piece of ass." He sneered a lopsided smirk and spit on the sidewalk. Marjorie's mother scooped up a rock from the side of the driveway and with a roar that came all the way up from her toes, threw the rock as hard as she could at the rear end of the car, denting the quarter panel.

"You'll be sorry, you bastard!" she screamed as the car peeled away from the curb and barreled down the street.

A long moment passed in which neither of them seemed to breathe.

"Mother?" Marjorie asked tentatively.

Her mother steeled her shoulders back, thrust out her chin, looked at Marjorie and said, "I'll be moving in with my beau immediately following your graduation. You'll need to make arrangements for a place to live," and turned to walk across the lawn and up the concrete steps to the front porch of the house.

Marjorie stood frozen in place. Dumbfounded. She felt lightheaded as the news sunk in. She had nowhere to go.

Chapter Eleven — 1981 — Jesse

Jesse zipped up his gold graduation robe and straightened the knot in his tie. With the robe on, he was instantly warm, even in the air-conditioned house. Oh, man, it was going to be a long, sweaty night if commencement was held outside at Countryside High School's new football stadium. He took one last look in the mirror, lifted his cap and tassel with '81 dangling from the golden band, and left the bathroom.

"There he is," Jack said, aiming the 35mm Nikon as his son arrived in the living room. "Say 'I'm almost free'!"

Jesse grinned. "Hell yeah!" The flash snapped in his eyes, causing him to blink.

Marjorie crossed the room to answer the ringing phone.

"Hello? Yes, this is Mrs. Stevens. Mhmm? Yes, I understand and I agree completely. Thank you for letting us know. Bye, now." She turned back to face the others in the room. "Looks like rain, so the commencement exercises have been moved indoors to the auditorium. Only two guests per graduate, so just your father and I will be attending. Since Nana and Gramps aren't here yet, please let them know when they arrive. We'll all go out to dinner afterward as planned."

Kimberly and Sabrina did not appear disappointed.

"Congrats, brother, we'll see ya when you get back!" Kimberly said as she wrapped her arms around his waist for a hug,

"Hey, watch it, don't wrinkle the threads!" Jesse joked as he smoothed out the robe. "Come here and give your very old brother a hug, little bit." Sabrina gave Jesse a quick hug and tore off down the hall to strip out of the horrible, stiff dress and put on shorts.

"Sabrina, hang that dress up on the back of the door. We have reservations at Benihana in about two hours and you'll need to have your nice clothes on. Kimberly, please see to it your sister does so. We'll be back to pick all of you up at six-thirty. I know I can count on you," said Marjorie.

When they arrived at the school a few minutes later, Jesse jumped out of the back seat with a quick, "See you guys later!" and ran off to join his buddies. The graduates were all still unsure what exactly they were supposed to do, since they had rehearsed for the outdoor ceremony that was now being moved indoors. He figured he would just go along with what everyone else was doing.

"Hey, Jess!" Keith called. "Over here!" Jesse waved and made his way through the crowd of families and graduates to his friends Keith, Carlos, and Brent, who were standing to the left of the auditorium entrance. He was greeted with high fives and big grins. Brent's grin was particularly shiny.

Brent said, "Can you believe we're graduating?"

"I can't believe they're letting you graduate when you still have braces, dude. Are you even old enough to drive?" Carlos said.

"Hey, asshole, " said Brent, with a punch to Carlos' arm. Carlos punched back, laughing.

"Are you going to the party tonight at Beth's house?" Keith asked.

"Well, yeah, she lives in my neighborhood, so I'll be there," said Jesse. "But I'm going to dinner with my family first. I probably won't make it there 'til like maybe nine o'clock."

"That's when things are just gonna get revved up! You won't be missing anything," Carlos said.

Keith was struggling to get the cap to stay on his head, due to his natural curly afro. "This stupid thing. Does anybody have a pin or something?"

"Hang on, man, I think my mom carries shit like that in her purse. Back in a sec," Jesse said. He ran back over to his mom and dad. "Hey, Mom, do you have any bobby pins?"

Jesse jogged back over to his friends, who were in the middle of a conversation.

"...and I for one am glad they didn't give her a bigger gown. I stand in appreciation and admiration of her rack!" Carlos elbowed Brent as they snorted and pointed to a particularly voluptuous girl in their class. Her gown appeared a bit too small and her cleavage was on full display. Jesse shook his head and lifted the pins in his hand.

"Keith, turn around, man. I'll see if I can fix it." Keith turned. Jesse slipped the bobby pins through the cap and into Keith's hair. "Try it now."

Keith nudged the cap from both sides of his head. It was snug.

"Thanks, man." Keith rewarded his friend with a broad, white-toothed grin. Jesse met Keith's dark brown eyes. He felt a little flip low in his stomach and knew he was blushing. He looked away awkwardly.

"Uh, yeah, sure. No problem, dude."

The squeal of the outside intercom system made everyone wince and grab their ears. The principal spoke.

"Graduates and parents. Thank you all for coming here tonight. At this time we will ask for parents to proceed into the auditorium theater and take a seat. Graduates, please remain outside. Your homeroom teachers will be standing by the outer wall with their hands raised. Please line up with your teacher and get into alphabetical order as we practiced yesterday. You'll need to hurry as the weather is calling for rain at any moment. Thank you."

All four boys were in different homerooms, so they said their goodbyes. "See you at Beth's later!"

Jesse wouldn't have missed it.

***

Dinner with the family seemed to take forever. The food was delicious and the teppanyaki show at the hibachi grill was always entertaining. It was nice to be celebrated by the whole family. A couple of hours later, when they arrived back at their house, his mom brought out a half sheet cake decorated in the CHS colors of garnet and gold, reading 'Congrats Jesse! Class of 1981.' Everyone sang "For He's a Jolly Good Fellow," and they all enjoyed dessert. Jesse opened his cards, giving hugs to everyone. Slipping the money gifts into his wallet, he went to change into jeans for the party. He grabbed a royal blue Polo shirt from his closet. When his mom bought it for him, she told him it matched his baby blues. He'd rolled his eyes at the time, but now he grinned as he tucked the shirt into faded Levi's, buckled his braided leather belt, and tied his Nike high tops. In the bathroom, he combed his sandy feathered hair and added a little spritz of Ralph Lauren Polo cologne—to match his shirt, naturally—and left the house out the back door before anyone could stop him. Or so he thought.

After having said goodbye to his own parents, Jack was standing outside by the garage smoking a cigarette. He looked up at his son as he emerged from the back door.

"Hey, slugger. Where you off to?"

"Just a grad party. Walking distance. I won't be driving."

"That's good to hear. Listen, your mom and I are very proud of you, Jess. Made it all the way through high school without being arrested or getting anyone pregnant. That's a win in my book!" His dad laughed. The smell of whiskey and cologne commingled in the air between them. The night was fragrant with summer—cut grass, humid salt air, crickets chirping all around them.

"Ha ha, yeah, thanks, Dad. Listen, I'm gonna be la—"

"I just have one thing to ask you. Did you think I wasn't gonna find out?" Jack said. Jesse's heartbeat sped up a little. He felt mildly sick inside.

"F-find out wh-what, Dad?" Instant guilt and shame wrapped him up like the dark of the night around them. His hands were clammy. He felt burning tears at the ready behind his eyes. He *knew* he should have told his dad. At least him. Mom would not have handled it okay, but he felt like he'd made a connection with his dad as he'd gotten older. He wondered how he'd found out. Did Kimberly tell him? No, there was no way she would have. He intentionally and meticulously had nothing incriminating in his room. He never brought his friends around, even though he wasn't out to them, either. He had no idea . . .

"The dent, Jesse."

A long pause. Jesse let out the breath he didn't realize he'd been holding. "I'm sorry . . . dent?"

"Yes, son, the dent you put in the right rear quarter panel of my Charger. The car. Right here in the driveway behind me. Are you telling me you know nothing about the dent in my car? The one you borrow constantly? Come on, Jesse, I'm not an idiot."

Jesse felt his entire body relax. The tears he was holding back nearly flooded out in relief.

"Oh, Dad, I am so sorry. I think it must have happened in the parking lot at school last week. I'll pay to fix it, I promise."

"You got that right. How much did you get in grad money?"

"Around $500."

"I'll get a quote from the body shop and let you know. And next time, son, be honest with me. Don't make me call you out when you screw up."

"Yes, sir. I mean, no, sir. I mean, I won't. Can I just go now?" Jesse wiped his sweaty palms on his jeans.

"Yeah, go. I was gonna say midnight curfew, but since it's graduation, let's say one o'clock. Don't be late."

"Okay, cool, see you later!" Jesse ran down the driveway to the street before his dad could change his mind.

The party was in full swing when Jesse walked across the lawn to the front door. A sign on the door said to go around back, so he rounded the house and opened the gate. There, under a million tiny white lights, was most of his graduating class. The huge back yard and pool were ablaze like a stadium; the stereo pumping a popular reggae punk song.

The tide is high . . .

Jesse walked to the drinks table first. Mr. Starr had iced down cans of beer and soda in giant, aluminum tubs. In the center of the table was a plastic, three-tiered fountain flowing with deep red, fizzy punch, pieces of fruit bobbing in the lower bowl, surrounded by red plastic cups. Jesse grabbed a Budweiser and headed toward the pool. He said hey and high-fived a number of kids from his class, while looking for his three buddies. One guy got him into a conversation about muscle cars, because Jesse occasionally drove his dad's Charger. Jesse didn't want to appear rude, but cars pretty much bored him. He nodded a lot and looked over the talker's head to see if any of the guys had arrived yet. Before he knew it, his beer can was empty. He excused himself, walked over and grabbed another one. Maybe his friends were by the garage.

Sure enough, as soon as he walked to the far side of the yard, he came across a large group of grads, including Brent, Carlos, and Keith. From the looks of it, Brent and Carlos had been there a while and were feeling painless from the Budweisers in their hands. Keith held a Coke.

"Heyyyyy, there he is!" Brent said. "Jessss, whassup??" He raised his hand for a slightly sloppy high-five. Jesse pointed at Keith's soda and raised his eyebrows.

"I have my mom's convertible tonight. The one rule was no drinking. So . . . " Keith said, gesturing to the can in his hand.

"Ah, well, unless I can get busted for walking back to my house while drunk, no rules for me. Except curfew."

"Curfew?!" the three of them chimed together.

"Jeez, Jess, it's grad night! What the hell is wrong with your parents?" Carlos asked.

Jesse shrugged and played it off. "No big deal, really. I'm pretty tired anyway. Long day."

"Yeah, okay," said Brent, rolling his eyes. "Dude, you need to move away from that prison you live in like yesterday."

"Tell me about it. I haven't made up my mind what to do yet. I'm lifeguarding at Clearwater Beach again this summer. After that . . ." he shrugged. "My old man can get me a gig at Eckerd's, but I have to start in the warehouse stocking merchandise. Not exactly my dream job."

Carlos chimed in. "Yeah, my mind was made up for me. My dad wants me to take over the restaurant so he can retire. But—" He puffed out his chest, raised one finger, and did his best imitation of his father. "'Times are different than when I was a boy, mijo. You have to have a degree!'" On the last word, he jabbed his finger up in the air for added emphasis. The boys chuckled. "At least I have the summer free before orientation at USF."

Brent said, "Y'all know you're just jealous of me heading out to the wild west, baby! You have to come visit me at my uncle's place near L.A. No shortage of sun, surf, and babes." He wiggled his eyebrows that were as red as the hair on his head, and chugged the rest of his beer.

"Yeah, you might want to get rid of those tinsel teeth if you wanna include the babes part of that equation," Carlos said. Brent looked at Carlos with a completely straight face and slowly raised his middle finger. Carlos shot him one right back.

Jesse looked over at Keith. He knew this guy was destined for greatness. He had a perfect GPA and graduated near the top of their class.

"What about you, Keith?" The tall, slender, young Black man

looked at Jesse. He paused for a moment.

"I didn't have a chance to tell you guys yet. I was accepted into Dartmouth. Political Science. Pre-law."

"Oh, wow, that's rad, Keith. Congratulations, man!" They all pumped Keith's hand and slapped him on the back.

"What are you doing slumming it with us, dude?"

"Shut up, you guys are my friends, man. I just have a vision for my life. I figure, you're only young once, right? You've gotta reach for the stars while you can," Keith said.

Jesse was impressed, and felt a little directionless. He wasn't sure what in the world he wanted to do and wasn't even sure he had any marketable skills. He wasn't very good with his hands, so any kind of trade was out. He wasn't a brainiac like Keith, so pursuing higher education would probably be a waste of money. For now, he was content to drink his beer and hang out with his buddies on their graduation night. He could figure it out later. After all, like Keith said, you're only young once.

As time creeped closer to midnight, the partygoers became a lot more loose. Some kids in shorts, and some still in jeans, wound up in the pool. There were ferocious games of chicken going on with girls on top of jocks' shoulders, splashing and hollering, as the music volume grew louder and louder. Drinking gave way to munchies, and soon the food table was ravaged by dozens of starving grads. Some kids were making out in the shallow end of the pool, or the darker corners of the yard. Mr. and Mrs. Starr seemed unfazed by it all from their perch on their upstairs balcony. They just smiled and sipped their frosty cocktails.

The four friends were sitting on the grass cracking jokes about the idiots in the pool. Jesse probably should have stopped drinking after a few, but unfortunately, his better judgment had apparently taken the night off. Right around the ninth beer, or was it the tenth, he happened to glance at his watch and realized he had exactly fifteen minutes to walk home so as not to miss curfew.

"Oh, shit!" Jesse said."I gotta go home, you guys," which sounded more like yoo guysh. His attempts to stand up on his own were fruitless, and very hilarious to Brent and Carlos, who doubled over in laughter. Keith jumped up and put out his hand for Jesse to take. They hooked thumbs, wrapping their hands around one another, and Keith pulled Jesse up, stopping him from falling over.

"Whoa, there. Steady. You okay?"

"Mhmm, yep! I got dis."

"Guys, I'm gonna walk Jess home. Be right back."

"Aw, man, naw, I said I got dis," Jesse said, swaying on planted feet. Keith turned him toward the gate in the fence and they proceeded out. Jesse looked over his shoulder. "Night, doods. See you at da beach dis weekennn!"

Once out in the street, Keith handed Jesse a Sprite he'd nabbed from the table. Seeing Jesse struggle with the pop top, he opened it and handed it back. Jesse took a sip and belched. "Ahhhhh, thanks."

"No problem, let's just get you home."

"Thank you, Keith. You're a gentleman and a scholar," he said, raising the can up into the air, sloshing a bit down his arm. He giggled when he realized how true those words were. "Hahaha, you really *are* a gentleman and a scholar!"

Keith smiled. "Yeah, okay, man. I hear ya."

The night became soft away from the party house. No cars traveled on the quiet street. Jesse had no idea what came over him, as he reached over and took Keith's hand. His skin was softer than Jesse's, his fingers long and strong. Jesse randomly wondered if Keith played piano. He met Keith's eyes. Those deep, serious, soulful windows of Keith's eyes. His heart pounded like a drum keeping time with the rhythm of their walking. He felt the blood rushing through his veins, the night holding its breath.

Keith reached up and touched the side of Jesse's face. Jesse closed his eyes.

"Listen, my friend. I'm honored. You're a really good guy. And some day, the right man is gonna be holding this hand of yours. You're a great friend, Jess, but I'm not that man." Then he wrapped Jesse in a hug, squeezing him tightly for a brief moment, and let go. "Come on, let's get you home."

Later, Jesse lay on his bed. He lifted his eyes to the dark ceiling and closed them gently. Tonight he'd finally lived the first moment of truth in his life. And he breathed a silent thanks as he drifted off to sleep.

Chapter Twelve — 1981 — Kimberly

"Okay, places, everyone, let's run it again! Hurry, ladies, we don't have all day!" Mrs. Novotny said. The drill team director appeared to grow more exasperated as the long day of band camp dragged on. The dances they'd learned at dance camp earlier that summer were innovative and sexy, which was precisely what the band director, Mr. Haywood, did not want to see on his field at halftime. So, Mrs. Novotny and the four senior drill team officers spent days tweaking the choreography in order to make it more innocuous.

As the squad ran the routine yet again, Mrs. Novotny removed her sunglasses, pinched the bridge of her nose, then looked across the practice field, an expression of frustration on her tanned, lined face.

The boosters of the marching band and auxiliary had generously rented an entire floor of a hotel near The Pier in St. Petersburg for band camp. It was an ideal location, the ground floor rooms opening out onto an enormous field alongside Tampa Bay.

Kimberly took a moment and breathed it all in. Choppy waves on deep blue water, bright white seagulls crying out, and the intoxicating aroma of salt breeze mixed with sunscreen on a hundred and fifty students. If she closed her eyes, she could almost convince herself she was on a tropical island somewhere.

"Okay, that's lunch! Take one hour for food and hydration—plenty of it, understand? Stay with your camp buddy. I'll see you right back here at 1:00 pm sharp. Remember, if you're on time, you're already fifteen minutes late," Mrs. Novotny said.

Kimberly and her camp buddy, Cathy, grabbed their pompoms from the ground and ran to the room they shared with two other girls, twin sisters, Nicki and Rocki. The four girls were the only budding sophomores to have made the team.

Tryouts had been difficult. Kimberly had endured four callbacks before the judges were done. At the end of the day, the list had finally been posted on the door to the gym. Only four underclassmen made the squad, which formed an instant bond between the girls. The following Saturday, a meeting had been held regarding mandatory fundraising: car washes, candy sales, bake sales, magazine sales, all to raise money for dance training at the University of Florida, band camp at The Pier, and game uniforms. Moms volunteered to sew the custom uniforms, and measurements of all of the girls were taken that night. As one of the moms asked Kimberly to stand up straight and held the cloth tape measure snug around her waist, she'd started to feel the fluttering of excitement in her tummy. *This is REAL!* Being the youngest on the squad, the four girls stuck with each other at every event. They worked hard canvassing their neighborhoods and standing outside Winn Dixie to sell their home-baked goods. They'd done extra chores at home and turned in aluminum cans and glass bottles for refunds. Before long, each of them had saved enough money to afford both camps and all of the uniforms.

When the band boosters made the announcement that they would be footing the bill to rent the hotel at The Pier for camp, the kids whooped and hollered. It was exciting to think they would not only be drilling all day right by the water, but they would stay in a hotel, too! The directors and boosters were serious about giving the students every opportunity to create the best halftime show the band had ever delivered. Everyone involved wanted to make their school proud. Excitement built in intensity as the summer days ticked away closer to the day they boarded the charter buses for The Pier.

Now, as Kimberly cooled off with a damp washcloth in their hotel room awaiting her turn in the bathroom, she stared out the sliding glass door at the beautiful view.

"I still can't believe we're actually here. Oh my God!"

"I know," Cathy said. "It seems like it took forever to get here! I don't think Mrs. Novotny is happy with us, though. I'm having such a hard time with the new steps." She smacked her forehead. "I just keep trying to drill them into this thick skull of mine, but I can't get it."

"You will with practice, Cathy. We all will. Don't worry."

"I just don't want to get kicked off the team. I heard she kicked a girl off the squad last year for not wearing her hair right at competition. I mean, jeez, all she had to do was tell someone to help her fix it."

"Sounds like there was more to that than just hair," said Nicki. At 5'11", Nicki and Rocki towered over all of the girls, and a lot of the boys in the school, too. Kimberly felt like a pipsqueak next to them at only 5'4", and with shoulder length brown curly hair, she felt like a wallflower, too. She knew she shouldn't care about that and wasn't at camp to get a boyfriend. But . . . there was this one junior boy who played trumpet named Dave D'Angelo that she just couldn't get out of her mind. They'd had geometry class together last year and she'd been daydreaming about him for months. He was so cute with his shaggy blonde hair, dark brown eyes, tanned skin, even his braces were adorable! Sigh . . . if only she could get him to notice her.

"Hellooo? Earth to Kim," Cathy said. "It's your turn for the bathroom. Get your head out of the clouds, girl. What's his name?" Her roommates giggled.

"Nobody!" she said, blushing, shutting the bathroom door behind her. She faced her reflection in the mirror and grinned, silently making a promise to herself that Dave would know *her* name before camp was over.

***

For nearly two weeks, the Golden Cougar Marching Band and Auxiliary drilled and marched, practiced and sweated, suffered sore muscles, twisted ankles, and bruises. More than once the directors had to get in the middle of some heated exchanges between worn-out and frustrated students. While marching, Kimberly found herself constantly distracted trying to locate one particular trumpet player. More than once, she was chided by the senior officers for being out of step.

"Cool it, Kim," Cathy warned. "Don't get yourself kicked off the squad because of a boy. Concentrate, girl!"

On the last afternoon of camp, the entire group assembled to perform their newly polished halftime show in full dress for the directors and chaperones. The field show was adapted from the music of Led Zeppelin, The Who, and The Rolling Stones. Each musician played with nuance and fervor as they marched to form patterns on the field. Brass instruments replaced electric guitars. The drum line pounded rhythms to life. Multi-colored flags flapped and spun, rifles flew through the air beside the silver flash of batons, and the high kicks and twirls of shimmery dancers rounded out the scene. As the show came to its final crescendo, the drum majors raised their arms in salute to the audience, who leapt to their feet in thunderous applause. Parents whistled and cheered. All the hard work had paid off. The band was not only ready for the football marching season, but would prove formidable at local and state band competitions during the school year.

The best part were the faces of Mr. Haywood and Mrs. Novotny, a mixture of glee and surprise, as the students outperformed their highest expectations. Mr. Haywood expressed his pride in a 'job well done' speech, before releasing the students for one last night of fun before they packed up in the morning and headed home to Clearwater.

Dismissed to get cleaned up before the barbecue bash, the four girls raced to their room to shower, blow dry, makeup, and hairspray themselves from sweaty to presentable. Kimberly tucked her curls in on each side with small hair combs. She glanced in the mirror. After two weeks in the sun, her skin was tanned to a golden brown. For once, she thought she looked terrific in white cut-off jean shorts, a peachy pink tank top, and white sandals. She fastened on silver hoop earrings and slid a matching bangle bracelet on her wrist.

At the scheduled time of 6:30 pm, the four young dancers slid open their door to a wondrous sight.

On the field where they'd had fourteen days of grueling practices, the chaperones set up a large, tent canopy. Tables were draped in school colors with white lights illuminating the scene. Garnet and gold balloons hung upside down on the ends of long strands of curling ribbon, swaying lazily in the light breeze. Mouth-watering aromas of hickory-smoked barbecue filled the air. Caterers filled smaller tents with smoked meats, potato salad, macaroni and cheese, coleslaw, buttery yeast rolls, and icy beverages.

As the sun moved lower in the western sky over the glittering bay waters, and the hungry group settled in, Mr. Haywood stood to say a few words of appreciation.

"To all of you gathered here, I would like to say thank you. To the students for all of your hard work and dedication, to the drum majors for your inspiring leadership, and to the selfless boosters and chaperones, without whom none of this would have been possible." He led the group in a prayer of thanks for the dinner before them and for a safe and successful camp. After a resounding Amen, all shouted, "GOLDEN COUGAR BAND!"

Everyone tucked into delicious food and lively conversation. All around were smiling, tanned faces, which band officers and section leaders captured on instant cameras. Summer was nearly over.

Kimberly was chatting and giggling with Cathy at their table when she felt a tap on her right shoulder. She looked and was stunned to see the smiling face of Dave D'Angelo and his buddy, Nick.

"Mind if we sit?" Dave asked. Kimberly froze, her face instantly flushed.

"Sure!" Cathy said and the boys took seats. Cathy and Nick slid easily into friendly conversation. Kimberly was convinced everyone could see her heart beating outside of her chest. Sure, she *thought* Dave had noticed her during camp. She'd gone out of her way to locate him on the field every single day, and though she knew she was staring like a starstruck groupie, she couldn't help herself. He was just really dreamy. And so funny. And so sweet. But she'd not yet gotten up the nerve to talk to him. And now here he was, right next to her, and his mouth was moving and, oh my word, what was he saying?

"Kimberly Stevens, right? I know your brother, Jesse. He's a lifeguard at Clearwater Beach? Drives a '72 Dodge Charger?"

"Uh, hi! Um, yep. It's my dad's car, but yeah, he drives it sometimes." *Duh, he didn't need to know that, stupid.*

"Cool. I'm Dave." He stuck out his hand. "Nice to finally meet you." Kimberly took his hand and felt something electric pass between them.

"Ha ha, yeah, I know. I mean, that you're Dave, I mean." *Oh my God, shut up, you idiot!*

"It's pretty noisy under this tent. You wanna take a walk by the bay?" Dave stood up from his seat.

"Oh, sure, okay," she said, standing to join him. "Wait, I'm not supposed to go anywhere without my camp buddy."

Dave laughed. Kimberly was serious. "Okay, sure," he said, and looked over at his buddy. "Hey, let's take these fine ladies for a walk. Sound good?"

The foursome headed across the cooled grass toward the water's edge. They walked along the sea wall chatting, struggling to hear each other over the crash of waves against the wall. The night was balmy and breezy, palm fronds swishing overhead. Kimberly anxiously spun the silver bangle around and around her wrist, responding with shy smiles and one-word answers as Dave babbled about myriad topics. Her mind was spinning with too many thoughts at once—*I hope he thinks I'm pretty . . . I'm so nervous . . . I hope he doesn't try anything too . . . wait, maybe he won't try anything at all . . . I'm probably not even his type . . . jeez, what do I want anyway?* At some point, Kimberly realized there was quite a bit of distance between them and Cathy and Nick. Nervous, she started to slow her pace a little.

"Hey, keep up, curly!" Dave said, grabbing her hand. Again—electricity. She stopped walking and looked into his deep brown eyes.

"Can I ask you something?"

"Of course." He gave her hand a light squeeze.

"Why did you come over to talk to me tonight?"

"Kimberly, really? Did I get the wrong signal?"

"Oh, no! I mean, I just didn't think you . . ." She rocked on her feet and focused on the sidewalk. "Sorry. I'm so awkward."

"Hey," he said, touching her chin. "I think you're just fine." Dave leaned in toward her and Kimberly closed her eyes. She smelled rain and wood smoke and her brain went a little fuzzy as his lips softly kissed hers. Wow—those trumpet lips. She had been staring at them since last year in math class. And now they were on hers. And she thought her legs were going to give way.

"Whoops, sorry, dude!" Nick said, as he and Cathy approached from behind them. Kimberly's eyes flew open.

No, no, no, NO! Go away! I don't want this moment to ever end!

And POOF! Just like that, the magic evaporated. Dave dropped Kimberly's hand. She raised her fingers to her mouth, still feeling the sensation of his lips.

"Hate to interrupt, love birds, but we've gotta get back. They're getting ready to hand out the camp awards, and if we're missing, my ass is definitely grass," Nick said.

***

The following morning was Sunday, departure day from camp.

A chaotic buzz of activity ensued as hotel rooms were emptied, buses and trailers loaded, and the entire entourage made their way back to the high school, where all of the unloading would begin. All band members pitched in to unload before they were released to their parents to go home. Kimberly and the twins were hanging garment bags in alphabetical order in the drill team section of the uniform room, when Dave came in.

"Hey, curly. Need a hand?"

Kimberly smiled. "No, thanks. I think I've got it. But I appreciate it," she said. He stepped closer and put his hand on her shoulder.

"So, Nick's sister is having a party Saturday night. One last fling before she leaves for UF. Wanna come?"

"Yeah, that would be great! What time?"

"Seven. Here." Dave opened his sheet music folder, ripped a corner of paper, and wrote down his phone number. "Call me. I'll come get you."

"Cool," Kimberly said, as her insides beamed like a lighthouse.

Her task complete, Kimberly checked out with Mrs. Novotny, located her luggage on the sidewalk outside the band room, and looked for her parents' station wagon. Approaching the car, she saw her dad sitting in the driver's seat. Jack jumped out, ground out a cigarette under his shoe, and came around to help Kimberly load her things in the back of the car.

"How was camp, kiddo?" With his free arm, he squeezed her shoulders.

"It was good, Dad. I'm just exhausted. So ready for a long nap."

"Well, I know everyone's looking forward to seeing you." Then with a big smile, he said, "And we have big news."

"What? Tell me! Is everything okay?"

"Oh, yeah, everything is terrific. I just got a huge promotion. Eckerd handpicked me to open our new operations base in the southwest. This means a big, brand new house. And we can finally get rid of this old junker wagon. And you kids can definitely go to college now. And—"

"Wait, southwest? How long will you be gone?"

"Me? Oh, it's not just me, kiddo. We're all moving to Texas!"

Chapter Thirteen —1961 — Jack

"Junior! Put that guitar down and get out here. Or, would you rather not graduate today?"

"Coming!" Jack carefully lay the brown and gold acoustic Sears Harmony guitar, his most prized possession, on the foot of his bed. He put on his black leather Oxford shoes and slicked back his thick, dark hair with pomade from a jar on his dresser. Heading toward the kitchen to wash his hands, he bumped into his dad in the small hallway.

Jack flinched. "Sorry, Dad."

"Shake a leg, boy. Car's pulling out in five."

"Yes, sir." He washed and dried his hands, grabbed the black graduation robe and cap, and went outside to join his waiting family.

***

On the coldest day on record in the Appalachian winter of 1943, John Ellis Stevens, Jr. was born to his German immigrant mother on a bed covered in homemade quilts in her mother's house, with a midwife guiding the labor and a local doctor on call. His father, John Senior, would not meet his son for two years, after the end of World War II. By then, mother and son had developed a bond of steel borne of love and laughter. Greta spent her days singing songs to Jack and teaching him to sing them back. In summer, they picked blackberries, Jack standing on a wooden chair to help his mother make jam, poured into Mason jars. His grandmother, Freida, let him roll out the dough for her scrumptious pans of biscuits. Greta reveled in watching her beautiful boy grow and learn, living vicariously through Jack's toddler eyes. He was so curious and smart and loving. Greta believed Jack was a direct gift from God to keep her company and give her life purpose during the unspeakable war that took her husband and so many of the men in her tiny West Virginia farm town away. Small town life afforded isolation from most of the news of the war, so Greta had no idea what horrors her husband may be experiencing in the European Theater.

Upon his return, it was obvious John was a changed man. Once a kind, jolly soul with a twinkle in his eye, the soldier that came back to Greta was quick to anger. He had no patience for the slow way of life in their mountain town any longer. He couldn't stand the snowy days that stretched into weeks of drab gray skies and staying huddled around a cast iron stove in the kitchen for warmth. John had no interest in continuing life as a farmer, nor did he desire delving deep into a coal mine to make a meager, miserable living. Many evenings after supper, he would don a heavy coat and hat and make his way down the hill to a local watering hole, not returning until Greta and Jack were long asleep.

John displayed no affection for his young son, only jealousy of the bond between his wife and child. Try as she might to distract her husband from his anxiety and restlessness, to get him to see how cute and smart and clever their boy was, Greta had no influence over John's brooding. The boy would toddle over to the knee of his father, looking up into his face as he sat by the stove, smoking a hand-rolled cigarette, only to be nudged away by his dad's big, calloused paw and ordered to go play. Jack would run away whining to the safety of his mother's apron, wrapping his arms around her ample legs and burying his face into the soft, stained fabric. John called his son a mama's boy and chided Greta for spoiling him.

"You'll never make a man out of a measly sack of flour like him, Greta. Stop babying, him!"

Soon after Jack turned three, and the long, frigid winter turned into a budding, fragrant spring, John declared they were moving out of this 'God-forsaken town' and relocating to Florida. John had received a letter from an Army buddy about sales opportunities in insurance encouraging him to move his family to the Sunshine State. So, the family of three packed up and began the long trip down from the mountains to the southern shores.

After settling into a small home in St. Petersburg with one bedroom and an efficiency kitchen, Greta discovered she was pregnant again. They also discovered the insurance business was a fickle one. John made little to no money the first year, as he was essentially building sales for his superior while he learned the ropes, but not earning much commission of his own. Greta convinced him to stick with it and, little by little, he eventually did start to see his income increase.

After Donna was born, they were able to use John's GI home loan to purchase a two-bedroom stucco house with a one-car garage and a large, terrazzo Florida room with jalousie windows, and a back yard filled with thick, sturdy Saint Augustine grass. The series of fortunate events began to have a buoyant effect on John. He drank less and smiled more, he even laughed at some of Greta's tales of their old hometown and the characters within. And with a love he'd never shown Jack, he fawned over his chubby baby daughter. Frequently, when Greta couldn't locate either of them, she would follow the sound of the baby girl's giggles to find John and Donna in the backyard playing tickle monster on a blanket, or John tossing her up in the air and swinging her around like an airplane.

Refusing to use the nickname his mother had given him, John called his son Junior. It was a constant reminder of who exactly was the Senior—the man of the house. Any attempt Jack made at getting close to his father was rebuffed. John simply had no interest in anything regarding his son besides showing him who was boss. And if that meant a spanking or a smack now and then, so be it. Greta's hands were tied and her heart crushed as she watched the erosion of any sort of relationship between her husband and son.

***

The radio hummed quietly in the car through the quick, ten-minute drive to Northeast High School. Trying to calm his nerves, Jack counted the sabal palms that lined the streets. The trees rose twenty-five feet, dotting the divide between the WWII-era homes constructed of cinderblocks and stucco. His parents discussed President Kennedy and the war going on in Vietnam. Jack's father was no proponent of war, having lived his own nightmare, but believed staunchly in patriotism and service, and never missed an opportunity to say as much.

"As horrible as this conflict is, I sure am proud of those boys over there. We don't even know what we're fighting for, yet they're brave every single day. It's making men out of them." Jack felt the dig of his dad's words as they fell where they were intended. His eyes met Jack's in the rear view mirror. Jack turned his face and stared out the window.

I'll never be good enough.

After suffering for years as a child with shortness of breath and his heart fluttering in his chest, Jack had been diagnosed with mitral valve prolapse. Doctors advised he would probably need surgery to repair the valve at some point in his life, and he'd been classified 4-F by Selective Service, much to the relief of his mother. To Jack's relief, as well. Even if he'd been physically fit, he probably would have listed himself as a conscientious objector, which would have really set off the old man. He intended to focus all his time and energy into launching his career in music.

When he wasn't working at the gas station, that is, but hopefully not for much longer. He had an audition with a band out of Tampa this weekend who had advertised needing a singing guitar player and he intended to win them over. He'd been working on a bunch of songs, when his dad wasn't riding him to work in the yard or clean out the gutters or some other menial task.

The family walked together toward the high school gymnasium where the ceremony would take place. His mother was handed a program by the underclassmen at the door. She immediately flipped to the student names and located Jack on the page.

"Look, there you are! John Ellis Stevens, Jr. Oh, Jack, I'm so proud of you!" His mother leaned up and kissed her son on the cheek. Jack smiled, looking into the soft brown eyes of his mother.

"Thanks, Mom. I gotta go. See you guys afterwards." Jack ran to catch up with his classmates as they filed into the locker rooms and hallways behind the gym, just in time to hear the beginnings of the processional song, Pomp and Circumstance.

***

The following morning, Donna stood in the doorway of his bedroom as Jack was zipping up his military-style duffel bag, filled with all of his clothes and books.

"What do you mean you're moving out?"

"Just what I said. Tim from the gas station and I got a studio apartment near downtown. It's not much, but it's cheap. And the best part is—no parents. I'm eighteen, I've graduated, I'm outta here."

"Do Mom and Dad know?"

"I'm leaving them a letter."

"A letter? Come on, Jack . . . "

"What, Donna? You know why. Mom will just cry and beg me not to go and Dad'll argue and tell me all the reasons I'm not ready for this yet. I'll never make a move unless I just take the leap. So, I'm outta here. I'll come back and see you, I promise. Besides, you're fifteen now and about to get your learner's permit. You don't need me anymore. You're almost a grown up!" He ruffled Donna's silky, chestnut hair and grabbed his duffel bag to load it in the trunk of his car. He was gingerly placing his guitar case in the back seat, when his parents arrived home earlier than expected from grocery shopping, and pulled up next to him in the driveway.

"Junior, grab these sacks from the trunk and take them to the kitchen," his father said. Jack paused for a beat, then turned to the trunk of his parents' car to help. His mother smiled at him and went inside the house. A feeling of dread began to build in Jack's stomach. He had lifted out one of the paper sacks when he heard his mother yell.

"John! Jack is leaving! Stop him!"

"What are you talking about, Greta, he's right here," John said. His mother came out of the front door waving an unfolded piece of notebook paper.

"I'm talking about this. Jack left us a note in the kitchen. He's moving out." His father turned to look at his son.

"That so, Junior?"

"Yes, sir. I got a small place with a buddy near downtown. I'm old enough and I'm done with school, so—"

"So, what, all you think about is yourself? Did you ever consider we might need you around here? That your mother might need the help? That your sister needs her big brother? And how much money are you spending on this place? You barely make a dime at that ridiculous job at the gas station. Did you ever think maybe you could start paying us a little room and board to live at home? That we might be able to use the money? No, of course not. You never think about anybody but yourself. I can't believe I raised such a spoiled, selfish brat!" With that last word, he struck Jack across the jaw with his closed fist.

"John, no!" Greta screamed.

With the force of the blow, Jack lost his grip on the sack of groceries. An onion and a tomato came loose from the bag and rolled down into the gutter. Jack stood completely still. He took in a deep breath through his nose.

"That is the last time," he said quietly through clenched teeth. He bent and picked up the grocery bag, slowly setting it back in his parents' trunk, and began to walk to his car.

"Get back here when I am talking to you, Junior. Yeah, that's right, just run away like you always do." John sneered at his son, but did not attempt to follow him.

Jack got into the driver's seat of his car and looked at his mother, standing on the small patio in front of the door. He saw Donna behind her on the threshold, her hand on their mother's shoulder.

I'm sorry. He's your problem now.

Jack backed out of the driveway, and drove away from his family's home without so much as a glance in the rearview mirror.

***

"What's the other guy look like?" Coming in from the bright Florida sunshine, it took a moment for Jack's eyes to adjust to the dim light inside the Cabana Lounge. A guy holding a saxophone was standing on the low-rise stage and was the only other person in the room, which smelled of old booze and tobacco smoke. Jack reached up and touched his bruised jaw.

"Shaving accident," he said with a smile and held out his hand, which the saxophone player shook. "Jack Stevens."

"Pepe. Nice to meet you, Jack. Auditioning?"

"Yeah. Want me to set up here?" Jack motioned to the stage.

"Sure, go ahead. Ed's in the back. I'll go get him." While Jack unpacked his guitar and began to tune up, a tall man emerged from the back of the lounge. At 6'3" with black hair and dark circles under his ebony eyes, Ed Martini was intimidating. Jack swallowed, his palms sweaty. As soon as Ed approached the stage, his face broke into an ice-melting, gap-toothed grin. He extended his hand to Jack.

"How ya doing, kid? Ed Martini. Think you're gonna be my new strummer, huh?"

Jack returned the firm handshake. "That's the plan, sir."

"None of that 'sir' bullshit. Save that for your old man." He looked at Jack's acoustic guitar. "Kid, we play rock and roll. Jazzy blues. We have an entire horn section that will drown out that acoustic of yours. Do you have an electric?" Jack was crestfallen. He shook his head. "Well, have you ever played one?" Again, the head shake. "Okay, let me hear what you've got on this acoustic. Take a listen to your pipes. Then we'll see what we can arrange."

Jack put the strap around his back, stepped up to the mic, and started to strum a folksy Kingston Trio tune, "Tom Dooley," a sad ballad about the murder of a woman.

Ed leaned against his piano, arms folded across his ample chest, and listened to Jack's warm baritone sing the melody, break into a high harmony, and back to melody to end the song. He nodded his head and grinned.

"Okay, okay, pretty good stuff there, kid. Got something a little more upbeat?"

"You bet." Jack launched into a rousing Elvis Presley hit, "That's Alright (Mama)."

Other band members began filling the room, sitting at two-top round tables in front of the stage, tapping along to Jack's performance. He took this as a good sign. His confidence brimming, he put a growl in his voice and strummed his guitar with intensity. When the song ended, Jack wiped the sweat from his brow. He beamed with surprised appreciation at the applause. Ed approached Jack and handed him an older electric guitar.

"Kid, you go home and practice on this thing. Here's the music to a couple numbers we do. We're here every Tuesday through Saturday. Come back as soon as you're ready and we'll see how you do."

"Thank you, sir, uh, Ed. I won't let you down." Ed handed Jack a beat up case for the borrowed guitar. As Jack turned to leave the bar, a guitar in each hand, Ed called after him, "Say, kid . . . how do you feel about singing with a girl?"

Chapter Fourteen — 1961 — Marjorie

Marjorie placed her last piece of luggage into the back of Isabella's baby blue 1955 Dodge Royal and closed the door. The air was warm and muggy, typical of a sunny afternoon in June. She could smell the sea water from the bay as it made its way down her street like fog rolling in.

"That's it," she said, as she started to climb into the passenger seat.

"Do you wanna go say bye to your mama?" Isabella asked. Marjorie looked at her friend and shook her head. Isabella placed her hand over Marjorie's and said, "Hey, you may not see her again for a while. You sure?"

"I'm sure," Marjorie said. She looked over her right shoulder at the small house once more, then turned to face the windshield. "Let's go."

Isabella pulled away from the curb and down the street, heading to her parents' house a few miles away in Ballast Point. Marjorie smiled gratefully at her friend, then closed her eyes, taking in a calming breath. So, this was it. She was leaving home.

The girls pulled into the driveway of the Lopez house and drove to the back by the detached garage. Isabella's young sister and brother were playing in the back yard littered with brightly colored balls of all sizes, plastic bats, a sandbox with pails and shovels, a jump rope, and a couple of hula hoops. Mrs. Lopez was hanging freshly laundered sheets on the line with clothes pins, the basket of wet linens at her feet.

"*Hola, Mami!*" Isabella called from the open car window. Her mother's smile was radiant as she put the clothes pins back into her apron and walked toward the car.

"*Hola, mija*! How are you girls doing?" Mrs. Lopez hugged her daughter, kissing her cheek. "All packed, Marjie?"

"Yes, ma'am. Thank you so much for letting me stay here," Marjorie said. "It means so much to me. I don't know how I can ever thank you enough."

"Nonsense, sweet girl. You and Bella have known each other for, what, ten years now? You are like family. And we take care of family." She walked around the car to Marjorie and gave her a hug. Marjorie held on a bit longer, so rarely was she hugged. Mrs. Lopez touched Marjorie's cheek. "You stay as long as you like. Everything's gonna be okay, am I right?"

"Yes, ma'am."

Mrs. Lopez smiled. "Good. Come on, let's get your things inside and get you settled in Bella's room."

Later that evening, Marjorie took her place next to Isabella at the dinner table. She looked around at the happy faces of the Lopez family, passing dishes filled with delicious food—*arroz con pollo, frijoles negros, yuca con mojo*, fried *tostones*, and a fresh tossed green salad with ripe red tomatoes. Marjorie's mouth watered as she placed a little of each dish on her plate. The dinner plates were beautiful, brightly colored stoneware painted in vibrant reds, greens, yellows and blues. The conversation was just as vibrant. Mr. Lopez laughed, amused by his wife's shared antics of her day with the little ones, and listened intently to Isabella's animated tales of dealing with grouchy customers at her job at a local bakery. He smiled across the table at Marjorie.

"We're happy you're here, Marjie. How about that chicken, huh? Mrs. Lopez's cooking cannot be beat. It might be the reason I married her!"

"Oh, stop, Pepe! And here I thought it was for my brilliant brain."

"Ah, yes, *mi amor*, for your brilliant brain, too."

Marjorie took a sip of her milk and smiled. This is what a normal family was like. She could be content here. Although she knew it was only temporary, she felt herself already getting attached to the Lopez family. It was going to be really hard to say goodbye when she and Chip got married.

"So, Papi, I asked Mr. Alessi at work if he could hire Marjie, but they just don't have room on the staff right now since tourist season is over. Do you know of anyone hiring for the summer?"

Mr. Lopez stroked his mustache. "I'll keep my ears open, *mija*."

After dinner, Isabella and Marjorie were in the kitchen doing the dishes. A small transistor radio sat on the windowsill playing popular music. The girls danced as they cleaned, sudsy water slopping out of the sink, giggles filling the air. Marjorie sang along at the top of her voice to the Connie Francis hit, "Where the Boys Are." She was grinding her voice to Brenda Lee's "Sweet Nothin's," when the door to the kitchen swung open and Mr. Lopez came into the room.

"Remember what I said about keeping my ears open? Am I glad that I did," he said.

"Papi, did you find out something already? Just since dinner?"

"Seems I have. Marjie, how would you like to sing with a band this summer?"

***

Pepe and his wife, Ana, were having coffee one Sunday morning in September. The house was quiet as the kids were still sleeping. They spoke in hushed tones.

"I didn't want to pry too much into her business, but what actually happened?" Ana asked.

"Beats me. I still don't really know. It was the strangest thing. When they met, they couldn't stand each other. Jack said Marjie was a stuck-up society girl and Marjie said Jack was a thug from the wrong side of town. It didn't help his case that he always has a pack of cigarettes rolled up in the sleeve of his t-shirt and all that grease in his hair. And she acts kind of prissy holding the microphone with a handkerchief!" Pepe chuckled. Ana smiled and nodded.

"But once these kids started singing together, it was like magic. Their voices blended with the sweetest harmonies. Ed was thrilled. The crowds poured in every weekend to see them all summer. And then, poof! They miss rehearsal a couple of nights last week and don't show up for the gigs over the weekend. And what do you know? They pop up at the lounge on Tuesday afternoon flashing little gold bands, saying they'd eloped to Georgia. Ed was furious with them for missing all the gigs. But we congratulated them and told them to get back to work." Pepe shook his head.

"When she picked up all of her things yesterday afternoon, she just thanked me for letting her stay here. I gave her a hug, wished her well. I didn't ask any questions. What about Chip?" Ana asked in a whisper. "I wonder how she is going to break it to him." She thought for a moment, then gasped. "Oh my gosh, her mother will probably never speak to her again."

Pepe took a sip of his coffee, swallowed, and looked his wife in the eye. "That wouldn't be the worst thing that ever happened to Marjie." Ana took his hand in silent agreement.

***

Marjorie looked from the passenger seat of the convertible at Jack's black hair ruffling in the wind, sunglasses on, cigarette dangling from his lips, and thought, "What in the world have I done?"

It had all started innocently enough. Marjorie's audition went so well, she was hired on the spot as a backup singer and occasional female lead. The lead guitarist and singer was a pompous ass who wore his cigarettes in his sleeve like a greaser and Marjorie wanted absolutely nothing to do with him. And what had he called her? A prude? The nerve.

Then there was the night at a diner after a late gig when some local boys were coming onto Marjorie. Jack defended her honor, offering to fight them in the parking lot. Ed stepped in and put a stop to the whole debacle, but she began to see Jack in a different light. That led to her giving him her phone number at Pepe and Ana's, which led to several calls and a few dates, which led to Marjorie constantly dreaming about his sea green eyes.

One night, Jack surprised her by arriving in a slightly beat-up, but very clean, convertible he'd just gotten in a great trade. On the way to the beach to watch the sunset, she was impressed with the car and moved by how proud he was of himself. Kisses led to a bit of touching, then a lot more touching, until Marjorie stopped to come up for air.

"Jack," she said, breathlessly. "I'm a good Catholic girl. You know I can't do this without being married."

Which led to Jack hatching a plan. He showed up with his buddy Ted and Ted's girlfriend Brenda for a double date beach picnic. He told Marjie to pack a change of clothes in case they wanted to have dinner that night. But instead of the beach, Jack headed north on US-41.

"Wait," Marjorie asked. "The beach is the other way."

Jack's smile was mischievous. "I have a surprise, honey." Marjorie was all bubbles and nerves inside. What could he have up his sleeve?

When they stopped for gas, Ted took over the pump and Jack walked Marjorie to a grassy area with a few trees. In the shade of the oaks, he got down on one knee and slipped a gold band onto her finger. Marjorie threw her arms around his neck and happy cried as he smothered her face and neck with sweet kisses.

"So where are we going to celebrate our engagement?" she asked.

"Well, that's the other half of my surprise. We're heading to Georgia to get married today!"

Marjorie froze. She swallowed hard. "Today? But I can't possibly. I mean, look at me, I'm dressed for the beach!"

"You brought a change of clothes."

"Pedal pushers and a blouse. Not a dress! Definitely nothing I should be getting married in!"

"It's fine, honey," Jack soothed. "You'd look beautiful in a potato sack."

"And what about Isabella? She's my best friend. She should be my maid of honor! And her parents, and your parents, and our friends…"

"This is just a formality, Marjie. We'll have the church wedding later if you want with everyone there and a big party afterward. You name it. But this is all about you and me. Just us. Starting our life together. I can't wait to call you my wife." Jack tipped her quivering chin up and gently kissed her, and Marjorie's knees went weak.

Later that evening, Marjorie stumbled across the shag carpet of the Howard Johnson Inn as she slipped one shoe off, then the other. Jack steadied her from behind.

"Whoa there, little lady. Looks like you've maybe had a bit too much celebration champagne."

"Well, of course I have! I'm a *married* little lady now. I'm all grown up and I can have as much champagne as I want from now on!" she giggled, wrestling with her blouse, which was now wrapped around her face. "I jus' wanna get comfy for my *husband.* Come 'ere, husband!"

Jack carefully slipped her blouse over her head and grinned at his bride.

"I bought you something else." He reached into his overnight case, pulling out a tissue-wrapped package with a gold ribbon. "I thought you might want to have something pretty for tonight."

Marjorie slipped the ribbon off the paper, revealing a diaphanous negligee of white silk and organza. "Oh, Jack, it's gorgeous! I don't think I've ever had anything so pretty in my whole life." She held it up to her body and flopped down onto the bed behind her, crying.

Sitting next to her, Jack wrapped his arm around her shoulders. "Darling, what's the matter?"

Through her tears, Marjorie sputtered, "I don't deserve this. I don't deserve you. I'm not as wonderful and sweet and innocent as you think I am, Jack. I'm a soiled girl. I feel like I misled you and I'm so, so sorry."

Jack handed her a tissue for her running nose. "What are you trying to say, Marjie?"

"That you're not the first. My stepdad. He was—," she choked though the words. "He was a drunk and awful and he touched me and did things. Terrible things."

Wrapping her up in his arms, Jack gently shushed Marjorie. "It's okay, honey. It's going to be okay. He can't hurt you anymore. I'm here and I'll always protect you. You're my wife, now and forever."

She looked up at him, mascara running down her soaked, reddened cheeks. She shook her head. "You don't mean it. Nobody ever means it."

Jack turned her to fully face him and looked into her eyes. "Marjorie Stevens, I make you this solemn promise. I will never, ever leave you."

Now driving back to Tampa, their friends sleeping in the backseat, Marjorie wondered how this had happened so fast. She was madly in love with the man before her, but was it enough? Did he mean it when he promised never to leave her? He had no idea, because she'd never told anyone, about the things that happened in her mind. When the memories were pervasive, she found herself soothing in any way she could. Sometimes it was washing her hands over and over to get as clean as she possibly could. Sometimes she rocked back and forth hugging herself on the floor of the locked bathroom. Sometimes she snuck liquor into her coffee and sodas. Oh, to just be numb and make her brain shut up! Sometimes she had scary, terrible thoughts of finding a way to just go to sleep and never wake up. To make the memories go away. To make the shame go away. To end the constant thoughts of what a bad girl she was. Gazing at the shiny gold band on her finger, she prayed to the God who she hoped was still there to keep her from destroying the one good thing in her life.

***

The following year, Isabella stopped at her parents' house one

Sunday afternoon following church. They were having lunch before she headed back to her dorm at the University of South Florida. She was looking forward to the new school year getting underway the following day. Ana set about putting a basket of leftovers together for her, while Isabella sat at the kitchen table flipping through the Sunday newspaper.

"Oh, *Mami*, I almost forgot to tell you! I ran into Marjie last night. She and Jack were at the same gas station as me. Anyway, I haven't seen her in forever. She looks great and very happy. I guess they have a cute little place over in St. Pete. Jack was promoted to a store manager with Eckerd's and Marjie is working as a pharmacy clerk. Oh, and here's the best part—she's expecting! Their first baby is due in the spring. Isn't it amazing how life changes?"

"Yes, *mija*. It sure is amazing," Ana said, as she packed the basket. She said a silent prayer of thanks for her daughter, and asked God to look over Marjorie and her sweet baby. Whatever life had in store for the beautiful girl with the sad heart, Ana hoped it would at least be filled with love.

***

Marjorie had never felt this kind of pain in her life. Searing, ripping, hot-knife-in-the-gut kind of pain. She knew childbirth was going to hurt; she wasn't that naïve. She just never imagined it would feel like the claws of a tiger. She gripped the rails on the sides of the hospital bed and tuned out the nurses encouraging her to push.

Months earlier, she'd been elated to find out she was about to be a mother. Unlike a lot of newly pregnant women, she couldn't wait to see her tummy grow. She'd stood sideways in front of the mirror every morning checking for signs that the baby was getting bigger. She'd eaten her food with a flourish, giving in to every craving.

Forced to be frugal, Marjorie saved every penny she could toward fabric and patterns of maternity blouses by McCall's, sewing herself a few new ones each trimester. The brightly colored tops looked like circus tents on her at first, but she'd soon outgrown each one.

Jack frequently teased her about her belly and had spoken to the baby inside each night in bed. When she'd grown too big to feel comfortable, she'd stepped down from singing in the band. As she'd sewed the skirt for the basinet they'd found at a yard sale, she'd told herself she was going to give this baby more love than it could handle.

She would hug it every single day and tell it how perfect and precious and adored it was. Because every child should feel loved by its mother. *A new beginning,* she told herself. *Please let this be a new beginning for me.*

Marjorie's delivery date came and went. The obstetrician told her that was not abnormal in a first pregnancy. He allowed her go one week past her due date, then decided it was best to induce labor. When the Pitocin injections took effect, contractions came on like tidal waves crashing onto jagged rocks. Marjorie gripped and sweated and cried out in agony until finally she felt something break loose. Her head spun and buzzed inside like a wasp nest. She was completely spent.

"Mrs. Stevens, you have a beautiful baby boy," the doctor pronounced. When the nurse swaddled John Ellis Stevens III and lay him on her belly, she looked down at her son for the first time, and she felt . . . nothing.

For days, the nurses tried to help her breastfeed, but she felt alien and weird in her own body and the baby never latched on. For months, she let him cry himself to sleep and awake, unable to muster the ability to soothe him. The arrivals of Kimberly Marie and Sabrina Grace years later changed nothing. Something inside her had become irretrievably broken. Marjorie simply couldn't give what she never had.

Chapter Fifteen — 1976 — The Family

The Fourth of July brought with it the largest celebration of Independence Day in the Stevens family's collective memory. The Bicentennial was shaping up to be an enormous event all across the United States. Not simply traditional cookouts and fireworks, the country geared up for parades, concerts, celebratory marches, and sailing events spanning the entire week leading up to Sunday, July 4, 1976—the 200th anniversary of the adoption of the Declaration of Independence.

With no shortage of network broadcast specials, Jesse, Kimberly, and Sabrina sat glued for many a summer morning to the television, as much as they could get away with, singing along to *Schoolhouse Rock's* "I'm Just a Bill," and cheering on US Olympic athletes during the televised trials leading up to the Summer Olympics in Montreal. The entire country was swept up in one giant block party.

The bathing suit-clad Stevens family packed up the station wagon early Sunday morning and headed to Fort DeSoto Park for a day of fun in the sun, picnics all day, and fireworks at sunset. John and Greta secured a campsite with two picnic tables and plenty of space for multiple cars and a canopy-style tent to house a plethora of summertime food and a cot in case anyone desired a mosquito-free nap.

Donna arrived with her husband, Bill, and met Greta and Marjorie in the tent to help organize the day's fare. In a large Coleman cooler were hamburger patties and packages of Oscar Meyer wieners, Tupperware containers of deviled eggs, macaroni salad, and Greta's beloved Watergate salad, that the kids just called 'green stuff,' a fluffy concoction of pistachio pudding, pineapple, Cool Whip, nuts, and marshmallows. A Stevens family holiday wasn't complete without it. Assorted bags of chips and buns kept one end of the red-and-white checked tablecloth secure, while the other end was held down by red, white, and blue paper plates, napkins, and utensils.

Donna hugged her mother, talking over Greta's shoulder to Marjorie. "Hey, Marjie, got anything I can use to cut up the watermelon we brought?"

"Of course," Marjorie said, handing her a plastic cutting board and a large knife.

"Also picked up pies on the way down—blueberry and cherry. You know me and desserts."

"We can always count on you to satisfy our sweet tooth, Donna."

As soon as the car was completely unloaded, the kids tore off down to the beach.

"Kimberly, keep an eye on the baby!"

"Okay, Mom," she called over her shoulder.

"Jesse! Anything happens to that baby and it won't be pretty," Jack hollered after him.

"I got it, Dad, jeez."

"I'm not a baby anymore, I'm almost six!"

"Sabrina, stay with your brother and sister. No buts."

"Yes, ma'am."

Jack lit the charcoal in the grill, scooping an icy Pabst from the cooler while he waited for the coals to turn gray. John Senior unfolded woven, aluminum lawn chairs and met his son's eye.

"Junior."

"Dad." They shook hands. Jack raised the can in his hands to his father in the form of question.

John shook his head. "Jumped on the wagon for a bit. Touch of the gout. I'll take a Coke, though, if you got one." Jack bent down to the cooler, trying to locate a red can among the white ones. He popped the top before handing it to his dad.

"Kids are getting big so fast," John said, looking past the campsite at his grandchildren on the beach.

"Tell me about it. I'm buying new shoes like people change underwear."

"How old now?"

"Thirteen, ten, and six."

"Hard to believe. I remember when each one arrived. Seems like yesterday."

"Yep, me, too. Jesse'll be driving before I know it. Kimberly's a funny little thing, but such a handful for Marj. Sabrina's our little sweetheart. The other day, she—"

"Junior, I wanted to talk to you about something." He looked at his son, then back at the beach. Greenish-blue waves kissed the grainy shore, dotted with children in brightly-colored bathing suits, surrounded by floats and plastic toys.

"Sounds serious, Dad." The men turned to face away from the family for a bit of privacy as they spoke.

"Just wanted to address something that's been on my mind before we get into the swing of the holiday." John took a swig of Coke and swallowed hard, clearing his throat. "Junior, I know I wasn't a good father to you. I was hard. Mean. Tried to toughen you up. I drove a wedge between us and I regret that."

"Dad, don't worry about—"

"Let me finish, son, please. I see you going down the same road with Jesse. Before you make all the mistakes I did, especially the teen years, take a minute and listen to your old man."

Jack looked at his dad and nodded, taking a pull from his can.

"Jesse is different from you. Quiet. Thoughtful. He's a good kid, but I don't have to tell you that. We have patterns in this family. Cycles. Like it's in our blood, or something. My old man was a real bastard, as was my grandpa. As fathers, we followed the examples of our own." He looked into the eyes of his son. "I'm hoping you can break that godawful cycle, Junior. Fortunately, you had the good sense to leave before I screwed you up too badly."

"I'm okay."

John put his beefy hand on Jack's shoulder. "I can see that, son, and I'm . . . well, I'm proud of you. You're a better father than I ever was. Just go easy on Jesse. Let him be who he's gonna be. He'll always need you, but he doesn't need you to be a hardass."

"Got it. All I can do is try, Dad."

"That's all any of us can ever do, Jun . . . er, Jack."

Jack put out his hand. John lifted his hand from Jack's shoulder and put it on the back of Jack's neck, pulling him in for a brief, awkward hug.

"Shoulda done more of that," he said, clearing his throat again.

Greta, hands busy slicing tomatoes and onions, watched from inside the screened canopy, eyes welling.

"Ma, those onions get you every time," Donna said, handing her a napkin.

"Yes, yes, the onions," she said, dabbing her eyes and nodding.

***

Sabrina threw her pail and shovel down into the gritty sand and put her hands on her slim hips, her miniature belly curved out over her star-spangled swimsuit bottoms.

"I'm tired of building a sand castle. I wanna go on the swings."

Kimberly pushed damp curls out of her eyes. "Go ask Mom, then. Jess and I are gonna finish this." She turned her pail of wet, compressed sand upside down, dumping it onto their creation, pressing and smoothing it to resemble a castle tower.

"Fine, I will," Sabrina said, trudging up the shifting sand toward the campsite. She'd forgotten to put on her flip-flops and stepped on a sand spur. "Ouch!" She pulled the offending tiny ball of spikes out of her foot, watching more carefully as she trod up to the picnic table, looking for her red rubber sandals.

Marjorie and Donna were deep in debate about who was the more handsome swimmer—John Naber or Mark Spitz—paying no attention to the youngest Stevens. Greta reclined on the cot inside the tent, giving her eyes a rest, and never saw Sabrina. The men flipped burgers and dogs on the grill, discussing whether the loud-mouthed millionaire who'd just bought the Atlanta Braves would be able to hire a front office that could actually deliver a winning season. They didn't notice as the little girl strode right past them, headed for the playground.

Only one of the rectangular, metal swings was unoccupied. Sabrina picked up her pace to nab it before some other kid did. She ran past the wooden teeter-totter. She ran past the rainbow colored merry-go-round. Almost there, she looked up at the boy standing on his swing, holding onto the thick, steel chains, pushing himself higher and higher. She would later say that she never really felt it when the sharp corner of the metal seat made contact with the center of her forehead, knocking her backward to the ground, the gash beginning to bleed.

Jack looked up as a woman ran down the sandy path, holding the child against her and pressing a t-shirt against the girl's head. As she ran, the frantic woman called out, "Whose child is this?" Confusion made its way across the faces of all the adults as it took a moment to register the child was Sabrina.

"Oh my God, that's my daughter!" Jack screamed, scooping the unconscious girl from the stranger's arms. "What happened to her?"

"I don't know! It all happened so fast. She was running for the swing set, but a kid standing on one of the swings didn't see her and they collided. It was just an accident. Can I help?"

"You already have, ma'am, thank you," he said, cradling Sabrina against him.

"Oh my God!" Donna cried out, running to get ice in a towel.

"Dad," Jack said. "Please take us to the hospital."

"Yes, of course," John said, pulling his keys out of his shorts pocket, running for his car.

"St. Anthony's is the closest. Marj, you coming?"

Marjorie was walking the opposite direction of the car toward the path to the beach. She bent down and picked up a narrow, broken tree branch, holding it tightly in her fist.

As she headed toward her older children, she said, "I've gotta take care of something first. I'll meet you there."

No time to argue, Jack climbed in the passenger seat of John's car, rocking his daughter back and forth, keeping the ice pack Donna gave him pressed to Sabrina's head. As her husband and son pulled away from the site, the diminutive Greta stepped in front of her daughter-in-law, clamping down on the branch with both hands as tightly as she could, wrenching it away from Marjorie's hand.

"No!" she shouted into the other woman's face. "What the hell is wrong with you, Marjorie? You go be with the baby who needs you. This is not Jesse and Kimberly's fault. It was an accident. I'll take care of them. Go!"

Bill approached, placing an arm around Marjorie's shoulders. "I'll take you, Marj. You shouldn't drive right now." He guided her into the passenger seat of his car. Marjorie sat stiffly, her face as hard as stone.

Greta and Donna wrapped the cooked meat in foil and went down to the beach to tell the kids what happened. Kimberly folded into herself, tears flowing, rocking back and forth on the sand.

"Mom and Dad are gonna kill us," Jesse said.

"Nobody's killing anybody. They know it was an accident," Donna said, rubbing Kimberly's back. "Sabrina is gonna be okay. Everything will be all right."

"But they said—"

"I know what they said."

Jesse allowed his grandmother to hold him in her arms as they sat on the beach. She stroked his hair, kissing the top of his head. In her faded German accent, she said, "People say things they don't mean all the time. Trust me." She met Donna's eyes over the children's bowed heads. "It's all right. I promise you that."

***

Brilliant shades of purples, pinks and oranges spread across the horizon as the sun lowered in the western sky. Families sat scattered like seashells across the beach awaiting the Bicentennial fireworks from a barge near the Sunshine Skyway Bridge. Sabrina licked a lollipop, resting her bandaged head against her grandmother's shoulder, as Greta sang softly to her, gently swaying side to side on the beach blanket near the shore. Jesse and Kimberly sat on either side of their aunt Donna, holding the treasured gifts she'd brought for them — a pogo stick for Jesse ("Don't break any bones, big guy, or I'll be in big trouble with your mom and dad") and a large, leather bound journal for Kimberly ("Pour out all your secrets, Kim. They'll be safe in here"). Bill and John's lawn chairs were close behind them on the sand, the men sitting in peaceful silence as the waves lapped the shore.

On a beach towel near the blanket, Marjorie closed her eyes, resting the back of her head against Jack's chest, his arm wrapped around her waist. Nearly inaudibly, she said, "I don't know what came over me. I don't know if I'm cut out for this . . ."

Jack lit a cigarette, blowing the smoke up into the night sky. As the *thunk* of the first cannon released a glittering rocket into the dark, he said, "Don't worry. It's not gonna happen again."

Chapter Sixteen — 1996 — Kimberly

"Momma, are you waked up? Momma?" came the little voice from the playpen beside her bed. Kimberly rubbed her burning eyes and opened them lazily. She looked over to see her little angel standing up and smiling, blonde ringlets askew from sleep, her eyes bright. Kimberly smiled.

"Well, hello, sunshine! How's my big girl? Did you sleep good?"

"Yep."

"Are you hungry? Let's get you some breakfast."

"I hungies." She raised her arms to her mother and Kimberly lifted her up, hugging her tightly.

"Well, aren't you just the best thing ever to see when I open my eyes?" She rained kisses all over Julie's little face and neck as her baby girl giggled, and stood her on the floor to get her out of her pajamas.

"Come on, pipsqueak," she said, and they walked into the kitchen. She helped Julie up into her high chair, locking the tray into place. She poured out Cheerios and filled the baby's sippy cup with cold milk. While Julie ate her breakfast, Kimberly went back into the bedroom. She placed her hands on her belly, as though that would help ease the waves of cramps. She sat down on the bed, put her head in her hands, and sighed deeply, swallowing two Advil with a tepid glass of water beside the bed.

***

Kimberly pushed the stroller closer to the big blue mailbox, pulled the squeaky door toward her, and dropped the letter inside. She closed the door and thought, *It's done. No going back now.*

Kimberly swiveled the stroller and started to walk back to the apartment. In the morning light, the neighborhood smelled of baked goods and coffee. She surprised herself by smiling and turning the stroller back in the other direction. She would take Julie to the park. Her daughter loved the playground. She made sure Julie still had on her mittens, zipped her jacket up, and pulled her tiny knit cap down tight.

"Wanna go to the swings?" Kimberly asked.

"Sweens!"

"That's right! Won't it be fun?"

As they strolled along the sidewalk, Kimberly sang, "This little light of mine, I'm gonna let it shine . . ." Julie hummed and sang along to every third word or so, amusing her mother.

The park was still relatively empty at this time of the morning. Kimberly unhooked the stroller belt and scooped her daughter out. She chose a purple baby swing, and set Julie on the seat, pulling the upper part down the chains to secure her little one inside. Julie opened her mouth in a wide smile as Kimberly pushed her slowly, gaining a little more speed and height with each push. Julie clapped her mittened hands and said, "Higher, Momma!" She moved around to the back of the swing to push it even higher. As she reached to push the swing again, a cramp shot through her lower belly like a lightning bolt. Kimberly grabbed her stomach with both hands and dropped to one knee. The world tilted as her vision began to swirl. *Oh, no, no, no, please.* On both knees, she placed her hands on the ground.

"Just breathe through it, breathe, breathe," she whispered to herself. She felt warm fluid escape her.

"Momma! Momma, go higher! Momma?"

"It's okay, baby girl. I'm sorry, we need to get home now. Maybe we'll come back a little later, okay? Let's get you out of the swing."

Kimberly placed Julie back in the stroller. She slipped off her hoodie and tied it around her waist, tugging it down in back to cover the seat of her jeans.

At her apartment building, she bent to lift the stroller to ascend the stairs. Mr. García stood slowly and approached the young mother and her daughter.

"Kimberly, you okay? You're white as a sheet. I'll help you up." Between the two of them, they managed to get the stroller up the stairs. At her front door, she thanked him. He patted her on the shoulder.

"It's no problem. Anytime. Sure you're okay?" She nodded and unlocked the door.

Once Julie was settled in her playpen with plenty of toys, Kimberly changed her clothes. She never knew when this was going to happen and chastised herself for not being better prepared. She wondered if this was a sign the cervical cancer had progressed beyond stage II.

Chapter Seventeen — 1981 — Kimberly

Christy Caldwell was gorgeous. Not just pretty. Gorgeous. At sixteen, she stood at 5'7" with long, wavy auburn hair and deep brown eyes. Redheads are typically known for freckles and sunburns, but not Christy. Her tanned skin glowed golden and flawless, a perfect frame to her bright white smile. She was a stunner and well aware of it. She also came from one of the wealthiest families in The Woodlands, Texas. Christy was the most popular girl at McCarthy High School, and she had it in for Kimberly from her second day there.

Kimberly hated being the new girl. It was so unfair for her dad to move them *again*. While she was happy for his promotion, she didn't think he had a clue at all as to what he put his kids through every time they moved. And this time to a new state? Right before the school year started?

Which is exactly why it was so painful to be the new girl. For at least the first day, and usually many more days to follow, the focus was on her. Other kids stared and whispered. Kimberly was conscious of how she spoke, walked, breathed . . . it was excruciating. Eventually, the kids got used to her, or someone else moved to the area and became the *new* new kid. Either way, when the focus was finally off Kimberly, she felt like she could let out the breath she'd been holding for weeks.

"Honey, just find out what all of the other kids are into and show an interest yourself! You'll fit right in," Mom said.

"Kimmy, stand up for yourself. Don't let those kids push you around. Be tough, be assertive, be brave!" Dad said.

The more she tried to fit in, the more miserable she became.

***

It all started over a pair of blue jeans. Kimberly attended the first day of school wearing what she would normally wear in Florida: a t-shirt, shorts, socks and sneakers. She was so far removed from how they dressed in Texas, the dreaded spotlight might as well have been over her head, following her every move in the hallways that day. She made mental notes as she timidly watched the other girls around her. Button-down blouses with shiny metallic threads running through them, frilly cotton peasant blouses in neutral colors, all of them worn with blue jeans. And not just any blue jeans, but designer names like Jordache with the horse head logo, Gloria Vanderbilt with the swan, or Calvin Klein with the CK. Some girls wore Wrangler jeans with the distinctive W stitching on the back pockets or Levis with their telltale red or white pocket tabs. Shoes were platform strappy sandals or expensive snakeskin cowboy boots, which she soon found out were called "kicker" boots. Not the dingy white Converse sneakers adorning Kimberly's feet. And most definitely *not* shorts. Shorts were worn exclusively in gym class. She could have sworn she heard giggles down every hallway she walked. She wanted to crawl into a hole and die.

As soon as Kimberly got off the bus at her stop that afternoon, she ran as fast as she could and burst through the front door of their new house.

"Mom! Mom, where are you?"

"I'm in the kitchen," Marjorie said. Kimberly ran straight into the kitchen to find her mom weighing handfuls of ground beef, rolling them into balls, and pressing them into perfect hamburger patties with a Tupperware press.

"We need to go shopping. Like now. I don't have *any* of the right clothes for school. It was humiliating, Mom. You promised we could go school clothes shopping after we got to Texas. We've been so busy unpacking we never went. *Please!"*

"Okay, catch your breath, Kim. Slow down. Yes, I did make you and your sister that promise. I am making dinner right now, which is a bit more important. Certainly you have at least four outfits you can wear this week. We can take our time and go shopping this weekend."

Kimberly shoved clenched fists down the sides of her legs and said, "No, I do not! I have dressy clothes and I have t-shirts. Nothing in between. Can you just give us your credit card? We can go on the bus."

"They don't have buses running here like they did in Florida. I need you to be reasonable right now and wait until this weekend. It's only four days."

"Ugggghhhh, you do not understand!"

Marjorie washed her hands thoroughly with soap and hot water, and then began to wash them again. "There's a strip mall not far from here. You could walk. It would do you both some good to get out of this house and spend some time together."

Kimberly leaned against the kitchen doorframe, her arms folded across her chest.

"Fine," she sighed. "I'll take her with me."

"Good, that's settled. I have a Lerner's charge you can use. Just bring the card and receipt straight back to me. Your budget is twenty-five dollars each. You should be able to get a few things. Look at the clearance racks. They usually have some real finds." She pulled the matching wallet from her purse and slipped out a pink and white Lerner Shop card, handing it to Kimberly. "Stick to the budget and be back for dinner by 5:30."

Kimberly slid the card into the back pocket of her frayed jean shorts and yelled up the stairs. "Come on, runt, let's go!"

The temperature and humidity seemed different in southeast Texas. Hotter and heavier somehow. Kimberly slid a rubber band from her wrist and pulled her curly hair up into a fluffy ponytail. Squinting, she regretted not grabbing her sunglasses on the way out the door. Their new neighborhood was pretty and tree-lined with pristine sidewalks. The two-story wooden houses all had a modern flair with odd angles on the facades and roofs, most painted various shades of brown and beige with lots of big picture windows.

As soon as they rounded the corner of their street and were out of sight of the house, Kimberly slid a pack of Marlboro Lights and a small Bic lighter out of her other back pocket. It took a few tries to get the lighter to work, but she lit a cigarette and they kept walking.

"Since when did you start smoking? Did you steal those from Dad?"

"I didn't steal, just borrowed. I don't even know if I'm gonna like it. It's my first day." Kimberly drew the smoke into her mouth and blew it back out.

"Whatever. You don't even do it right. You're not supposed to just keep it in your mouth."

"You want to show me how to do it right, Miss Big Shot?" Kimberly held the pack over to Sabrina.

"Ew, no! I am never smoking those disgusting things. They stink. Is this why you agreed to take me with you? So you have an accomplice?"

"No, idiot. It's because I'm sure you're going through the same crap I am being the new girl. We're gonna need to stick together. It would be nice to make a friend or two, but at least we already have each other."

Sabrina eyed Kimberly warily. "Why are you being nice to me?"

Kimberly looked at her little sister. Sabrina was rapidly approaching thirteen and was almost as tall as Kimberly. Sabrina had been told frequently by her parents that she was going to be a looker, with her smooth, black hair and wide blue eyes. Where Kimberly tanned easily, Sabrina had porcelain skin, taking after their mother. Since they were small, the kids were always being reminded to put sunscreen on 'the baby' before they went outside.

"I'm not being all that nice. I just know how it is, that's all."

"Well, thanks," Sabrina said. She snapped a golden hibiscus flower from a bush to her left and sniffed it. "I caught Mom snooping again."

Kimberly wheeled her head around to face Sabrina. "On me?"

"Nope, on me this time. She was digging through my dresser drawers when she thought I wasn't home. What did I ever do to make her not trust me?"

"It's not just you, Brie. She doesn't trust anyone. I think having grown up with a mother like hers, she's a giant mess inside. Just do as I told you and don't leave anything where she can find it. Hide your diary, girl."

The girls reached the side of the strip mall and stepped onto the covered sidewalk. They took their time, in no hurry to get back home for dinner. They walked past stores that Sabrina could probably identify with her eyes closed just by how they smelled. The drug store smelled like vitamins and isopropyl alcohol, the greeting card store smelled like candles and new paper, the ice cream shop smelled like fudge and peanuts. When they opened the door to Lerner's, the smell of new clothes excited Sabrina instantly. She didn't get to go school clothes shopping very often. Being the youngest usually meant a lot of hand-me-downs. But now they had Mom's credit card. She immediately ran for the wall filled with cubby holes of folded jeans, all different shades of blue and in different styles and sizes. As soon as she arrived at the wall, though, she saw the sign: New 'Designer' Jeans - $19.99 each. Disappointed, she showed her sister.

"Look at these prices. I'm not going to be able to afford anything at all."

"Okay, first of all, let's get away from 'designer' anything. We just don't have that kind of budget. So, let's go over to the clearance racks and see if we can find some cute things."   Sabrina followed her sister to the other side of the store. After weeding through piles of jeans and tops, and trying on outfit after outfit, they were able to pull together two new outfits and a pair of shoes each.

Back outside on the sidewalk, Sabrina happily bounced the heavy shopping bag against her leg.

Kimberly said, "Hey wait, just one more stop." She pushed open the door to the ice cream shop, pulled a $5 bill out of her back pocket, and told the teenage boy behind the counter, "Two vanilla sugar cones, please." Sabrina looked at her sister, stunned. Who was this person and what had she done with Kimberly?

The next morning, Kimberly carefully chose a frilly, cinnamon-colored, cotton peasant blouse and her new jeans with copper and beige silk piping on the back pockets. They weren't designer, but they fit her well and she could pair quite a few tops with them. She finished the look with her new rusty leather platform sandals, pulled her hair back in combs, and put on some lip gloss.

"Bye, Mom!" she called as she ran out to meet the school bus.

Kimberly was walking down the hall of the science wing, looking at her class schedule, when she heard a snotty, slightly raspy female voice say, "Is she kidding me with those jeans?" and another, higher, nasally voice respond, "Ugh, I know. She must have shopped at a yard sale. Gross."

She stopped walking and looked over her left shoulder, just in time to see a tall, beautiful auburn-haired girl and her blonde pal brush past her holding their noses. Kimberly stood perfectly still, feeling heat rise up her neck and into her face.

I will never be good enough.

Kimberly closed her eyes and took a breath, looked at her schedule again, then up at the classroom next to her. She entered the room just before the second bell sounded and found a seat near the windows.

"Watch out for that one, you guys. You'll probably be able to smell her jeans from here." The kids in the back of the classroom giggled.

"Way to start the day, Miss Caldwell," Mrs. Harrison said. "Your smart mouth is always a pleasure. Please take your feet off of the seat in front of you and sit up. Beginning roll call, respond loudly enough so I can hear you, please."

Kimberly pulled her pencil out of her notebook and kept her eyes focused on her desk. It was going to be a long year.

***

Sabrina lay on her stomach on the creamy, speckled carpet in their family room doing a jigsaw puzzle of the Eiffel Tower. She glanced out the sliding glass doors at the gloomy rain washing the patio and soaking the new vinyl deck furniture. She wondered if the cushions should be brought in from the rain, then brushed that thought aside, as that would require getting up and doing something. Rainy Saturday mornings were for lazy, mindless things. Like jigsaw puzzles of the Eiffel Tower for the tenth time. She crossed her feet at the ankles and let them drop to the floor, then back up again as she worked on the puzzle. She'd read in a magazine somewhere that this was a good exercise for your tummy.

"Hey, do you think I should try out for drill team next year?" Sabrina asked. Kimberly lay on the sofa with her head propped up on the armrest, a paperback novel in her hands, blocking her face from view.

"Why the hell would you want to do that?"

"Because I like it. I loved watching you and your friends practice those dances in Florida. I think I could definitely do it. You don't think it's stupid?"

"I think it's a giant waste of time. Do what you want, Brie. Just don't try to rope me into anything."

Sabrina rolled her eyes. "I wouldn't dream of disturbing you, Your Highness."

Kimberly put her book on her chest and looked at her little sister. Long legs, silky hair—she definitely had "the look" most of the girls on drill team had here in Texas. Maybe Sabrina should try out. And maybe Kim would, too. Nobody needed to know.

***

From her upstairs bedroom, Kimberly hollered down to her sister. "Sabrina! Go get Dad in the garage and tell him Jesse's on the phone. Long distance from Florida. Hurry it up!" She resumed her conversation. "So, you're doing okay then? Is the apartment you guys got expensive?"

"Yeah, things are fine. There's four of us living here so it's not too bad. I got a second job at Crawfish on the Causeway bartending at night, so I'm banking some cash. It helps that Dad left me the station wagon. At least I don't have to worry about a car payment."

"That's true, but you won't be impressing any dates any time soon. Mom was not about to drive Dad's Charger every day to work. You should see her new ride. It's a fancy-schmancy Cutlass Supreme. Smells all new inside. Hey, I miss you. It feels really weird and empty without you. You're coming for Christmas, right? You'll like the new house. Mom decorated the guest room downstairs like it was your room. Hope you still like *Star Wars*."

"What? Oh my God, you gotta be kidding me."

Kimberly belly laughed. "Hahaha! Just joking, just joking, but you should have heard your voice! It's a nice room, like all plaid and blue and brown and stuff. Hey, did you call because you're gonna tell—"

"No, not yet. Maybe when I am there in person. I don't know. Hopefully I can make the trip if Mom and Dad send me a ticket. Plane fare at Christmas is pricey."

"Let me work on Dad. I'll let you know. Hey, write me back, dumbass. I've sent you like five letters already."

"Yeah, yeah, in all my spare time. I'm still lifeguarding, too, you know. I'll try, Kimmy." They heard a click and their dad's voice on the extension in the kitchen.

"Hey, Jess! You doing okay, slugger?"

"Okay, getting off. Love you," Kimberly said.

"You, too, brat. Be good." Kimberly placed the white plastic phone onto its cradle, picked up her pen, and rolled back over on her bed to continue writing in her journal.

***

The backyard of the Stevens home was bleak in late February. Jack sat smoking in a deck chair, fragrant woodsmoke and earthy dampness surrounding him. The occasional wind gust chilled the tips of his ears and nose. With no fence to mark the property line, the forest went on for miles. Hundreds of 80-foot loblolly pines had shed their needles, blanketing the ground in a sea of rust-brown. Jack would have to wait until spring to rake them and make room for the dead grass to revive itself. He snuffed out his cigarette in the ashtray on the side table and took a sip from his longneck bottle. He was considering purchasing a leaf blower to hasten the chore, when he heard behind him the door from the family room sliding open. He turned to see Marjorie step outside in a navy woolen peacoat, jeans, and hiking boots, with a thick ivory scarf wrapped around her neck, carrying a steaming mug. She hooked Spooky to his run, attached between the corner of the house and the back of the garage, and the black lab took off like a rocket into the needle covered yard, curiously sniffing everything in sight.

She chuckled as she sat in the matching chair on the other side of the table, her mittened hands warming on the mug. "He would chase his own shadow if the run was long enough." She sipped from the mug.

"Coffee?"

"Irish. I thought a nip would help the coffee do its job."

Jack withheld comment. "Long day at the pharmacy?"

"A bit. I had to stay a little late to fill prescriptions for Monday since tomorrow is my day off. How was your Saturday?"

"Pretty good," Jack said. "Dropped the girls off at the movies, did an oil change on the Charger, took Brie to her friend's house for a sleepover, and had to listen to Kimberly bug me the whole way home about going car shopping."

"What did you tell her?"

"That I won't even entertain the notion until she's saved enough to cover half the cost, which, of course, requires her to get out of this house and get a job. She continues to throw the argument in my face that we gave Jesse his car and it's '*so not fair, Daaaaad,*'" Jack said, whining in a dead-on impression of his teenage daughter. Marjorie laughed and sipped from the mug.

"Did you explain yet again that the situation was different?"

"No, I'm not wasting anymore breath on that. It's getting old. She knows she needs to get off her butt and get a job. No handouts around here. I don't care how much better we're doing financially. That's none of her business anyway."

"I agree. Good things are *earned*, not just given. What has she done to deserve anything good? Oh, hey, I was thinking. Now that I'm working again, we can definitely afford that honeymoon we never got to take. I've been looking at brochures from the travel agency next door to the drugstore. Want to take a look when we go back inside?"

"I was just sitting here thinking about how we probably need a fence for the backyard and that I may want to buy some more lawn equipment, especially with spring coming. And don't forget, I'm still paying off your credit card debt."

"Jack, please, let's not have that discussion again. We're having a nice evening so far." Jack tipped the bottle and filled his mouth with the last of the foamy lager. He lit a cigarette, blew the smoke out through his nostrils, and looked at his wife.

"You're right. I'm sorry. I know you've been trying."

Marjorie put her hand on top of Jack's and squeezed. "Thank you, honey. Speaking of Jesse, have you heard from him lately? I was so disappointed he wasn't able to come out for Christmas. I guess at the height of tourist season, he really can't get away from his job."

Jack shook his head and tapped the cigarette on the side of the ashtray. "Nope, he hasn't called in a while. Just busy, I guess."

"So, where is Kim tonight anyway?" Marjorie asked.

"Last I saw, she was holed up in her room writing in that giant journal of hers. Maybe she'll publish that thing one day and make herself a bucket of money. Meanwhile, she needs to go to work. I'm really sick of seeing that mopey face of hers around here all the time."

"I'm a little sick of the doom and gloom, too. The only way she's going to make friends again is to get out of this house once in a while. Look at Sabrina! Our little church mouse having more of a social calendar than Kimberly. I never thought I'd see that happen. If she doesn't snap out of her funk, she's gonna be very lonely for the rest of high school. Nobody wants to hang out with a loser."

"Loser? A bit harsh, Marj. It *is* quite a switch for the girls, though. Brie's becoming quite a beauty, too. Kim doesn't have that going for her, but she's smart and pretty funny, when she's not being so sarcastic. I'm

94

gonna go in and get another brew. Need anything?" Marjorie shook her head. Jack slid open the door and went in to the warmth of the house, pausing in front of the blazing fireplace, warming his hands.

Above the deck on the second floor, Kimberly quietly slid her bedroom window closed and flopped down on her bed to write the overheard conversation in her journal. The backs of her eyelids burned as she fought her emotions. She pinched the insides of her thighs hard to get herself under control.

I'll never be good enough.

***

"You're all set, right?" She looked over at Sabrina sitting in the passenger seat of Kimberly's tiny blue Ford Courier pick-up truck, the only thing of which Kim was very proud.

The truck had been sitting in the side yard of their neighbors ever since the Stevens family had arrived last summer. Kimberly hadn't seen it move once. One afternoon as she was walking home from the bus stop, she saw old Mr. Lance watering his gardenia bushes.

"Excuse me, Mr. Lance?" He looked up and tipped the bill of his Houston Astros ball cap to her.

"Hey there, little lady. What can I do you for?"

"Well, sir, I was noticing your truck there and that you don't seem to use it. I wonder, does it run okay?"

"That little thing?" He chuckled and motioned for her to come into the yard. "Let's take a look see at her," he said, pointing to the truck. "I bought this little gal back in 1972 brand new as a graduation gift for my boy, Brian. Shoulda seen his face when I handed him the keys that morning. Youd'a thought I'd'a given him a Ferrari! He sure loved her. Called her Blueberry. Used to look for any reason to leave the house so's he could take her for a spin. Loaded up the back with his buddies and off they'd go, the good Lord knows ta where."

"What a great gift! I can understand how excited he was."

He laid his hand on the passenger door and peered inside.

"Yep, he shore was."

"So, why did Brian leave the truck here?"

Looking back at Kimberly, his smile faded.

"One night around Christmas that year, Brian took off in his buddy's new hot rod. They was goin down the dirt roads out east to see if'n he could drag race that spitfire of his a little bit. His buddy won some races. Let Brian give it a whirl. My boy never come home. The po-lice said he lost control goin way too fast. Musta hit a pothole or who knows what and caused him to flip over and over."

His eyes were lost in a faraway memory as he ran his hand back and forth along the top of the truck door.

"Blueberry ain't moved since. I ain't had the heart. Ethel said I should sell her if I weren't gonna start her up and run her now and then. Said I cain't do that neither."

Kimberly's heart was heavy. She felt terrible for her sweet neighbor. "I am so sorry, sir. I had no idea."

"Course you didn't, now, young'un. How wouldja? I reckon yer lookin for a car yerseff now, am I right? You seem about that right age."

"Yes, sir. Dad said we can look for a car if I can save up half the money. I don't have a job yet, but I'm gonna look for one soon. I'm hoping by the summer I can find a car that I can afford. I didn't mean to bother you about the truck, Mr. Lance. I'm really sorry."

"Naw, naw, little lady, don't you worry. Tell you what. I think ol' Blueberry been waitin for jes the right owner. If you'd be willing to hep me get her motor all spruced up and purrin like a kitten, we can call her even. Whadda you say?" His smile was wide and genuine. He set down the garden hose, wiped his leathery hand on his jeans, and held it out to Kimberly. She grinned and shook his hand.

"You mean it? Really? This is so great, Mr. Lance. Thank you! I'll go talk to my dad. When can we get started?"

"Well, how's about this weekend? You said you ain't got a job yet, so I'm guessin you have some free time?"

"Yes, sir. I'll be here Saturday morning bright and early. Thank you so much!" Kimberly said. She turned and sprinted to her house, her curls bouncing as she ran.

That night at the dinner table, Kimberly shared with her family the exciting proposal Mr. Lance had made.

"Can you believe it? He's just going to give me the truck."

Mom set her fork down. "Kimberly, what do you know about working on a motor? You're a girl."

"How very 1950's of you, Mother," Kimberly said. She shot a look across the table that said, "Watch me."

"Hey, mind your mouth, smartass," Jack said. "Marj, I say let her do it. Who cares if she gets a little dirty? She'll be learning some valuable mechanics that might serve her later in life. Plus, a free truck?"

Kimberly beamed. The truck was practically hers.

***

Every Saturday and occasional weeknights, Kimberly went next door to Mr. Lance's garage to work on Blueberry. She learned how to change the oil, replace the battery, install a new water pump, and flush the brake lines. She prided herself in having to scrub grease from underneath her finger nails in the kitchen sink at night, as her mother looked on, cringing.

Every time they started the truck, Mr. Lance would explain what the different sounds meant.

"Ya hear that whine? Means the timing belt's gonna snap on ya. We'd best replace it." Another mechanical lesson learned.

After a couple of months of maintenance, Mr. Lance slid into the passenger seat and dangled the keys at Kimberly.

"Well, come own, girl, less take her for a test drive." Kimberly's grin was lit with a thousand watts. They took a spin around the neighborhood. Mr. Lance was patient as he taught Kimberly to work the clutch and slide the gearshift into place. For an old truck, it ran as smooth as butter.

When they arrived back at his house, Mr. Lance refused to take the keys from Kimberly's outstretched hand.

"No ma'am, I do believe those belong to you now. You gonna want to replace the tires soon. I'll be happy to learn ya that too, jes let me know. Meantime, congratulations, young'un. You done earnt you a truck!"

"You mean it?" Kimberly was so overwhelmed, she threw her arms around a stunned Mr. Lance and gave him a big squeeze. "Thank you so much, sir. I can't tell you how grateful I am."

Mr. Lance was visibly moved. "Jes take good care of her. Do my boy proud." His smile was a bit watery as he patted the dashboard one last time and opened the passenger door. "I'll get the paperwork all signed for ya. It's in the kitchen. Back in a minute."

"Wait, Mr. Lance?" Kimberly held the key ring on the palm of her hand. "I know the round key is for the doors and the square key is for the ignition. What is this little key here?"

Mr. Lance pulled a pair of glasses from the breast pocket of his coveralls and peered closer. "Well, I'll be. I plum forgot all about that. This here key goes to a lockbox Brian kept behint the driver seat. Pull that lever yonder and it'll come up."

Kimberly lifted the lever on the side and the seat tilted toward the steering wheel. Behind the seat on the floor of the pickup was a steel lockbox with two latches and a handle in the center of the lid. She lifted out the box, pushed the seat back down to its locked position, and set the box on it. Mr. Lance gave her a nod and she fit the small key into the lock and turned. Popping the latches, she began to open the lid. At the look of anticipation on Mr. Lance's face, she thought better of it and slid the box over to him. He should be the one to see what his son had left behind.

Mr. Lance opened the lid and paused for a moment, emotion clouding his weathered face. It was the first time the box had been opened by anyone but his son. There hadn't been much time for Brian to build up things inside the box before he passed. With arthritic, calloused hands, Mr. Lance delicately lifted out the one thing inside: military dog tags on a chain. He tightened his fist around the tags and looked at Kimberly.

"I give my tags to Brian when he was small. Weren't no use to me no more after the war. Thought he loss 'em a long time ago," he said and wiped his hand across his forehead. "Well, I'll be . . ."

After a long moment, Mr. Lance closed the box, sliding the dog tags into the pocket of his greasy coveralls. He fastened the latches and slid the box back to Kimberly.

"Here ya go, little lady. A box fer all yer hidden treasures."

Kimberly touched the back of his hand tenderly. "Thank you, sir. I really mean it."

A few minutes later, she walked through the kitchen door of her parents' home in all her dirty, sweaty splendor, jangling the keys and carrying a steel box. Marjorie looked up from peeling a cucumber over the kitchen sink.

"So, it's all yours, huh?"

"Yep! Just gotta take care of the title thingy."

Kimberly bounded up the stairs two at a time to her room. She needed to strip off her nasty clothes and get a shower. She had places to go and things to do in *her* new truck. But first and foremost, before she did anything else, she walked around to the far side of her bed and lifted the corner of the mattress, sliding out her journal. She placed it inside the steel box, locked it up, and slid it under her bed.

"You're safe now."

***

"Yep, I'm good," Sabrina said. It was a bright, hot Saturday morning. Kimberly pulled into the bus loop in the back of the junior high school to drop Sabrina off for drill team auditions. She reached over and put her hand on Sabrina's shoulder.

"Listen, just trust your body. You know the steps cold. Just feel the music, ignore everyone around you, and smile, smile, smile 'til your cheeks hurt. Got it?"

"I got it," Sabrina said. "They said we'll be done by 2."

"I'll be here. Knock 'em dead!"

Instead of turning left out of the school toward home, Kimberly made a right and headed to the high school gym.

The girl she approached at the check-in table wore the coveted uniform of the high school drill team.

"Hi!" the girl said. She tossed her long blonde ponytail and smiled brilliantly. "Name?"

"Kimberly Stevens."

The girl looked at her list and said, "Here you are. Looks like you have number 102." She uncapped a black marker and wrote the number on a large sticker that she handed to Kimberly "Just stick this to the front of your shirt. Don't forget your number, because the judges will be using it all day to call you. Make sure to listen to all announcements and be prompt to every event. Good luck!"

102? Kimberly wondered just how many girls were trying out for the squad. This was going to be harder than she thought. She followed the signs taped to the hallway walls and made her way to the girls' locker room by the gym.

When she entered the locker room, she saw dozens of girls wearing white t-shirts and crimson nylon shorts, the school colors. Kimberly looked down at her own clothes. She was wearing a typical Saturday outfit—purple tank top and white shorts. What the heck? Was there some kind of memo that went out about a uniform? Fortunately, she noticed a few girls wearing other colors, but they were from the younger class. Kimberly was the only incoming junior not in school colors. She was mortified.

Hearing laughter, she looked to her right. Christy Caldwell and her group of friends were gathered, pointing and chortling, quite porcine.

"Looks like someone can't read. What's the matter, Goodwill? Didn't you see the tryout signs all over the school this week? It's how the judges are going to know who's in what grade. Dumbass," Christy said. Kimberly felt her neck and face turn beet red.

"How much time do we have? Maybe I can call my mom?"

"Too late, stupid," said the nasally, blonde friend, Teena Worthington. "They'll just know you have no idea how to follow rules."

"Yeah, smooth move, Ex-Lax," Christy said.

The bell to the intercom chimed and everyone shushed each other to get quiet.

"Good afternoon, ladies, and welcome to auditions for the 1982-83 McCarthy High School High Steppers! The High Steppers have an honored tradition of promoting school loyalty, unity, and pride. You're here because you believe you have what it takes. And we believe in you, too! In just a few moments, we'll begin calling your dance groups by number. When we do, line up in numerical order in the hallway. You'll be judged on dance ability, dance memory, and overall appearance and attitude. So, get out there and do your best. But most of all, have fun! Best of luck to all of you!"

Appearance. Kimberly's stomach knotted up. She knew she was doomed. Why was she even here? At that moment, Mrs. Wilson, the director, came through the door, instantly commanding the locker room.

"Ladies, I need all of you to keep the talking to a minimum so you can hear the numbers called over the intercom. This is particularly important as the day goes on and selected dancers are narrowed down. Please stay in the locker room at all times unless your number is called, at which time you may proceed into the hallway. Always line up in numerical order. Am I clear?"

"YES, MA'AM!" the girls responded.

A few minutes after Mrs. Wilson left the locker room, the bell to the intercom chimed.

"Numbers one through twenty-five, please line up in the hallway." Christy was in the first group to leave the room. Kimberly noticed that girls from both age groups were lining up together. The numbers must have been assigned by last name. They were definitely not separated by class. *Whew, maybe they won't notice my clothes.*

When Kimberly's group was called, she pushed through the locker room doors with 24 other girls, all frantically looking at each other's numbers in order to line up correctly. Once in place, another volunteer opened the door to the gym and the girls were led inside.

Mrs. Wilson was standing behind a long table in front of the wooden bleachers, joined by four other judges. With the gym acoustics, her voice carried easily.

"Ladies, form a single line shoulder to shoulder facing the judges' table. Now space with arms fully extended meeting fingertips. Good. Now, even numbers, step forward one full stride. Odd numbers, step backward one full stride. Very good, ladies. First, you will perform the routine you have learned to Donna Summer's 'Last Dance.' Second, you will perform the high kick and contagion routine you have learned. Remember your steps, your posture, and most of all, project your beauty through your dazzling smile! Don't be distracted if the judges walk around and between you to get a closer look. Are you ready? Let's dance!"

Kimberly just knew they could see her heart pounding right through her shirt. Her ears were ringing and her breath was coming in fast bursts. She closed her eyes, breathed in through her nose, then out through her mouth slowly. When she opened her eyes, Kimberly smiled as wide as she could, turning her chin up, focusing on the top bleacher. She imagined fans sitting up there and she was dancing just for them.

The music was pumping and Kimberly lost herself completely in the song. If this was her only opportunity to perform this routine, she was going to leave everything on that gym floor. She whipped her head, tossed her hair, thrust her arms, spun her body, and kicked so high she could nearly kiss her shins. The routine ended in a split facing the judges, right leg forward, arms fully raised in a V. Kimberly was so relieved the routine was over, she tossed her head back and gave them a smile to rival a sun's ray. After the troupe came together for high kicks and contagions, they were thanked by the judges and asked to wait in the locker room.

"The judges may want to call some of you back in to see your dance or kick form, or just take a look at your posture and presence. Please pay attention and listen for your number to be called."

The locker room was a beehive of activity. Girls were clustered about singing songs, practicing dance steps, or eating the sack lunch they had brought. Kimberly had brought lunch, too, but she was too nervous to eat it. She found an unoccupied corner of the room, pulled a soda out of her back pack and sipped it, mentally doing the routine over and over, just in case she got a callback. She closed her eyes, deep in focus, and the intercom bell chimed again.

"Please listen up. The following numbers need to line up in the hallway for the first round of callbacks: 7, 10, 16, 21 . . . " Girls were dropping whatever they were doing and running as fast as they could into the hallway. "86, 88, 94, 95, 102, 107 . . . " Oh my God! They called her number! Kimberly jumped up, tossing her soda into the nearest trash can, and ran out into the hallway to fall in at the back of the line. It was a very long line of at least sixty girls.

The volunteer shushed all the girls and said, "I'll send you back into the gym by tens. Stay out here quietly so you do not disturb the judges inside. No talking."

The first ten callbacks entered the gym. As soon as the door was closed, Kimberly realized she had to use the bathroom. *Oh great, why does this always happen when I'm nervous?* She tried to overcome the sensation mentally, thinking of everything but what her bladder was hollering at her to do. She started shifting from foot to foot, then softly bouncing up and down. The volunteer walking the hallway came up alongside her.

"Are you okay? Do you have to use the restroom?" Kimberly

nodded her head yes.

"I have to go, too. I'll go with her," said a nasally voice behind her. Of course, Teena would be at the back of the line. Her last name started with W.

"Good attitude, number 121. Thank you. You two hurry up and get straight back here," said the volunteer. Kimberly looked at Teena tentatively.

"Come on, stupid, hurry up! I have to go, too," Teena whispered. Kimberly stepped out of line and followed Teena down the hall, away from the other girls, and around the corner. "It's that door right there. It's a single one for teachers. You go first, and I'll watch the door for you. Hurry before I pee in my pants!"

"Uh, okay, thanks," Kimberly said. She opened the door and as she stepped into the bright sunshine, she realized it wasn't a bathroom at all. This was a door to the blacktop outside. "Hey, wait a second . . . " she began, when she felt Teena shove her hard from behind out onto the asphalt.

"Happy trails, you idiot," Teena said, as she pulled the door hard to slam it closed.

Kimberly grabbed the doorknob. Locked. She banged on the door as hard as she could. "HEY! LET ME BACK IN!" It was no use. Nobody was going to hear her.

Kimberly took off running as fast as she could toward the bus loop, which was all the way around the opposite side of the gym. She pumped her legs as fast as they would carry her. Her foot caught the lip of a pothole in the parking lot and she went sprawling toward the hot pavement. The heels of her hands and her knees hit hard. Kimberly cried out as she slid. She jumped up and continued to run, wiping the dirt and gravel from her hands onto her white shorts. As she ran, she cursed herself for not paying better attention, she cursed herself for being so trusting, she cursed herself for working so hard and then blowing the one chance she had to feel like she belonged . . . anywhere.

The bus loop finally came into view and Kimberly ran across it with determination, heading toward the door she had entered hours before. Blessedly, the door was still open. She ran toward the gym hallway and arrived just in time to hear Mrs. Wilson saying, "Number 102? Where is number 102?" Sabrina stopped short before colliding with the director, gasping for air and wiping the sweat from her forehead.

"I'm right here, Mrs. Wilson," Kimberly said, panting.

"What in the world happened to you?"

"I was pushed outside. I didn't know what door it was and it locked from the inside and I couldn't get back in. I had to run around the building."

"I don't care what your excuse is. You obviously were fooling around and not doing as you were instructed. No member of my squad is ever disobedient and no member is ever late. You may call your parents to come and pick you up. Go gather your things," Mrs. Wilson said, and turned on her heel to go back into the gym.

"Wait, what?" Kimberly said.

So that was it. It was all over. She put her hands on her knees to catch her breath for a moment, then entered the locker room, head down. Locating her small backpack in the corner, she dumped the food into the trash and left the room, trying not to notice the other girls whispering.

She felt numb as she approached her little blue truck. Sitting inside the stifling cab, hot tears flowed down Kimberly's face, dampening the collar of her tank top. Why had Dad made them move to this stupid place? Why couldn't she have stayed in Florida where she had friends instead of here where everybody hated her? She would never fit in. She would never be happy. She would never be enough.

Kimberly saw Sabrina waving as she pulled into the junior high bus loop, beaming from ear to ear.

"I made it, Kim! I can't believe it! Thank you so much for your help. I know I couldn't have done it without you!" She slid across the seat and gave her big sister a squeeze. "What did you do while I was at tryouts?"

"Went to a movie at the mall. A sad one," she said, putting the truck into gear and easing out onto the street, making the left turn for home.

***

Hamburgers sizzled over charcoal embers, mixing with waves of chlorine and sunscreen in the air as neighborhood kids of all ages splashed and dove at the community family pool day. Dads manned the grills, spatulas in one hand, cold brews in the other, attempting to teach the fine art of flipping perfect burgers to their nearly-adult sons, who feigned paying attention while not so inconspicuously checking out the teenage, bikini-clad beauties from the block.

Jack parked the Charger in a spot alongside the chainlink fence near the locker rooms.

"Kim, take that bowl of potato salad to the ladies at that long table over there and explain Mom has a migraine and won't be joining us. Brie, see if you can find at least one lounge chair we can use. Put our beach bag on it. I'm gonna see if anyone needs any help at the grills."

After dropping off the salad and accepting sympathies for her mother, Kimberly joined Brie near the deep end of the pool. She'd been able to score two chairs and was spreading striped beach towels across them. Kimberly sat down on one of the chairs in a huff, pulling her ball cap low over her sunglasses and tugging her open button-down shirt closed across her middle.

"Why didn't you wear a suit? You're gonna sweat to death out here," Sabrina said.

Kimberly looked down at her tube top and cutoff shorts, crossing her ankles and bouncing a flip-flop against the bottom of her foot.

"Just worry about yourself, nosy. Maybe I don't feel like getting in the pool, okay?"

"Jeez, fine. Why don't you go back home then?"

"And hang out with headache lady all day? I'd rather have bamboo shoved under my fingernails."

"There's an image," Sabrina shuddered.

"I plan to make my escape sometime between eating-o'clock and Dad's-buzzed-thirty."

"Where are you going?"

"None of your beeswax." Kimberly closed her eyes and Sabrina took the cue to shut her mouth. She pulled a tube of sunscreen out of the beach bag and began rubbing it onto her shoulders.

"Look out!" someone yelled, and before Sabrina could react, a beach ball hit her square in the nose and landed in her lap.

"Oops, sorry!" someone giggled. She saw a group of teenagers in the middle of the pool, some with their arms up waiting for her to throw the ball back in. She tossed the ball up into the air and hit it with the butt of her hand, volleyball style. It sailed perfectly through the air back to the group.

"Hey! Come in and join us!" said one of the splashing kids. Sabrina looked over at her dozing sister, shrugged and thought *why not?* She removed her oversized Florida Gators t-shirt, revealing a blue and black one-piece bathing suit, and jumped in the pool.

Jack approached the chairs twisting the cap off a longneck, a cigarette dangling under his mustache.

"Kim, see that guy by the grill in the red shorts with the ample gut?"

Kimberly looked back the way her dad had come. "Yeah?"

"That's Mr. Morley. He owns the Oak Ridge movie theater. I told him you were looking for a job and he's willing to talk to you Monday afternoon. Go over there after school and fill out an application."

"What if I don't wanna work at the movie theater?"

"Little girl, that was not a suggestion. It was not a request. It was a direct order. You need a job and you need to get your butt out of the house."

"Fine," Kimberly said.

"'*Gee, thanks, Dad, I appreciate your help!'*" Jack mocked.

"I hate it here, Dad."

Jack wrapped his arm around Kimberly's shoulder and squeezed. "Hey. Look at me. You haven't even given it a chance, honey. Now that you have your truck, nothing's stopping you. Get out there and make some friends. You'll forget all about Florida before you know it. You owe it to yourself to at least try."

"Whatever."

"I'm going back over to help cook. Come eat something."

The lifeguard blew the whistle to signal adult swim. Kids of all ages grudgingly left the pool and grabbed their towels on the way to the food tables. Sabrina ran to the chairs, her wet feet slapping the cement.

"Wanna come with me to get a burger?" she asked her sister, drying her face and hair.

"Nah, you go ahead. The line's too long anyway. I'll get something later."

"Suit yourself."

Kimberly watched as families gathered at picnic tables on the grass outside the pool deck and ate lunch. She wistfully recalled their family picnics at the state park in Florida and how much fun she used to have playing on the beach and around the campsite all day with her brother. Her heart ached to be little again. To have Jesse by her side. To be holding hands with Dave again. To feel like she still belonged. Like she mattered. Loneliness lay in the pit of her stomach like a stone.

Hours later, out of sheer boredom, Kimberly wandered over to the food tables. What was left was picked over and looked fairly unappetizing. Kimberly snagged a bag of barbecue chips, and swiped a root beer from the bottom of a cooler full of melting ice. She was wiping her freezing hand on her shorts when someone spoke behind her causing her to jump.

"You want a Koozie for that?"

"I'm sorry, a what?" Kimberly turned to see a tanned, shirtless boy with blonde hair as curly as hers, a shark tooth necklace resting on his breastbone.

"A Koozie." He picked up a short foam cylinder from the table, took the can from her hand and slid it into the cylinder. "It'll keep your drink cold."

"Oh, thanks. I've never seen one of these before."

"Well, now you have. I'm Woody. Haven't seen you at the pool before. You just move here?"

"Last year. I don't get out much. I'm Kim."

"Nice to meet you, Kim. I'm gonna go hang with some of my friends over there." He pointed to a copse of trees outside the fence and out of sight of the pool. "Wanna come?"

"Why not?" Kimberly followed Woody, taking a look around to locate Sabrina, who was ogling a magazine with a few girls her age at an umbrella table, and her dad, who was probably a six-pack in with the other dads joking in lawn chairs around the pool. She wouldn't be missed.

A glance at Jack's watch revealed they'd been at the party for four hours already. He excused himself to relieve his lager-swollen bladder. Inside the men's locker room, the urinals were taken by some teenage boys, so he slipped into a stall and locked the door.

"Can you believe the tits on that one in the tube top?"

"I hear ya. Woody's probably gonna cop a feel while we're gone."

"Yeah, take your time. Two hits off that j and she was already soaring."

"Never saw her here before. What's her name again? Kim?"

"Yeah, says she moved here from Florida. I hear chicks from there are easy. Figures Woody gets all the luck."

Jack flushed the toilet and left the locker room in full stride, looking all around the pool for his daughter. He called Sabrina over to the side of the pool, pulling her away from her game of Marco Polo.

"Have you seen your sister?"

"She was right over there," she said and pointed to the chairs, now sitting empty.

"Never mind, I'll find her." Jack scanned every face in and around the pool. He walked over to the food tables and coolers, but she was nowhere to be seen. Movement caught the corner of his eye by a small group of trees. He walked briskly through the grass toward the trees.

"Kim!" he called out. "Kimberly! Where the hell are you?" A few teenagers scattered at the sound of the angry adult voice.

Jack came around the corner to see his daughter, high as a kite, on the ground, her legs pretzeled with a boy's, his mouth on hers, and his hand deep inside her tube top. "Knock it off right now, you two!"

The boy jumped and pushed Kimberly away, clambering to stand and run. Jack grabbed his wrist as he tried to make a break for it.

"If I ever see you around my daughter again—"

"S-sorry, sir!" he sputtered as he took off running.

Kimberly slowly pulled her button-down shirt back on. Her eyes, glazed and red, opened and closed dreamily as she giggled. "Dad. Hey. Look. I'm snapping out of my funk."

***

The sun had long set as Marjorie sat at the dining room table rubbing her temples, her elbows resting on the placemat in front of her. Jack came downstairs and sat at the table, speaking in a low voice.

"She's sleeping it off."

"She is unbelievable."

"Marj, she's sad. She hates it here. She told me today."

"That's no excuse for behaving like a common streetwalker."

"Maybe we should get her into counseling."

"What for? What she needs is an ass-whooping, but she's too old for that now. We should take that truck away."

"Then how is she supposed to get to work? We need to be reasonable."

"Reasonable? Her behavior is deplorable! She oughta be ashamed. I cannot believe I raised a daughter like her."

Jack took a deep breath and let it out slowly. "We'll discuss this when you don't have a headache."

Ascending the stairs behind Marjorie, Jack was careful not to spill the steaming cup of herbal tea in his hand. He patted her back as she turned toward the master bedroom.

"Rest well. I'll be in bed shortly," he said. He tapped quietly on the middle door in the hallway.

"Kim?" No answer. "She must still be asleep," he muttered to himself. He turned away to go down to the kitchen and dump the tea, but thought better of it. "I'll just leave this on her nightstand."

Jack turned the knob and gently pushed the door across the shag carpet. Kimberly's room was dark except for the shaft of light from the hallway across the floor. Jack set the mug down next to her alarm clock. 10:45 pm. He reached out to pat his daughter's shoulder and only a bedspread met his hand. Switching on the bedside lamp, he cursed at the empty bed.

Quickly descending the stairs, Jack threw open the front door to see the driveway. Blueberry was gone, too. How had they not heard the truck start up?

Back upstairs, he found Sabrina curled up on her bed reading a paperback, her wet hair wrapped in a towel.

"Brie, does Kim have some place she likes to go? To get away? Or someone she hangs out with?"

Sabrina sat up in bed. "Why? What's wrong?"

"She's not in her room. She must have snuck out. The truck is gone."

"Oh wow—I have no idea, Dad." She thought for a quick moment. "Wait—maybe the lake—"

"Lake Conroe? It's huge. Any idea where on the lake?"

Sabrina sprung from the bed, flinging the towel off of her head and grabbing a scrunchie, while she stepped into flip-flops. "I'll come with you. I think I know where she might be."

Exiting I-45 at FM 1097, they headed west toward Lake Conroe.

"There's a little area up here called Fisherman's Cove. I came here with her once after she had a fallout with Mom. There! On the right. Turn here."

Jack turned onto a dirt road that wasn't much more than a path. Slowly, he navigated the car closer to the lake using his high beams, while Sabrina shined a flashlight around the base of the trees.

"There's Blueberry!"

Jack pulled up next to the truck and stopped the car. The thick, damp night clung to their skin as they approached. Kim wasn't in the cab or the bed of the truck.

"Down to the water," he whispered, taking the flashlight from Sabrina. She followed closely behind her dad holding onto the hem of his t-shirt. Nearer the lake, they heard the plop, plop, plop of rocks being tossed into the dark, murky water. Kim sat on the bank, her knees drawn up under an oversized sweatshirt.

"Kim, it's Dad and Brie," Jack said softly.

"I heard you pull up."

"Mind if we sit with you?"

"Whatever."

Crisscrossing her legs, Brie sat on her sister's left side, rubbing her lower back. Jack lit a cigarette and took the other side.

"Dad, I—"

"Wait. Me first. You told me today you hate it here. I get it. But acting out and running away aren't going to fix the situation. I really think getting out of the house every day and working, making new friends, will help you. And maybe you could speak to someone? A counselor?"

Kimberly looked at her dad and shook her head.

"No, you don't get it."

"What am I missing?"

"It's just not that simple. I need to get away from Mom. She's my biggest problem. *She's* the one who needs therapy."

"I don't think that's very fair, Kimberly, she—"

"Please don't plead her case to me, Dad. She hates me. I mean, she might love me because she's my mom, but she certainly doesn't like me. She treats me and Brie completely differently. I'm miserable in that house."

Memories of his own struggles at home when he was eighteen came flooding back. "I understand more than you know, kiddo. Listen, give the job a shot. It'll get you out of being in the house so much, and you'll be able to save for your own place. I'll talk to Mom. She doesn't hate you, she's just hard on you. You know how she was raised. She really doesn't know any other way to be."

"Which is why she needs therapy."

"Let that be my concern, not yours. Meanwhile, let's get you home. The mosquitoes are feasting on us."

"Home. Great. More lectures from her."

"Your mother took a sedative for her migraine and went to bed. She doesn't even know we're out here."

Kimberly was visibly relieved. "I appreciate you coming to find me. I didn't even realize I wanted you to." Jack wrapped his arms around his daughter's shoulders and kissed the top of her head.

"If you ever pull this shit again, the truck is mine, you understand?"

"Yeah, I get it." They stood up, brushing off sandy bottoms. "Brie, ride with me?"

"Sure. I don't think you're a flight risk with me in the truck." Sabrina winked at her sister.

"Hey, Kim, how did you get Blueberry out of the driveway without making a sound?" Jack asked.

"Neutral. I Fred Flintstoned it."

Jack tipped his head back, "Ah," he said, privately appreciating the ingenuity. "But how did you get down there from upstairs?"

"Garage roof," Kim and Brie answered together.

Jack stared at Sabrina. She raised her hands in surrender. "Hey, don't look at me! She's the one who taught me."
"Get in the damn truck. I'll follow you home."

***

Saturday of Memorial Day weekend was a busy morning of chores at the Stevens house. Jack was putting the last coat of stain on the new fence out back. Marjorie surrounded herself with boxes and cans as she organized the pantry. Sabrina ran the vacuum from the living room toward the foyer and noticed the UPS truck pulling away from the driveway.

"Kim, there's a package for you!" she called up to the second floor.

Kimberly bounded down the stairs. "Oh, I bet it's my cap and gown!" she said, grabbing the box to look at the return address. "Yes! One step closer to being out of that school!" *And out of this house.*

Kimberly took the box upstairs to hang the robe so she could steam out the wrinkles. The deep hunter green nylon was shiny and extremely creased, but it was a thing of beauty. Just a few more days and she would stride across that stage and be free of McCarthy High School forever. She hadn't thought about her future much past the summer. The only colleges to which she'd applied had politely responded with no interest in having Kimberly in the student body. She figured she would probably have to take some classes at the community college to get a few credits under her belt, then she could make a plan in a year or two. She was young — there was no hurry.

Except for moving out. She had to do that as soon as possible. She was sick to death of all the rules around her. She and her mother were like oil and water, and it was getting worse. The psychology class she took this year had clarified some of her mother's behavior. It had all started to make sense—the way she could be perfectly fine one minute then lose it the next. The way she spied on Kimberly and Brie, always paranoid, thinking they were up to no good. The way she flipped out when the dishes weren't put away just so, or Kimberly brushed crumbs onto the floor, or they didn't hang up their coats in the closet immediately upon coming in from a cold day. It was exhausting being around her. At the very least, she was probably obsessive compulsive, but she could possibly be manic depressive, too. Either way, her mother was a miserable person and the fact remained—they never got along and they never would. Time to find a way out of here.

Kimberly was looking through her closet trying to decide what to wear under her graduation robe, when her dad knocked on the door.

"Kim, you got a minute?"

"Yep, come in." Her father pushed open her bedroom door. The sunlight coming through the blinds lit up her dad's face. For the first time, Kimberly noticed her dad was starting to show his age. His dark hair was graying at the temples and a little throughout his mustache. He had laugh lines around his eyes and deep grooves along his forehead. *I'm probably to blame for some of that gray hair.* He spun her desk chair around to face her and sat down. Kimberly plopped onto her bed, tucking her feet underneath her.

"You haven't said much to us about what your plans are after high school. I know you didn't have much luck with the college applications. How are things going at the movie theater? Do you plan to work there all summer?"

"I guess so. I won't be there forever, though. I was thinking I might take some classes at Lone Star College to get some credits. I don't know."

"Well, I have a proposition for you. Eckerd is expanding out west, opening new stores in Arizona and New Mexico. I've been designated to spearhead the openings. I'm putting together a team to interview and hire staff, canvas fliers in the surrounding neighborhoods, stock the stores, that sort of thing. It would mean heading out there shortly after graduation. You'd work for me, but report to my subordinate. It doesn't pay great but it's a chance to get away for the summer."

"Wow, really? Where would we stay?"

"The company's putting me up in a condo in Tucson. You'd live there with me. I'll be making a few trips back here, leaving you there on your own, so I'll need to know you'll behave." Jack locked eyes with Kimberly and tipped his chin inward, raising his eyebrows.

"Scout's honor," she said, raising three fingers in a salute.

"It's not gonna be easy. If you do well, I'll see if Eckerd would be willing to hire you full time here in Texas. You in?"

"Dad, seriously? I didn't do anything to deserve—"

"Listen, I know what a hard working kid you can be. I saw you get that truck back up and running with Mr. Lance. I think you'd be a great addition to my team. And it'll get you out of this house. Besides, what else are you gonna do this summer?"

"Thanks, Dad. I promise I won't let you down. How long before we leave?"

Her dad stood up and headed for the door.

"I'm flying out there tomorrow to sign the lease on the condo and take a look at the properties, but I'll be back in a couple of days. You and I will fly out in two weeks. After your graduation. Get ready to work hard." He turned and left her room.

Kimberly balled her fists and hugged them tightly to the front of her thumping chest. "Holy crap, I cannot believe this."

"Believe what?" Sabrina asked. She stood in the doorway to their adjoining bathroom, one towel wrapped around her, another one in her hands, drying her hair.

"I'm going to Arizona with Dad to work on a team that's opening new stores. All summer! I can't even believe it." Kimberly began pacing her room. "I need to call and quit the movie theater. I need to get packing."

Sabrina smiled. "That's nice, Kim. Have a great time," she said, and closed the bathroom door behind her, leaning against it. She rolled her head to look at her reflection in the mirror. In a soft voice, she said, "A whole summer with just me and Mom. Yay. Maybe Jesse wants company . . . "

Chapter Eighteen — 1984 — Jesse

The driving rain was not letting up.

Keeping a close eye on the weather reports of the newly-formed tropical storm spinning out in the Atlantic Ocean, Jesse and his business partner had not yet made the decision to delay the grand opening of the bar the coming weekend. As was usually the case in Daytona Beach, the storm was likely to blow through in a matter of hours, but the owners of Two Dudes Bar & Grill could not be too cautious. The investment in the bar was enormous. If they postponed the opening for even a week in the summer, it could mean thousands in lost revenue. Some of the food that now stocked the coolers could be moved to the freezer, but the fresh produce would have to be scrapped. They'd be further in the red before even opening the doors. Then again, if they opened and the storm hit or even skirted Daytona, they would be jeopardizing the safety of their patrons and would have to consider the liability and possible structural damage. It was a difficult call to make, and it was only Monday.

"So, Tom, you're the master dude. The man with the plan. What do you think?"

Tom Harding was the primary investor and president and CEO of MTH Ventures, Inc. A British expat, he owned Crawfish on the Causeway in Tampa, a bar and grill that morphed into a nightclub in the late hours on the weekends. His longterm business goal was to open a waterfront bar and grill in each of the major beach tourist cities in Florida. Recognizing Jesse's knack for running a smooth bar shift and engaging the clientele, Tom began to groom him for management. Jesse worked double shifts multiple times a week to learn the ropes. It became apparent after only a few months that Jesse possessed keen business acumen. After a profitable year, Tom offered him a promotion to general manager of the property. Tom was a fair businessman who offered higher-end wages and treated the staff with respect. He hired only the most talented, hardworking people. Those who showed their dedication were rewarded with paid time off, health benefits, and profit sharing; all rarities in the hospitality industry. The result was a loyal, happy staff and a constant stream of customers, locals and tourists alike. The lines that formed for the nightclub on weekends became legendary. And at twenty-one, Jesse was running the show.

Late one weeknight, Tom and Jesse were totaling the evening's receipts in the upstairs executive office when Tom mentioned he was looking at a property in Daytona Beach.

"Kind of a dump, really. Previously owned by an old man who drank all his profits and the bank foreclosed. It has a lot of potential, though. Lots on either side are available. I have a real vision for the future of the place."

"Sounds like a great deal. Guessing you have to act fast to snag such prime property. When are you planning to make the offer?

"Already have. Just waiting to hear from my attorney."

"Congrats! I hope it's a huge success for you."

"Well, Jesse, there's a reason I brought this up. Each of my future properties will be set up as limited liability corporations under the umbrella of MTH Ventures. I'd like to have other investors who are willing to be hands-on with operations, not just to hire managers and staff. Investors tend to be more committed. To have a stake in the success. I believe you share my vision of how I like to run my business."

Tom rose from his chair and circled around to the front of his desk, leaning against it. "I'd like to offer you a twenty-five percent stake in the new property, with an option to buy in more as you're able. And I'd like you to run it."

Jesse met Tom's eyes, realizing the offer was genuine.

"Tom, I don't know what to say. That's a huge vote of confidence and I really appreciate it. But I don't have the kind of capital—"

"Before you say anything more, let me show you the most recent valuation of Crawfish." He picked up a report from the desk and handed it to Jesse. "Also, here's your latest profit sharing statement."

Jesse looked at the current value of shares and swallowed hard. He didn't want to appear too shocked in front of his boss, but it was a bigger number than he ever expected.

"Don't misunderstand, I am not demanding a partnership. This is simply an offer. I'm more than pleased with how you're running Crawfish. I'd love to have you stay here indefinitely. But this is an opportunity for you to have something of your own. To be more than a manager. I can't guarantee the enormous success we've had here, but I feel very positive about the potential. Eventually, you'll want to buy a home, start a family, right? I'm offering you security. A future. It's a big decision. I don't expect you to answer this moment. Take a few days. Let me know."

Jesse exhaled the breath he didn't realize he was holding and leaned back in the chair, running a hand through his sandy hair. He thought about the conversation he would have with his parents. How he would be his own boss. How he would be set for life if this thing took off. And just maybe now he could have that other conversation with them that he kept putting off. He stood up, extended his hand to his boss and smiled.

"Tom, meet your new partner."

***

From behind the brand new, highly-lacquered oak bar under a giant thatched Tiki hut, the partners kept their eye on the raging Atlantic through pounding rain. To their relief, the roof of the hut showed no signs of leakage. The contractor had assured them it could withstand high winds and rain. So far, he was true to his word. The concrete floor was damp with mist coming through the open sides of the hut. Delivery of furniture for the outside section of the property had been delayed until the storm blew over. A stage in the far corner for live music was still covered, small puddles of rain forming on the heavy plastic tarp.

Tom took a swig of sparkling water from a bottle and turned to look at the radar on the television hanging over the bar.

"Hard to predict what these things are gonna do, Jesse. I say we give it a few more hours. I'm leaning toward delaying the opening another week, though."

"I was thinking the same thing. I'll let the staff know as soon as we decide. Let me call the liquor distributor and delay the shipment for now," Jesse said, and reached for the phone next to the cash register behind the bar. It rang before he could pick up the receiver. Startled, he answered. "Two Dudes Bar & Grill, can I help you?"

"Hey, Jess, it's Brie. How ya doin?" It was difficult to hear his little sister with the rain coming down so hard.

"Hey, Brie. Not so great at the moment. We have a tropical storm threatening to shut down our opening and my partner and I are in the middle of making arrangements. What do you need?"

"Oh. Okay. I didn't realize. I was just wondering if I could come stay with you for a little while this summer? Maybe help you in the restaurant?"

Jesse sighed, pinching his eyes shut. "Now's not a good time, little bit. Maybe next summer when we're up and running. We have a lot of work to do and I can't babysit you, too."

Sabrina was indignant. "I am *not* a baby that requires sitting, Jesse."

"You are also *not* an adult that can be left alone, Sabrina. Don't be a brat. We can talk about this another time."

"Fine. Bye."

"Wait, are you okay? Is everything okay out there?"

"Yes, it's fine. It's all fine. I'm great. Whatever. Have fun with your bar. Bye."

Jesse heard the dial tone as the connection ended. He sighed again as he hung up the phone. Little sisters . . . jeez.

Chapter Nineteen — 1984 — Kimberly

On Saturday night, when Kimberly and her dad carried their luggage through the front door of the fifth floor condo in Tucson, her jaw dropped. It was the prettiest apartment she had ever seen.

The foyer opened onto a large, L-shaped living area. Deep brown leather furniture and dark walnut tables filled the room. A balcony wrapped around the outside, accessed by numerous French doors.

A spectacular view of the Tucson Mountains took Kimberly's breath away. She dropped her suitcase and ran to open one of the doors to the balcony. Leaning on the railing, she looked below at an Olympic-sized pool surrounded by chaise lounges and umbrella tables. Oh, she could certainly get used to this!

Jack stood alongside her at the railing. "Beautiful, isn't it? You should see it in the morning at sunrise."

"Dad, it's gorgeous. Thank you for letting me come with you."

"Don't thank me yet. You're going to be working hard, I promise you that."

"I know, I know. But, jeez, look at this place!" She walked back into the living area and spun around, her arms extended wide.

"Come on, let's get you settled in your room. You have tomorrow to relax, maybe go to the pool. We get started first thing Monday morning. The company stocked the kitchen for us, but I was thinking we should go out for a nice, big steak tonight. What do you think?"

"Twist my arm," Kimberly said, picking up her suitcase and heading down the hallway that led to the bedrooms. Both were master suites with private balconies and en suite bathrooms with giant jacuzzi tubs. Kimberly had never seen such luxury. She was never going to want to go back home.

***

Slicing into a juicy, medium rare ribeye at the Silver Saddle Steakhouse, Kimberly listened as Jack described what the operation this summer would entail. Eckerd was opening four new stores in the Tucson area. Her responsibilities would include making appointments for staff interviews, helping stock shelves with inventory, and canvassing the local neighborhoods with fliers announcing the grand openings. Jack would introduce Kimberly to her supervisor on Monday, a man named Richard Hollister, who worked in operations at the Conroe distribution center back in Texas.

"You'll like him, Kim. He's a funny, easy going guy. Reminds me a lot of me."

"Ha ha, as if, Dad."

"What, you don't think I'm funny, or you don't think I'm easy going? Which is it?" Jack said, grinning.

"Neither. You're just . . . Dad," she said, rolling her eyes.

Jack picked up his Miller Lite and took a swig. "Kimberly, I can't say enough how important this opportunity is. I hope you enjoy yourself and learn a lot while you're out here. You might want to follow in your old man's footsteps. You never know."

"We'll see, old man. Can I order dessert?"

***

The next morning, Kimberly awoke to the rich aroma of freshly brewed coffee. She rubbed her eyes, stretching underneath the fluffy down comforter. The sun was just beginning to rise and the sky outside the glass doors was turning a stunning coral pink. She caught her breath and sat up, enchanted. She glanced over her shoulder at the digital alarm clock on the nightstand.

"Five-thirty in the morning? What am I crazy?" She got out of bed, stepped into her slippers, and went to brush her teeth. Shuffling down the hallway toward the kitchen, she stretched her arms overhead and yawned.

"Dad?"

"Out here," Jack said from the balcony. Kimberly poured herself a cup of coffee, adding whole milk and too much sugar. She sat next to her dad, bending her legs to put her slippered feet on the seat, the wrought iron chair cold on the backs of her legs.

"What am I doing up so early? The sky is amazing, though. You weren't kidding."

Jack nodded and took a drag from his cigarette. The quiet morning soothed Kimberly, a light breeze fluttering the curls around her face. The coffee warmed her from the inside as she stared at the mountains. The vista changed every minute the sun rose. It was as though they were in a living painting, the artist continually dipping the brush into new colors.

Far off in the distance, Kimberly heard a rumble. Low and soft at first, but the sound continued to grow. As it got louder, Kimberly turned to her dad to ask what that was when overhead, seemingly out of nowhere, soared two military jets in formation. The balcony shook. Kimberly felt the rumble in her chest. She jolted and spilled a little coffee on her pajama top.

"Holy cow, what was that?"

"Jets from Davis-Monthan Air Force Base. I didn't know they flew on Sunday mornings, too. I guess the military doesn't take a day off, does it?"

The jets faded from Kimberly's view.

That might be one of the coolest things I've ever seen.

***

Practically asleep on the chaise lounge by the pool, Kimberly lay on her belly in a baby blue checkered bikini, listening to the soothing sound of the waterfall flowing into the pool. Her brown curls were scooped off of her neck in a banana clip. Although the thermometer outside their condo read one hundred five degrees, it didn't feel as stifling as the heat in Texas or Florida. The air in the desert was so much drier, her sweat evaporated almost as soon as it surfaced on her skin. She took a deep breath, inhaling a mix of chlorine and coconut oil. She had almost drifted off when she heard a splash in the pool.

Shielding her eyes from the sun, her attention was captured by a man swimming laps. He completed four lengths of the broad pool without slowing.

Huh. Impressive.

Getting caught staring would be embarrassing. She chose to get back to her nap. Her eyes were closed and her breathing slow. The slap, slap of someone with wet feet approaching roused her.

"This seat taken?"

Kimberly opened her eyes, squinting against the glare. She

registered the figure of the swimming man but couldn't see what he looked like in the bright sunshine. He gestured to the chaise next to hers.

Oh, brother.

"Uh, nope, not taken."

"Great, thanks." He tossed his towel over the propped-up head of the chair and sat down, reclining. For a long moment, nothing was said. Uncomfortable, Kimberly attempted to resume her nap. Dozens of empty chairs surrounded the pool and he chose to lie on the one next to her.

Is he flirting with me? What in the world am I supposed to do with this?

"Did you just move in?" he asked.

Kimberly kept her eyes closed, her head on her bent arms, facing away from him."Yes and no. Just got here yesterday. I'm only staying for the summer."

"Oh, cool. Did you hear those jets this morning? Pretty jarring. I was sound asleep. I almost fell out of bed."

Kimberly chuckled. "Yeah, pretty sure I have a permanent coffee stain on my pajamas." She sat up, retrieving her sunglasses from the table between them. Time to check out this man who clearly wanted her attention. She reclined in her chaise and gave him a quick once-over.

He was tall, easily over six feet, mid- to late-twenties, his dark hair wet and wavy. Ray-Bans hid his eyes, but his smile was nice, complete with one cute dimple on the right side. Orange and white Ocean Pacific swim trunks complemented his tanned skin and she noticed he had very long feet.

That's why he's such a good swimmer—he has built-in flippers!

Before she could stop herself, she let out a giggle, and quickly covered her mouth, embarrassed.

"What's so funny?" he asked, smiling. *Dimple alert.*

"Oh, it's nothing. I was just thinking about—so, do you live here?"

"For now. I'm on assignment. But I don't want to talk about work."

"Yeah, I get it. Who wants to think about work on a Sunday?"

"Exactly."

She noticed him glancing at her left hand. Wow, how old must he think she is if he's checking to see if she's married! He took off his sunglasses and the greenest eyes she had ever seen were looking back at her.

Why in the world would a guy like this be interested in someone like me? Maybe he was just being nice, seeing as there was nobody else around to talk to.

"I know this is a little forward. I'm new around here, too. Do you have dinner plans tonight?"

Kimberly swallowed. He wasn't just being nice. He was definitely interested.

Dear God, what am I supposed to do now?

She was pretty sure everything about her screamed 'nerd'. No way in hell would her dad ever agree to let her go out to dinner with some strange guy on her first day in Arizona.

"I do have plans tonight, but maybe another time?" Kimberly said. Okay, it was time to get out of here before she said something stupid and blew it.

He nodded. "Sure. Another time." He put his sunglasses back on and held out his hand. "I'm Rich, by the way. Rich Hollister."

Oh, shit.

She took his hand and shook it. "I'm Kimberly Stevens. And, apparently, you're my boss."

***

Monday morning was a bit awkward. Kimberly didn't want to give her dad the wrong idea about Rich approaching her at the pool, so she'd said nothing to him about it. Jack introduced them at the store. She shook his hand professionally and said, "Pleased to meet you." Rich didn't blow her cover. He just smiled and said, "Likewise." *Oh, that damn dimple.*

Day one proved to be a busy one. Kimberly spent the entire morning on the phone calling applicants and scheduling interviews. In the afternoon, she helped unload boxes of inventory and began to stock shelves. Pharmacists were considered the store managers and would be interviewing for all of the staff positions. Her dad only needed to sit in on the interviews for shift manager positions. At his request, she scheduled all of those interviews for the following day. Since Rich had a rental car, he and Kimberly would be using that time tomorrow to pass out fliers in the neighborhoods nearby.

She fixed spaghetti and salad for dinner that night, and after cleaning the dishes, excused herself to take a shower and turn in. Yawning, she made her way down the hallway to her room, hearing Jack pick up the phone to call Marjorie. After a long, hot shower, she tucked herself into bed and began to write in her journal. Although weary from the long day, she had no idea how she was going to sleep. She was a bundle of nerves.

***

A beautiful sunrise welcomed Kimberly again when she opened her eyes. Despite her concern the night before, she'd slept like a baby. But now remembering why she was concerned in the first place, the nerves started all over again. A sudden ball of energy, she bounded out of bed.

She dressed in a turquoise Polo shirt, flipped up the collar, and tucked it into acid washed jean shorts. Nike high-tops with magenta laces completed the ensemble. She applied magenta eyeshadow and turquoise eyeliner with lots of mascara, topping it off with bright pink lip gloss. After fluffing her curly bangs with a pick comb, she pinned the sides of her hair back over her ears with barrettes. The finishing touches were her homemade, neon pink guitar pick earrings. She hoped her look said 'fun girl,' not employee.

"Morning, Dad," she said. Jack sat at the table on the balcony having his morning coffee and smoke.

Glancing up at Kimberly, Jack sputtered into his coffee. "Uh, hey, Kim." He wiped his mustache, grinning behind the napkin. "Remember, I have interviews with managers all day. You'll be working with Richard today."

"Yeah, I remember. Don't worry. I'm sure we'll get a lot done."

"Worry? I'm not worried. The two of you'll do fine," Jack said. He went inside and picked up the tie he'd draped over a barstool, wrapping it under his shirt collar and looping it into a neat knot. Pulling his money clip from his pocket, he peeled off a ten dollar bill, placing it on the bar. "Here's lunch money. Be sure to stop and eat. Drink plenty of liquids. The desert air is much drier than what we're used to."

"Got it," Kimberly said, pocketing the money.

"One thing's for sure, Richard won't have to worry about losing you in a crowd. Very colorful ensemble today."

"By colorful, you mean awesome, right?"

Jack winked. "Yeah, that's what I meant."

***

By lunchtime, Rich and Kimberly had passed out nearly half the fliers to nearby homes. Rich parked at the corner of every street and they split up, each canvassing one side of the street. Mostly they rubber banded the papers to the mailbox flags, but if they saw a homeowner, they would tell them all about the new Eckerd Drug store opening in the area, and to be sure to come in for all kinds of specials and free surprises for the grand opening next weekend.

"Mark your calendars. We wouldn't want you to miss out. It's a family experience—bring everyone you know!"

When they met back at the car, Rich suggested they try a taco place for lunch they'd passed a couple of hours back.

"I saw it yesterday and the parking lot was full. I take that as a good sign."

They ordered tacos in soft white corn tortillas and Cokes and sat down at an outside table. The breeze was welcome on a hot desert day, proving much cooler under the shade of the umbrella.

"Thanks for not saying anything to my dad about meeting me at the pool. I didn't want him to get any kind of impression of you before we worked together."

"Noted. I had a feeling. I've known your dad for about a year. He's a good guy. I have a lot of respect for him."

"Thanks, I appreciate that."

"He trained me in operations when I arrived at Eckerd. Handpicked me for this assignment."

"Oh, nice!" Kimberly said.

Wait, he handpicked me for this, too. Maybe I'm not as big of a letdown to him as I thought.

She smiled.

"So, what do you do back in Texas?" Rich asked.

"I work at the movie theater in Oak Ridge, or at least I did before I quit to come out here for the summer. Dad says if I do well, he'll recommend me for a job with Eckerd, which would be rad. Hopefully it would pay more than I make now. I also like to write."

"Oh, really? What do you write?"

"Poetry mostly. Some short stories, but I never seem to finish them. And I keep a journal. It's huge. Probably gonna take until I'm ninety years old to finish it," Kimberly said.

"Love to read some of your work some time. I majored in English lit. I was a bit of a writer myself until I realized that unless I was going to be a professor, there wasn't much in the way of a career for me in literature."

"What kinds of things did you write?"

"Plays, actually. Wrote some stupid ones when I was a kid. Really got into it in high school. The drama club performed one of mine in my senior year. I minored in theater arts, but at the college level it was much more difficult. I gave that up. Wrote it off as a childhood hobby."

"Oh, I'll bet your plays are good! Do you have any of them with you?"

He laughed. "No, no. They're all shoved in a box stuffed in my parents' attic in Dallas. As far as I'm concerned, they'll never again see the light of day."

"Oh, that's too bad. I would love to read one."

"You're just humoring me. Trust me, they're pretty lame." An easy silence passed between them as they enjoyed the good food and weather.

"I appreciate you asking me to dinner. But I have to ask . . . do you know how old I am?"

"To be honest, I thought you were around my age when I met you at the pool. But, yes, I know you're eighteen."

"And a half. I'll be nineteen in the fall."

Rich grinned. *Dimple alert, dammit.* "And a half."

"Does that change your mind about having dinner?"

"Oh, Kimberly, I don't think it's a good idea. I'm your supervisor. Pretty sure it would be frowned upon."

"What if my dad was there?"

"You want us to have dinner with your dad?"

"Technically, I want you to have dinner with us. At our condo one night this weekend? I'm a pretty good cook and my dad can grill the hell out of some meat. Let me run it by him and see what he says. Deal?"

Rich frowned, thinking for a moment. He wiped his hands on his napkin and met Kimberly's eyes. *Oh my God, those dang eyes.*

"Okay, let me know what your dad says. I would be honored to have dinner with the two of you."

"Sweet! I'll talk to him tonight."

They tossed their trash into a receptacle by the parking lot and walked to the rental car.

"Off to finish pressing flesh with the public," Rich said.

"Yep, onward, Jeeves!" She crossed her fingers and closed her eyes.

Please let Dad say yes.

***

"No," Dad said.

"But why not?" Kimberly whined.

"Because it's Eckerd policy not to fraternize with your employees. If I invite him here, that's two of us violating policy."

"But, Dad, this situation is different. We're out here on assignment. What's he supposed to do, eat alone every single night he's here?"

"I don't think Richard's social life is any of my concern."

"Oh, come on, Dad. You don't have to be such a stickler out here. I'm sure the powers that be would completely understand. We're a team. Shouldn't we act like one?"

Jack thought for a moment. "I guess the rules could be relaxed a little for the success of the team. Okay, he can come for dinner on Saturday night. But let me extend the invitation. It would definitely be inappropriate coming from his employee."

A grin tugged at Kimberly's mouth, but she stifled her enthusiasm. "Thanks, Dad. He's a nice guy. What should we serve?"

"Let's worry about that later in the week. I need to go over these interview notes. I'll be on the balcony." He picked up the pile of paperwork and his Miller Lite longneck from the bar. "Thanks for dinner.

The tuna casserole was almost as good as your mom's."

Kimberly hummed to herself as she washed the dishes. She couldn't wait to write every detail in her journal.

***

The doorbell rang and Kimberly ran from the kitchen to answer it. At the door, she stopped. Took a breath. One last glance in the foyer mirror. Her turquoise and silver dangle earrings looked lovely against her tanned skin, she thought, pleased. She opened the door to find Rich standing on the welcome mat holding a bouquet of multi-colored gerbera daisies and a bottle of scotch.

"Hi there!" she said."Please come in."

Rich followed Kimberly into the dining room.

"These are for you and this," raising the bottle, "is for your dad." Kimberly took the flowers from his hand.

"Why, thank you. They're beautiful. Dad's on the balcony grilling the ribs, if you'd like to join him. Beer?"

"Sure, that'd be great."

Kimberly handed him a cold bottle of beer and started looking through cabinets for a vase.

"This will do nicely," she said, and began to fill a crystal pitcher with water. She closed her eyes and breathed slowly, her insides as squirrely as a nervous cat. Placing the vibrant flowers in the table's center, she began filling it with side dishes—potato salad, baked beans, corn on the cob, and corn bread. She would warm up a blueberry pie for dessert. Checking the place settings one last time, Kimberly opened a bottle of beer and joined the men on the balcony.

"…going really well so far," Jack was saying.

"I agree," Rich said. "Everything seems to be running smoothly. We're slightly ahead of schedule. Great news for the grand opening of the first location next weekend."

"What is that in your hand, little girl?" Jack asked.

"A beer," she said. "It's legal in Texas, Dad."

"Well, you're still too young in Arizona. I don't recall you ever having a beer with your old man before."

Uh-oh. This could get embarrassing.

He tipped the neck of his bottle toward Kimberly. Surprised, she tapped the neck of her bottle on his.

"Cheers!" Kimberly said.

"I guess you're not such a little girl anymore. Take it easy. It can hit your head fast if you're not used to it."

"Got it," she said, raising her bottle in salute.

After a delicious barbecue dinner, the three of them sat out on the balcony enjoying the evening in the desert sun. Even on a full stomach, Kimberly was starting to feel her third beer. Her giggles were a little too loud. Her eyes felt a bit droopy.

Rich stood up to excuse himself. "This has been really nice. Thanks for having me over, Jack. Ribs were delicious. Kimberly, terrific dinner. Your dad is spoiled having you here."

"Ha! Well, you know . . . " she said, trailing off, her thought unfinished.

Jack stood and shook Rich's hand. "I'll walk you to the door, Richard. Thanks a lot for the scotch. I'm sure I'll enjoy it."

Kimberly wandered down the hallway toward her room, elbows bent, hands near her shoulders, in case she started to pinball. She brushed her teeth, washed her face, changed into pajamas, and got into bed before her dad tapped on the door.

"Kim, you okay?"

"Yep, fine, Dad."

"Nice job on dinner. It was nice of Richard to join us."

"Yep." Kimberly felt her eyes closing.

"Sleep in tomorrow. See you in the morning."

***

In her dream, they were having an earthquake. The building was shaking and beginning to fall apart, pictures flying off the walls, glasses in the kitchen breaking. Oh my word, it's so loud! Kimberly gasped and her eyes flew open just in time to hear the Air Force jets fly overhead.

She groaned. Damn those stinking jets. What time was it? She peered at her clock. 6:30 am. Doesn't the military ever sleep? She rolled out of bed and splashed cool water on her face. It was far too early to wake up on a Sunday morning. She crawled back under the covers and closed her eyes.

Hours later, she awoke feeling groggy with a very dry mouth. She sat up and sipped from the glass of water next to her bed. 11:45. Holy crap! She hadn't slept this late in forever.

After freshening up, she went to the kitchen and opened the refrigerator. Pulling out a Sprite, she popped it open, took a long, fizzy gulp, and went to look for her dad. There was a note leaning against the pitcher of flowers.

Kim: Got a call from Mom late last night. Her mother and stepfather have been killed in a car accident. She is flying back to Tampa for the funeral. I'm going home to be with Brie for a few days. Richard has a good handle on things—follow his lead. I'll be back soon. Here's a credit card for emergencies only. Maybe lay off the beer while I'm gone. Love, Dad.

Kimberly sat down on the dining room chair with a thud. She barely knew her mother's parents, yet she was jarred by the tragic news. She went to the phone and dialed long distance to her family's house in Texas.

"Hello?"

"Brie, hey, it's me. Is Mom there? Is she okay?"

"Yeah, she's packing. Going to meet Dad at the airport in an hour. I think she's okay. Wanna talk to her?"

"Please." Sabrina yelled from the kitchen up the stairs that Kimberly was on the phone. Marjorie picked up the extension in the master bedroom and Sabrina hung up.

"Hello, Kimberly," she said, her voice strained. Though Marjorie had no relationship to speak of with her mother, the news had to have pierced her heart.

"Mom, I'm so sorry. What happened? When did you find out?"

"My aunt called. It happened a few days ago. They were rear-ended in a traffic jam on I-275 in Tampa. The semi-truck that hit them never even braked. Five cars were smashed. No survivors." Kimberly shuddered at the image.

"That's horrific! Are you okay? Do you want anyone to go with you?"

"No, no, it's fine. I'll be okay. I'm kind of numb right now."

"Maybe you should call Jesse. See if he can come be with you for the funeral."

"I don't want to bother your brother with this. He's very busy with the new restaurant. It will all be fine. I appreciate your concern, though."

"All right, Mom. Take it easy. I'll talk to you soon."

"Be good, Kimberly," Marjorie said.

"Love y—" A dial tone buzzed in her ear and Kimberly hung up the phone, her heart heavy.

***

Kimberly tried to open her eyes, but they were burning, her eyelids crusty. The pillowcase pressed against her cheek was slightly damp. She opened and closed her mouth a couple of times, and grimaced. What was that nasty taste in her mouth? She needed a gallon of water and a gallon of mouthwash, not necessarily in that order. She attempted to roll over, but the pounding and whooshing in her ears made her lie still. *Ugh, what is going on with me?*

GASP! What time is it? Oh no, oh no . . . She opened one eye and looked at the clock. 10:30 am. On Monday morning. She was late. She was so screwed. Her dad was going to kill her. Why in the world didn't she set her alarm?

And then it all came back. The shame. The humiliation. The nightmare of the night before. She pulled the covers over her head and mumbled, "Fuck it."

***

After hanging up the phone with Marjorie the day before, Kimberly had closed her eyes, mentally sending her mother comfort. She'd looked out the French doors at a beautiful, cloudless day. She'd lived at sea level her entire life, so the view of the mountains enthralled her. Sometime this summer, she was going to have to talk her dad into going on a hike.

After a bowl of cereal, Kimberly took a quick shower and put on a magenta and black bikini. She scooped her hair up into a high, curly ponytail and slathered herself with tanning oil. She packed a cooler with cheese and crackers and a few beers, whispering *sorry, Dad*. Grabbing her pool bag, she shoved the latest novel in a series by V.C.Andrews into the side pocket, put on her flip-flops and sunglasses, and headed down for a relaxing day in the sun.

A few people had begun to gather poolside. Fortunately, no residents under the age of 18 were allowed in their complex, so she was sure to have a quiet morning to lay in the sun and read without the sounds of kids splashing and hollering. Kimberly found a chaise in a corner away from the others. The beach towel soft under her, she opened her paperback. It wasn't long before the warmth of the desert sun lulled her to sleep.

"This seat taken?" a familiar voice said. Kimberly jumped, her book falling to the pool deck.

"Oh, hi! You keep asking me that," she said. Rich smiled and sat down on the adjacent chair. He stretched out his long legs and opened the newspaper he'd brought.

"Thanks again for dinner last night. It was really nice of you and Jack. I hope we can do it again sometime."

"Sure! I don't think that'll be a problem."

"Will he be joining us by the pool today?"

"My dad? No. He had to go back to Texas. Family emergency. He'll be back in a few days. So, I guess it's just you and me getting the store in order this week."

"Is everything okay?"

"Yeah, I mean, we're all okay, but my mom's mother and her husband died in a car accident."

Rich sat up, taking off his sunglasses."Kimberly, I'm so sorry to hear that."

"Thanks. It's kind of not that big of a deal. I mean, it is for my mom, I guess, but none of us were close at all. I think the last time I saw them I was in kindergarten. I appreciate you being sweet, though." Kimberly reached into her bag and pulled out her white Swatch watch, checking the time. 2:07 pm. Not too early to toast their memory, she supposed. She slid the cooler out from under her chair, popped the tops off of two of the bottles of beer and handed one to Rich.

"To my mom's parents, may they rest in peace," Kimberly said, lifting her beer in salute.

"To your mom's parents," Rich said, taking a sip, his face solemn. No dimple this time. They sipped their drinks quietly, watching the other people sitting at umbrella tables having lunch and cocktails, lounging on chairs reading magazines, and bobbing around in the pool. It was truly a beautiful Sunday. Kimberly felt her muscles loosen as the beer relaxed her. She realized she and Rich barely knew a thing about one another.

"So, I wanna hear more about your childhood in Dallas," she said, and the conversation began to flow.

They stopped chatting long enough to take a quick dip in the cool water. Back in the chairs, Rich tipped his bottle, draining the last of it. Six empty bottles stood like soldiers between them.

"Should I go get some more from my place?"

"Oh, sure, get more! I have some snacks in here, too. We can share when you get back," she said.

"Back in a flash."

Kimberly watched him walk away, a lazy smile on her lips. The summer sun was pretty potent and she was feeling drowsy. She would probably need to drink some water, too. Looking across the pool deck at the little building housing the restrooms, she spied a water fountain. She made a mental note to stop there later. Inhaling deeply, Kimberly was intoxicated by the aroma of tropical oils and lotions, like a warm piña colada.

Kimberly rolled over onto her belly and began to let her mind wander. She daydreamed about what would happen when Rich returned. Maybe he would rub oil on her back. She imagined feeling his large hands lightly massaging her muscles, down her spine to her bottom, down the backs of her legs. A tiny moan of pleasure slipped out, thinking of how good it would feel to have a man touch her.

She'd been so depressed after leaving her boyfriend behind in Florida that she'd avoided dating altogether. She knew she would never give a shit about any of the stupid boys in Texas. But Rich was not a boy. Rich was a man. And a super hot one at that. She reached around her back with one hand and untied the string of her bikini, letting the strings fall to her sides. She didn't want to get a tan line on her back. She also hoped his hands would find their way to sides of her breasts. Her body tingled just thinking about it.

"Are you sleeping?" he asked.

Kimberly startled for a moment, then smiled. "Not yet." Rich put an open bottle on the deck under chair, close enough for her to reach without having to sit up. *So thoughtful.* He reclined in his chaise, picking up the newspaper.

"Did you say you brought snacks?"

"Yeah, in the cooler," she said, the alcohol making her tongue feel a little thick. Rich reached under her chair and opened the cooler to find a sandwich baggie containing a few slices of cheddar and some small wheat crackers.

"This is what you brought? Girl, that's not even enough for you, much less both of us. Let's go up to my place and make some sandwiches."

"Mmmm, sounds good . . . " The oil rubdown was going to have to wait. She reached back with both hands, her face pressed into her towel, and retied the string of her bikini, grateful he hadn't mentioned it.

When the drinks were empty, they packed up their belongings. Kimberly was light-headed and trying not to show it. Rich gathered all the bottles and threw them in the trash near the water fountain. She stopped for a long drink, reminding herself to ask for a glass of water when they got upstairs.

Rich's condo was not quite as luxurious as the one she was sharing with her dad. A one-bedroom unit, it was cozier, the balcony half the size. The furnishings were simple but nice—a small, beige sectional in the living area, round glass table with seating for four in the dining area. The air conditioning was a welcome relief from the heat. Chill bumps rose on her skin. Her head was pleasantly buzzing as she stepped out onto the balcony and lit a cigarette.

"I didn't realize you smoked."

"Oh, right. Is it a problem?"

"Suit yourself. Let me see if there's an ashtray in the kitchen somewhere," he said, rifling through cabinets. He found a small, black plastic ashtray and took it to her. "I have ham and Swiss, okay with you?"

"Absolutely. I'm starving," she said.

Rich brought lunch out to the balcony along with two more cold lagers. Kimberly didn't want to refuse and seem like some kind of baby, but she was definitely buzzed. She accepted the plate on her lap and tapped the neck of his beer with the neck of hers.

"Cheers!" she said.

"Back atcha."

They chatted while they had lunch. Kimberly was sure she was just babbling, but he was engaging, continuing to ask questions about her childhood, their move to Texas, what she aspired to.

"Did you hear those damn jets again this morning?" she asked.

"I did," Rich said, laughing. "So annoying. I guess they have a goal not to let anyone in Tucson sleep past dawn."

"I agree!" Kimberly said, raising the bottle to her lips again. "But can I let you in on a little secret?"

"Of course."

"I think they are sweet as hell. Completely badass. I wouldn't mind being in the military if I got to be around those things." Rich sat back and looked her, amused.

"Really? Wow. I did not expect to hear you say that."

"Crazy, right? I don't know why. They just fascinate me."

"Well, then maybe you should."

"What do you mean?"

"I mean, if that's what you want to do, that's what you should do. Follow your dream. Why not?" Rich looked at her with those damn green eyes. Kimberly thought about it for a moment. In her relaxed state, her filters fell away and she opened herself up to this virtual stranger.

"Why not is because my parents would flip out if I said I wanted to join the military. Well, Dad would. He has me out here in Arizona proving myself so I can follow in his footsteps, since there's no way Jesse ever will. I finally feel close to my dad in a way I never have and the last thing I want to do is disappoint him. Mom doesn't honestly give a shit what I do as long as I stay out of her hair. I think she really only cares about Sabrina anyway. I don't know . . . " Kimberly paused. "Sorry, too much info, I'm sure."

Rich stood up, so Kimberly did, too, a bit on the wobbly side. They took their empty plates and bottles and headed in to the kitchen.

"You know what I think? I think you're only given one chance at life. Pretty sure enlistment is usually just four years, similar to a college commitment. You get paid and you get benefits. If you want to find out what those jets are all about, that's what you should do. If you decide you don't like it, it's only temporary. You can follow another dream."

Oh my God, smart is so sexy.

Rich opened the fridge.

Inhibition washed away by the beer, and her body filled with desire for this man, Kimberly untied her bikini top and let it fall to the linoleum floor. She stepped forward to press her naked breasts against his back, wrapping her arms around his waist.

"Whoa," Rich said. He pulled her hands apart, turning to face her. She held onto his hands and leaned up to kiss him, but he pulled their joined hands up, placing them in front of her mouth to stop her. The look on his face was not lust. It was shock.

"Kimberly, I'm sorry. I did not mean to give you the impression that . . . Oh, God. I'm engaged to a girl back in Texas. I'm so sorry," he said.

Kimberly grabbed a kitchen towel and covered her chest. Her body wide awake now, flooded with embarrassment. Tears welled in her eyes as she snatched her top from the floor, found her bag, and fled the condo, slamming the door behind her. She ducked into a stairwell, refastening her bathing suit top, breathing heavily, humiliation burning her face.

Oh, Jesus, what was I thinking?! I am such an idiot. Of course he doesn't want me. Why would he? I am such a Stupid. Little. Girl.

Back at her unit, she fumbled for the keys in her pool bag. Inside, she closed the door, locked it, and leaned against it, steadying herself. Dropping her bag and keys to the floor, along with Rich's kitchen towel, she stumbled to the kitchen. She splashed her face with cold water, hoping to flush the shame right down the sink.

Reaching for a paper towel, she saw the unopened bottle of scotch on the counter next to the microwave oven. She opened the cabinet above it and pulled out a small orange juice glass. Cracking the seal on the scotch, she poured the amber liquid into the crystal cut glass until it almost reached the top. She wrinkled her nose as the pungent aroma hit her.

"Down the hatch!" she said to herself, and tossed the drink to the back of her throat, swallowing it all at once. Her body shuddered as the warm sensation from the liquor spread through her belly. She retched a little bit, putting her fist over her mouth to hold it in. "Buck up, little girl.

Don't be a wimp!" She poured herself another glass.

***

Scotch, Kimberly thought, nauseated, and willed herself to get out of bed. She sat up slowly, groaning, and saw that her journal was open. Her drunken, nearly unintelligible scrawl filled a number of pages. Even in her highly inebriated state last night, she'd made a decision. She closed her eyes and breathed slowly. She walked down the hall to the kitchen, lifting the phone receiver from the cradle.

***

The sun was nearly gone from the western sky as her father stood on the front walk. The cab driver pulled away from the curb. Kimberly dragged both suitcases through the grass, avoiding his eyes.

"One week. That's all you lasted. One week," he said.

"What can I say, Dad? I'm kind of a loser." She brushed past Jack through the front door, not allowing him to help with her luggage. Physically and emotionally drained, she tossed the condo keys and the credit card onto the foyer table and went upstairs. Sabrina came out of her room as Kimberly reached the landing.

"Hey, what are you—"

"Don't get too used to me. I'm leaving in two weeks for boot camp."

Chapter Twenty — 1984 — Kimberly

Kimberly rode in the back seat of her mother's Cutlass to the airport. She was somewhat touched that her dad came back from Tucson to see her off. Maybe he just wanted to make sure Kimberly was actually going to follow through. His eyes met hers in the rearview mirror and she diverted her gaze to watch the sights of Houston speeding by outside the car window.

"So, tell me again, why Navy and not Air Force, like the planes we saw in Arizona?" Jack asked.

Kimberly sighed. "Pretty sure we already went over this. When I got off the plane, I asked the cab driver to take me to the closest recruiting station. When we got there, the only recruiter still at the office was Navy. He told me that the Naval air force is larger than the Air Force itself, so, Navy it is."

"Kimberly, I just have to ask you again, and I really would like the truth. Did you have sex with that young man in Tucson? Is that what this is all about? I have a strong intuitive wisdom about these things," Marjorie said.

"Mother, there's a fine line between intuitive wisdom and acute paranoia. For the tenth time, no, I did not sleep with him. Not that it's any of your business."

"Kimberly Marie, watch your tone with your mother," Jack said. Kimberly rolled her eyes, crossed her arms over her chest, and continued to stare out the window. Just a few more miles and she may never have to see these people ever again.

"It's fine, Jack. Let her take it to the grave if she wishes. Only she can deal with the shame of her behavior. She's a grown woman."

Jack glared at Marjorie, annoyed by her cold insensitivity. He had already explained to her that he'd spoken to Richard upon his return to Tucson, who had been a gentleman about the situation. He'd said that there had been a miscommunication between the two of them and when he'd explained he was engaged to be married, she became upset. When he'd gone to pick her up for work the next morning, she didn't answer the door. That's all he knew. Jack respected Richard's discretion and trusted his version of the events. He had no reason not to. Whatever had happened, he refused to press Kimberly on it. Her decision was made. She'd signed a contract with the United States government and made a commitment. It was done. The reasons didn't matter.

"What did you say your job in the Navy is going to be? Will you be working with their version of those jets?" Jack asked, attempting to break the tension in the car.

"Surprisingly, I got a very high score on the entrance exam, that ASVAB I told you about? The recruiter told me I could pretty much pick any rate in the Navy that had open jobs available. I can't train to be a pilot without a college degree. I decided to work in life support maintenance, since Mr. Lance taught me so much about mechanics. Speaking of that . . ." Kimberly slid the small key off her key ring, tucking it into the pocket of her jeans. She tossed the keyring up front. It hit the space on the seat between her parents with a clink. "Give Blueberry to Sabrina. Tell her to be careful with her."

"Teaching her to drive a stick—that's gonna be an adventure," Jack said. "Life support, huh?"

"Aviation life support technician. According to the recruiter, not many women are in that job. I'll be servicing planes with oxygen, air conditioning and pressurization, and the coolest thing—maintaining ejection seats and canopies. If anything, I figure I won't get bored."

"That's for sure. Well, I'm impressed with your choice. Listen, the best thing you can do for yourself and your career is to never give up. Just hang in there no matter what happens. Especially through boot camp. I heard from a buddy of mine that they call it that because it's designed to weed out those who can't cut it. They get 'booted' out," Jack said.

"I know, Dad."

"Are both of you crazy?" Marjorie asked. "Am I the only one that realizes what's happening here? Kimberly is just running away. Hiding on a major scale this time. Whenever things get hard—"

"You know what, Mom?"

"Kimberly . . ." Jack warned, as he pulled into the airport departure lane.

"No, Dad, I'm sorry, but I am sick to death of this shit. You have issues, Mother. You're a self-focused, narcissistic, obsessive-compulsive, manic depressive. It's your world and the rest of us are just living in it. You have no idea how long you have been hurting me. How about my whole life! If it wasn't a belt on my butt, it was your hand on my face, or your words directly to my heart. You are *mean*, Mother. You still have a shot not to completely ruin Sabrina. Don't fuck it up."

Kimberly jumped out of the car, slamming the door behind her, so as not to see the stricken, enflamed face of her mother in the front seat.

Jack closed the driver door. "Kim! You don't want to leave things like this with your mother."

"Leave things like what, Dad? Don't blame this on me. She's crazy. I couldn't be happier about leaving. If you're smart, you'll do the same thing."

Jack popped the trunk and pulled his daughter's suitcase out, setting it on the sidewalk. He shook his head.

"Little girl, sometimes you need to engage your filter." He wrapped her in a hug that felt like finality. "Be smart and take care of you, ya hear?"

Five hours later, she was wishing she was still in the comfort of that car.

***

"ON THE LINE. NOW, RECRUITS! GET YOUR ASSES OUT OF THE RACK AND GET YOUR TOES ON MY LINE, DO YOU HEAR ME?" Some little boy was stomping through the Quonset hut filled with iron bunk beds and flimsy mattresses, banging on an aluminum trash can lid like a gong, and screaming at the top of his lungs. What the hell was the line?

He looked up into the face of a bleary-eyed, groggy girl who was around 5'4" and was green around the gills, as though she was about to throw up.

"Do you have some sort of hearing problem, Recruit? I said, ON THE LINE!" He pointed down at the floor at the long line of red tape that ran the length of the room in front of both rows of bunks. "Put.Your.Toes.

ON THE LINE. Now, Recruit!"

The nauseous girl stepped up to the red tape. Just as the screaming boy moved past her to yell at another recruit, she ran to the trashcan with no lid on it and promptly puked up her guts. Kimberly and the other women in close proximity wrinkled their noses, some retching in solidarity. Nobody helped the vomiting girl. They kept their toes on the red line out of sheer terror.

Outside was pitch black. Sunrise was still a long way off. Kimberly would have looked at her watch, but they had taken it. Along with every other piece of jewelry she wore, and anything else of value, and her makeup, perfume, cigarettes, anything considered frivolous. Everything had been boxed up when they arrived. They wrote their names and addresses on the outsides of the boxes and the Navy was shipping them all back home. Kimberly said a silent prayer of thanks for the foresight to lock her journal up in the lockbox under her bed at home. If anyone were to have access to that journal, she would have been mortified.

Once stripped of nearly everything but the clothes on their backs, the women were each given an olive green duffel called a seabag. They were taken to get gym clothes, which would double as pajamas, chambray blouses and bell bottom dungarees. Each recruit was assigned a stencil of their last name along with black and white permanent paint markers. They were measured for their dress uniforms and told to keep the seabags closed and await further instructions. By the time they arrived at the Quonset hut, it was nearly 2:00 in the morning. Most recruits were exhausted and fell wearily onto the various bunks, falling asleep instantly despite the noise of 80 women in a large, cavernous space. Some were too keyed up to sleep. Some were absolutely terrified and questioning their sanity at that moment. Then the screaming and banging started, throwing everyone into a complete state of confusion.

Kimberly heard a tall woman with a deep voice say, "Hey, that's not a little boy, that's a really short woman!" They all turned and looked at the person causing all the ruckus. It was, indeed, a really short woman. She was Filipino American, with very short, jet-black hair, and a fierce holler. She was wearing a short-sleeved, white uniform blouse with white slacks over shiny black shoes, and had an impressive number of chevrons on her sleeve patch.

"Recruits, I am Petty Officer First Class Sharp and your company commander. You will call me ma'am, or Petty Officer Sharp, understood?" In response came a low rumbling from the women with their toes on the red line.

"I CANNOT HEAR YOU. AM I UNDERSTOOD?"

"YES, MA'AM!" The walls of the Q-hut nearly shook from the deafening sound.

"I will be your company commander along with Master Chief Petty Officer Kuhn. You will call him sir, or Master Chief, is that clear?"

"YES, MA'AM!"

The CC turned and strode with purpose toward the end of the hut. She turned back toward the recruits. Gesturing to the left side of the room, then the right, she said, "This line fall in behind me, that line behind them, single file. You will follow me to our barracks, which will be your home for the next 8.3 weeks, if you have what it takes to be in my Navy. No talking. Not one word. Zip it, or there will be consequences for all of you. From this moment forward, you live and die as a team. Understood?"

"YES, MA'AM!"

And so it began.

During the first few days, recruit officers were picked by the CC's to lead the company. Due to Kimberly's high ASVAB score, she was chosen as the company yeoman, or secretary. Her duties would include keeping track of all 80 girls at all times, and reporting a muster to the CC's first thing in the morning and last thing at night. So, she was required to be awake before everyone else and was the last one in bed. Losing precious minutes of sleep in boot camp proved to be draining, but Kimberly steeled herself, determined not to quit this time. Not to fail.

The days were extremely long, beginning with physical training before dawn each morning, and again in the afternoon; learning how to fold their clothes to fit in limited space on a ship; and make a perfect rack (Navy for bunk) as though they were in ship's berthing. They had classroom studies, swim qualifications, firefighting for shipboard training, tear gas exposure, and drilling in the marching field over and over and over. It felt a little like high school marching band with none of the fun.

Every Friday night was mail call. All of the women would gather with freshly showered heads and sit relaxed on the floor reading letters and opening packages from loved ones, after they'd been inspected by the CC's, of course. Kimberly received two letters the entire time she was in training. One from her dad and one from Sabrina. She sent home the information packet regarding boot camp graduation, including local hotel information and the strict schedule to which the ceremonies would adhere.

Nearly nine weeks later, on the morning of Pass In Review, the graduation ceremony, Kimberly marched across the field with her company, pulling up the rear as the yeoman. She held her head high and proud, following barked orders from the recruit CPO. Standing at parade rest for nearly half an hour while the Base Commander addressed the attendees, Kimberly scanned the crowd looking for anyone resembling her family. She hadn't received word from any of them, but that wasn't unusual.

Once the newly graduated sailors were dismissed, they marched in formation back to their barracks. Smiles and hugs filled the space as most of the women hurried back outside to meet up with their families.

Kimberly spent the entire last weekend of boot camp in the barracks packing for her next duty station. Nobody had come. She could understand her mother not showing up, but her dad? Her brother? Disappointment throbbed painfully inside.

The next morning, when Airman Apprentice Stevens was handed her orders and a plane ticket to Naval Air Technical Training Center in Millington, Tennessee, something had calcified within her. Her heart's door to her family had closed.

***

During her time in Millington, she wrote to her dad one last time requesting he use the enclosed money order to ship her the lockbox. Aside from that request, she had no further contact with her family. Following four months of intense technical training as an AME (aviation mechanic egress, or life support technician), Kimberly was assigned to Air Test and Evaluation Squadron One (VX-1) at Naval Air Station Patuxent River, Maryland. As it was in training school, she was the only female in her squadron shop. She quickly proved herself worthy of the position. She was technically savvy and had mechanical ability as good as, or better than, any of the men with whom she was assigned.

Kimberly didn't get assigned to work on fighter jets, as she'd first been attracted to in Arizona. VX-1 was a test and evaluation squadron for five different platforms of anti-submarine warfare aircraft. The squadron was in constant motion with plenty to learn each day, especially in her early years of enlistment. She focused on each platform, learning every step of the daily and turnaround inspections to the point where she could nearly do them blindfolded, gaining qualifications to operate flight line vehicles, servicing both liquid and gaseous oxygen bottles for all of the aircraft, and surprising herself by how unafraid she was to climb up the side of the fuselage of a 34-foot tall aircraft or to handle explosives every day. The job was complicated and rewarding, and her hard work did not go unnoticed. Kimberly was selected for various detachments—short-term ancillary assignments for small, specialized groups within the squadron—accompanying their aircraft to military bases across the globe. She found that promotions came more easily than she'd expected.

However, she built a solid wall around herself and her heart. She would allow no one in. It was safer to just do the work, do it well, and go home each night. Keep your head down and don't draw attention to yourself. One good thing about the military, in Kimberly's eyes, was that there really wasn't time to become attached to anyone at the squadron. People came and went with such frequency that it was easy to be a loner. To hide.

Until she met Allison, that is.

Allison Johnson was a hard as nails, tiny, blonde spitfire of a woman from Key West, Florida. When Kimberly mentioned that nobody is actually *from* Key West, they just migrate there, Allison responded that she was the daughter of migrants from Long Island, New York, which gave her the dual personality traits of taking no shit and not giving a shit.

Allison said that Johnson may or may not have been her family's real last name and that her dad had some shadowy, mysterious friends, who may or may not have politely suggested migration to the Keys when Allison's mom was pregnant with her, which actually made her one of the rare Key West natives.

A third class petty officer, Allison worked in the ordnance shop—another job that few women aspired to. She and Kimberly got along like a house on fire, and Kimberly had to admit to herself she was grateful for the companionship.

On a cool December evening, Kimberly and one of her fellow

AME's climbed down from the rotor head of an SH-60B Seahawk onto the flight line and removed their cranial headgear, strapping them to the belt loops on their coveralls by the chinstraps. Kimberly hoisted the ladder onto her shoulder through the rungs and her partner grabbed the toolbox. They headed toward the squadron to load up the tools in the shop.

"Ahh, thank the good Lord for this cool night. I'm sweatin' like a pig in a butcher shop," Mike said.

"Careful, your Kentucky is coming out again, Patterson," Kimberly said, laughing.

"Nobody does mountain southern like me, that's for dang sure. Where you headed this fine Friday night?" (which came out fahn Frahday naht)

"You know me. A six-pack and a book is about my speed. After how hard we worked this week, it might progress to a twelve-pack."

"Oooo, your life is so excitin', can I come?"

"Yeah, yeah, you know you're just jealous. You have to go to your apartment and deal with roommates and a girlfriend. I have the solitude of my barracks room *and* my roommate is on leave for two weeks. I intend to drink, read, and sleep as many hours as possible, and not necessarily in that order."

Back in the Paraloft, the shop housing the parachute riggers and life support technicians, Kimberly hung the ladder on the wall, while Mike had the toolbox checked by the work center supervisor.

"If you find yourself wanting to see actual people, Stevens, you know where to find us."

"I do. Have a good weekend, man."

The supervisor got their attention. "Stevens, Patterson, Haig, Lorde, and Cooper—you are all secure for the weekend. Coop, you're on duty, so keep it clean and stick close to home. See the rest of you Monday. Be good. And if you can't be good, be good at it."

After her shower, Kimberly threw on sweats and grabbed a cold one from her dorm-sized refrigerator. She was just getting settled into the corner of her bed against the wall, when three sharp knocks broke the silence.

"Oh, man, really?" She walked over the door and opened it. "What?"

"*'What?'* That's how you greet me? What the fuck, over?" Allison pushed her way into the room carrying a bottle of Irish whiskey and a salad. She was wearing plaid boxer shorts and a long-sleeved Navy hooded sweatshirt, her short blonde hair under a ball cap that said Alpha Female.

"Whiskey and salad. Dinner of champions," Kimberly said.

"What? I have to watch my girlish figure *and* get severely trashed tonight because Frank is back with that hoebag ex of his and I just can't deal. So, *you* are doing shots with me. And, *no,* you do not get to argue."

"Allison, Frank is a weenie who isn't worthy to breathe your air. What you ever saw in him in the first place is way beyond me."

"He has a giant schlong and he's easy on the eyes. Good enough for a month or two, right? I just didn't expect to actually feel anything for the bastard. So! What do we have here? Beer and a book? Seriously, Kim? Your roommate is gone for two weeks and you're not blaring music and dancing topless yet? Ugh, I came just in time to save you from yourself."

Allison looked through Kimberly's cassettes, grabbed Cheap Trick's *Live at Budokan,* and cranked it up on the stereo. She danced across the room to Kimberly's shelves, snagging two solo cups, and twisting off the cap to the bottle of Jameson. "One finger or two?"

"Go big or go home, lady."

"Yes! I have taught you well, young Skywalker." They tapped plastic cups and downed the booze, grimacing and grinning at the same time. "Holy shit, I love this stuff. Nectar of the damn gods. Okay, one more, then I seriously have to eat this food or I'll be face down before sundown." Kimberly found a bag of Cheetos on her shelf and had a snack herself.

"Hey, let's go somewhere tonight!" Allison said.

"Nah, I've had a long week. I really just want to stay here and chill out."

"Oh, come *on!* You can be such a bump on a log, Stevens."

"I know. But you love me anyway."

"Jury's still out on that, Kemosabe. Hey, do me a solid and meet me halfway. We can go to the Cellar Door pub in the next barracks over. This way we can walk and not have to drive. You haven't been out in weeks. Come onnnn." Allison folded her hands prayer-like and put on her best angel face, complete with batting eyelashes.

"Okay, okay, we'll go to the Cellar Door. But I want to be home and in the rack by 11. No bullshit. No buying me shots at the last minute. No starting a new game of pool or darts. No money in the jukebox at 10:55. Got it?"

"Jeez, lighten up, grandma. Fine, in the rack by 11. Lemme run get some jeans on. Back in a flash!"

Allison threw the salad in the trash and ran out the door yelling behind her, "Do not crap out on me, Stevens! Get some damn jeans on!"

Kimberly rolled her eyes and shook her head, laughing as she closed the door. She was pretty sure she had some clean jeans somewhere.

The first thing Kimberly noticed when they opened the door to the basement bar was that it was dead. Friday night and hardly anyone was there. Probably because most sailors and marines took off on Friday nights for the bars on Solomon's Island or on quick weekend trips to get away from the base for a while. At the little pub in the barracks, only about ten people decided to party close to home.

The second thing she noticed was one of the guys shooting pool. He was playing his pool cue like an air guitar, had a cigarette dangling from his mouth, and was currently on a roll, making every attempted shot on the table. It was like watching billiards ballet.

Allison saw Kimberly staring, elbowed her and wiggled her eyebrows. "Come on, let's get a drink and go see what's new on the jukebox. Dorky dude isn't going anywhere."

"I am strangely attracted to dorky dude," Kimberly said, and followed Allison on the short walk across the room to the bar.

A legendary watering hole on base, the Cellar Door was a basement pub located in the barracks next door to theirs. At full capacity, which was frequently every week night, the pub served around 50 people, closing at midnight. Two cork dart boards adorned the walls on either end of the room with chalkboards in between for scoring. The big draw were the four pool tables in the center of the room. High-backed stools surrounded the pool tables with small high top tables in between, just big enough for an ashtray and a couple of drinks. The bar was at the far end, a straight shot between the pool tables from the bottom of the cellar steps. It was constantly lit up with various colors of funky holiday lights, as there was no natural light down there. No top shelf choices were available, but this was not the place for picky patrons.

Allison slapped a fiver on the counter. "Two Bud Lights and the change is yours," she said, with a wink. The bored bartender appeared underwhelmed. He handed them their bottles.

"Do my ears deceive me? Did I hear you say the word 'attracted'? Catch me, Rhett, I think I might faint!" Allison raised the back of her hand to her forehead and blinked rapidly for effect.

"Oh, shut up, idjit," Kimberly said, giggling. Their faces aglow by the jukebox, they pressed the buttons to flip through the selections. "Bon Jovi for sure. And U2. And—"

"Hey, quit bogarting all the choices, greedy gut. I got this. Go get us a table."

Kimberly chose to sit near a different pool table so as not to appear too obvious. She did want to check this guy out, but no way did she want him to realize it. He was not tall, maybe 5'9", with a slender frame, ropy muscles in his forearms. His thick brown hair was in a typical Navy cut— longish on top, close cropped all the way around. He had a mustache and deep brown eyes that squinted while he aimed his cue, but twinkled when he laughed at his buddies. He wore a red and black plaid lumberjack shirt, hanging open over a white tank top that clung to his flat stomach, tucked into faded Levi's. As he circled the table, she noticed the laces in his hiking boots were untied. Dorky dude was quirky, too.

Whitesnake blared from the jukebox as Allison jumped up into the high stool. "I swear you pick these stupid high chairs just to see me look like a toddler."

Kimberly laughed out loud. "Ha! Maybe I do." She lit a cigarette and sipped her beer, willing herself to stay focused on Allison and not the pool table.

"You do know who that is, right?"

"Dorky dude?"

"Yeah, him. He is the LPO in the line shack. Second only to Chief Stewart. I think his name is TJ or JT or something. Last name Allen. Saw it on his coveralls in the coffee mess. Second class electrician, but a badass plane captain on the H-60's."

"Wow, you seem to know a lot about him."

"You hear all kinds of shit working midnights. People get bored and hang out in the coffee mess. Ordys don't do a lot of installations at night, so I'm in there a bunch. Oh, and I think he's *single*," Allison said, sing-singing the last word: SING-gullllll.

"Oh, really . . . hmm." She turned to look at him again and was surprised to see him walking their way, patting his shirt and pant pockets. He came right up to Kimberly, looked her in the eye, and her heart stopped.

"Lost my lighter. Bum a light?" he asked.

Kimberly handed him her small purple Bic, knowing her face was flushed red. He flicked, lit his smoke, and placed it back in her open palm in a handshake.

"JT. Much obliged."

"K-Kimberly. You're welcome." He winked and walked away. Without moving a muscle, she whispered, "Catch me, Rhett, I think I might faint."

Over the next few hours, Kimberly allowed JT to purchase her a few beers, only if he bought for Allison, too, and they engaged in light flirting. Mostly, Kimberly tried not to stare at him while she and Allison cracked each other up with stories from their past. Every twenty minutes or so, he came over and asked for a light, locking eyes with Kimberly each time, her insides doing flip flops.

"Cinderella hour approaches," said the bartender. "Last call." JT looked at Kimberly from across the smoky room and raised his eyebrows, miming a drinking motion with one hand. She shook her head and raised her palm to him. She mouthed 'thanks, though.' She and Allison finished their drinks and slid off their stools. Waving goodbye to JT and his pals, they ascended the basement stairs into the crisp, cool night.

"It's past eleven," said Allison.

"I know."

"You didn't turn into a pumpkin."

"I know."

"You met a cute guy."

"I know."

"And I don't think Prince Charming ever lost his lighter," Allison said. Elbowing Kimberly, she pointed to the group of guys walking toward their own barracks. She saw JT light a cigarette and slide the lighter back into his jeans pocket. Kimberly smiled and looked at her watch. 12:05 am.

"It's past midnight," Kimberly said.

"Yeah? And?"

"And I'm officially twenty-two. Happy birthday to me," she said, smiling at the back of the man in the plaid shirt.

***

"AME's, Maintenance," came the voice over the intercom they lovingly referred to as the bitch box.

"Go ahead, Maintenance," said the supervisor.

"Send Petty Officer Stevens down to see Chief Conroy asap."

"Roger that," he said. "You heard him, Stevens." Kimberly grabbed her cranial and pushed open the door to the Paraloft, hanging a left in the hangar, and made her way toward the Maintenance Control office. Sounds of tools and shouted conversations filled the huge space. Currently, a giant P-3 Orion and an S-3 Viking were housed in the hangar being thoroughly cleaned, rivet to rivet, for a tiger team inspection from CINCNAV in Washington, DC. The inspection happened to each aircraft in the test and eval fleet periodically. Kimberly was assigned to the S-3 tiger team along with Mike Patterson. They had been working double shifts for weeks to get the bird ready for the crucial inspection. It was hard, tedious work, but quite an honor to have been chosen for the team.

Kimberly pushed open the door to Maintenance and approached the counter. The airman behind the desk looked up.

"Reporting to Chief Conroy."

"Wait one, Petty Officer Stevens," he said and picked up the phone. He hung up, motioned to Kimberly's left and said, "Chief will see you now." Kimberly proceeded down the hallway, past the first two offices with half-walls of wired glass, and entered the small second office on the right. The Chief Petty Officer looked up from her desk. Dark hair pulled back in a tight, shiny bun, her hazel eyes were warm as she smiled at Kimberly.

"Have a seat, Stevens."

"Thank you, Chief."

"I appreciate all of your hard work on the tiger team. JA-17 looks pristine. We have an excellent chance of scoring an outstanding on the inspection, which would mean a meritorious unit command medal for all of the sailors in our squadron. So, kudos to you and the team."

"Thank you, Chief."

The woman rose to her full height of 5'10" and walked around her desk in a form-fitting khaki uniform. She leaned against the front of her desk, crossing the ankles on her seemingly endless legs, and folding her hands on her lap, fingers devoid of rings. "I've called you in specifically because your orders are coming up soon. I know you've been in touch with the Bureau of Personnel in DC about upcoming available billets in the S-3 community. But I know that you do outstanding work on the H-60's as well. I've been advised there are numerous billets coming open in Mayport near Jacksonville, Florida. The H-60 is my community and I'll be heading down there myself, attached to HSL-60 squadron. If you'd be open to those orders, I'd be happy to put in a good word." Kimberly was dumbfounded. The chief was requesting her to work in her command.

"Chief, I don't know what to say."

"Stevens, there are very few women in the H-60 community out in the fleet and I'd like to see that change. You're well aware that females have to work twice as hard to prove themselves in our Navy, and I never fail to be impressed with your ability and overall demeanor. You come highly recommended by your shop LPO, as well."

"I'm honored, Chief. Thank you. I'd like to go to Mayport. I'm originally from Florida. It would be like going home."

The chief flashed her million-watt smile. "That's settled. I'll call BUPERS and let them know. They'll be contacting you soon. And the results don't officially come out until tomorrow, but let me be the first to congratulate you on your promotion, AME2 Stevens."

"I made second class?"

"You did, and with points to spare. Your pay raise will take effect immediately." Chief Conroy stood up and extended her hand. "Congratulations. Well deserved."

Kimberly shook her chief's hand and was dismissed. She was in a daze walking through the hangar to the Paraloft.

"Whoa, whoa, hold up, little filly. Watch where you're walking."

Kimberly looked up in time to avoid a collision with JT as he came through the stairwell door. "Penny for your thoughts."

"I just came from seeing Chief Conroy. I'm putting on second."

"Congratulations, girlie, you definitely earned it."

"And I'm going to Mayport."

"On detachment?"

"No, orders. I leave next month."

"Do you know what squadron?"

"She didn't say for sure. I'll find out soon, but I think HSL-60."

JT smiled. "What a coincidence. So am I."

***

Although their assigned barracks at Naval Station Mayport were co-ed, they were for unaccompanied service members and rooms were single gender only. Though she didn't express this to JT, Kimberly was relieved. Only six months into dating, she felt it was a little too soon to be sharing housing. Working together at the squadron, they saw each other constantly. Kimberly was still trying to get a foothold at the new command. There would be time for things to progress later.

Being assigned to a seagoing fleet squadron was very different from the shore duty command she'd just left. Sorties were flown each day. Detachments were always at the ready. Deployments of larger groups of personnel for six-month periods were on constant rotation. Daily and turnaround inspections were non-stop. Kimberly felt as though she was on top of the birds as much as she was on the ground. It was a fast, busy pace and she thrived in it.

Unfortunately, she was yet again the only female in her shop. This time, though, she felt resentment from her fellow AME's rather than respect. Helicopter squadrons notoriously had all-male shops. Females tended to be assigned to the tool room or Maintenance Control, not turning wrenches alongside the men. Kimberly was breaking a barrier and she was well aware of it.

AME3 Andy Coleman and AME2 Brett Lewis tried to play rookie jokes on her, sending her to the tool room for a left-handed torque wrench or a bucket of CO_2, or telling her to blow into a blazing hot pitot tube as part of a turnaround inspection. She never fell for the hazing, but they sure got a kick out of hoping she would. Each day was an exercise in holding her head high and focusing on the work.

"Hey Stevens, you do the daily on zero-two today?" Lewis asked.

"Yes. I signed off the VIDSMAF worksheet. It's on AME1's desk for inspection."

"You cleared the RT, right?"

"I'm sorry, the what?"

"The RT. Didn't you learn anything at that pansy-ass squadron you came from? Follow me." Lewis fastened a cranial to his head and pushed through the door of the Paraloft, heading to the flight line. Kimberly followed suit and trailed a few steps behind him.

Once at the helo, Lewis grabbed onto a hold and jumped up into the cabin. Kimberly waited for him to move all the way inside then joined him. He pointed to a tube held by clamps along the bulkhead.

"The RT. Did you clear it?"

Kimberly pulled the daily card from the pocket of her coveralls and scanned it. There was nothing on the card that mentioned an RT, much less requiring her to do anything inside the cabin. All of the steps for an AME daily inspection required her to be on top of the helo underneath the rotor blades.

"Lewis, this isn't part of a daily."

"I'm telling you it is, Stevens." Kimberly could hear chuckling from a few mechs gathered outside the aircraft.

"Look here, you take the tube out of the clamp like so." He pulled the tube away from the bulkhead and swiveled it toward her. "Then you blow into it as hard as you can to clear any clogs. You neglected this step on your daily. Take care of it now. Go ahead."

Kimberly looked at the tube. Something wasn't right. She'd never heard one thing about this in any of her training.

Then it hit her. RT—relief tube. Or, more commonly called the piss tube.

"Sorry, Lewis, I wouldn't want to take away your primary duty in the shop. That just wouldn't be right. Blow away, asshole." She jumped down onto the flight line as six or seven mechs laughed out loud and scattered.

Nice try, dickhead.

***

JT and Kimberly began working opposite shifts—she was on days in the Paraloft, he worked nights in the line shack. They looked forward to weekends with enthusiasm and spent every waking moment together. Jacksonville was a busy city with lots of things to do. They would hop in his black Ford F-150 pickup and take off for the beach, windows down, country music blasting. Some Saturday evenings, they would head to The Landings on the St. Johns River for live music, good food, and icy drinks. Mostly, they spent what time they had together sharing their pasts, exploring each other, and falling in love.

JT stood for Jason Todd, but nobody had ever called him anything but JT since he was born. He loved fishing, hunting, football, and, as he would say, both types of music—country *and* western. She loved to read, write in her journal, take long walks, and watch old movies. She adored holding his hand, he adored kissing hers. He was goofy and outgoing where she was serious and quiet. He was a good ol' boy from the Texas hill country and she was a native Floridian. The old saying was true— opposites attract.

Besides their love and admiration for each other, the main thing they had in common was their work ethic. Both of them worked long, hard hours, never quitting the job they'd started until it was complete, even if it meant staying into the next shift. They got to know the pilots in the squadron well and took very seriously the job of keeping their birds safe for flight and their pilots alive and well. They both garnered respect from the upper ranks, but Kimberly continued to have issues with the guys in her shop. JT reassured her 'this too shall pass,' and told her not to let it bother her too much.

"They steal my tools so that my box never passes inspection. They 'accidentally' walk in on me when I'm in the changing room, then report to AME1 that I'm flashing them. So far, everything they've done has been fairly harmless bullying, but I'm concerned that they'll graduate to something more serious. Something that will endanger my safety or someone else's."

"Have you reported these things to AME1?"

"JT, it's hard enough being taken seriously as a woman. Do you think I want 'tattletale' associated with me, too? I might as well paint a giant target on my back."

"Then all you can do is let it roll off your back. Watch your six. Do your job as perfectly as you can. They'll get tired of it, you'll see."

Kimberly wasn't so sure.

***

Just before Thanksgiving, they were informed a large detachment from the squadron would be deploying on a six-month cruise in the Mediterranean Sea a week after Christmas. The HSL-60 det would be attached to a destroyer as part of a battle group. JT was one of the preferred plane captains as well as a valuable electrician, so he was assigned to the det. As women were not permitted on combatant ships, Kimberly would be required to stay behind on shore duty during the deployment, along with all of the other females and the less essential males. The main focus of the squadron for the next month was readiness of the aircraft and personnel for the cruise. It was all Kimberly and JT seemed to discuss when they were together.

Walking along the Riverwalk one unseasonably cold Saturday night in December, JT held tight to Kimberly's gloved hand. He spoke about how often he would write while he was gone, that he would buy her fun presents in every port, that he was already looking forward to seeing her meet the ship when he came back.

"JT, I don't even want to think about this tonight. It's just so hard."

He nodded and said, "Understood."

She wore a white turtleneck under a black leather jacket, her jeans tucked into black boots. Her white cable knit scarf was wrapped snuggly under her chin, but she felt the chill coming off the river and shivered. JT let go of her hand and put his arm around her, pulling her close.

"Cold, girlie?"

"Yeah. I didn't think it was gonna be this cold down here tonight. Even with all these layers on, brrr! I'm a wimp."

"You are not. Just maybe need a little more meat on your bones is all."

Kimberly smiled up at him. "See, that's what I love about you. I'm far from skinny."

"You are perfect."

"And you, sir, are biased." They found a cozy bar, ordered an Irish coffee for her, a cold longneck for him, and took them to a small booth in the corner. She took off her gloves, putting them in one pocket of her jacket. She reached into the other pocket to pull out her pack of cigarettes and felt something odd inside. Grabbing ahold of it, she pulled out a small, deep red velvet ring box. "What in the hell . . .?"

Smiling, his hands trembling, JT slid into her side of the booth, removed the box from her hand and looked into her eyes.

"Ever since the night we met last fall in Pax, you've been the most important person in my life. You're smart and sassy and funny and strong and beautiful. You're exactly the type of girl I am gonna be proud to take home to my mama. I can't imagine how hard this deployment is going to be without you. I wanted you to have a constant reminder that no matter what happens, I'm in love with you." He touched the side of her face and she closed her teary eyes, pressing her cheek into his palm. When she opened them again, he was holding the open box in front of her. "Kimberly, as soon as I get back, will you do me the honor of becoming my wife?"

Nestled inside the box was an emerald ring with tiny diamond baguettes on either side. It was the most beautiful thing Kimberly had ever laid eyes on. She couldn't speak. She could barely breathe. She nodded her head and the tears broke free, flowing over her apple cheeks to her broad smile. He slid the ring onto her finger and wrapped her up in his strong arms, holding her tightly to him.

"Don't ever let me go," she said, her face buried in his neck.

"I love you," he said.

"I love that you love me," she said.

Just down the Riverwalk, JT squeezed her hand as they stood near the lobby of a grand hotel. He looked at her and she nodded.

Lying on the bed, Kimberly looked up and saw nothing in the world but his eyes. His beautiful, dark brown eyes, that twinkled when he laughed. His mischievous eyes that teased her with just a look. He held both of her hands tightly on either side of the pillow, his eyes burning into hers, his love so raw.

"Jason," she whispered as he entered her, changing her forever.

***

Kimberly checked her mailbox and flipped through the envelopes.

Bills for her car payment, the private phone line in her room, her credit card, and a package from Allison that she could not wait to open. She missed her friend so much it hurt. Still no letter from JT this week. The last one she'd received was three weeks ago at the end of February. She assumed they'd been unable to pull into port and do a mail drop in a while. She would probably receive a pile of letters all at once. She sure looked forward to shutting herself in her room to become immersed in the words from her fiancé. She was bored with filling page after page of mundane daily life in her journal every weekend.

When she entered the lobby of the barracks, green and white decorations were plastered all over the common room. Oh, right—Saint Patrick's Day. The barracks was assigned to a number of squadrons, so there were sure to be plenty of people celebrating. She intended to avoid that event altogether. She walked up the stairs and down the hall to her room. As a second class petty officer, she was entitled to a private room. She reminded herself every time she entered the space how lucky she was not to have to deal with a roommate any longer. She closed her eyes and took a deep breath. This was the only place she felt she could breathe, to completely relax and be herself. She felt a little sorry for JT living in berthing with racks stacked three high along long bulkheads of a destroyer.

"It's only temporary, babe," she said to the memory of his face in her mind. "You'll be home this summer and we'll finally get our own place." She glanced at the deep green stone in her ring and smiled to herself. She couldn't wait to become Mrs. Kimberly Marie Allen.

She got comfy in a t-shirt and sweatpants, tossing her dirty dungarees into the hamper. She poured herself two fingers of Irish whiskey into a clear plastic rocks cup and opened a cold beer, placing the drinks on her nightstand. On the bed, Kimberly curled her feet under her and sliced into the box from Allison. Immediately on top was a letter from her best girlfriend.

Hey Stranger! It's been way too long. Before you read any further, get yourself a shot and a beer. If you already have, consider yourself high-fived. Now you may proceed haha. I know we said we were gonna get together while JT is on deployment, but with as busy as both of us are, we may just need to settle for letters and an occasional phone call. I never know what time is good for you, what shift you're working, etc. Just call me and leave a message with your schedule and we'll work it out.

Here's the latest gossip from Pax . . .

The ten-page letter went on to report who was dating whom, who was no longer together, who was pregnant, who had gotten sent to restriction, and so on and so on. Kimberly giggled through the entire letter, rereading it twice, while refreshing her drinks. She could practically hear Allison's voice in her head with each word. She ached to see her and give her a hug.

Kimberly pulled out a thick Manila envelope from the box. Written on the outside: *How did I wind up with all of these? I thought you would enjoy the memories.* Inside were dozens of photos, most of them showing Kimberly and Allison together, which had been pretty much all of the time—birthday parties in the barracks lounge, dancing at the E Club, squadron barbecues and volleyball games, weekend trips to Washington DC, laying out on the base beach on the Chesapeake Bay, a trip to Kings Dominion in Virginia, squadron Christmas parties. She became overcome with emotion, smearing mascara into the cuff of the top sheet as she wiped her face. She hadn't realized until this moment how truly lonely she was. Allison and JT had become her only family. She was so grateful to have them in her life.

Allison had also included two t-shirts and a pair of shorts that Kimberly must have lent to her and forgotten about. Under the clothing was the last item in the box: A tin box about six inches square. Kimberly cut a slit in the pieces of tape on each side and opened it. Inside was a stack of 4x6 blank, folded notecards, a stack of envelopes, and two books of stamps, along with a note on a corner of a piece of notebook paper: *In case this isn't obvious enough—WRITE ME!*

Kimberly laughed through her tears. She placed everything on her bed and crossed the floor to the bathroom for toilet paper to blow her nose. One glance in the mirror made her grimace, then laugh again. *Thank goodness I'm alone!* She opened her fridge for another beer. Shit, she'd already drunk the last one. She'd have to remember to stop at the convenience store on the way home from the squadron tomorrow.

She was about to sit on her bed to look at the contents of the package again, when she heard a knock at the door.

"That's odd," she mumbled and made her way to the door, a bit loopy. *I really should have eaten dinner.*

Opening the door, she saw a face she never expected outside of her room. "Coleman. What do you want?" It was more of a statement than a question.

Andy Coleman stood in the hallway, his 5'7" frame appearing smaller in civilian clothes, his tight, coarse amber curls exposed without a cranial or squadron ball cap. He held two solo cups and bore a sheepish expression.

"Hey, Stevens. Kimberly. I was down at the party and I didn't see you, so I thought I'd come up. I know me and the guys have been a little hard on you and I wanted to say I'm a jerk and I'm sorry."

"Okay, fine, you're sorry. No argument from me. Look, I'm tired, I'm gonna—"

"Come on, Kimberly. I wanted to explain something to you. And I brought a little peace offering," he said, raising one of the cups toward her. "It's some really good mojo punch from the party. Can I come in for a minute?" She hesitated for a moment then opened the door to let him in, leaving it open.

"Five minutes, Coleman. I have to work tomorrow."

"Thanks. I won't stay long. Want to try the punch?"

Kimberly took one of the cups from his hand and sniffed, wrinkling her nose.

"Ugh, what's in that?"

"I think it's mostly rum and fruit juice with a shitload of fresh fruit. Also some grain alcohol."

"Sounds like death in a cup. I'll pass," she said, placing the cup on a small round table. She picked up her rocks cup and raised it to her lips, finding it empty. "Dammit. Hang on."

"What are you drinking? I'll get you a refill." She gestured to the whiskey bottle on the shelf in the tiny kitchen area, then sat back down on her bed. Coleman smiled, took the cup from her hand, and walked over to pour her drink. "You hear from JT much? How are they doing in the Med?"

"Fine. Same old same old. Working hard, not enough ports, food sucks, life on a destroyer." She took the cup he offered and took a sip. "Why are you here again, Coleman? What did you want to tell me?"

Coleman took a seat in a chair next to her small table and lifted his cup. "Cheers—Happy Saint Patrick's Day!" She looked at him, a little confused, and took a sip of her drink.

"And?"

"Like I said, I know we've been giving you a hard time and, well, I guess it's kind of played out. We aren't gonna do it anymore. It's obvious you deserve to be in the shop. You're smart and you work hard." Kimberly began hearing a buzzing sound in her ears and a flush came over her face and neck.

"Do you hear that?" she asked.

"Hear what?" Coleman said, just as Kimberly's eyes rolled back and she fell to her pillow. He jumped up from his chair and leaned over her."Kimberly? Stevens! You okay?" He tapped her arm, her forehead. "She's out."

Brett Lewis came through the open door carrying a Polaroid camera, and closed the door quietly behind him.

"Hurry up. I don't know how long that shit lasts," Lewis said. They pulled off her t-shirt exposing her bra. Coleman unbuttoned his jeans and dropped them with his boxers to the floor. Lewis lifted the camera. "Ain't no way this bitch is taking LPO over me," he said, as the camera began to click and whirr over and over.

***

The alarm clock bleeped louder and louder. Kimberly groaned and smacked the clock as hard as she could, launching it onto the floor and into silence. Oh my God, she had a monster of a headache. It felt like a bass drum booming behind her eyes. Her mouth was like sand and her teeth felt furry. Even her throat was sore. She sat up and the room spun to the right. She placed her hands on either side of her head to try to stop the spinning. Jumping out of bed, she ran to the bathroom as fast as she could just in time to be sick into the toilet. When her stomach calmed down, she splashed cold water onto her face. While the shower warmed up, she brushed her teeth, gargling with mouthwash.

As she passed the mirror over the sink, it hit her. She was in her bra and sweatpants. That was exactly backwards from normal sleeping attire. How much of that whiskey had she had last night? She glanced over at the shelf in the tiny kitchen. The level on the bottle looked the same as it had last night when she had poured her last . . . wait. She didn't pour her last drink. That had been that asshole Coleman. Why had she let him in her room anyway? What in the world was she thinking? She didn't remember him leaving. Her eyes darted to her bed in a panic, but it was empty. She sighed, relieved. She shuddered at the thought.

She walked over to the small round table. A red solo cup and her plastic rocks cup, both empty. She tossed them in the trash. She saw the package from Allison spilled on the floor, photos scattered. She must have kicked it off the bed in her sleep. Her t-shirt was on the floor next to the bed. The liquor must have hit her extra hard on her empty stomach. And her emotional outburst probably hadn't helped. She was absolutely drained and felt lousy. She probably had a cold coming on with her throat so tender.

Picking up her phone, she dialed the shop.

"HSL-60 Paraloft, Petty Officer Walker speaking."

"Hey, Walker, it's Stevens."

"Sup, girl?"

"Listen, I feel lousy. Headache, sore throat, nausea, I might even have a fever. I'm gonna need a leave chit for the day. Can you pass that on to AME1? He can call me if he needs to. I'll be in the rack."

"You got it. Feel better. See you Monday."

"Thanks, man." Kimberly got into the soothing shower, inhaling the floral scent of her shampoo, soaping herself from head to toe. After toweling off, she put on a clean t-shirt and shorts, scooped up all of the clothes and towels and tossed them in the hamper. She picked up the contents of the package from Allison—wow, it hurt her head to bend over—and put everything on the round table. As she crawled back into bed and pulled up the covers, she thought *I really need to dial it back on the drinking.*

***

Monday morning, the squadron was buzzing with activity, even with such a small skeleton crew. While the majority of personnel were on deployment, the sailors left behind took on major projects of refurbishing—painting walls and floors, cleaning out closets and filing cabinets, giving the entire hangar and its offices a facelift.

The coffee mess was crowded, so Kimberly scooted in and got a place in line to buy a cup of hot tea. She noticed a few guys in coveralls in the corner gathered around the community bulletin board, elbowing each other. Maybe someone was selling a muscle car or something. As the line moved, snaking closer to the board, she tried to see what they were looking at out of curiosity.

One of the mechs stepped away from the board just as she approached. He grinned and smacked his buddy's arm, nudging his head toward Kimberly. They tipped their squadron ball caps to her and walked out of the coffee mess cackling. Kimberly furrowed her brow and rolled her eyes. Weirdos.

Closer now, she looked at the cork board. In the lower right corner was a Polaroid photo tacked up with a push pin. From a distance of about six feet, she could see that it looked like someone performing oral sex. The right buttock and part of the penis of the man were visible, as well as the hand cupping the back of the woman's head. As she got closer, she was horrified to recognize the curly brown hair. For a brief moment, her body froze and her brain shut down. She reached out and jerked the photo from the board, stuffing it into the pocket of her dungarees. Trembling, she pushed her way across the line of sailors and shoved open the door to the coffee mess. She made her way across the hangar in a daze, opening the door to Maintenance Control. Ignoring the airman calling out to her from behind the counter, she walked down the hallway to the last office on the right. In shock, she shook violently as though blasted by an icy wind. She threw the photo down on the desk, her jaw chattering as she spoke.

"Ch-Chief C-Conroy, I respectfully request a t-transfer."

Chapter Twenty-One — 1991 — Jesse & Kimberly

Spring break in Daytona was nuts. Packed with high school and college kids from all over the country on vacation, they swarmed Two Dudes Bar & Grill like locusts every night of the week, thrashing and grinding to live music in the outside Tiki hut that opened onto the beach. Kids of all ages produced fake ID's of all ages. Jesse and Tom strictly trained their staff to check every single ID carefully, even those of the folks with silver hair.

"You never know," said Jesse."You might make their day. No ID, no drink. Period."

The last thing Two Dudes needed was to lose their liquor license over selling a drink to a teenager. During March, they only allowed their most senior staff to work the bar, and that included Jesse.

Dinner rush on Thursday night was just winding down. With a little breathing room available before the night crowd packed the patio, Jesse ducked into the owners' office for a quick sandwich and a Coke. The intercom buzzed.

"Jesse, call on line 1. It's your sister." Jesse wiped his mouth, picked up the receiver and pressed the blinking red button.

"Hey Brie, I was gonna give you a call on Sunday. It's crazy here during spring break. How's Miami? You all settled in yet?" There was silence on the other end of the line. Jesse had nearly hung up when he heard a low, gravely voice.

"It's me, Jess. It's Kim."

Jesse almost dropped the phone. "Kimberly, oh my God where are you? How are you? Are you still in the Navy?"

"Yes, I'm on leave right now. I wanted to know if I could come stay with you for a few days. Things are kind of bad at the moment. I need to get away."

"Of course. I mean, I am working non-stop during spring break, but you're welcome to crash at my place. Where are you? When will you be here?"

"I'm at Mayport Naval Station. I can be there in about two hours. I'll tell you everything when I get there."

"Come straight to the bar. You were able to track me down, so I'm sure you can find it. It's Two Dudes on A1A on the south end near Port Orange. Ask for me at the hostess stand inside. Kim, I can't believe I'm going to see you. Be safe getting here."

"Thanks, Jess. See you soon."

***

They kept their voices low as the rest of the beach was deserted at 2:00 a.m. Sticky, salty breeze cooled their faces. Waves splashed onto the sand and receded, as more folded over to take their place. Jesse poured Kimberly another glass of wine from the bottle nestled in the sand between them just outside the Tiki hut. They were sitting low on beach chairs, toes buried in the sand. The bar closed at midnight on Thursdays and the crowd was finally, blessedly gone. While the staff finished up cleaning and stocking for the upcoming busy weekend, Jesse listened to his sister's story.

"So, Chief is in contact with BUPERS to see if I can get a transfer. She asked me if I wanted to press charges. Even with the photos, there's no proof it was him, but you can see me as plain as day. I don't look unconscious. I have no way to prove that, either. It would mean standing up for myself in a court-martial with the burden of proof on me. It would be a he said/she said scenario. I just want to put this all behind me and move on. I can't believe this happened to me. And I *cannot believe* I can't do a damn thing about it."

Jesse thought quietly before he said anything. "What about your fiancé? You said he gets back in three months. Don't you think he'll stand by you? Don't you think he'll want to go wherever you go?"

Kimberly looked at her brother with tears in her eyes. "That's the worst part of all of this. Even though he knows the hell I've been through with these guys, it's hard to fight photo proof. And even if he did believe me, I don't think he would ever want to be with me again. How could he?

I'm damaged goods. I know the image is seared into *my* brain. Imagine how it would be for him? I have no idea how many copies there are. He'll definitely see it. I'm sure that was the point. He's an amazing man, but even he can't unsee something like that. It's over. I don't know what made me think I ever deserved anyone that good in my life."

Jesse reached for her hand and squeezed. "Kimmy . . ."

"Anyway, they called that asshole in for questioning on Monday. I'm positive he's lying his way through the whole thing. I immediately put in for leave and called my best friend up in Maryland to see if I could go stay with her. But she lives in the barracks and has a roommate. She said, 'You know you need to call your brother,' and she was right. I called information and got the number." Kimberly looked at Jesse."You didn't have to let me come here. It's been almost seven years."

"I know, Kim. I wish you had let us know where you were. I missed talking to you so much."

"Can I ask you something?"

"Of course, anything."

"Why didn't you come to my boot camp graduation? It was in Orlando, only a quick drive for you. It's the only thing in my life I'd ever done of any importance. Why weren't you there?"

"Because I never knew about it."

"What? I sent all of the information to our parents. They had all the details."

"They never said a word. I mean, I know it's my fault for not asking about you, but I had no idea you were even in the Navy until long after your boot camp was over. Mom said she hadn't wanted to bother me while we were launching the bar. I'm so sorry, Kim."

"Mom. Yeah, that doesn't surprise me one bit," Kimberly said, filling her mouth with wine and staring out at the waves of the Atlantic Ocean.

"I know, our parents are a piece of work. I had to tell myself a long time ago that they are both damaged by their childhoods. They're doing the best they can," Jesse said.

"Dad's great, but Mom? Do you honestly believe she's doing the best she can, Jess?"

"I have to. I had to forgive them in order to survive. I needed to

165

live my truth. To look inward for acceptance and love, not outward. I certainly wasn't going to get it from them."

"So, you told them?"

"I tried. It was weird, awkward. Dad said I was probably just going through a phase and Mom cried and asked what she had done to ruin her son. What *she* had done? *Ruin* me? It went about as well as expected. I left. I haven't been back since. Then I got a phone call from her that sealed the deal."

"I would ask if you're kidding, but I know better."

"Yeah . . . she wanted me to know how sick inside she was because she had a son who thought he was a daughter. I told her that's not how it works—I'm not transgender. She said, 'this whole lifestyle thing is a choice,' and that I'd made the wrong one. Again, I told her she was mistaken. I can't help how I was born. Then she flew into a rage and said, 'That's rich—blaming your parents for your defective brain.'" Jesse sighed and washed his hand over his eyes. "She ended the call with, 'I no longer have a son.' I said, 'I'm sorry you feel that way. I love you, Mom,' and hung up. That was that."

Kimberly wrapped her hand around her brother's and squeezed back.

"I'm so sorry, Jess. Had she been drinking?"

Jesse looked at her and laughed. "What do you think?"

She looked into his freckled face, his light blue eyes. "Maybe I gave them too much credit pushing you to tell them all the time. She's never gonna change."

"Maybe, maybe not. I hope she does. I hope Dad comes around, too. Think of all the time they've missed out on with their kids."

Kimberly brushed her bangs out of her eyes. "You know how our family is—out of sight, out of mind. Like it's in our blood or something. And I honestly don't think they ever really gave a shit, Jess. It's never been about us with them. I think we were a giant inconvenience. Well, except maybe Brie."

"Oh, I don't think she's as much of a 'golden child' as you might think. She has her issues with them, too."

"Ha, right. I'll believe that when I see it." She drained her glass. "Anyway, I have to figure out what the hell to do next. I'm so grateful you're letting me stay with you."

"Of course, hon. Listen, I think you need to talk to your fiancé about this. You might be underestimating him. You need to give him the benefit of the doubt. Don't run away again."

"I'll think about it. There's time. He won't be back for three more months." She closed her eyes and leaned her head back against the chair, inhaling tangy sea breeze.

"We're both tired. I'm going to have a word with the general manager, then I'll get you back to my place. You need a good night's sleep."

***

Kimberly awoke with a start, trying to remember where she was. She was lying on a double bed in a bright, airy room under a navy blue comforter. The room smelled of sandalwood and orange spice. One lone print of a sailboat at sea hung on the white walls. She looked on the nightstand and saw a glass of water and two aspirin next to a lamp, a bowl of potpourri, and a digital alarm clock. 9:48 am.

She sat up and swallowed the aspirin with a sip of water, then stretched her arms overhead and legs straight out in what JT would have called a 'complete body yawn.'

JT. How was she ever going to be able to explain this to him? She sighed, absentmindedly spinning the emerald ring around her finger. She stood up and looked out the window. The view from the guest room in Jesse's 10th floor condo consisted of nearby home roofs and the condo parking lot below. She located her toiletry kit and opened the bedroom door, making her way into the guest bath.

Jesse was sipping coffee on the balcony when she came into the living room.

"Hey. How'd you sleep?"
"Like a log. There's coffee?"

"Yep, help yourself."

Kimberly poured the hot brew into a Two Dudes Daytona Beach mug and joined him on the balcony.

"I gave Chief Conroy your phone number for my leave contact. She'll be calling me here as soon as she learns anything from BUPERS. Is it okay if I stick around here today?"

"Of course. Whatever you need to do. Tom's taking the early shift so I won't head to the bar until around four o'clock, but I do have some errands to run. I have an answering machine if you want to come with me."

"Thanks, but I think I'll stay close to the phone."

"Do what you have to. I'll be back in a couple of hours. Help yourself to the sparseness that is my kitchen."

***

Kimberly smoked nearly half a pack of cigarettes while staring out at the ocean. She chewed her nails and bounced her legs nervously, the cordless phone in her lap. She switched from coffee to ice water to help quell her nerves. Everything in her future hinged on what the chief petty officer had to tell her. Why didn't she just call already?

The phone rang just after noon.

"Is this Petty Officer Stevens?"
"Yes, it's me, Chief. Thank you for calling."

"No problem. Stevens, I want to let you know that AME3 Coleman is denying everything, even being in your room that night. Without you pressing charges against him, we really can't go any further. I spoke with your detailer at BUPERS. You're up for orders again in about four months with your reenlistment coming shortly afterward. Until then, there's nowhere for the Navy to put you. So, you have three choices: You can come back to base after your leave is up and press charges, you can work in a different shop in the squadron until you're up for orders, or you can forgo reenlistment and take an early out. You're nearly at eight years service, so your commitment has been fulfilled. I'll give you time to think about it and make up your mind. Please contact me at the squadron as soon as possible next week so we can get the paperwork started. And, Stevens, I'm so very sorry this happened. All of it. I wish things were different." Kimberly was grateful for the chief's clinical delivery of the news. It helped keep the emotion churning in her stomach in check.

"I understand, Chief, and thank you. I'll call you next week. Have a good weekend." She hung up the phone and looked down at the frothy green ocean. She lit another cigarette, slowly exhaling the smoke.

Jesse came through the front door, arms loaded with grocery bags. He went into the corner kitchen and spoke over the long bar into the living room as he unloaded each bag.

"I wasn't sure how long you'd be staying so I picked up a few things. Plus, I have no idea what the hell you eat, so there's stuff for salads, sandwiches, bacon and eggs, cereal and milk. I figure you can eat dinner with me at the bar. Sorry you came at such a busy time."

Kimberly stepped back inside the condo and went to the kitchen to help. She smiled at her brother. She had missed him so very much. He still looked like the same sandy-haired Jess, just a bit taller and filled out. His hair was to his shoulders. He had a surfer boy, tousled look. His eyes were still kind.

"What?" he asked, holding a quart of whole milk.

"They called. I have a decision to make. I'll let them know next week."

"Do you want to talk about it?"

Kimberly shook her head. She put a box of crackers and a bag of Doritos in the pantry. "Fair enough," Jesse said. "We'll need to head out of here in a couple of hours. Wanna take a walk on the beach?"

"That sounds really nice."

As they walked in and out of the breaking surf, sand squishing under their feet, they talked about everything they'd been up to since they saw each other last. It took some doing, but Jesse was able to draw Kimberly out of herself. When she talked about her best friend and her fiancé, she was animated and seemed happy. She shared some hilarious stories. He was so happy to hear she had found love. It broke his heart to think she might lose that love now.

"And what about you? Seeing anyone?"

"Me? Are you kidding? Who has time? My whole life is the bar. If you weren't here right now, I'd probably be there already today. Tom isn't in town all that often but he always spends spring break here in Daytona. It's our busiest time of the year. He likes being part of the craziness."

"What happens if you meet someone?"

"Oh, I've met people but nobody special. I am in a deeply committed relationship with my work," he said, laughing. Jesse looked out across the ocean so Kimberly couldn't see him swallow over the lump in his throat.

***

"Order up!" The plates began to stack up under the kitchen's heat lamp. Saturday nights, the expeditor was frequently in the weeds as Two Dudes Bar & Grill stayed packed. Spring break usually lasted a month in Daytona, and in mid-March of 1987, it was just revving up.

"I'll take it," Jesse said, lifting three plates according to the ticket and placing them on his arms. He delivered the food to a table in the Tiki hut near the stage, asking if he could bring them anything else at the moment. When he turned to walk away, he thought he heard someone calling his name.

"Jesse. Jesse, is that you?" He followed the voice to the stage, and met eyes with a man holding cords in one hand, a bass guitar in the other. Jesse held out his hand.

"Hi, Jesse Stevens. I own this chaos," he grinned. "I see you're in the band tonight?"

"Don't recognize me, do you?" The man grinned back. "Not surprised. It's been a helluva long time."

Jesse looked more closely at the man. Long, dark, layered waves of hair surrounded a chiseled face with piercing brown eyes. A black tank top fit his v-shaped torso nicely, tucked into black Levi's over Doc Marten boots.

Mmm, I sure wish *I knew this guy . . .*

The man chuckled and set the bass on a stand by a Peavey amplifier. "Maybe it would help if I said we were playing AC/DC tonight. The best band ever."

Jesse gasped. "Oh my God, Max!" Before he could think, Jesse wrapped his arms around his old friend in a tight hug. "How've you been? Shit, it's been, what, ten, twelve years?"

Max slapped his friend jovially on the back and backed up to look at him. "Yeah, something like that. Things are good. You own this place?"

"Yes, with a partner. For about four years. I can't believe I'm looking at you right now."

"I know. Dude, it's kinda out-of-body." He laughed.

Jesse looked at his watch. "Hey, I know you're setting up for sound check. We're completely in the weeds. Let's catch up after your set. I'll buy you a drink. Cool?"

"Cool."

The bar was so jammed that first Saturday of spring break, Jesse didn't have time to breathe until after closing. It was the first time Max's band had ever played at Two Dudes, and they were excellent. The crowd was slamming all night to covers of Bruce Springsteen, Rush, Eric Clapton, and, yes, AC/DC.

Jesse was making a restocking list behind the bar when Max approached, hands shoved into the pockets of his jeans. Jesse's face lit up as his friend took a seat.

"What's your poison?"

"Bud Light draft and a shot of Jack."

"Coming right up." Jesse poured, grabbed himself a can of Heineken, and the men walked out of the bar to the beach. They sat down in the sand and clinked beverages.

"To old friends," Jesse said.

"Cheers." Max tossed back the shot, setting the glass in the sand. "It's been a long time, Jesse. Sorry I lost touch."

"No apologies, man, so did I. Been in Daytona all this time and haven't even looked for you. That's my bad."

"Nah, it's all right. I see how busy this place is. You probably have no time for anything besides work. Looks like that's treating you well."

"Can't complain. Pretty happy here."

He looked into Max's eyes. It was hard to believe he was seeing his first crush in person right now. Those damn butterflies again. "It's so good to see you. How are your brothers? What have you been up to all this time?"

Max took a swig from the cup of foamy brew. "Mike and Danny are good. Both married, building families. I'm just playing gigs with these guys. Nobody special." Jesse's heart beat a little faster.

"I had no idea you were in this band. I booked through your lead singer. Cool name — Voltage. Homage to your favorite band?"

"Yeah, you got me."

Jesse fought the urge to say *I wish I did,* to grab Max's hand, to kiss him here on the dark beach.

"Crowd was really digging your show tonight. This won't be the last time we'll hire you. We've got a busy season."

"Guess that means I'll be seeing more of you, dude."

"Guess that does."

"Hey, boss!" the bartender hollered from the hut. "Band's looking for the pay wagon."

"Be right there!" Jesse stood up, offering Max his hand. Both standing, they locked eyes and Jesse felt his stomach tilt. "Tell your singer I'll be out with a check in a minute."

"Got a pen?"

Jesse pulled a Bic out of his pocket. Max clicked it, opened Jesse's palm, and wrote a phone number. "Call me."

For the next six months, Voltage played every other Saturday night at Two Dudes and gained quite a following. Long after the spring break crowd was gone and the oppressive heat of the summer offseason took over, they packed the Tiki hut with local fans of all ages. Groups of bikers ordered buckets of longnecks and staked out multiple tables eating, drinking, and banging their heads all night. Gaggles of groupies tossed back shots of melon balls and lemon drops, gyrating in front of the stage while making eyes at the sweat-soaked musicians. Students from nearby Embry-Riddle and Bethune-Cookman Universities hung out to jam and, hopefully, pick up some of the rejected groupies. Voltage rocked cuts from the 70's and 80's, playing songs as old as "Good Times Bad Times" by Led Zeppelin, as current as "Cult of Personality" by Living Color, and everything in between.

Near midnight on each of those Saturday nights, the bartender would holler at the crowd, "Last call for alcohol then it's time to go, people! You ain't gotta go home, but you can't stay here!" The bar became swarmed with thirsty patrons waving bills in the air in case the bartenders didn't see them. By closing time at one o'clock, the crowd would shuffle out and the staff would begin cleaning and stocking. Jesse gave a check to the band as they broke down their set. By 2:00 am, everyone was gone.

That's when Jesse and Max would disappear onto the beach.

Drinks in hand, they would stroll in the dark to a small alcove hidden by dunes in the sand near the Atlantic. Jesse would run his hands up Max's back into his long, thick hair, grabbing fistfuls at his neck as Max devoured Jesse's mouth, his body, like a starving man, tightly wrapping themselves around each other.

One late night, they lay on the sand, catching their breath, holding hands. Stars glittered above them in the dark sky, the ocean crashing into the shore.

"Come back to my place tonight."

"I can't."

"It's been months, Max. This is really nice, but you deserve better. Come home with me."

Max sat up, looked down at Jesse, running his hand down Jesse's chest. "Jess, I said I can't and I meant it. Look, I haven't been completely honest with you."

Jesse closed his eyes. "Just say it."

Max looked far away at a tiny light out in the ocean. "Her name is Wendy. She's eight months pregnant, which is why she doesn't come to the shows. We're getting married."

Jesse said nothing.

"I'm so sorry. I am *such* an asshole."

"Yeah, you are, Max. Yeah, you are."

Jesse stood up, brushing sand off of his pants, throwing his shirt back over his head. He began to head back to the bar, then turned back around to face Max. He pursed his lips and inhaled deeply. "Because I'm *not* an asshole, I hope you have a very healthy baby. I don't ever want to see you at my bar again."

Two weeks later, Voltage arrived with a new bass player. The lead singer told the crowd their boy Max was on his honeymoon. Groupies made sounds of disappointment, but instantly embraced the new, gorgeous Black man holding the four-string guitar, as he launched into the powerful bass line intro of "City of Love" by Yes. In moments, they'd forgotten all about Max. Unlike the man behind the bar with the newly hardened heart.

***

"Earth to Jess. You in there?"

"What? Oh, yeah, sorry, what were you saying?"

"Bro, you were miles away just now. You okay?"

"Yeah, yeah, fine. A lot on my mind this time of year."

"I was asking about Brie. What's she up to?"

Jesse took a sip from his bottle of water to clear his head. "Brie—uh, let's see. She lived at home for a while and eventually got sick of the parents."

"Big surprise."

"She came over here and worked in the bar for a bit, like most of one summer. She was obsessed with keeping her beach body fit, of course." Kimberly rolled her eyes. "So she started taking classes at the Y. Fell in love with Pilates. Next thing I know, she wants to become an instructor, so I loaned her money to get certified. She and another student decided their best shot at a wealthy clientele and steady business was Miami."

"Miami, huh?"

"Yeah. That's where she is now. Haven't heard from her in a while and was actually planning on calling her this weekend to see how things are going down there. She'll be so happy to hear your voice. Let's give her a call tomorrow."

"Sounds good," Kimberly said, staring out over the glistening water. Gulls swooped and dove all around them making their loud caw. The ocean air moisturized her skin. She felt her muscles relax for the first time in days. Jesse lived in paradise. She could understand why he loved it here. Walking on the beach every day would be like a slice of heaven.

Back at the condo, Jesse took a shower to get ready for work. In the guest room, Kimberly found the small key on her keychain and unlocked the steel box that went everywhere with her. She took the journal out to the balcony, sat down, and for the first time in a week, began to write.

Jesse came out of the master bedroom buckling the belt on his jeans, his damp hair left to air dry. Kimberly detected a whiff of Polo cologne. She smiled to herself, so glad some things never changed.

"Hey, not much time left if you want to get a shower."

"If it's okay with you, I think I'll stay here and write. I'm feeling pretty beat."

Jesse nodded his head. "Yeah, I get it. Long night ahead for me, so I'll lock the door behind me. There's a spare key in the drawer next to the sink if you need to go anywhere. And call the bar if anything earth shattering happens. Otherwise, see you in the morning. Late morning, okay? I'll need to sleep in." He winked at her as he left the condo.

***

Jesse woke up to the smell of bacon. He smiled. He could get used to having someone here taking care of him. He threw on shorts and opened his door.

"I hope there's coffee," he said, then stopped. On the bar was a plate of bacon and scrambled eggs with toast cut into triangles and a glass of orange juice sweating beside it. Stuck to the water droplets on the glass was a note:

Thank you for everything. I mean it. Tell Brie hi. I'll be in touch when I figure shit out. Love you~~Kimmy

Jesse dashed into the guest room just in case, but the bed was neatly made. Kimberly was gone. Again.

Chapter Twenty-Two — 1988 — Sabrina

A deep amber glow rose in the morning sky as Sabrina crept barefoot in cut-offs and a t-shirt through the front door of her parents' home, carrying strappy, blue, 3-inch heeled sandals on two curled fingers. Her cap and gown sat at the bottom of a tote bag along with the sundress she'd worn beneath it, and her purse. She closed the door silently, carefully, and turned to sneak into the downstairs half-bath to survey the damage.

The mirror was unforgiving this morning—her long, ebony hair askew from its ponytail, wisps loose around her face, mascara smeared raccoon-like under both eyes, a bluish-black bump forming on her forehead. She touched it tenderly, wincing. Lifting off her t-shirt, she slipped her bra strap down slightly to reveal the angry, red friction burn diagonally from shoulder to waist, a result of the seatbelt. She soaked a washcloth in cool water and pressed it to her forehead, lowering herself to sit cross-legged on the vinyl floor. Resting her elbows on her knees, she settled her head in her hands.

The bathroom door opened slowly, her mother's voice low.

"Get yourself together and come speak to your father and me in the living room."

Sabrina deposited her things at the foot of the stairs and sat across from her parents in a wing-backed chair.

"Are you okay?" Jack asked.

"I'm fine. Just a little bumped and bruised."

"What happened?" Marjorie asked.

Highlights flashed through Sabrina's mind—graduation ceremony, dinner with parents, 'no curfew tonight, have fun!,' meeting pals at a defunct drive-in theater, beer kegs and champagne bottles, donning shorts and a t-shirt, keeping the heels on to be sassy, Shan Crawford also finding the heels sassy, dancing around a bonfire, Shan Crawford's back seat, 'Brie, you shouldn't drive,' 'I'm fine! It's only ten minutes away,' trouble seeing in the dark, tree coming out of nowhere, waking up, splitting headache, no blood, everything hurts, take the damn shoes off and get home, sshhh, don't wake Mom and Dad . . .

"I had an accident, but I'm fine. Just sore."

"Where?"

"Here in the neighborhood somewhere. I walked home."

"Blueberry?"

"Yeah, I don't think she made it."

After surveying the damage to the truck, Jack returned to the house to call a tow truck. The little blue pickup was found firmly kissing a large pine tree in the corner lot at the entrance to their subdivision. Jack offered to take care of the damaged grass and tree, but the generous neighbor declined the offer, relieved to hear his daughter was okay. Blueberry, however, would be retired. The truck would be at the dump in a matter of hours.

Later, Jack and Sabrina drove home from the emergency room. All tests showed no brain or other internal injuries. She would only be sore and bruised for a few days.

"What were you thinking, Sabrina?"

"I don't know. It was dark when I got off the freeway."

"Mom can't even speak to you right now, she's so angry."

"It's just a truck, Dad."

"You think the truck is what's upsetting her?"

"Well, I'm fine, so it must be the truck."

Idling at a stoplight, Jack looked at his daughter. "Do you seriously think either of us care about a stupid truck? You could have severely injured yourself, Sabrina, or even died. *That's* why we're upset. A truck is just a thing. It can be replaced. You cannot."

Sabrina looked out the window and mumbled, "How am I supposed to get to work at the boutique?"

Jack tightened his grip on the steering wheel, the muscles in his jaw working. "I think you're going to have to figure that out on your own, Sabrina."

Marjorie stood in the kitchen, leaning against the corner of the countertop, sipping hot, black coffee. She met Sabrina's eyes as they entered through the garage door.

"Go to your room."

Jack shared the results of the tests at the hospital with Marjorie, as Sabrina ascended the stairs to her bedroom. Well this summer was officially gonna suck.

***

"Why do you have to take me to the movies? I don't understand why I can't borrow one of the cars," Sabrina said, arms folded across her chest. The heat from the Texas summer evening on the backyard deck did nothing to melt the frostiness coming from her mother.

"You've got to be kidding me, Sabrina."

"Mom, the accident was weeks ago. I've learned my lesson. You know me well enough to know that's true."

Marjorie leaned toward the chair across the table from hers where her daughter sat, her eyes twitching. "Child, I don't believe I know you at all anymore. I've bent over backward your entire life making sure you were well taken care of and happy. All your needs were met, most of your desires fulfilled. You've always been easily the most well-behaved, best mannered of my children. I trusted you, Sabrina, and look what happened. I let you go out without a curfew and you drive drunk and destroy your sister's truck."

"It was grad night! I wasn't *that* drunk and Kimberly gave *me* that truck."

Her mother's voice shot across the space between them like a bullet. "Do *not* interrupt me when I am speaking to you. Since you made the decision to act without common sense, without regard to rules or concern for your parents' feelings, you've also managed to destroy my trust in you." Marjorie slid a cigarette from her case, twisting the clasp closed. Flicking the lighter, she blew out the smoke, twitching eyes fixed on Sabrina. "It's a funny thing, trust. It takes a lifetime to earn and merely moments to lose."

"Mom, I know I had a lack of judgment that night, but am I going to be punished forever? I mean, they call them accidents for a reason."

Marjorie's face remained frozen in place as she said, "Sabrina

Grace, I had hope for you, but it appears you've turned into a version of your sister. Not only will I not be driving you to the movies, thanks to your smart mouth, consider your social life over for the summer. You will go to work and come home, is that clear?"

Sabrina's mouth dropped open, her eyes wide. Sweat trickled down her back. "Mom, I'm eighteen!"

"We have rules under this roof, young lady. One of the biggest being to respect your parents. Seeing as you seem unable to do that, it might be time for you to reconsider your living situation."

Sabrina shot up from her chair. "Are you kicking me out of the house?"

"I'm merely making things simple for you. Follow the rules or don't. Your choice. When you don't, there are consequences."

"I cannot believe this. I'm gonna call Dad."

"Your father is on a conference call with China at the office. You will not be bothering him. He and I are in agreement on this, anyway. Now, go to your room."

Sabrina slammed the sliding glass door behind her, the wall shaking in her wake. She stomped up the stairs, angry tears threatening to leak from her eyes.

I'll show her.

In her room, she dragged one of her nightstands over to the closet and climbed on top, reaching into the far corner of the closet shelf. Underneath a stack of sweaters, her fingers wrapped around a leather wallet. She pulled it free, backing carefully down off the nightstand.

On her bed, she counted out the cash in the wallet, the checks she'd received for graduation, and all of her paychecks from the boutique. She dug her calculator and a notebook out of her backpack and started to do calculations. Not quite enough yet. Tomorrow, she would open a bank account. If her calculations were correct, she should be able to buy a car and move out in about nine months. She replaced the wallet with the page of calculations tucked inside and slid the nightstand back into place.

Now the big decision . . . where to?

Sabrina changed out of jeans into shorts and a tank top, pulling on her Reeboks and securing her hair into a high ponytail. As she bounded

179

down the stairs, she heard her mother yell something from the porch but she ignored it.

"Going for a run," she yelled back, as she closed the front door behind her.

***

Jack lifted the last duffel bag to place it in the hatchback of his daughter's Toyota Celica. "Oof, this is heavy. What do you have in here, bricks?"

"Nope, books," Sabrina said, grinning.

"Same thing. You all set for cash?" Jack pulled his wallet out of his back pocket.

"I'm okay, but thanks. Save it for when I call you destitute and groveling."

Jack met Sabrina's eyes. "Go inside and make things right with your mom before you pull out, okay?"

Leaning into the passenger side of the car, she opened the cooler to make sure she'd remembered ice for her drinks and opened the road atlas to the first page she needed, heading south, then east. Closing the door, she leaned against it, twisting her dark hair into a bun. The sun was barely up and she was already warm.

"Nope, I'm good."

"Brie."

"Dad, I love her, but she makes it impossible to like her." She wrapped her arms tightly around her father and squeezed until her arms ached. He kissed her cheek and placed his hands on her shoulders.

"Are you sure you can drive 15 hours straight by yourself? I'm very concerned."

"I'm a big girl, Dad. I'll make plenty of stops. I have a calling card for emergencies." She walked around to the hatchback, giving one last look at her belongings, then closed it tight.

"I just wish you'd've let Jesse fly out and drive back with you."

"He's busy. It's almost Memorial Day weekend. I. Will. Be. Fine. Please don't worry. I'll call you when I get there."

"No matter what."

"No matter what. Promise." She made a criss-cross motion across her heart. She started the car, the turbo roaring into life. She put on her sunglasses and turned to the open window. "Hey, Dad? Don't ever change, okay?"

From the window beside the front door, Marjorie watched her daughter's white sports car back out of the driveway, a rare tear escaping her eye.

***

After a long night of waiting tables at Two Dudes, Sabrina was bushed. While thrilled that Jesse promoted her from hostessing after a month, and really digging the cash in her pocket every night, she wasn't convinced the aching feet and back were worth it. Dealing with some of the customers was a nightmare, too.

"Oh, miss! My fries are cold. Can you have the kitchen make a new batch?"

"Excuse me, miss? I ordered this salad with the dressing on the side. I can't eat this. It's drowning."

"Um, miss, my burger is supposed to be well-done and it's mooing."

Just once, she so badly wanted to say, "My name is not Miss, it's Sabrina. Just deal with it, you bunch of spoiled tourists." But she kept her mouth shut and rolled her eyes in solidarity with the cooks with every plate she returned to the kitchen.

Weeknights working tables in the Tiki hut were by far the best. The unforgiving summer evening heat drove most patrons inside. While the tips weren't as good, Sabrina loved the slower pace and danced along to live music as she headed to and from the kitchen. Jesse hired some great local bands. The music ranged from rock to reggae, from folk to country, and most of the band members were pretty friendly to the wait staff. Sabrina made a point of asking the musicians what they were drinking and made sure they never had to go to the bar themselves, which usually resulted in a nice tip from them at the end of the night.

Staying at Jesse's was also a bonus. He didn't ask her to pay any rent and she ate most of her meals at the bar, so her expenses were low. When she offered to chip in, he told her to just keep socking away her money and to make a plan. In other words, don't plan to be here forever. And she didn't.

Rosario frequently pulled shifts with Sabrina. A recent high school grad as well, she wore her hair and her jeans tight and sported the Puerto Rican flag on the front bumper of the bright red Ford Escort that matched her lipstick.

Sabrina got a kick out of her pissed-off kitchen tirades in Spanish.

"*Hijo de puta* . . ." Rosario said, muttering under her breath.

"What did you just call that guy?"

"Don't worry about it, *chica*, I'll tell you later. But it wasn't a term of endearment, I promise you that."

Sabrina covered her ears. "Contributing to the delinquency. I will not be a party to this!"

Rosario snapped a towel at Sabrina's hip. "Oh, shut up, you lily-white virgin."

"Only my ears, girlfriend, only my ears."

Jesse walked past them at the salad prep station. "What about your ears, Brie?"

Sabrina flushed and focused on assembling the four salad plates for table fourteen. "Nothing, boss. We were just talking about piercings." Rosario and Sabrina looked wide-eyed at each other and burst out laughing as Jesse left the kitchen. "Oh my God, you're gonna get me in trouble!"

"Hey, I can't help it that you're a little hoe with a big mouth!"

Nights in the Tiki hut, Rosario cracked up at Sabrina's attempts to sing along with the live music. Sadly, Sabrina's dip in the gene pool didn't include her parents' vocal talent. Walking past Sabrina waiting for drinks at the bar, Rosario covered her ears.

"Now it's *my* turn to complain about my virgin ears. Stick to waiting tables, Pat Benatar. Hell ain't for *children* up in here, just for my *hearing*."

Sabrina giggled. "It wouldn't be fair to mankind for me to have *all* of God's gifts, now would it?"

On their days off, the girls met at the beach, spending hours man-watching and sharing their dreams. Sabrina coated herself in sunscreen every hour, but her fair skin always burned a little.

"I wish I tanned like you, Rosie."

"Ha! No, you don't, princess. Trust me. The pain of a sunburn only lasts a day."

Sabrina pinched the only flesh on her belly that wasn't flat. "Ugh, I am eating way too many fries at Dudes. None of my clothes are gonna fit."

Rosario lifted up onto her elbows on the old patchwork quilt and looked at Sabrina.

"What world do you live in and how do I send you a ticket outta there? Are you insane? You are *flaca*—skinny. More like skin and bones. If anything, you need to start lifting weights. Get some meat on that skeleton of yours." She rolled her eyes and flipped over onto her belly. Mumbling into the crook of her arm, she said, "I don't wanna hear one more word like that outta your mouth, *comprendes?"*

"Fine. I'll shut up. But . . . there's a class at the Y called Pilates. Ever hear of it?"

"Puh-what-eese? Sounds like some kinda Greek god or something."

"I know. Weird name. It's controlled movements to improve strength and flexibility. Sorta like yoga without all the spiritual stuff. I was reading in Cosmo that all the top actresses in Hollywood are doing it. And they look amazing."

"All the actresses in Hollywood need to eat a cheeseburger, Brie."

"I'm thinking of signing up."

"Be my guest. I'll meet you for pizza afterward."

After three weeks of classes, Sabrina was hooked. The Y didn't offer all of the specialized Pilates equipment, so she did some research to find out where she could go that was fully equipped. She found a brand new, private studio in Port Orange, near the bar. It was pricey, but she could afford a few sessions to see if she liked it. Oh boy, did she ever. Within weeks, she began to tone and strengthen. Her body felt leaner. She could have sworn she'd even gotten taller.

Before long, pulling shifts at the restaurant began to interfere with the time she wanted to spend at the studio. When she realized the only reason she was working at the bar was to fund her Pilates classes, she had a talk with Jesse.

"So, they offer certification classes. My instructors say I'm a natural. If I could charge what they do per session, I could make a very good living, Jess."

"Sounds good to me. Looks like you've found your calling. Are you telling me you're quitting the bar?"

"Well . . . here's the thing. I know you want me to get my own place, and believe me, so do I."

"Hey, I'm not *that* bad of a roommate, am I?" he teased.

Sabrina chuckled and smacked her brother's arm. "Oh, stop it, that's not what I meant and you know it. The classes are expensive. I've been saving nearly all of my money. But if I spend all of my cash on certification, I'll have to start saving all over again for a place to live."

Jesse nodded. "I get it. You're in a Catch-twenty-two. No worries. Let me know how much the classes are and I'll loan you the money."

"You will?" Sabrina hugged her brother's neck. "You're a godsend, Jesse. What about paying you back though?"

"Get through the school first, get settled, start building a clientele. Then we'll talk about it."

"I don't know what to say. You're an angel. Are you sure we're related?"

Six months later, Sabrina Stevens, certified Pilates instructor, loaded up her Celica, and pointed the car south toward Miami. She was on her way.

Chapter Twenty-Three — 1991 — Kimberly

After accepting the early out from her enlistment, clearing off the base was more swift than Kimberly would have thought possible. She'd already packed up her barracks room. All of her belongings were in the trunk of her car. She received a check-out card and drove around base to various places to have it signed off—the library, sick call, the Navy Exchange, the post office. She withdrew all but $100 from her checking account. The career counselor advised her she was entitled to unemployment benefits upon separation, so that would buy her some time to get settled somewhere. When she returned to her command, she turned in the signed card, signed her discharge papers, and she was free to go. Nearly eight years of service ended in an afternoon.

As she headed back to her car, she removed her uniform cover for the last time and tucked it under her arm.

"Hey, you are out of uniform, sailor. That is unsat," came a voice from behind her. She wheeled around to see Chief Conroy approaching, a bittersweet smile on her face.

"Chief. Thanks for seeing me out."

"This is hard for me, Stevens . . . Kimberly. You are a damn fine AME. I will always be proud to have served with you. I wish I could convey to you how frustrated I am that I can't do more to bring the men to justice who abused you."

A tear rolled down Kimberly's face as she fought to maintain decorum in front of her superior. Chief Conroy put a hand on her shoulder.

"I promise you this: I will fight until my last day in this man's Navy to see things change. My only hope is that you'll speak to someone about this. Get some counseling. If nothing else, please know that I believe you. And I believe *in* you. I always will."

Kimberly choked on her words. "Thank you, Chief."

"Call me Susanne. And don't be a stranger, okay? You know where to reach me. Take care, Kimberly. As they say, fair winds and following seas." She turned and strode purposefully back to the squadron. Kimberly was relieved not to have received a hug, or she would have completely lost herself in front of God and everyone.

Kimberly drove off base and stopped at a grocery store, choosing cheese, crackers, grapes, apples, and a twelve-pack of beer. She pulled her silver 1987 Toyota Corolla into the parking lot of the Days Inn, unlocking the door to the room she'd booked for a week, and placed her groceries in the tiny fridge.

Sitting in an uncomfortable wooden chair, she cracked open a cold can of beer, hoisted it in the air, and to no one said, "Here's to Kimberly Marie Stevens. Former sailor. Fair winds and following seas, loser."

She grabbed the stack of envelopes that had been stuffed into her mailbox, arranging them by postmark, the earliest one on top. Return address AE2 JT Allen. As she opened the letter from the first envelope and saw the familiar handwriting, it hit her hard. He was going to find out. And she was convinced he would never want to see her again. She had *never* deserved him. She never deserved anything good in her life. What was it her mother always said? Good things are earned, not just given. She'd definitely not earned his love. How could she have been so stupid?

Her heart shattered into a million pieces. She clutched the letter to her chest and crawled onto the bed, burying her face into the bedspread. It was over. Her career. Her Navy family. The love of her life. It was all over.

***

For days, Kimberly lay in bed in the hotel room, alternating between sleep and mind numbing television. Until one morning when she awoke feeling mostly human again. She felt hungry. She wanted to shower. She wanted to be outside and feel the sun on her skin. It was time to move on.

She showered and dressed, packing up her things and returning them to the trunk of the car. Checking out of the hotel, she thought, *Where to first?*

In order to apply for unemployment benefits, she needed to stay in her home of record state, so she wouldn't be leaving Florida. Her parents had moved back to Clearwater years ago after her dad was promoted to Vice

President of Operations for Eckerd. However, she didn't plan to use their address any longer. She was a grown woman who could take care of herself.

At the post office, she signed up for a PO Box, paying for a year in advance. She sat in a booth at Denny's for a couple of hours having breakfast and reading the want ads and apartments for rent in the newspaper. Leaving her server a healthy tip, she thanked her for her patience in 'renting' the space to her for so long.

She was going to have to find a place to live before she could interview for jobs. The only place within her budget was a small one-bedroom apartment in a rundown brown brick building just outside of downtown Jacksonville. The maintenance man was very friendly and showed her the unit. It wasn't much, but Kimberly could add touches here and there to make it her own. Mr. García explained that he collected the rents for all four units and paid it directly to the landlord, who came by once a month. She would need to pay first months' rent and a security deposit up front, so she paid him in cash from her purse.

"Is it possible to go month to month rather than signing a lease? I believe this is only going to be temporary," she said. Mr. García nodded, telling her it would be fine.

Next, she stopped at Bell Telephone and paid to have service in her new place. They even provided a phone. Then she went to the closest Goodwill location to see if she could find a bed and a sofa and arranged to have them delivered the following morning. By the end of the afternoon, she felt pretty accomplished, and pretty broke. She took a deep breath. Everything would be okay.

Sitting on the floor of her mostly empty apartment, Kimberly unlocked the metal box containing her journal. She sifted through the box of belongings from her trunk. She pulled out the stationery tin from Allison, all the photos she could find, and all the personal letters she'd received. In a corner of the cardboard box, her fingers touched on the small maroon velvet box. Swallowing hard over the lump in her throat, she slipped the emerald ring off her finger and nestled it into the insert in the box. She lifted the dog tag chain from her neck and slipped it over her head. Placing all of the items in the stationery tin, she closed the lid tightly and held it to her chest. Last, she placed the tin, letters, and photos in the lock box, latched and locked it. A form of closure. It would have to do.

By week's end, Kimberly discovered her experience in the military did not translate well into the civilian world. Nobody needed an aviation life support technician in their offices and she had no experience with anything else. Not bookkeeping, not customer service, not anything marketable, apparently.

She was sitting in Denny's again sipping a Coke, leafing through the want ads, when the server who waited on her previously stopped at her table.

"Hey there, I remember you from a week ago. Nice tip, thanks."

"Oh, no problem. You were very kind to let me take up your table for so long. I may be guilty of that again today."

"Listen, don't worry about a thing. It's not like we have $200 checks at these tables. Take your time. I'm Penny. Can I get you anything?"

Kimberly chuckled softly. "Thanks, Penny . . . maybe a job?"

"Are you serious? We're always hiring. Want me to bring you an application?"

Kimberly thought for a moment. "Sure, why not? I've never waited tables, but I can certainly be trained."

"Great! I'll get the application for you and see if the manager is available to talk to you. Wait right here."

"Oh, I'm not going anywhere," Kimberly said, smiling.

***

The Christmas shopping rush seemed to be nonstop from Black Friday all the way through Christmas Eve. Denny's was a 24-hour restaurant and there were hungry shoppers during the holidays no matter what time of day it was. Kimberly didn't mind the fast pace at all. Her shifts flew by and the tips made up for her aching feet every night.

At 10:00 pm, she gave the check to her last four-top, adding a couple of candy canes, and wished them a Merry Christmas. She slipped off her apron and went into the kitchen to clock out. Her manager called her to the back office before she made it out the door. He handed her an envelope with her name and Merry Christmas written on the front.

"A little something from us to you. Have a merry Christmas and we'll see you on the 26th. Enjoy your holiday."

"Thank you, Jim. I appreciate it. Merry Christmas to you and your family." She turned to leave, her face solemn.

"Everything okay, Kimberly?"

"Yes, everything's fine. Just a little wiped out from the holidays, I guess. See you soon." Kimberly folded the envelope and slipped it into her front pocket with her tips. As she drove to her apartment, she thought about Christmas Eve when she was a kid. The Stevens clan would gather around the tree and open one gift each, usually pajamas. Dad would pull out his guitar, complaining about not having callouses on his fingers anymore, and they would sing songs into the night. Mom always shooed them to bed before midnight saying Santa wouldn't come if the kids were awake, even when they were teenagers.

She checked her mail and her spirits immediately lifted. Inside was a red envelope from Allison, the only person who had Kimberly's address and phone number. In the apartment, Kimberly took a shower, put on pajamas, and curled up on the lumpy couch with a bottle of whiskey and her two envelopes. She took a swig from the bottle. "Merry Christmas to me," she said.

The envelope from work contained a fifty dollar bonus. She smiled. Maybe she would use some of it to call Allison long distance tomorrow for Christmas. She opened the card from Allison. On the front it said *Santa doesn't exist and the Tooth Fairy is your parents.* Kimberly burst out laughing and opened the card to find a long letter from Allison and a long distance calling card. She was finally getting out of the Navy and going back home to Key West.

Here's all my contact information. By the time you get this card, I will be there. Call me, lady! I love you. ~~Alli

Kimberly immediately rubbed the silver coating off the back of the gift card to reveal the PIN and grabbed her phone. It took a minute to activate the card and call her best friend for Christmas Eve. Even at the late hour, Allison was awake and waiting by the phone.

"There you are, jeez! I was hoping it would get there in time for you to call me tonight. Are you in jammies already, grandma?"

Kimberly giggled. "Yep, you know it. Bottle at the ready. Go big or go home, lady!"

"Atta girl."

"How are things back home? You all settled in?"

"Oh, yeah, it's like I never left. Tell you one thing, though. I gotta get my own place pronto. I feel like a little kid back in my parents' house."

"I hear ya."

"Why don't you come down here? Make a fresh start?"

"I don't know, Alli—"

"Come on, Kim. Think about it. You would be with *me*, your favorite bad influence! And you wouldn't ever have to worry about running into those assholes from your shop again. What did you say their names were?"

"Andy Coleman and Brett Lewis." She shuddered saying their names aloud.

"One phone call, lady. That's all it would take. You say the word."

"As tempting as that sounds, I think I'll pass on hiring the hit." Kimberly laughed, a little creeped out to think her best friend could be serious.

"Just sayin. So, lift your glass, grandma."

"Lifted."

"To life. I'm so friggin happy you're in mine."

Kimberly's eyes filled. "Ditto, lady. Merry Christmas. God, I miss you."

***

The humid air was heavy on a warm morning as the Memorial Day holiday approached. Kimberly was looking forward to clocking out and going to the beach. She usually drove down to St. Augustine to avoid all the sailors in Jacksonville. She was tired from working all night but when the sun came up it always gave her a second wind.

Sun, sand, and surf, here I come!

"Did you think I wouldn't find out?" a voice said from the lobby in front of the hostess stand. Kimberly froze. Her heart thumped. She turned to see him standing in the lobby in a dark brown t-shirt, jeans, and hiking boots. She caught her breath and looked at the apron in her hands. She swallowed hard.

"JT. My shift is just ending. Wait for me outside. I'll just be a minute," she said, unable to meet his eyes.

As she pushed open the back door, her head swooned and she felt as though she might pass out. Shame and humiliation enveloped her. She took a steadying breath. For a moment, she thought about quietly getting in her car and driving away, but she knew he would be back. He had found her. There was nowhere to escape. She steeled herself to face him, and began to walk around to the front of the building.

JT was parked under a tree in the side parking lot, sitting on the lowered tailgate of his truck. He smoked slowly, watching Kimberly walk toward him. She could feel the anger seething from him. She didn't want to have this conversation in the parking lot of her job.

As she approached, she held the palms of her hands up in a sort of surrender and said, "Before you say anything, can we please go somewh—"

JT flicked the cigarette away and jumped down from the tailgate. He wrapped her up in his arms and slammed his mouth against hers, kissing her deeply. His hands rubbed every inch of her back as though recalling memories through his fingertips. He held her face in his hands and finally broke the kiss to look into her eyes. He held her there for a long moment, staring hard into her face. She didn't move. She didn't breathe.

"Why?" was all he said.

Sitting in the cab of his truck, the air conditioning cooling the morning heat, she sat very still and listened to his broken heart pouring out in his words. He told her they hadn't gone to the Med at all, but had been in the Persian Gulf in support of Operation Desert Storm, and hadn't been allowed to let anyone know. He tried to get as many letters out as he could, but it was a rare occurrence for a tender to come and offload the mail. He said he'd received the Polaroid in an anonymous envelope and was crushed. He'd planned to come back to Mayport in a fury and end everything with her. But as time went on, he knew something wasn't right. By the time they got back in May, she was gone and due to the Privacy Act, nobody would give him any current information. He wrote to her old PO Box on base but no forwarding address had been left and his letters just came back. As a last ditch effort, he contacted Allison in Pax, but she refused to tell him anything.

"That girl is a vault, Kimberly. I knew you could have gone anywhere in the world. I had absolutely no idea how to begin to find you. So, I gave up. I volunteered for various detachments to get away from here and I signed up for the next deployment. We're leaving in two weeks for Bosnia."

"So, how did you find me?"

"I was out having a drink at the Fleet Reserve and it hit me. I know you have no relationship with your parents but I thought maybe if I could track them down, they might be able to offer a clue as to where you were. I remembered your dad was some bigwig with Eckerd and I know their headquarters is in Clearwater, so I called every single Stevens in the phone book in the area. I got lucky when I hit the J's. Your mother—not a nice person, by the way—said she had no idea where you were, but some mail had come for you from Unemployment."

"But I changed my address. Dammit. They must have used my military home of record anyway."

"Probably. It apparently listed a current place of employment as Denny's at a Jacksonville address. She told me maybe I should start there. She also said if I found you to tell you that it's 'long past time to end this ridiculous stand-off,' whatever that means. So, here I am. And all I want to know is why? Why didn't you stand up for yourself with those assholes? Why did you disappear? Why didn't you trust me enough to confide in me and give me a chance to defend you?"

Kimberly looked at JT for a long moment, processing all that he'd just told her.

"Because you were so proud of having a girl like me on your arm. But after what happened? Once you saw those photos? How could you stay with me? I'm damaged . . . soiled. I don't deserve you. I never did," she said. JT closed his eyes. She could see the muscles working in his jaw as he clenched his teeth. He threw the truck in reverse and peeled out of the parking lot. Kimberly hurried to put on her seatbelt.

"JT, what are you doing? Where are we going?" He said nothing as he drove angrily toward the river. He pulled into the parking lot of the hotel near The Landings, the very place they'd sealed their love for each other what seemed like a lifetime ago. He got out of the truck and came around to open her door.

"Come with me," he said.

***

For two weeks, every moment they weren't working, they were together. JT convinced her to swallow her pride and let him come to her apartment. If he was disappointed, he never let her know. He wasn't there to look at the furnishings anyway, he assured her. Their hands explored each other's bodies, memorizing. Their eyes never parting until they fell asleep in each other's arms.

The day he had to leave for deployment, he parked his truck at the barracks. She drove him to the squadron in her Corolla.

Standing beside her car in the parking lot, JT took her left hand and raised it to his lips, kissing the ring and her fingers beneath.

"As soon as I get home, girlie."

"Yes, as soon as you get home."

"I'll write as soon as I can."

"I'll answer."

"I love you."

"I love that you love me."

***

The emerald ring sparkled on her hand as Kimberly read the newspaper after her shift. She'd already clocked out, so she changed out of her uniform shirt and took a seat at the bar to have breakfast. She was always hungry these days.

She took a mouthful of scrambled eggs and laid her fork down on the plate, flipping through the paper with both hands. A small article on page two of the A section caught her eye. She blinked and wiped her eyes in order to read the words more clearly. She tapped lightly on the arm of a stranger in a flannel shirt sitting next to her at the bar.

"Excuse me, sir. I'm so sorry to bother you. Can you please read this article and tell me what it says? I don't seem to be able to focus." Her eyes had welled up, blurring her vision.

The man leaned closer to get a better view of the newspaper. "Uh, sure, miss. It says "SH-60H Helicopter From HSL-60 in Mayport, Florida Crashes in Humanitarian Mission in Bosnia and Herzegovina. No Survivors. It also says the names of the service members are being withheld until notification of next of kin. Could it be someone you know?"

Kimberly pushed herself back from the bar, no longer hungry. Leaving a five dollar bill on the counter, she stumbled toward the lobby door. She raised her hand to shield her eyes, her ring twinkling in the morning sunlight. Then everything went black.

"Miss? Miss, are you okay?" The man in the flannel shirt knelt next to Kimberly on the floor of the restaurant, lightly shaking her by the shoulder.

"Oh no!" Penny said, calling into the kitchen. "Jim, Kimberly fainted!" She ran to Kimberly's side.

The customer said, "She asked me to read something to her in the paper about a helicopter crash in Bosnia. It was a crew from here in Mayport. I think maybe it was someone she knows?"

"Oh God. Her fiancé. Thank you for your help, sir. We'll take it from here," Penny said.

The manager rushed around the counter with clean, folded towels in his hands. Placing the towels gently under Kimberly's head, he spoke to Penny.

"Call 911 and please clear everyone from this area so we can afford her a little privacy."

"You got it. Folks, if you can please go back to your tables, we are handling the situation. Please back away. Thanks so much." She grabbed the cordless phone from the hostess stand to dial emergency. "Jim, a customer told me she just read in the paper that her fiancé was killed in Bosnia."

Jim's head bent toward his chest. He sighed. "Dear heavens. Poor girl."

Kimberly's eyelids fluttered as she slowly regained consciousness. She looked up into the concerned face of her manager.

"What happened?" she mumbled.

"You passed out, Kim. Can you try to sit up?" He supported her back and shoulders from behind. "Here, take it slowly."

Jim eased Kimberly into an upright position. Her head dizzy and pounding, she placed a hand on her forehead.

"Do you have low blood pressure? Diabetes? I can get you a glass of orange juice."

"No, no. It's not that," she said, woozy. Kimberly met Jim's eyes. "I'm 9 weeks pregnant."

"Oh, Kim . . . oh, dear girl. Your fiancé . . ." He wrapped his arms around Kimberly as she collapsed sobbing into his chest. He patted her back paternally. "Don't you worry. Everything's gonna be okay."

She choked out her words. "Nothing's ever gonna be okay again."

Chapter Twenty-Four — 2012 — Julie

Julie blotted her face with a tissue and continued to read the words from her mom.

There is so much I want to tell you. So much I wish I could share with you while looking at your beautiful face. Almost everything you need to know about me is contained in the two boxes. I was a single mom with a toddler, no money, no job, living on public assistance. I couldn't provide you the safe and happy life you deserved. I couldn't ask my family for help. So, I did what I had to do. I left them no choice. I knew Jesse and Sabrina would do the right thing where you were concerned. I asked them to let me take care of things my way and not to interfere. Please don't be angry with them for honoring my wishes.

I hope your life has been so happy and full of wonderful moments. I wish I could see the young woman you've become. I know that my family hasn't always been a good one. I don't know why we always hurt the ones we love, baby girl. We have a long, unpleasant history of causing each other pain. I guess it's in our blood. It's a vicious cycle. I hope that you will be the one to break that cycle for the Stevens clan. I hope that you are the shining light the family needs. I have a feeling you will be. Please know that no matter what, I have loved you from the moment you began to grow inside me and I will love you even after I'm gone.

Always~~Mom

Julie looked at the page behind the letter, creasing her brow. It took a moment to figure out that she was looking at a letter of suggested course of treatment from her mother's doctor. She folded the letters and placed them in her lap. She closed her eyes and took in a deep breath. It was as though her mom reached across time and space from wherever she was and touched Julie's soul. She ached to know her.

Sabrina spoke softly from the doorway. "Jules, you okay?"

Julie nodded, melancholy filling her face. "Yeah." She turned and met her aunt's kind eyes. "Aunt Brie, my mom had cancer." Sabrina stepped quickly across the terrace to sit next to Julie, her eyes wide.

"What? What did she say?" Sabrina scanned the doctor's letter. "Cervical cancer, stage II." She sighed. "Oh my God. Why didn't she come to us for help? We could have provided her with the best doctors, the best care . . ."

"I don't know. She says in her letter she couldn't go to her family for help."

Sabrina looked stricken as it appeared a memory came to her. "Oh, God. Our last phone conversation. She was coming to me for help and I turned her away."

Julie gasped and looked at her aunt, incredulous. "What are you saying?" Sabrina placed her hand over Julie's.

"Jules, it was a different time. We'd been through a lot with Kimberly and we'd agreed with my mother to be firm where she was concerned. We realized too late what a horrible mistake that was. Kimberly had a habit of disappearing when things got difficult. I guess we never dreamed that would happen once she had you."

"She said that she needed to handle things her way. I'm assuming she means taking her own life."

"It's what we've always assumed, too, Julie. She asked us not to try to find or stop her. And, honestly, back then we had no idea where to even begin to look for her. She was very good at shutting all of us out of her life."

Julie pulled her hand away from her aunt. "What is wrong with you people? Aunt Brie, what exactly happened that night? The night she left?"

Jesse spoke up from the doorway. "I believe you need to hear that story from me."

Chapter Twenty-Five — 1996 — Jesse

"Hey there, I thought I heard you come in. Long day, huh?" Taylor crossed the beige living room carpet to meet Jesse at the end of the kitchen bar for a kiss. Jesse put his hand on Taylor's jaw, taking in his deep brown eyes, his smooth, bald head, his soft beautiful lips. It was nearly midnight.

"Have I told you lately how wonderful it is to come home to a man as incredible as you?" Jesse asked.

"Have I told *you* lately how much I wish you were coming home to me in a *new* home?" Taylor said, his dimpled grin mischievous. Jesse playfully swatted his behind.

"Not this again, honey. I know, I know, I've had this condo forever and it's dated. But I've told you I don't want a mortgage. Rates are too high right now. Besides, I like living at the speed of cash. If I can't pay cash, I can't afford it. And the house I want us to grow old in? I can't afford it. Yet."

Taylor sighed and wrapped his arm around Jesse's waist, pulling him close. "Fine. Kiss me and make it better, handsome." Their lips met softly, then parted, the kiss deepening. Jesse pulled back, placing his hands on Taylor's chest.

"Give a man a minute to breathe, lover," he said with a wink. He gently placed his hand on the back of his partner's neck and rested his creased, freckled forehead against Taylor's dark, smooth one. "How was your day?"

"Oh, it was good," Taylor said, as he pulled away and walked toward a small table in the hall. "I may finally be under contract with that million dollar listing in Jupiter. Fingers crossed!" He picked up the mail from the foyer table and walked back to Jesse.

"Nicely done. I know you've been working hard on that one. What buyers this time?" Jesse asked.

"Some obnoxious couple from Fort Lauderdale. That's okay, I don't care who buys the dang house, as long as my commission is in the bank. Babe, we'll be paying cash for our own place before you know it. Here's the mail. Something in there from Jacksonville." Taylor walked into the kitchen and opened a cabinet, taking down two glass snifters for a brandy nightcap.

Jesse flipped through the envelopes, coming to the one with a post mark from Jacksonville. He looked at the return address.

"Oh my God, that's where she's been," he mumbled softly.

"What's that?"

"My sister," Jesse said, and sat down on the couch to open the envelope.

Chapter Twenty-Six — 1996 — Kimberly

At midnight, Kimberly double checked that everything was in place. Tin stationery box taped with thick electrical tape sitting on top of the lock box on the sofa, letter to Jesse resting on the very top, Sabrina's underneath. Diaper bag and backpack on her bed, packed with everything Julie would need, resting inside her car seat. Plenty of milk, cereal, and snacks in a soft-side cooler on the counter in the kitchen, cold packs inside.

She lifted her own pack, hoisting it onto her shoulders, straps securely in place. She checked her front pocket. Disappointing that a ring that beautiful had only gotten her $900 from the pawn shop. It was better than nothing.

She didn't dare touch her daughter and risk waking her. She looked into the shadowy room from the open bedroom door. The little angel was sleeping soundly on her side, blonde curls across her face. Everything inside Kimberly cried out for her baby. She longed to hold her one last time, to sprinkle her tiny face with kisses, to nuzzle her sweet smelling neck.

Kimberly ran to the couch and buried her face in the plaid blanket. A guttural wail came from her throat. Her mouth dropped open, a flood of tears years in the making gushed forth, her body racked with grief for several minutes.

Dammit, Kimberly, get it together. You know this is best. Do it right this minute or you will blow it.

Kimberly gathered her courage, blew her daughter a silent kiss, and left the apartment, locking it behind her. She slipped the key into an envelope addressed to Mr. García, and left it under the cushion of his front porch chair, the corner sticking out enough so that it would poke his leg as he sat down in the morning.

"Thank you," she whispered, and strode briskly away from the building.

***

Mr. García tilted the small sauce pan and poured warm milk into a coffee mug. He added a splash of spiced rum and a dash of cocoa. Taking a sip and nodding in satisfaction, he began to take a seat in his recliner by the front window of his living room. He missed his Lisita making this concoction for him as she did for so many of his sleepless nights over their 49 years together. *Rest peacefully, mi amor,* he thought, looking at their wedding photo on his bookshelf. He kissed his fingers and sent it to her in heaven.

Just as he sat down, he heard footsteps on the rusty iron stairs. Only they weren't going up, they were coming down. He found that odd, as he knew Kimberly and her daughter were sleeping. It took his old bones a moment to get out of the chair. He peeled back the corner of the curtain and saw the back of someone in a black hoodie and jeans with a backpack heading away from his front porch.

"How very strange," he said, muttering to himself. He opened the front door and walked out into the night. He could no longer see the person so they must have been moving quickly. He scanned the area around his chair and little table. Everything looked in place. And then he saw it—something white sticking out from under his seat cushion. He pulled the envelope out and took it inside to get his reading glasses.

As he read the note, he sighed sadly. "Oh, no, Miss Kimberly. Oh, please be okay," he said.

Dear Mr. García: I had no choice and needed to leave. While you do not owe me any favors, I hope to ask just one of you. Can you please call this number and speak to my brother, Jesse? Please give him our address here. He will handle everything. Thank you for being such a wonderful neighbor. I will really miss you. Please take care of yourself and stop smoking those stinky cigars. Love~~Kimberly

"Oh, *niña*. What have you done?" He went back into his home and crossed the small, carpeted room to his kitchen phone. He didn't pay the late hour any mind as he dialed the number Kimberly had given him. It rang only once. The person on the other end was clearly waiting for his call.

"Hello! This is Jesse Stevens, who is calling?"

"Sir, my name is Juan García. I am the maintenance man and neighbor of your sister, Kimberly. She left me a note to call you and give you our address here in Jacksonville. I'm not sure what has happened but I think I saw her run away from the building a few minutes ago." Suddenly, he gasped. "Oh, *Dios mío*, she was alone when she left."

"Julie!" Jesse said. "Can you get to her and make sure she is safe? Please, sir!"

"Yes, yes, of course, I will go up and check. Our building is at the corner of Forsyth and Davis in Jacksonville. Brown brick, four units. You can't miss it. Where will you be coming from, Mr. Stevens?"

"Jesse, please. I'm in Daytona. I'll be there in about an hour and a half. This is my cellular phone. You can call it anytime. I'll pay for any charges."

"Jesse, I am going to go now to check on the baby. I will call you back."

Mr. García took the steps as quickly as his body would allow. He unlocked the door and raced to the bedroom, finding Julie fast asleep in her playpen. He breathed a sigh of relief and leaned against the doorframe to steady his beating heart.

Jesse sounded breathless when he answered the phone again, like he was running. "Mr. García, is she okay?"

"Yes, Jesse, she is sleeping soundly. Kimberly packed her things. There is a note here for you with some boxes. I will stay here and keep everything safe until you arrive. Please don't worry and drive safely."

"Thank you, sir. I'll be there as soon as I can."

Jesse hung up the phone and screamed inside the car. "Goddammit, Kimberly, what in the hell have you done now?"

Taylor reached over, resting a calming hand on Jesse's forearm. "Breathe, love. I've got you. We'll figure this out together." Jesse placed his hand over Taylor's, meeting his eyes. Then he threw the car in gear and raced north on A1A.

***

The azure sky was interrupted with bold strokes of orange, as the day dawned on the Atlantic horizon. Sabrina answered the phone on the second ring and heard Grey groaning next to her.

"What time is it, jeez?"

"Go back to sleep, honey," she said, as she slipped out of bed. "Jesse, do you have any idea what time it is?" Sabrina whispered into the phone as she left the bedroom.

"Yes, Brie, I'm aware. I waited until the sun came up to call you."

"Well, that was considerate. What happened? Are you guys okay?"

"Yes, we're fine. We're heading down your way from Jacksonville."

"What? Why?"

"Well, you know how you guys have been trying for so long to have a baby?"

"Yes . . .?"

"Congratulations. It's a girl."

***

The aroma of freshly brewed coffee swooshed out the door of Sabrina's condo as she opened it for her brother and his partner.

"Oh dear God," she whispered, grabbing the handle of the baby carrier that held her sleeping niece and withdrew back inside. "Come in."

Grey stood in the kitchen doorway. "Coffee?"

The men nodded. "Thanks, Grey. I'll come fix it," Taylor said.

After placing the baby in the guest room, Sabrina joined Jesse on the sofa, morning light flooding the room.

"I don't understand," she said.

"That makes two of us."

"The note you read me over the phone makes it sound like she killed herself, Jesse."

"I know. It does. I don't even have the faintest idea where to look for her."

Sabrina covered her eyes with the heels of her hands. "This is all my fault. I was horrid to her on the phone. I'm absolutely sick inside."

Placing an arm around her narrow shoulders, Jesse said, "Blaming yourself is pointless, Brie. You aren't responsible for her behavior." He pulled an envelope from his jacket pocket and handed it to her. "She left this for you."

Sabrina tore open the envelope.

Brie: The only thing in my life that I ever did right was give birth to the most beautiful baby on the planet. If I know Jesse, she's probably in your care as you read this. Thank you is not strong enough for the gratitude I have knowing you and Grey will give Julie a wonderful life. It was meant to be. Just do me one favor, please? Every night, give her one extra kiss from her momma. I love you, little sister. I always have. ~~Kim

A moan of grief escaped her throat as Sabrina handed the note to Jesse and buried her face in his shoulder. A few moments later, the cries of a waking toddler brought Grey from the kitchen. He held Sabrina's hand tightly as they walked down the hall toward their precious and unexpected gift.

Chapter Twenty-Seven — 2012 — Julie

Julie pulled the lid off the tin stationery box and began removing items one by one. All of her mom's military insignia, her dog tags, a banded stack of letters, Julie's birth announcement, hospital baby bracelet, and a lock of hair. Bittersweet tears broke through smiles as she lovingly touched each piece. Her long lost mother felt as though she was right before her in the form of artifacts from a life so long ago.

Aunt Brie and Uncle Jesse sat close to Julie on the terrace, emotion crossing their faces as she shared the pieces of her mom's past. Julie opened the deep red velvet box to find it empty.

"Huh. That doesn't make much sense, does it? Why would she keep an empty ring box?"

The stationery box now empty, Julie popped the two latches on the metal box, but it was locked. She sifted through all of the items again to see if she'd missed something.

Auntie Charlotte came out of the kitchen with a tray of coffee service. "Can I interest anyone? It's decaf." She poured a few mugs. Uncle Grey and Uncle Taylor each took a coffee. Uncle Jesse lifted his beer in a polite decline. Aunt Brie said, "I think I need a brandy."

Uncle Grey spoke up. "I'll get that for you, hon."

Julie unbound the letters and began to shake each one to see if there was a key inside. She saw a letter from her grandpa, her aunt, a few from someone named AO3 A. Johnson, but most of them were addressed from AE2 JT Allen. No key in any of them. Just letters.

Then it dawned on her. She opened the ring box again and lifted out the velvet insert. Nothing on the bottom of the box, but the insert was heavier than it should have been. She flipped it over and saw a piece of the same tape that bound the tin box. She peeled it away and discovered a small key. Julie smiled. This was it.

She fit the key into the lock of the box and turned it. The lock opened. Inside were photos. So many photos. Julie's hand flew to her mouth as she saw her mother's face over and over again. What an absolute treasure trove! While she didn't know who a lot of the people were in the photos, it didn't matter. There was her mother, young and vibrant and beautiful. She saw where she got her curls from. And she definitely had her mother's eyes. She began to pass the photos around to her aunt and uncle, who shared them with the others. Emotions ran high — it had been so long since any of them had seen Kimberly.

"I got my wish," Julie said.

"What's that, honey?" Aunt Sabrina asked.

"I got to see my mother again."

Sabrina lay her hand softly on Julie's shoulder. "Yes, you did. You look so much like her, too."

"Who's the baby in this picture? Is that me? That's not Mom, though, is it?" Julie held up a photo of a little one toddling in front of a sofa. The child's mother is sitting, legs curled to the side, crocheting what appears to be an afghan, a faraway look in her eyes. Sabrina took the photo and tenderly touched the image of the woman.

"No, honey, that's not you. It's your mom. You definitely looked the same as little ones. This woman on the sofa is our mother. Your grandmother." She reaches out and tucks a loose tendril of Julie's hair behind her ear. "You never knew her. And, truly, neither did I."

Chapter Twenty-Eight — 1999 — Sabrina

Booming bass vibrated the electric charged air, the sounds of Prince, along with Earth, Wind & Fire, Gloria Estefan & Miami Sound Machine, and Will Smith kept the New Year's Eve guests dancing and grooving from room to room in the Hanover's high-rise condo. Lights burned in every room, champagne flowing on this once-in-a-lifetime evening. They were ushering in a new millennium. From their vantage point high above the city, all of Miami was ablaze in celebration and anticipation of the year 2000—Y2K, as it was referred to in the media. While tech companies worldwide planted people by their servers out of fear of disaster when the clocks rolled over, nothing could dampen the party atmosphere in South Florida.

Charlotte brushed through the metallic doorway streamers into the kitchen, the heel of her five-inch stilettos catching on one and pulling it free from the rest.

"Sorry about that, Brie," she said, bending her knee to better reach her heel behind her and remove the entwined decoration.

Sabrina swiped her hand in an 'oh please' gesture and hugged her friend carefully, so as not to ruin their expensive coiffures and makeup. She backed up a step, taking in Charlotte's skin-tight, purple-sequined cocktail dress in admiration.

"Wow, girl, you are the most stunningly beautiful Black woman in all of Miami tonight!"

"Why, thank you, my ivory sistah. Look at you! The goddess in silver." Sabrina's long, black hair was twisted into a chignon, bangs framing her oval, ivory face, smoky eyes and deep red lips. Diamonds twinkled at her ears above a silver lamé, halter-style jumpsuit.

"You only ring in a millennium once, right? So glad you made it!" Sabrina said, handing Charlotte a glass of Veuve Clicquot. Clinking glasses, "Cheers!," the women made their way into the dining room for a shrimp and avocado toast canapé on a passed tray.

"I wouldn't have missed it for the world. Sorry I was kept late at the office. I'm sure Grey's told you about the big sexual harassment case we have coming up."

Sabrina sipped her champagne and nodded, speaking up over the music. "Of course. I know you guys are busy, but it's a holiday weekend. You need to let down your hair tonight." Charlotte's silky hair was pulled back tight away from her face, a cascade of curls flowed to her shoulders.

"Well . . . it's halfway there," she winked. "Where's Grey?"

"He just got back from Mrs. McPherson's downstairs. Julie's sleeping down there for the night."

"Oh, dang, I missed her all decked out in her party dress. Please tell me you got pictures."

"I did. She didn't want to take off 'the princess gown,' so Grey took pajamas with her downstairs. We let her stay up so late tonight. I hope she won't give poor Mrs. McPherson a hard time about changing clothes."

"Too cute. Let's go mingle!"

Charlotte and Sabrina made their way through the throngs of guests, introducing each other to people invited through Richardson Hanover or folks Sabrina and Grey knew from the country club. Charlotte was pulled into a conversation with the mayor of Cutler Bay, as Sabrina glided away. She spotted Grey at the bar cart near the terrace, pouring himself a scotch. Slipping a narrow arm through his, her diamond tennis bracelet dazzled under a white droplight.

"There's my beautiful bride," Grey said. He gently kissed her cheek, breathing in the light floral fragrance on her neck. "You look remarkable, Brie." Sabrina's smile shone brighter than all the lights in the place.

"So in love with you, husband." Grey slid his arm around Sabrina's slender waist and guided her onto the terrace, greeting guests as they made their way to the far end of the railing. Away from the music and conversation, they looked down at the beauty of the city they called home. The bay danced, painted in multi-colored lights, breeze cooling their faces.

Grey turned to Sabrina and raised his crystal Baccarat tumbler. "To us. You, me, and Jules. May the new year find us healthy and happy, and all of our needs met."

Sabrina raised her champagne flute. "To us. May we always be as in love as we are tonight and may we raise one helluva girl." Staring into each other's eyes, they drank.

"We thought we might find you lovebirds out here." Jesse and Taylor approached, drinks in hands, smiling. Sabrina moved to hug her brother.

"Oh, Jess! I'm so happy you made it. When we spoke yesterday, I wasn't sure you would."

"Same here. It's a big night for us at the bar, too. But Tom's there and Taylor and I felt it was important to be with our family tonight." Sabrina put her hand in Taylor's and squeezed. He lifted her hand to his lips, kissing it.

"Madame, may I say you are simply ravishing this evening."

"You may, and thank you. You ain't so bad yourself, sir." She stepped back to take in the dapper gentlemen in their silk suits and ties. "You two clean up nicely. Sorry the dress code wasn't your usual board shorts and t-shirt, bro."

Jesse laughed. "No worries. Taylor loves an excuse to dress me up."

"Yes, I do. And you should do it more often. So hot."

"Quite a crowd you guys have here tonight."

Grey nodded. "Agreed. A few more than I expected," he said, raising his eyebrows at his wife.

"What can I say? Once Charlotte and I started making the guest list, we realized how many people whose business and friendship we were grateful for this year. We just couldn't bring ourselves to leave anyone off the list."

"Clients and friends I completely understand. But the mayor of Cutler Bay?"

"He's a hometown friend of Charlotte's and a super nice guy. I'll introduce you to him and his wife. They're lovely people."

"Such a posh affair, sister. Crystal, china, passed hors d'oeuvres and champagne, a whole waitstaff. Your sound system rivals mine at the bar. Are you sure we're related?"

Sabrina rolled her eyes. "Oh, stop it, Jess. You two aren't doing so badly yourselves. Soon to open a second location of Two Dudes and you're finally building the house of your dreams. We couldn't be happier for you."

"The only thing that would make *us* happier is if we could legally get married." Jesse placed his hand on the back of his partner's neck.

Taylor looked away from his love to Sabrina and Grey. Raising his Waterford flute, he toasted. "To the new millennium. May we all be free to be who we are and love who we love in the eyes of the law."

"Hear, hear!" The sound of the clinking glasses was interrupted by the ringtone of Jesse's cell phone.

"I'm sorry, you guys. It's probably Tom at the bar. I'll take it over here," he said as he moved toward the glass doors of the condo. Removing his phone from his breast pocket, he saw the familiar number on the screen.

"Dad. Hey. It's, uh, nice to hear from you. Happy New Year. I'm at Br—"

"Jesse," he said in a choked voice. "It's your mother. You and Sabrina need to come home."

Chapter Twenty-Nine — 1999 — Jack

"Chilly tonight," Jack said, as he added another log and stoked the embers in the fireplace. "Supposed to get down to forty-eight. You want another whiskey? Or maybe some herbal tea instead?"

On the sofa, Marjorie adjusted the hunter green afghan, pulling it closer to her chin over her pajama top. She tinkled the ice in her glass. "Whiskey," she slurred.

Jack nodded, taking her glass to the bar to refill it with a little less of the amber liquid this time.

I'll talk to her about all this drinking tomorrow. Just let her have this one last night. It's New Year's, after all.

He settled into his leather recliner and picked up the remote. "What do you think? Should we watch the Dick Clark special or should we really go crazy and watch the MTV thing? The kids would be so proud."

"Don't talk ta me about the shildren. Nah tonight."

Jack took in a deep breath and slowly let it out. "You're right. Sorry. Hey, it's only 8:00. You wanna play some backgammon? Maybe I'll even let you win." He grinned and took a pull from his beer bottle.

"I'm juss gonna go da bed," Marjorie said, draining her glass. "Wash whatever you want." She struggled to pull herself into a sitting position, allowing the blanket to slip to the hardwood floor. Standing was going to be an issue, much less walking. Jack leapt to his feet, wrapping an arm around her waist and leading her down the hall to their bedroom.

"Honey, can I help you get into some clean pajamas?"

Marjorie sat on the edge of the bed. She raised her unfocused eyes to her husband. "Juss leave me be."

"Okay," Jack sighed. He closed the door quietly behind him. Placing his palm on the wooden door, he whispered, "Sleep peacefully, Marjie."

Flipping through the plethora of New Year's specials on television, Jack tuned them out and began to reminisce. He thought about their children as babies. How each one had its own different personality from the time they opened their eyes. Jesse—so sure of himself, yet so gentle. Always taking care of his sisters. He had truly failed him in not embracing his son for exactly who he was. Sabrina—so driven and independent. Such a kind soul, if a little spoiled, but what a beautiful, successful woman. Kimberly—a lump formed in his throat, emotions filled his eyes—his feisty, fearless smartass. Of the three, she'd always reminded him most of himself. Goddammit, it made no sense. Why wouldn't she have come to him in the end? Why would she take her own life? Had she truly not known how much he loved her? How much they *all* loved her? Who was he kidding? He had failed her, too. He'd chosen Marj over the kids. Once they were out of the house, he focused on his relationship with his wife, because that's what his logical mind told him he should do. His kids would be fine. They were grown, on their own, they didn't need dear old Dad nosing around.

But Marjorie—the news of Kimberly's death four years ago nearly destroyed her. She'd been in a spiral ever since. Nothing helped. Not counseling, not constant love, not visits from Sabrina, nothing. She hadn't worked in nearly three years, quit taking care of the house, then herself. He stood by, helpless, watching his wife gradually become a shell of her former self. A body with no spirit, a dead heart. And it broke his.

Jack blew his nose into a tissue. He raised his bottle. "To my baby girl, Kim. I miss you so much. May you be at peace wherever you are."

After a snack of cheese and crackers, Jack looked at his watch. Nearly 10:00. He should check on Marjorie, give her a kiss, make sure her covers hadn't slipped off in fitful sleep. Opening the bedroom door, he made a mental note to spray some oil on the creaking hinges tomorrow. The room felt cold. He lifted the edge of the down comforter from the foot of the bed and pulled it up over his sleeping wife. As he bent to kiss her in the dark, his nostrils wrinkled at an acrid odor.

Oh, no . . . she's gotten sick in the bed.

Jack moved to turn on the bedside lamp and his toe hit an object on the floor. He picked it up. Her prescription bottle of Ambien. It was empty. *What the hell . . . ?*

"Marj. Marjie, wake up." He shook her shoulder. He leaned over and placed his lips on her forehead. It was cold. Too cold. "MARJORIE, WAKE UP!" he screamed into his wife's face. "Oh, God . . . oh, my God. No, honey, no! Come on, wake up!" Frantic, he grabbed the cordless phone from the nightstand and dialed emergency.

"911, what is your emergency?"

"It's my wife. I think she overdosed on medication. She's very cold."

"Sir, is she breathing?"

"No," he cried.

"Can you detect a pulse in her neck or wrist?"

"NO!"

"Sir, I'm sending an ambulance to your home right now. Please try to stay calm. They will be arriving in a few minutes. Will they be able . . ." Her voice faded from Jack's hearing. He let go of Marjorie's bluish hand and picked up a piece of paper from the nightstand. In barely legible scrawl:

Jack, I love you deeply. Tell them I tried.

Picking up the phone again, he hit speed dial #2.

"Jesse, it's your mother. You and Sabrina need to come home."

Chapter Thirty — 2012 — Julie

Sabrina set the photo down on the table.

"Do you miss her, Aunt Brie?"

"My mother? Yes, honey, sometimes I really do. I miss the woman she used to be. She was so tortured in the end."

"I wish I could have known her."

"Me, too, sweet pea." She took in a breath and blew it out, shoving the memory from the forefront of her mind. "Hey, what do you say we see what else is in the box?"

Julie removed the last thing from the lockbox, a large and heavy journal. It was leather bound and locked as well, but the tiny key dangled from the end of the bookmark ribbon.

Sabrina's hand flew to her face. "Oh my God, there it is. Kimberly's journal! Remember that, Jess?"

"Of course I do. That girl went nowhere without that journal. I didn't realize that's what was in the lockbox all these years. I mean, it looks like a tackle box. For all I knew, she was really into fishing."

Sabrina rolled her eyes. "Really? Come on, brother." She placed her hand on the journal in Julie's lap. "Jules, I'll tell you in all the years we were teenagers, your mom wrote in this journal every single day she could. If anything holds the key to her life, it's this book. But a little word of warning, Kimberly was amazing and I adored my sister, but she was no angel. Some of the things you read in here might be a little much."

Julie looked at her aunt. "I'm not a baby, Aunt Brie. I think I can handle it. You guys mind if I take this in my room?"

***

"Well, this has been quite a night, you guys," Charlotte said. "Brie, if you don't need anything else, I'm going to call it a night. Please keep me posted on any revelations in the Mystery of the Giant Journal, okay?"

Sabrina hugged her tightly. "Good night, my friend. I'm so glad you were here."

Charlotte smiled and wished everyone a good night. "See you at the office on Monday, Grey." He closed the front door behind her and locked it.

"Glad you guys decided to stay the weekend, Jess. It means a lot to Julie having you here," Grey said, once back on the terrace.

"We wouldn't have missed it. I was the keeper of the boxes, after all. I just hope she can handle all of this okay. Pretty heavy stuff." Looking at Taylor standing by the railing, Jesse patted the seat cushion next to him on the loveseat.

"She's a great kid. Wise beyond her years," Sabrina said. "I think she'll be okay. God, it was so good to see Kim again in those photos. Looks like she had a blast with her Navy buddies. I wonder if one of them is Julie's father?"

"She did have a fiancé back in the day, hence the missing ring," Jesse said. "Julie took the letters in her room, but I think it was the JT Allen person in the return addresses. Pretty sure that was the name she mentioned when she stayed with me years ago. Kimberly never said who Julie's father was, but I have a feeling he's the guy."

"You're probably right," Sabrina said. "It broke my heart that she had her baby all alone and never told any of us anything until Julie was nearly six months old. I mean, I know she struggled and Lord knows she was the most private person I've ever known. I can't believe she had cancer and never told us. Our poor sister. She must have been absolutely devastated. Her shoulders so heavy. Things could have been different if she'd come to us sooner. She was a proud woman. She never wanted to rely on anyone else. It took a giant act of courage and humility on her part to ever ask for help. And, no thanks to Mom, I blew it the last time I spoke to her. I've lived with that regret for all these years. I wish I had the opportunity to make it up to her."

"You did, sis," Jesse said. "You took her daughter in and raised her as your own. You afforded Julie a life she would never have been able to have with her mother. Kimberly was a terrific woman but she made some really shitty decisions. You and Grey saved Julie from a lifetime of heartache."

"I know we provided a comfortable home and lifestyle for her, Jess, but that girl has lived with a broken heart her entire life. Nothing I could do would ever take that away."

Taylor said, "Well, maybe that huge journal of Kimberly's holds some answers for Julie. That would be the best birthday gift she could receive—some closure." They all murmured their agreement.

"It's getting late, you guys. I'm gonna turn in," Grey said. He stroked the back of Brie's cropped dark hair.

Grey slipped off his shoes and padded barefoot down the hallway, loafers in hand, toward the primary suite. He closed the door behind him and entered the darkly paneled gentlemen's closet, depositing his shoes on a shelf. Slipping his cell phone out of his pocket, he swiped through his contacts and tapped on the long buried name.

"Because it's her daughter's 18th birthday," he responded to the voice on the phone. "I haven't received anything from you in many years. Did she—" Grey held his breath as he listened. "I see. I think it's time. I'll text you her number." He ended the call. After forwarding a contact card via text, he placed his phone on a shelf and began undressing for bed.

Chapter Thirty-One — 1997 — Allison

A light breeze from the southern side of the Key blew in, fluttering the white sheers in a lazy dance by the open glass doors. Allison slipped her phone into the pocket of her jean shorts and came through the door carrying a newspaper and bucket of shells.

"Mmm, it smells good in here. What are you making?"

"Just a pot of chili and some jalapeño corn bread. Hopefully I have an appetite when it's done. Girl, you run out to get a newspaper every single day. What's so important?"

"The news, Nosy McFlozy. I like to be kept informed."

"Ha! Since when? Oh, never mind. Put the bucket of shells on the porch.We can go through them later. They'll be so pretty inside that table top on the lanai."

"Yeah, they will. And all handpicked by yours truly. No thanks to you, ya slacker."

"If you had any idea how to even boil water, I wouldn't have to toil over the stove every day and I could join you on the beach."

"Oh, kiss my ass, you know I can cook. Like . . . toast, maybe?" They looked at each other and broke up giggling. Allison rubbed the scarf on Kimberly's head and sat down at the white wicker and glass table in the breakfast nook. "How ya feeling today? Seriously."

Kimberly put a hand on her stomach and smiled, half-heartedly. "Today's one of the better days."

"Just think, only one more round of chemo. Maybe this one's the charm, my friend."

"From your lips to God's ears, lady."

***

The previous year, Kimberly had shown up on Allison's doorstep at dawn. She'd collapsed into her best friend spilling the entire, heartbreaking story. She was a broke, single mother who couldn't go back to work because childcare was expensive and impossible with her shifts constantly changing. She had been diagnosed with cervical cancer and could not afford treatment. Her child's father died serving their country, but Kimberly had made a stupid, prideful mistake by not listing him as Julie's father on the birth certificate. She'd felt at the time that her unborn child was the only thing she had in life that was just hers and would not give her JT's name. She couldn't see the point at the time. She just knew her heart would break every time she had to explain why Julie's last name was different from her own. And she had no desire to break his parents' hearts, too. It was best to just keep Julie to herself.

As things became harder and harder, she'd come to a sad realization. Her daughter needed much better than the miserable life Kimberly provided. She'd known her whole life that she didn't deserve good things, and couldn't believe she'd fooled herself into believing that she did. Her plan had been to go to Miami and leave Julie safely with her sister and brother-in-law, as they were wealthy and as of yet unable to have children of their own. She pawned the only thing she had of value, her engagement ring, so she could afford the trip to their home. She had not revealed her diagnosis to anyone because she wanted to be accepted as family, not out of pity. But her sister had turned her down.

Something told her to go to Key West instead. To say goodbye to Allison. So that's why she showed up at dawn, unannounced, and without her daughter.

Allison had taken in the entire story without interruption. When Kimberly completed her tragic tale, Allison said, "Say goodbye? Where are you going?"

Kimberly had looked deep into her friend's eyes, then said, "I'm sorry. I don't know what else to do." She'd reached into her backpack and pulled out a full bottle of a prescribed painkiller. "I was going to—"

"No, ma'am!" Allison said, and took the bottle from Kimberly's hand. "We are gonna figure this shit out." She poked a finger at Kimberly's chest and then at her own. "You. And. Me. I've got you, lady. Don't you ever forget it. You're going to get some sleep and we're going to figure it all out. We will go and get Julie—"

"No!" Kimberly said. "This fucking cancer is gonna kill me. She doesn't need to see me die like that. Let my sister and her husband raise her. She is so tiny, she'll never remember any of the bad stuff where I'm concerned. She'll only know me through photos and memories my family shares. Hopefully, they'll be kind in my death. Maybe they'll even have her call them Mom and Dad and leave me out of her entire story. It's for the best. This is non-negotiable, Alli. Promise me."

Allison had held Kimberly's hands in her own. She'd considered long and hard this plea of her dying friend. This woman who was closer to her than anyone in her life. About the enormous sacrifice she was making for a better life for her daughter. Who was she to deny her? Just as she would never have tried to talk anyone out of putting their child up for adoption, she had no right to interfere with Kimberly's plan for her child now.

"Okay, listen to me. We'll do this your way. But will you promise *me* something? If I arrange it for you, will you please see an oncologist down here? And a therapist?" she said, rattling the prescription bottle.

"Only as long as the money I have lasts. When it's gone, that's it. Here. I don't even want to deal with it." She'd pulled her wallet out of the backpack and given it to Allison. "But I don't see the point. Without JT or Julie, I don't care anymore."

Allison pulled her friend to her, stroking the back of her curly locks with the palm of her hand as tenderly as she could. "I know, grandma," she'd said.

Kimberly kept good on her promise and saw an oncologist. A course of treatment was established and Kimberly began chemotherapy and radiation. She was in therapy twice a week and started on an antidepressant. Slowly, things began to improve. That was fourteen months ago and yet Kimberly still struggled with the insidious enemy ravaging her body.

Allison had never used a dime of Kimberly's money. She'd placed the wallet in a drawer of her nightstand for safekeeping. She'd paid all the medical bills with her savings, and when that ran out, she'd done the only thing she knew to do—she looked in Kimberly's wallet for her family's contact information. Then she took a walk on the beach to collect shells, and called Grey.

"Mr. Hanover, you don't know me, but—"

"Who is this? How did you get this number? It's private."

"I'm Kimberly's best friend, Allison. From the Navy. And I found your number in her wallet. Please don't hang up. I need to tell you what happened the night she left Julie in Jacksonville."

After a lengthy explanation, including Kimberly's resolve and frame of mind, she got to the reason for her call. "And now the course of treatment seems to be working a little. She's making progress. I've depleted my savings, so I'm humbly coming to you to ask for your help in paying her medical bills. I know you don't owe her a thing, but she is Sabrina's sister. And Julie's mother. She needs help and I don't know where else to turn. I should add that she's adamant nobody knows she's here. That she's even alive. Especially Julie. She feels it's much better for her daughter's well-being this way."

"I see," Grey said. "Allow me a few days to think about this. I'll call you back at this number within the week. Goodbye."

Allison closed her phone. She sighed and slumped her shoulders. Shielding her eyes from the sun, she looked up at the sky as if she could find the answers somewhere in the puffy white clouds. She was about to pocket her phone and go back to the house when it rang again, startling her. Grey called back to tell her he was going to help. He wanted her to have all of the bills sent to a PO Box and he would take care of them anonymously. However, she was not to have any contact with him that he didn't initiate.

"It took months for Julie to stop crying for her mother every night. All Sabrina and I want for her is a happy life, and we feel fortunate that we were chosen to provide that for her. It would be too painful and confusing for her to be in touch with Kimberly, not to mention the pain it would cause my wife and her family, so I absolutely agree with Kim's wishes. They believe she's passed on and they've made their peace with that. This agreement stays between you and me, period."

Allison silently mouthed 'thank you, thank you, thank you.'

"I'll handle everything but there is to be no direct contact with me whatsoever, do you understand? I'll reach out to you when necessary and *I'll* decide when this arrangement ends . . . or nature will. Trust that everything will be fine on my end. I give you my word."

"Thank you, sir. I understand and I'm grateful," Allison said. The call ended. Allison pocketed her phone. The breeze from the ocean swept her blonde bangs out of her eyes and she closed them against the wind.

Please forgive me if I've done the wrong thing.

***

At the kitchen table, Allison scanned the newspaper until an article caught her eye.

Wreckage of Missing Boat Washes Up in Saint Augustine - No Bodies Recovered

St. Johns County Sheriff has released a statement regarding the discovery of the wreckage of a fishing boat that washed up in St. Augustine on Tuesday. The boat has been identified as belonging to one of two missing service members from Mayport Naval Base, Petty Officer Second Class Andrew Coleman. It appears to have been destroyed in an explosion. No bodies were recovered in the wreckage. All search and rescue efforts have been called off.

Allison folded the newspaper and placed it on the table. She closed her eyes and drew in a long, slow breath.

"So, when's dinner?"

Chapter Thirty-Two — Julie

Breakfast on Saturday morning was cream cheese stuffed French toast and bacon, at Julie's request. Even Sabrina broke from her normal breakfast of a protein shake to have a few bites of decadence. Julie figured she'd better load up before her day on the beach with her girlfriends. Looking around the table, she smiled. What a lucky girl she was to be surrounded by so much love. Her aunt and uncles had made her birthday fantastic. And now, she had an entire book of her mother's words going all the way back to when she was a little girl. Such a gift. Julie had fallen asleep after reading the first few pages the night before, but intended to dive in as soon as she got into bed tonight.

"Hey, squirt—can I still call you that now that you're all old and everything?" Uncle Jesse asked.

Julie laughed. "I would be utterly heartbroken if you didn't. I wish Grandpa was here. He comes up with the wackiest nicknames for me."

"Yeah, that's kinda how Dad rolls. I'm sure as soon as he gets back from his 'pub tour of Ireland—'" Sabrina said, making air quotes "—that wild horses couldn't keep him away. These roses he sent you are gorgeous." She leaned toward the center of the table to inhale the fragrance of the fluffy Esperanzas. "What time are your friends coming to get you?"

"They said nine, but knowing them it might be ten before they show up. You know how we women love our beauty sleep!"

"Then you ladies must be snoozing all the time because y'all are fabulous," Taylor said.

"Says the most fabulous man I know!" Julie leaned over and kissed her uncle's cheek. She popped a bite of syrup-soaked bacon into her mouth. "Oh, man, this is so delish. Thanks a ton, Aunt Brie."

"No sweat, honey. Whatever the birthday girl wants. Remember—

dinner at Jaya tonight. Reservation's at seven."

"Got it." Julie stood to take her plate to the sink when the back pocket of her frayed denim shorts began to buzz. "Probably Carlee saying they're gonna be late. What'd I tell you guys?" She slipped the phone out of her pocket with her free hand. "That's weird. I don't know this number. Hello? Yes?"

The plate slid from her hand to the floor and shattered.

"Jules!" Sabrina leapt from her chair to pick up the sticky shards. The pale face of her niece as she dropped back into her chair stopped Sabrina cold. "Who is on that phone?" she demanded.

Julie looked at all the faces of her family surrounding her.

"It's my mom . . ."

Chapter Thirty-Three — Kimberly & Allison

Allison took the smartphone from Kimberly's hand and replaced it with a tissue. After a moment, she placed the phone on the wicker nightstand and picked up a tube of mint-orange lip balm. Kimberly was careful not to nudge the oxygen line cannula from under her nose as she dabbed at her spilling eyes. Allison traded the tissue for the tube of balm and Kimberly smoothed it over her lips, composing herself, her head nestled into three down pillows. Tugging on the quilt, Allison pulled it up closer to Kimberly's chin and smoothed back the wispy hair framing her face. She looked into her best friend's eyes with tenderness and silently smiled.

It was a long moment before Kimberly spoke, her voice a mixture of softness and leathery gravel.

"Sixteen years."

"Yes."

"She sounds so grown up."

"Well, she is."

"How long since we saw her last?"

Allison thought for a moment, looking out the bedroom window at the ponytail palms, nudged lazily by the morning breeze.

"If memory serves, the last time you convinced me to make the trip was about six years ago. We watched her softball team take a beating to get knocked out of a tournament, and you wanted so badly—"

"To run into the dugout and hug her and tell her everything was gonna be okay."

"You should have, you know," Allison said.

Kimberly shot her a look, holding Allison's eyes with her own.

"You know better than that, lady."

"Do I? What exactly do I know, Kim? I have never, not once, understood your absolutely pigheaded resolve not to be with your daughter in all of these years."

Kimberly closed her eyes, weary. "Not this again."

"No matter how many ways you try to explain it away, in my mind, it makes zero sense."

Exasperated, Kimberly covered her closed eyes with the palm of her hand and said, "Julie has had a fantastic life with my sister. She's content, loved, wants for nothing. I could never bring myself to take that all away from her."

"Oh, that's rich, considering what you *did* take away from her. How the hell do you know she wants for nothing? Material things, maybe, but what about her mother? Don't you think she wants you? Needs you?"

"Stop, please. I don't have the energy. Leaving her was the best thing I ever did for her."

Allison slowly shook her head. Softly, she said, "How can you say that, grandma?"

"Because I was a piece of shit, okay? A mistake. Useless. Everything I touched turned to garbage. Giving her to Sabrina and Grey to raise was probably the only responsible, intelligent decision I've made in my entire life."

"Choosing to give birth to her after hearing of JT's death was your best decision, Kimberly. If you'd just swallowed your pride and allowed people to help—"

Using all of her strength, Kimberly propped up on one elbow and grabbed Allison's arm.

"I tried! Allison, you know I tried. I had nothing and nobody left."

"You had me."

"I know. And I wasn't even going to come here."

"But then you did."

"I was very sick. I had no idea how much longer . . ." Kimberly lay back down against the pillows, hair damp with perspiration, her breathing labored.

"But the stem cells gave you so much more time. I'm sorry. I shouldn't have brought it all up again," Allison said, crossing the room to pour a cool glass of water for Kimberly from a pitcher near the window. Slices of lemon swirled as she poured, the scent of citrus tangy. Sitting back down on the edge of the bed, she handed Kimberly the glass, turning the bent straw toward her lips.

"Kim, you should know something. After you ended your call with Julie, I texted her our address."

Fear and betrayal crossed Kimberly's face. "I cannot believe you—"

"Because it's time. Way past time. She's an adult now."

"But my family. They'll be furious with me. I can't even imagine what my monster of a mother will have to say."

"That's just something we'll have to face—together. I was complicit in your decision, after all. I have to answer to them, too."

Kimberly's hands shook as she handed the glass back to Allison. Her voice breaking, she asked, "Are they coming?"

Allison shrugged. "I sent the text only a few minutes ago. I haven't heard back. I'd imagine they're processing right now. Despite things you've told me about your past, I believe they're very good people, Kim. They took in your daughter with no questions asked. They honored your wishes and never tried to find you."

"They thought I was dead."

"That's true. But now that they know you're alive—"

"Barely."

Allison sighed and clasped her friend's hand. "I'm sure they'll want to see you. Especially Julie."

"I never should have let you talk me into calling her," Kimberly said, eyes brimming.

"I think they'll surprise you . . . pleasantly."

PART TWO
Sunday

Chapter Thirty-Four — Julie

Sunday, February 13, 2012

 My first entry. I've never kept a diary before. After reading most of my mom's journal last night, I was inspired to get my thoughts and experiences on paper. It was an incredible gift she left me. My head is still spinning from the events of yesterday.

 Let me back up for a second though. I turned 18 two days ago. I was orphaned by my mom and taken in by my aunt & uncle when I was 2. Everyone in our family believed my mom had killed herself. It's a long story that I'll explain later, but we found out yesterday that she's still alive . . . because she called me! She didn't sound all that great. She's very sick. She was diagnosed with cancer before she left me and I guess it's finally taking its toll.

 I'm still trying to wrap my head around the fact that she's alive. And that she never came back for me when she got better. I mean, she must have gotten better if she's still alive all these years later, right? I know there's a long story there and I can't wait to hear it. I need to hear it. I need to see her face to face and listen to what she has to say. I don't know how much time we have left.

 There are so many emotions flowing from my family members right now. It's extremely uncomfortable. Uncle Jesse is seething. Uncle Taylor keeps trying to comfort him and give him space at the same time. Aunt Brie has waves of emotion hitting her every few minutes that range anywhere from tears to anger to disbelief, I guess, because she keeps shaking her head and closing her eyes, sometimes balling her hands into fists, sometimes staring off into the distance. They called Grandpa yesterday to tell him the news and now he's cutting his trip short to get home and see her, too.

 And all of them are worried about me. I can see it in their eyes when they look at me. They're all being so careful, like they're afraid I'm gonna shatter any minute now. Truthfully? I have so many emotions that I'm mostly numb. But if I'm being honest, I'm also kind of excited. Kind of like about to cross a balance beam for the first time or walk a tightrope between two rooftops excited. A mixture of my heart is gonna burst from happiness and I think I'm gonna throw up from nervousness.

Uncle Jesse is about to pull over at Tiny's gas station in Islamorada. I'm gonna jump out with Aunt Brie and buy a Coke. I'll write more later. We're halfway to Key West.

Chapter Thirty-Five — Key West, FL

The Key West Express jet-powered catamaran from Fort Myers Beach glided up to their company dock on the Gulf of Mexico side of the island. Part of the crew leapt out into the damp morning to wrap thick nylon rope around large iron cleats mounted to the dock, taking care not to slip on the damp, paint-chipped wood. The remaining crew handed various sizes of rolling luggage to awaiting passengers who were anxious to get started on their sun-soaked, boozy vacations.

The bearded man slipped on Ray-Ban mirrored aviator sunglasses and maneuvered past the waiting tourists, right hand tight on the leather pack slung across his back. Wordlessly he moved his slim, blue-jeaned body, slicing through the crowd, descending the metal ramp to the island that gonged under each step of his heavy, worn flight deck boots. The warm, humid morning wrapped around him like flannel, causing him to rethink his typical attire.

On the terminal sidewalk, he lit a cigarette and looked out over the choppy Gulf waters. Hard to believe only a thousand miles of deep, blue sea separated him from his former home.

"Sir?" His shielded eyes met with a young islander, one foot in his taxi, the other on the ground, his accent placing him further into the Caribbean than here. "I asked if you need a taxi?"

Shaking his head, he ground the cigarette out in the butt-laden sand of a community ashtray beside his knee.

The islander pointed to the man's feet. "Be careful, sir. Your boots are untied."

He gave a quick, two-finger salute to the driver, tightened his grip on the strap of his backpack, and stepped off the curb. Turning the corner, a blue and white neon sign advertising Bud Light drew his attention. Each of his long strides ended in a scuff, as the heels of his slightly loose boots hit the pavement. Slipping his iPhone from the back pocket of his faded Levi's, he noted the time. 11:29 am.

"It's 5 o'clock somewhere," he mumbled to himself, and proceeded to the open air bar across the street. Weathered wooden pillars, no doors, adorned the facade. A few dedicated imbibers speckled the barstools already in the morning hour. Nazareth's "Love Hurts" piped around them from somewhere inside the dark pub. He emitted a bitter chuckle at the irony.

"Well, that's appropriate," he mumbled again, with a shake of his head. Sliding the pack from his shoulder, he placed it under an empty stool, one booted foot on the rung, one on the floor.

A diminutive, mocha-tanned bartender toweled the space in front of him with a veined, arthritic hand, slapping down a coaster. Her deeply-lined face held friendly eyes the color of the sea behind them, framed by frizzy, blonde hair with mousy, graying roots dusting her bony shoulders. Louie's Watering Hole shouted at him from across the chest of her bright pink tank top.

"What'll it be?" she asked, her voice reminiscent of campfires and gravel roads.

"Bud draft and a shot of Beam," he said, wiping away the sweat beginning to form on his brow.

"Bud Light draft okay?"

"It'll do."

Placing the drinks on the bar in plastic cups, she eyed his jeans and boots.

"Not dressed for the occasion, are ya?"

He tossed the bourbon down his throat, grimacing, and chased it with a long pull of the cold draft. "Apparently not."

"It's a little warm for February. Hope you packed some shorts in that bag."

He lifted his beer in response and turned to face the street. Tourists in sun visors and flip flops buzzed along the sidewalk in lazy patterns, window shopping, swilling beverages and posing for selfies. He sipped his beer and closed his eyes behind his sunglasses, feeling his shoulders relax for the first time in days, morning sunshine warm on his face. He breathed deeply, the briny air soothing—taking him back to the beach he frequented so many years ago with his beautiful girl lying by his side, the call of seagulls surrounding them.

Finishing his drink in one long swallow, he lay a twenty on the bar and bent to scoop up his pack.

"That's all you," he said.

The bartender picked up the bill, sweeping the empty cups into the trash can below the bar. "Thanks, boots. Hey, I didn't catch your name."

"I didn't toss it.

She grinned. "Fair enough. Have a nice stay on our fine island. Come back and see us."

With another two-finger salute, he ambled down the sidewalk toward the historic district, boots scuffing the pavement. Sweat trickling down his back, he made his way down Duval Street toward the Atlantic Ocean. According to Google Maps, his destination was still a number of blocks ahead. Everyone around him was bedecked in island garb or beachwear, feet in sandals, drinks in hand. He knew he stuck out like a sore thumb in this vacation destination. But he couldn't care less. He was no longer concerned about anything or anyone. He came to the island for only one thing—to disappear. And he knew of no better place on earth to do that than Key West.

Chapter Thirty-Six — Julie

We just checked into the hotel, this cute place called Almond Tree Inn right in the center of town. I'm sharing a room with Aunt Brie, since Uncle Grey has a huge case to work on and couldn't make the trip with us. It's really pretty—a little living room, two queen-sized beds, and a huge bathroom with sliding doors. We have a little front porch with a table and chairs and a gate that leads to the pool. I have a feeling we're not spending much time here though. Uncle Jesse says we can walk—it's only a couple of blocks to Catherine Street from here.

We don't know how advanced my mom's cancer is. I feel like we need to get over there as soon as possible. But after I got the text from her friend with their address, Aunt Brie called her back. Allison explained that Mom wasn't up to speaking to anyone else at the moment, but encouraged us to come see her if we could. She said mornings were usually better— that she tires out by evening. It's early afternoon now, so we'll probably wait until tomorrow to go see her.

I don't know if I can take it. I'm a nervous wreck. My hands are sweaty and shaking. My heart is racing. I'm probably having a panic attack. I have no idea what in the world I'm gonna say to her. I keep looking at the photos from the box she left for me for my birthday, but I know she probably won't look like that anymore. It's been many years and she's very sick. I don't want to say the wrong thing and upset her. But I feel like I have every right to tell her exactly how I feel. I'm trying to gather my thoughts but my mind is on overdrive. I'm so angry, so nervous, so anxious.

I'm sitting in the little living room writing in this journal to try to calm down and get ready for them to tell me it's time to go see her. They're outside talking things over. Being her older brother and her younger sister, Uncle Jesse and Aunt Brie have so much they want to say to her and so many questions. Uncle Taylor, Jesse's husband, is totally neutral and playing peacemaker out there. He never met my mom—she disappeared before he had the chance. Normally, I'd be offended to be left out of this conversation, like I'm being treated like a little kid or something, especially since she's my *mother, after all. But right now, I'm grateful for a few minutes alone. I never, ever thought this day would happen, even though I wished for it every single birthday for as long as I can remember.*

I brought my mother's journal. I keep reading passages in it trying to picture her as a younger woman, a teenager, a little girl. Some of the things she wrote remind me so much of me and my friends and things we've done. But some of the things . . . it makes my heart just hurt for all that she went through in her life. And now to be dying?

Ughhh, I get so pissed off thinking I could have known her sooner. I could have had a life with my mom! I know she had her reasons, but I swear, I would never do that to a child of mine. Ever. I mean, don't get me wrong, I've had a really great, nearly perfect life with my aunt and uncle. But I would trade every last moment to have spent it with my mom instead.

Okay, I'm gonna put the pen down now and blow my nose. This was supposed to be calming me down. It's not working.

Chapter Thirty-Seven — Kimberly & Allison

"Do you think you'd like to try to sit outside for a little while?" Allison asked her best friend. "It's warm and breezy out. Might feel good to get a little sun on your skin."

"Yeah, you're probably right," Kimberly said. She pulled the duvet away from her body, her once muscular and curvy figure gaunt under fuzzy pajamas. As she sat up to swing her legs over the side of the bed, Allison stepped closer to offer a hand. Kimberly demurred. "It's okay. I got it. I need to do things by myself while I still can."

"Okay, grandma," Allison said.

"Literally, not ready for the wheelchair yet, lady. I'll take the walker for now. Oh, and no pain meds yet today." Kimberly grinned, bracing herself on the handles of a walker next to the bed, her legs lacking the strength of even one week ago, but they still worked. A small oxygen tank sat on the seat of the walker, a line running to the cannula under her nose. She moved gingerly to her closet, pulling out a creamy linen swing top and loose drawstring capris.

"Good for you, Wonder Woman. I'll leave you to it. Need anything, just holler. I'll make us drinks."

Allison closed Kimberly's bedroom door behind her, bare feet padding across the Spanish tile to the kitchen of the two-bedroom bungalow they'd shared for sixteen years. Regina, the hospice nurse, told them Kimberly had no diet restrictions. A little heartbreaking to hear, as it indicated how close to the end she really was.

No pain meds meant she could have a small cocktail. Allison splashed a tiny bit of Aviation gin over crushed ice in two highball glasses. She added fresh limeade from a pitcher in the refrigerator and stirred, garnishing with a lime wedge and a sprig of fresh mint. Carrying the drinks through the French doors off the breakfast nook, she placed them on a table on the travertine lanai by a small wading pool in the backyard. She checked the thermometer in the pool to make sure the heater was on. Ninety-degree water would be soothing, if Kimberly decided to get in later.

Hearing a noise, she looked up to see her dearest friend moving confidently across the threshold of the doors, a smile on her face, a beautiful scarf of ivory, turquoise, and salmon silk wrapped around her head where her thick, brown curls used to be.

"Oooo, mojitos. Yum."

"Well, Mo-Allisons. Gin's more refreshing than rum, dontcha think? It's a beautiful day. I thought, why not? Look at you, all island chic."

"Just thought I'd be ready in case, you know, Brad Pitt or George Clooney stop by."

"Good thinking." Allison winked, lifting her glass to sip the cool concoction.

"When are they coming?"

"Brad and George? They said they'd pop in for cocktails before dinner. You still have time to get your diamond jewels on."

"My family."

Allison lowered her glass and wiped her lips. "I told them you're at your best in the mornings. I haven't heard from them yet. I promise I'll let you know."

Kimberly nodded and focused on her glass, lifting it to her mouth with both hands.

"Again, I'm sorry, Kim. I should have asked before I sent our address to them. After all this time, it really should have been your decision whether you wanted to see them or not."

Kimberly placed her drink on the table and raised her hand. "No, no. I'm the one that spoke with my daughter and broke that giant block of ice. I'm glad you handed me the phone. I'm just nervous. They all have every right to hate me."

"Listen, I think they're all probably overjoyed that you're still alive—"

"For now."

Allison's lips pursed in a grim line. "Yes, for now. But having believed for so long that you'd taken your own life . . . I can't speak for them, Kim, but I'm guessing this is not only an enormous shock, but a huge relief. Especially for Julie."

"I don't know that I'll ever make her understand."

"I don't believe that's your job right now. I think you just need to love her with all the time you have left."

Chapter Thirty-Eight — Jack

The Dublin Airport was teeming with travelers on an early Saturday evening, but Jack's brain didn't register any of them. He had one thing on his mind—his long-dead daughter, his baby girl, was *alive!* He hadn't been successful in getting a quick flight back to the US. All he could book on such short notice was a pricey KLM flight through Amsterdam, a journey that would take him many hours, but was worth every second—every penny.

A few hours previous, he'd just finished his lunch—shepherd's pie and a Guinness—in The Black Rose pub near Dublin city centre, and stepped out into a cold, gray afternoon, when his phone had rung.

"Sabrina, me dear! Guess where I am right this minute."

"Dad. I have some jarring news. Wherever you are, are you sitting down?"

Jack thought better of reentering the raucous pub. He'd spied a bench a block away and began to weave through the crowded sidewalk toward it.

"Brie, you're scaring me. What's happened?"

"Yesterday was Julie's birthday—"

"Oh, dammit! I completely forgot to call her. I ordered flowers earlier in the week, did she get—"

"Yes, Dad, she got them. They're gorgeous. That's not why I'm calling. A few minutes ago, we were having breakfast when Julie received a call on her cell. From Kim."

"Kim who?"

"Kimberly, Dad. Your daughter. My sister. Julie's mother."

Jack's equilibrium tilted. He fell heavily onto the wrought iron bench. "Sabrina, that's not funny."

"I know it's not. I'm not kidding. She's alive. She's been living in Key West all this time."

"I . . . I don't understand, what the—"

"Look, I know it's hard to wrap your head around. Believe me, we're all in shock. I'll explain more later, but where are you? How soon can you get a flight to Key West? We're heading down there tomorrow morning. Can you meet us? We'll get you a room."

"Of course! I'll get on the internet immediately and book a flight. I'm in Dublin. I'll text you the information as soon as I can."

"Good. Just get here as quickly as possible. She's sick, Dad. Cancer. It's pretty advanced. I don't have any further details."

"I'll be there if I have to move heaven and earth. Sabrina, keep me constantly posted. I'll see you as soon as I can."

Jack sent Sabrina a text once he was seated at the KLM gate.

KLM flight in an hour, thru AMS, connect ATL

Be in KW 5 pm tomorrow.

Best I could do.

Sabrina responded:

No worries, be safe

We'll send a car for you

Call me from AMS

Jack buckled his seat belt. His body was electric with nerves, mind racing. How could this be possible? Did she fake her death? No, if he remembered correctly, they'd all been led to believe she'd committed suicide, but that didn't mean it was a deliberate ruse on Kimberly's part.

He washed his hands over his face. Sixteen years. Had she really been in Key West this entire time? Just a day's drive from his home in Clearwater? Emotions began rapid firing like a Gatling gun. Shock, anger, sadness, elation—but mostly regret. There was so much he'd done wrong back then. For many years, he blamed himself for Kim's death, and then the tragic death of his wife, Marjorie. It had taken a decade of therapy, and reconnection with his children, to make it possible for him to move on, leaving the misplaced guilt behind.

Although it had been many years since Jack had touched the hard stuff, he asked the flight attendant for a tiny bottle of Crown Royal and a glass of ice. These were going to be the longest thirty hours of his life.

Chapter Thirty-Nine — Key West

After a half hour's walk that felt like much longer in the heat, the man in Ray-Bans finally arrived at his destination. Located on the Atlantic Ocean near the point furthest south in the United States was the magnificent, historic Southernmost House, a Queen Anne Victorian-style mansion. Built in 1897, the mansion had hosted five US Presidents and numerous celebrities and dignitaries throughout the previous century, and had even installed a speakeasy during Prohibition and a nightclub in the 1940's. A private residence for many years afterward, Southernmost House was currently operating as an eighteen-room bed and breakfast, with a five-room detached guest house for long-term rental, affording the most privacy. Exactly what the man wanted.

Ascending the wide, tiled front steps of the mansion's enormous porch, he took in the oversized wicker chairs under ceiling fans, blades moving in a slow spin—quintessential Key West. He entered the foyer through large walnut and glass doors and approached the desk.

"Hello, sir, and welcome to Southernmost House. How may I help you today?" asked the perky front desk clerk, her dark, high ponytail swinging with enthusiasm.

Placing his pack on the ground and removing his wallet from his back pocket, he lay his credit card and driver's license on the counter.

"I have a reservation. Name's Allen, two L's, one E. Jason Allen."

Typing swiftly on her computer, the clerk, whose name tag read "Daisy," pulled up his information.

"Yes, here you are, sir. I see you've reserved our Lopez House for one month, is that correct?" He nodded. "Wonderful. It's a spectacular space with a private entrance and beautiful views. The room requires a fifty-percent deposit, that I see we've already collected, so you're all set."

"I'll be paying in cash when I check out."

"Of course! That's fine. We won't charge your card, just need it for security. Give me a moment to scan these cards, then I'll show you to the house. Meanwhile, may I offer you a welcome beverage? Champagne, wine, a cold beer?"

"A beer would be great, miss."

"Absolutely!" Turning, Daisy said, "Teddy, please fetch Mr. Allen a cold beer."

"Coming right up, sir," Teddy said.

Daisy scanned the key card and opened the door of the guest house. Bright, natural light poured through French doors and many windows. Various patterns of Cuban tile adorned the floors of each room. Four-poster beds were plush and inviting. He would be comfortable here.

"Catered breakfast is served each morning in the main house. If you need anything at all, please don't hesitate to allow us to accommodate you. I hope you'll enjoy your stay, Mr. Allen. Here are your keys."

"JT, please. Thanks, uh, Daisy. Much obliged." She closed the door softly as she left the room. "Shower and a nap," he said to the empty room. He sat down on the king-sized bed, testing the firmness. Then lay back, his head in the center of the bed. And, in moments, fell fast asleep.

Chapter Forty — Julie

Just like I thought, we won't be going over to see my mom tonight. Grandpa's flight from Ireland gets in soon. I guess Aunt Brie told him she would send a car to pick him up, but Uncle Jesse says he needs to get out of here for a minute, so he's going to pick him up. Uncle Taylor and I are on the internet checking out restaurants for dinner, although I don't think anyone has much of an appetite tonight. Aunt Brie just said, "As long as they have wine . . ." So, it looks like we'll probably try a little Italian place that's around the corner from the hotel. Uncle Taylor has excellent taste in restaurants, so I'm sure we'll enjoy it as much as we can, all things considered.

I have no memories of my mother that don't come from photographs. Maybe when I see her tomorrow, it'll jar something loose. I hope so. I'd love to remember anything at all from the time I was with her. I was reading a little more of her journal today. Sounds like she and my grandmother didn't get along. At. All. From the sound of it, Grandma wasn't a very nice person. I've been told she had a miserable childhood and took it out on everyone around her. Makes me so sad. I wish I could have known her, too. I've seen a few photos of her with me when I was really small, like shortly after I came to live in Miami. She was like a blonde version of Aunt Brie, only not as thin. She had kind of a puffy face, but pretty blue eyes. I've tried to pull up any memories of her that might be lodged in my brain, but I can't. I was just too little. All I know is she wasn't close to any of her kids. It's tragic.

Having grown up without my mom, I've always known in the back of my mind that life is very short. You never know if tomorrow is gonna come, so people should always try to let bygones be bygones, agree to disagree, kiss and make up, pick your metaphor. Staying angry and apart, especially with family members, is a giant waste of precious time and doesn't serve anyone. Maybe I'm just super positive, or super naïve, but I feel like there can never be an issue so big that it's completely unforgivable. Human nature is far from perfect. People say and do things when they're hurt that they regret. It would serve us all so much better if we could take a breath and forgive, or apologize. Aunt Brie says I'm gonna change the world some day. Uncle Grey tells me never to pursue politics—that it will ruin my giant heart. But I don't know about that. Our current president has a giant heart and he seems to be handling things okay. Of course, I think his wife and two little girls keep him grounded.

Anyway, I just know that I want to help people. I'm thinking of going into medicine. I'm kind of a math and science geek. I've applied to six colleges and I'm just waiting to hear back. My dream school would be any of the ones in Boston. I love it there—it's one of my favorite cities ever. I've applied to Boston College, Northeastern, and Wellesley. Fingers crossed! I've also applied at University of Miami (Uncle Grey's alma mater—he calls it The U), Duke University, and Georgetown in Washington DC.

But since this is for my eyes only and I can be perfectly honest . . . I'm thinking of taking a year off before I go to school. I want to travel without my aunt and uncle. I love them, but I'm an adult now. It's time to get some stamps on my passport by myself. I've also been doing a lot of reading about underprivileged parts of the world. They need our help. There are so many organizations I can join to go and lend a hand. And I would learn so much! I know if I bring it up to Aunt Brie and Uncle Grey, they'll just discourage me and tell me to wait until after undergrad. I've heard the argument before that if I lose academic momentum now, I may never go to school. Which I happen to think is ridiculous. I mean, shouldn't I know how my own brain works? Uncle Grey is a lawyer and he appreciates preparation and facts. I'm gonna do all the research and put my case together before I approach them.

But before I do anything, I'm going to meet my mother.

Chapter Forty-One — Kimberly & Allison

Having finished a steaming bowl of Allison's homemade vegetable soup, and even a piece of avocado toast, Kimberly pushed back from the table in their breakfast nook.

"Well, lady, you outdid yourself this time."

"The secrets are my homegrown tomatoes and herbs. One of the best things I ever did was start those giant pots out back."

Kimberly chuckled. "Remember when you couldn't even boil water? You've come a long way, sister."

"If I'd known all those years how much I was going to enjoy cooking, I'd have started a long time ago."

Kimberly looked deadpan at Allison. "Yeah . . . no, you wouldn't've."

Allison laughed. "You're right. I mean, I had *you* spoiling me all those years."

"And I barely knew my way around a kitchen. Thank the stars for cookbooks."

Looking at the clock on the stove, Allison said, "It's five o'clock. How's your energy level? Feel like taking a stroll on the beach?"

"I feel really good tonight, honestly. Must be that secret soup. Let's go see Dustin and Geno at Grand Vin."

Allison's face broke into a wide grin. "Seriously? You surprise me, grandma. I need to make that soup more often."

"Well, I don't want to waste this beautiful outfit since Brad and George stood us up. Besides, it'll be good to see the boys."

"Grand Vin it is. I'll go get your shoes."

***

The wine bar was a quick two blocks walk away from their house, but they took it at Kimberly's walker pace. Located in a two-story island-style home on Duval Street, complete with wrap-around porches and outdoor seating, it was a tourist draw. But locals ventured in, as well, to enjoy the hilarious and entertaining hospitality of the owners, Geno and Dustin, a married couple transplanted from Chicago. But more than just selling wine to patrons, the men were well-respected for their community involvement. They were devoted volunteers of Equality Florida, the largest civil rights organization dedicated to securing full equality for Florida's LGBTQ community, and were known for truly living the Key West motto—One Human Family. It was a tight knit community and they took care of any islanders who needed help, day or night, without question. Allison and Kimberly met the couple shortly after their migration to the island and they'd been dear friends ever since. When Kimberly's cancer came screaming back, Dustin and Geno stepped up instantly, rallying the community to hold fundraisers, coordinating meals to be brought during treatment, anything they needed. Allison and Kimberly were beyond grateful for the couple.

As the women slowly took the stairs—Kimberly holding the railing, Allison holding her small oxygen tank—Dustin rushed out of the front door to assist.

"Kimmy! Oh my goddess, where have you been? This place just does not sparkle and shine without you, darling. Here, take ahold of me, precious." Kimberly leaned in to kiss Dustin's cheek and wrapped her arm through his.

"Well, hi there, handsome. Long time."

"Allison, my love, hand me that oxygen bottle. Come on over here, girls, your chariot awaits." Dustin led them to a large table outside at the far end of the lower porch. He got Kimberly settled and stood across from them. "It's a beautiful night made gorgeous by the two of you. What can I bring you tonight?"

"How about a bottle of that delicious Sancerre you introduced us to? We'll cork whatever we can't handle." Allison winked at Kimberly.

"And a glass of water, please, Dustin?" Kimberly said.

The night was like velvet—the air soft and rich, the lights on Duval

Street glowing golden as the sun began its descent in the western sky.

Geno emerged from inside the bar carrying a platter of cheese and crackers and Kimberly's water.

"How delightful! Two of my favorite women have come to grace us with their beauty on a Sunday night. Snacks on the house, ladies." He leaned in to kiss their cheeks and took Kimberly's hand. "Kim, you look ravishing. How are you feeling tonight?"

"Better than usual, honestly. I don't know what's gotten into me, but I have the energy of a teenager."

"Wonderful! And the pain?"

"Manageable."

"Marvelous. Here's Dustin with your crisp, luscious Sancerre. We have a large party inside, but we'll be back out to check on you in the shake of a lamb's tail. *Ya mas!*"

"Cheers back atcha," Allison said, lifting her glass. She sipped the cool wine and sighed. "It really is a nice evening. I'm so glad you're feeling up to venturing out. Here's to you, grandma. May you have many more of these evenings."

Kimberly touched her glass to Allison's with a ting. "Hear, hear. To many more."

They sat in silky silence, the night warm and breezy around them, watching tourists and locals move along the sidewalks, holding hands, pointing into store windows, downing preposterously large cocktails. Normally a cacophony of noise and activity, Duval Street was relatively tranquil for the moment. A slight melancholy spread through Kimberly's soul. She would miss this.

"Oh, I forgot to tell you. I ran into Kat from the DAS at the grocery store. They really miss you there."

Before illness had taken its latest aggressive turn, Kimberly had been an advocate at the Domestic Abuse Shelters in Key West and Marathon. She counseled and advocated for survivors of abuse, working full time, sometimes twenty-four hour stretches. It was her passion. Those women were kindred spirits and had her heart.

"I miss them all, too. Especially Kat. I need to give her a call . . ."

***

"Hey there. First day?"

Kimberly looked up from the bench in the lobby of DAS, where she was waiting to be welcomed by HR with lots of paperwork and, hopefully, training. It was 2002—not quite a year after the US had been attacked on September 11, 2001. She knew two things—she'd been given a new lease on life with the miracle stem cell treatment she'd received, and that she was meant to give back, to pay it forward. Her heart led her to apply as an advocate for the abused, but her brain kept telling her she was terribly unqualified. All she really had going for her was a heart full of empathy and a strong desire to make things better for those who'd been wronged. Not to mention, she was one of them—a survivor of abuse. In her case, sexual assault at the hands of fellow sailors in her Navy squadron. She'd hoped it was enough. The interview had gone really well. Kimberly had told her story, warts and all, and the director was enthusiastic about her addition to the team. It felt good that someone had confidence in her ability to be an asset—to possibly make a difference.

She was met with the bright smile and laughing hazel grey eyes of a busty brunette in jeans, a v-neck t-shirt, and motorcycle boots. When she offered her hand to shake, Kimberly noticed beautifully colored tattoos painting the landscapes of her arms.

"I'm Kat. Well, Katherine, but only my mother gets away with calling me that."

"Kimberly. My friends call me Kim."

"Well, Kim, I believe we'll be friends from now on. Follow me. I've been assigned to mentor you for a few weeks. First things first—do you drink coffee?"

"I do."

"Good woman. Let's grab a cup. And, second, let's go to HR and get your credentials. This building is kept secret. We have precious lives to protect. We don't advertise its location at all. The only way in and around here is with your ID. Keep it on you at all times."

"Got it." Kimberly liked the sound of this place already. They took very seriously their mission to serve and protect the women and children that came to be in their care. She knew she'd made the right decision in coming here . . . on so many levels.

A few weeks into training, Kat invited Kimberly to dinner at her place.

"Don't get the wrong idea, I have a partner. And your significant other is more than welcome to join us. I just think it would strengthen our work relationship to get to know each other on a personal level—to share our stories. If you're uncomfortable with the invitation, say the word. No offense will be taken, I promise."

"I'd be honored to come, Kat. Thanks for asking. I don't have a romantic partner—I live with my best friend. But I think I'll come alone, if that's okay? She's pretty busy and pinning down a free evening in her schedule might be difficult."

"Sounds good. I'm glad you're coming. Here's the address and I've written the directions from here. Tomorrow night, say, around seven?"

Kimberly arrived at an unassuming duplex in Marathon with a bottle of cabernet and ten minutes to spare. Her tires crunched in the shell driveway as she pulled up next to a gorgeous pair of Harley-Davidson motorcycles.

"Right on time," Kat said, meeting her in the driveway. "Come on in, girl. Hope you like gumbo." Kimberly followed her coworker into a cozy living room with velvety, overstuffed, chocolate brown sofas and numerous lush green plants. The heady aroma of thick Cajun soup made her mouth water.

"Mmm, I *love* gumbo. Do you use chicken, sausage, or shellfish?"

"Yes," came the smiling response from the woman coming from the kitchen, wiping her hands on a towel. She tucked the towel in the back pocket of her jean shorts and held out her hand.

"Kim, meet my queen, Luci. My love, this is Kim, my new coworker."

Luci's long, thick curls were swept into a ponytail that ran down her back, her caramel skin smooth and, unlike her partner, unadorned. Her bright green eyes twinkled as she shook Kim's hand.

"We're so happy you could make it, Kim. Hope you're hungry. Can I take the wine?"

Kimberly looked at the bottle as though seeing it for the first time. "Oh, yes! Sorry. Yes, here you go. I don't know if cab goes with gumbo."

"Honey, *everything* goes with gumbo. And to answer your question, I use all three—chicken, andouille, and shrimp. And there's a little kick of fire, if you can handle it." Kimberly detected a Louisiana twang to her accent.

"Oh, absolutely. Are you from New Orleans? I lived in Houston when I was younger and your accent sounds familiar."

"Born and bred, sister. Good ear. Dinner'll be ready in about 20 minutes. Y'all visit."

"Kim, how about I open the wine with dinner," Kat offered. "Meantime, what can I get you to drink?"

Kimberly looked at the bottle in Kat's hand. "Whatever you're having sounds great."

"Miller High Life it is. Have a seat." Kimberly sank into one of the sofas, immediately feeling at home. Kat handed her a cold longneck, taking a seat on the opposite couch.

"Director mentioned you're a survivor. Same here. Want to talk about it?"

Kimberly took a long draw from the bottle and swallowed. "Yeah. Military sexual assault. I was in the Navy."

"Marine Corps here. Someone you worked with?"

"Yep. Drugged my drink and took photos of me 'performing' oral sex," Kimberly said, using air quotes. "No memory of it, small mercy, and nothing happened to him. I requested a transfer but wound up taking an early out instead."

Kat held Kimberly's eyes with her own. "I'm so very sorry that happened to you, Kim. So sorry."

"Thanks. I mean it. Do you want to talk about what happened to you? Someone you worked with, too?"

Swallowing her beer, Kat said, "Mhmm." She set her bottle on the coffee table. "Yeah, I was getting harassed by some redneck assholes at a barracks party. I wasn't out then—don't ask, don't tell, right? The guys couldn't appreciate that I wasn't charmed by their pathetic come-ons. I just wanted to hang out, have a few drinks, be sociable. I'd only been at my command a few months. The more they drank, the more obnoxious they became, until one of them went too far and ripped the necklace I was wearing right off my neck. His drunk ass claimed it looked like a microphone and he accused me of being undercover NCIS."

Kat rolled her eyes, picked up her beer, took a pull, and went on. "So this 'knight in shining armor' sergeant comes to my rescue. Says it's not safe for me in the barracks. Says he has an apartment off base and he'll get me out of here. For my safety, of course. Classic 'don't let 'em take you to another location' scenario. Only, I'm so rattled by the whole thing, and just buzzed enough to be irrational, that I agree and go with him. He stops for more beer on the way, telling me to drink more, that it'll calm me down."

She snorts out a bitter laugh. "I mean, I was eighteen, fresh out of my parents' house in New Jersey. I was so gullible. I passed out cold on his couch and came to in the middle of the night with my sweatpants down around my ankles and him inside me. I thought it was a dream at first. When I realized what was happening, I shoved him off of me as hard as I could, screaming. I think he was shocked that I woke up and interrupted him. He scrambled for his clothes and told me he would take me home. But I ran out of there and called a cab from a payphone on the corner."

"Oh, god, Kat . . . I'm so sorry. That's horrible."

"Yeah, thanks. I guess I was lucky that he wasn't violent with me. I didn't know anyone well enough to trust them with what had happened so I called my recruiter back in Jersey. He said he would advise me to put in for leave and get away from there as soon as possible. To let things blow over. Because, in his words, the asshole outranked me by many stripes and nobody was gonna believe me over him. He said I didn't want to put myself through a he said/she said scenario. That any defense JAG officer would rake me over the coals. I'd gone to the guy's apartment willingly. I had a lot of alcohol in my system. So, not knowing any better, I did what the recruiter told me to."

Kim closed her eyes, nodding. She understood completely.

"What he *should* have advised me to do was get my ass to the base hospital immediately for a rape kit. To ask the medical personnel to call the MP's. To file charges against that prick. But things were so much different back then. It was the early '90's. There were very few enlisted women in the Marine Corps and we still weren't allowed to serve on combatant ships."

"I remember," Kimberly said.

Kat drained her bottle, setting the empty on the coffee table. "So, I told myself if I couldn't make things better for women in the military, the next best thing I could do is work for a shelter. To do the *right* thing for women who are abused. I've been at DAS for years and I don't intend to ever do anything else."

"Thank you for trusting me with your story, Kat."

"Kindred spirits, girl. We only have each other, right? Now, let's go dig into my woman's amazing grub. You'll be so happy you came on gumbo night."

***

Allison leveled her gaze, meeting Kimberly's eyes.

"Everything okay, grandma?"

Kimberly nodded. "Mm. Just lost in thought."

"How're you feeling about tomorrow? Seriously."

"Mixed."

"I get it."

"Part of me is so excited to see everyone, I feel like I could soar into the sky. Most of me is nervous as hell. I'm steeling myself for what they might say. Preparing to just take it, whatever comes my way. I deserve it."

Allison took her friend's hand and held it tightly.

"I completely understand. I'll be there. I've got you."

Kimberly squeezed her friend's hand gratefully. "Thank you, lady. I honestly have no idea what I would have done without you."

"You'll never have to find out."

Kimberly dropped Allison's hand suddenly, fingers flying to her mouth. Her eyes grew large. She gasped.

"What? Kim, what is it? You okay?"

"I think I'm delirious. I know I'm seeing things. No more wine for me, Alli, let's just cork it and go home."

Allison swiveled her head trying to see what had Kimberly so spooked.

"What in the hell did I just miss?"

"It's insane. I almost don't want to say it out loud. I think I just saw JT."

Chapter Forty-Two — Jack

Drained from a long layover in Amsterdam, Jack slept nearly the entire ten-hour flight to Atlanta. Between nerves and alcohol and not enough food, by the time he buckled into his business class seat, he was as wobbly as a wet noodle. As soon as the plane was airborne, he tipped back his seat and dropped into dreamless sleep.

As the lights came on in the cabin and flight attendants announced the arrival back in the States, Jack opened his eyes and stretched. He needed a giant bottle of water and a toothbrush. Quickly, he freshened up in the lavatory and took his seat again. Just a two-hour stop in Atlanta then he'd be on his way to Key West.

Kimberly.

He still couldn't believe it.
The phone conversation he'd had with Sabrina from the Amsterdam Schiphol Airport had been brief. She'd told him all she knew—that Julie's phone rang at breakfast yesterday morning and it was Kimberly, she told Julie she'd been living in Key West and that she was now grievously ill with advanced, aggressive cancer, that she was sorry she hadn't contacted her all these years, that she hoped Julie would forgive her and that she felt she had made the best decision she could have in order for Julie to have a good life. Julie had been in shock during the call and was merely able to say "uh huh" a lot, tears streaming as soon as they hung up. The call had been short—Brie said five minutes or so—then the text came with the address. Brie had grabbed the phone from Julie and called back but it was Kim's friend, Allison, who answered. She'd demanded to speak to her sister, but Allison said she wasn't up to it. She suggested they come to Key West to see Kim and say goodbye, since time was not on her side. After making plans for the trip, Brie had called Jack and told him the news.

It had only been yesterday, but it felt like a week ago. Despite sleeping on the plane, Jack didn't feel rested. He was a giant swirl of emotion. He needed to see his daughter with his own eyes in order to accept that it was truly her. Because he simply couldn't wrap his head around the fact that she wouldn't have been in touch with her family, especially her daughter, in sixteen years.

Jack bought a chicken sandwich and a Coke at a kiosk and found a seat in the terminal near the gate to his final flight. While he ate, memories came to him like an old movie reel—bringing newborn Kimberly Marie home from St. Anthony's Hospital in St. Petersburg, baby Kimmy crawling on the braided rug in the living room, toddler Kimmy chasing Spooky the black lab in the backyard, the time Kim missed her own birthday party because Marj grounded her, teaching Kim and Jesse how to water ski during spring break at Fort DeSoto Park, teenage Kim brooding after the family's big move to Texas, the pride in her eyes when she restored her little blue pickup truck, her shame after screwing up a summer job in Arizona after only a week, her steely resolve when she left for the Navy, her contrition when she showed up on their Clearwater doorstep with a six-month old baby and no husband . . . sadly that's where the memories ended. Jack winced with regret.

***

On a hot, sticky Saturday evening in mid-August, Jack and Marjorie sat under whirring ceiling fans on their lanai, smoking cigarettes and enjoying after-dinner cocktails. They were discussing the MLB players' strike and whether or not they believed President Clinton was innocent of the sexual harassment accusations when he'd been governor of Arkansas, when Jack heard the doorbell.

"Who in the world would that be?" Marjorie asked.

Jack put out his cigarette and set down the tumbler of bourbon.

"No idea, but I'm about to find out."

He opened the door to see his middle child for the first time in ten years (had it really been that long?) holding a carseat carrier with a sleeping baby inside.

Jack looked from Kim's face to the face of the beautiful child, her blonde curls plastered to her forehead and cheek in the sweat of sleep.

"Dad?" Kim said, as tears rolled down her thin face.

Jack took the carrier from her hands and gently lay the snoozing baby on the foyer tile. He wrapped his arms tightly around his daughter and pulled her into the house, joining her in a tear or two.

"Oh, Kim," he said into her ear. "What took you so long?"

"What the hell are *you* doing here?" Marjorie said from the living room, hands on hips, a slight liquor sway. "Let me guess. Need money?"

"Marj!" Jack admonished.

"No, Dad, it's okay. Hi, Mom. I came to introduce you to your granddaughter."

"Oh, well, that's nice. Got out of the Navy, got knocked up, and I don't see a ring. Perfect, Kimberly. We're so proud."

"Marjorie, that's enough."

Marjorie turned unsteadily on her heel and shuffled back to the lanai.

"Kim, I'm sorry. Let's go talk in the living room. Are you hungry?" Kimberly lifted the car carrier and shook her head. She followed her dad to the sofa, setting the baby between them.

"She's beautiful, hon. What's her name?"

"Juliana Susanne. I call her Julie. She was born in February. Nine pounds. Biggest baby born in that hospital the entire weekend. She's an absolute angel, Dad."

"She sure looks like it." He tenderly smoothed the ringlets from her face and whispered, "Hi there, little nugget. I'm your grandpa. And I already love you so much."

Kimberly wiped a tear with the back of her hand.

"She's never gonna change, is she, Dad?"

Jack looked toward the lanai then back at his daughter.

"She doesn't mean it, Kim. Her reactions are . . . they come from a place of pain."

"Did you ever get her into counseling?"

"Honestly, she's been better since all of you kids moved out. I hate to say that, but it's true. Things have been okay here."

"Why doesn't that surprise me? It was always us. We were the source of all her anger."

"No, I promise, you kids aren't the source. You're just the target."

Kim stood to leave. "Well, I tried. I'm done here. If you want to see me and Julie, we're living in Jacksonville."

Jack pulled his wallet from his back pocket. Taking out a folded receipt, he grabbed a pencil lying on top of a crossword puzzle book on the end table.

"Here, write down your address and phone number for me. And, please, don't go yet. Spend the night. It's a long drive back there. I'll deal with your mother."

"Thanks, but no thanks. I don't want to stay under the same roof as her. She's a monster."

"Kim, she's really not. If you could only see—"

"Dad, I'm not the one who needs to see anything. You are." She scrawled her address information quickly and lifted the carrier from the sofa. "I don't have a phone right now. I'll let you know when I do. This was a mistake, coming here. I miss you, but I'm not doing this with her. I may be broke and an unwed mother, but at least I have self-respect."

Jack followed Kimberly to her Corolla sitting in his driveway. He pulled all the bills from his wallet and tucked them beside Julie in the carrier. "It's not much, a couple hundred bucks, but hopefully it'll help. Please think twice about leaving right now."

Kimberly looked into Jack's eyes, hoping for some glimmer of resignation, some flicker of agreement and understanding.

"Kim, honey, I'm all she has. I made her a promise." Kimberly shook her head and sighed, averting her eyes.

After buckling the carrier into the passenger seat facing backward, she kissed her father for the last time. If he'd known, if he'd only had some kind of crystal ball moment, he would have held her tight, memorized her face, not let her go.

***

Even now, these many years later, Jack felt the sting of shame burn his neck and face. He should have stood up to his wife. He should have insisted Kimberly and the baby stay. The regret of his failure to take care of his daughter and granddaughter in that moment still haunted him. For this, and so many other reasons, he owed Kimberly an apology. And tomorrow morning, by some strange stroke of fate, or luck, or kismet, or whatever it was, he finally had the opportunity to give it to her.

Chapter Forty-Three — JT

He awoke with a start on the unfamiliar bed. Feet still on the floor, lying on his back. His body rebelled as he sat up, wanting to stay in the reclining position.

"How long was I out?" he wondered aloud, pulling out his phone. 5:02 pm. "Okay, now I really need that shower. Then food."

Hot water melted his stiff muscles. As he wrapped a towel around his waist, his stomach began to growl. He couldn't recall the last time he'd eaten. Nabbing a snack bag of pretzels from the mini-bar *(that'll probably cost me five bucks)*, he scarfed them down, attempting to appease the hunger pangs.

Dressed a bit more appropriately for the tropical climate, he wore a t-shirt and jeans, but chose sneakers instead of boots, untied, naturally. He was going to have to do some shopping. After food.

Approaching the front desk, he saw the young man from earlier behind the counter.

"Evening, Teddy."

"Good evening, sir. How may I help you?"

"I need a dinner suggestion. Something close. With big portions."

Teddy smiled. "I have the perfect place for you. Head toward the Gulf on Duval. In a couple of blocks on your right, there're steps leading up to a courtyard of shops. Back in there, you'll find The Pasta Garden. Authentic, New York-style Italian food with big portions and a really friendly staff."

"That'll work. Thanks, Teddy."

"Absolutely, sir. Enjoy!"

JT tapped the brim of his ball cap and donned his Ray-Bans. He crossed the street, a big bowl of pasta and a beer on his mind.

Even on a Sunday night, the sidewalks were filled with tourists, but it was a subdued crowd. JT could only imagine what a Friday or Saturday night was like around here. Surely, it would be easy to lose himself in the throngs. He passed a sunny yellow eatery called Banana Cafe, La Te Da Bar and Restaurant (*great name*), The Rum Bar, and Grand Vin Wine Bar. No shortage of places to have a meal and drink the night away. And he was only a couple of blocks down the street. Overheated and exhausted earlier in the day, the majority of Duval Street had been a blur when he'd first walked to the inn. If he had enough energy tonight after his meal, he was going to explore the rest of the thoroughfare. Maybe double back and have a cocktail at The Rum Bar. He had nowhere to be and nobody to answer to.

He smiled to himself and pulled the bill of his cap lower. It was not going to be difficult at all to disappear on this island.

JT asked to be seated at an outside table on the furthest end of the patio. The weather had cooled a bit as the sun went down and the evening air was comforting. He ordered a bowl of spaghetti and meatballs, garlic bread, and the largest draft beer they could bring. Off the beaten path in the courtyard of shops and restaurants, he couldn't do much people watching. Most of the patio tables were occupied in the pleasant weather. He savored the cold Peroni draft and took note of the other diners. A man and woman with silver hair were having pre-dinner cocktails and salads, a giggling Latino couple fed each other steamed mussels, a party of five—a teenage girl babbled like a brook to a middle-aged gentleman with salt and pepper hair (*probably her grandfather*), who appeared enraptured; a slender, dark-haired woman pulled on a cardigan, sipping a glass of red wine; two men—one Black, one white—held hands, matching wedding bands, quietly listening to the girl. That wasn't something a native Texan saw every day.

Good for them. Live and let live. Freedom is one of the reasons I served my country.

With a steaming bowl of pasta and a fresh brew placed in front of him, JT tucked in and allowed his mind to roam. The last time he'd had pasta this good was in the Med.

***

In early 1996, the destroyer to which JT's Navy helicopter squadron deployment was attached had docked in Naples on its way back to the US. He'd been separated from his squadron for nearly three years on military humanitarian missions—first to the Bosnian War, then to the civil war in Somalia. Early into his time in Bosnia, he'd come highly recommended and had been selected to maintain the helos for a special ops det. Exceptionally skilled and on top secret orders, he was reassigned from his squadron to an outfit of Navy SEALS, charged with maintaining both of their Sikorsky H-60's. Civilian communication was prohibited in or out of the secure camps and there was no such thing as downtime.

Three years was a very long time.

JT had been both war weary and anxious to get back to the States—back to his fiancée, the most amazing woman he'd ever known. That is, if she would still have him. He'd been completely unable to contact her. He couldn't send mail. They couldn't make phone calls. He may as well have been on Mars all those years. He knew that she understood deployments, having been stationed in the Navy with him. But she didn't understand top secret missions, being detached from your squadron for years, being unable to send or receive mail, call home, not even a Red Cross telegram was allowed, unless it had been a dire emergency. He could only hope that no news was good news.

Docked in Naples, JT had left the ship as soon as the gangway was in place and sailors were secured for shore leave. The aromas from the port in Naples cascaded over him like a waterfall. Coffee, garlic, baked goods, cigars, wine . . . he couldn't wait to indulge all of his senses. But priority one was finding a payphone and using the calling card he'd purchased onboard the ship.

JT had asked the international operator five times to please check the number he'd given her and please try again. Every single time, she'd said the number was disconnected. He was heartbroken. Maybe she'd run out of money or maybe she'd moved. Either way, he'd known one thing for sure—she'd given up on him. And he couldn't fault her. But, by God, he was gonna fight for her. As soon as he got home, he was going to find her and beg her to take him back. He'd found her once before. He would find her again. And he wasn't going to take no for an answer.

Kimberly. His Kimberly.

When he'd finally made it back to Mayport and was secured for leave from the squadron, it was late February. He'd snagged his truck keys from the LPO, cursing *loudly* when the truck groaned and sputtered before the engine roared to life, and drove like a bat out of hell to Kimberly's tiny apartment in a rundown brick building on the north side of Jacksonville. He'd bounded the wrought iron stairs two at a time and banged on the door. Again. And again. He'd tried to peer through the windows, but couldn't see past the vinyl mini-blinds. He'd been about to sit down on the walk in front of her door and camp out until she came home, when an older gentleman came up the stairs.

"Help you, *señor*?"

"I'm looking for someone who lives here. Or at least I think she still does. Kimberly Stevens?"

The look on the old man's face told a different story.

"I'm sorry to tell you this, but she's gone. She left a few weeks ago. Who did you say you are?"

A few weeks??

JT met the man on the staircase and offered his hand. "JT Allen. I'm her . . . friend. From the Navy. Do you happen to know where she went?"

"Juan García. Nice to meet you. I'm sorry. I can't offer you any information."

JT hung his head, sighing deeply. "Thanks for your time, sir. Much obliged."

He descended the stairs, footsteps as heavy as his heart. Standing on the corner by his truck, he noticed a convenience store about a block away. He walked past a cafe and bakery, a pawn shop, and a Chinese restaurant. Inside the convenience store, he bought a six-pack of Budweiser and two packs of Marlboro Lights. On the way back to his truck, a thought occurred to him. He turned back and entered the pawn shop, a bell tinkling over the door. A large, no-nonsense, red-bearded man in a flannel shirt stood behind the counter.

"Whadda ya say, hoss? You buyin' or sellin'?" he asked.

"Looking for something in particular. You sell jewelry?"

"Every damn day. Whatcha lookin for? Watch? Chain? Maybe something for your lady?"

"Yeah, the last one. A ring."

The large man smiled and pulled a big, jangling key ring away from his belt on a retractable cord. Fitting a key into a case, he'd pulled out three trays of rings and laid them on the glass counter.

"Anything strike your fancy?"

JT scanned the rows of rings hoping, hoping. Then he saw it. A two-carat oval-cut emerald ring with tiny diamond baguettes on either side.

"This one. This is the ring. What can you tell me about the person who sold it to you?"

Suspiciously, the man eyed JT. "Why? You a cop?"

"No, sir. Far from it. I'm the guy that gave her that ring."

"Who says I paid a woman for it?"

"Okay, look. I'm trying to find the woman that sold this ring. Don't you have to get a driver's license or some form of ID when people pawn shit?"

"None a yer business. You want the ring or not? I ain't got all day."

"How much?"

"Two thousand. Cash only."

JT had set down the grocery bag, pulled out his wallet and opened it, knowing he never carried that much cash, and hadn't been back in the States long enough to even go to his bank.

"I'll be back in twenty minutes. Don't sell that ring."

"We close in an hour. Shake a leg, hoss. And bring ID."

Half an hour later, JT had sat in the cab of his truck staring at the ring. She'd definitely needed money. But where would she have gone? He removed the stainless dog-tag ball chain from inside his shirt. Pulling one end free of the clasp connector, he slid the sparkling ring onto the chain. It fell against the tags with a clink. He wrapped it tightly in his fist and closed his eyes.

"Wherever you are, Kim, I swear I'm gonna find you. Don't give up on me yet."

***

Across the state, in a ranch-style home within an affluent

neighborhood, a message played on an answering machine.

"Mr. and Mrs. Stevens, this is JT Allen again. I apologize for calling so often. If you could just call me back at 904-555-8789, I promise I won't take much of your time. I'm just trying to get any information you may have on Kimberly's whereabouts. It's very important that I reach her. This is my private phone in my barracks room. I have an answering machine, so feel free to call and leave a message anytime. Thanks again." *Beep!*

Marjorie pushed delete for the seventh time this week, finally unplugging the phone from the machine. She walked out to the lanai, the tumbler of vodka in her hand swinging in time with her hips.

"Jack? We really need to get a private number . . ."

***

When JT looked down, his bowl of pasta was nearly gone. So lost was he in memories, he could scarcely recall eating it. But his belly was full and he was ready for the check. He looked around the patio for the server. Taking off his ball cap, he ran his fingers through his hair—much longer now that he was a civilian. He was overdue for a haircut and a shave, but that wasn't going to happen. All the better for disappearing. Nobody he knew would ever recognize him now.

Out of habit, he tapped his chest through the t-shirt, feeling the reassuring clunk of the emerald ring against the dog tags.

As the server left his table with the cash for his bill, he stood up, placing the cap back on his head. He met eyes with the teenage girl picking at a salad at the table for five. She gave him a shy grin and he smiled back, giving her the two-finger salute. *What a beauty*, he thought, as he made his way back to Duval Street.

Chapter Forty-Four — Julie

Grandpa's here! It feels like forever since we last saw him. He went on his Ireland Pub trip just after Christmas. Leaving for that trip was the happiest I'd ever seen him. He packed up his guitar and some clothes and took off! He said, "Nugget, I'm gonna go to every single pub I see and ask if they'll let an old man from the US play some guitar for the folks. And if they say no, I'll have a pint and move on to the next one." Aunt Brie and Uncle Jesse said he hadn't played since they were teenagers. They teased him, asking who did he think he was, Jon Bon Jovi or something? Haha! Well, I happen to think my grandpa is way more handsome than that guy, but I could be biased.

We had dinner at the Italian place Uncle Taylor found. It was okay. Mostly, we talked. Grandpa wanted to know everything about my phone call with my mom and I shared every single word of it—what she said, how she sounded, everything. I was pretty much in shock when she called, so I don't know if I remembered everything correctly, but I guess it doesn't really matter. We'll all be seeing her tomorrow.

Oh my word, we'll all be seeing her tomorrow. I'm never gonna sleep tonight.

Grandpa shared some stories of his adventures in Ireland over the past 6 weeks or so. Turns out a lot of those pubs welcomed a Yank (as they called him) entertaining the locals. He says probably because he didn't ask for any money. But a bunch of folks paid him tips, which I thought was nice. He said it usually only amounted to enough for him to buy a pint and a meal, then he would move on to the next pub. It's so good to hear how much fun he'd had. I might have been the only one listening, though. Well, me and Uncle Taylor. Aunt Brie and Uncle Jesse appeared lost in thought. I know they're nervous and upset about tomorrow.

Oh, yeah, and there was this really nice man at the restaurant who ate by himself. He gave me a salute when he walked out, which I thought was kinda charming. Like, who does that? I thought it was kinda weird that he ate with sunglasses on, though, even after it got dark out.

I sent a text to Allison asking what is a good time for us to come tomorrow. Haven't heard back yet.

I'm too restless to sleep, so I'm gonna go sit by the pool and read my mom's journal some more. I really can't wait to meet her. Please let me have the right words.

Chapter Forty-Five — Kimberly & Allison

"I told you it was insane," Kimberly said, resting her head against the down pillows on her bed. "I think my mind is evoking faces from the past. Is that an end-of-life thing? No more alcohol. It's doing weird things to my brain."

Allison sat in a bedside rattan chair, holding a damp towel from Kimberly's bath.

"No, grandma, I don't think it was the booze. You've only had a small amount. I think you're just tired. You've had a lot of activity today."
"And I'm a nervous wreck about tomorrow."

"To be expected."

"What if, for some strange reason, my mother comes with them? I mean, she probably won't. She loathes me. But what if she does? I'm not prepared for that kind of ugliness, Alli."

"Then I won't allow her in the house. That's a promise."

"You? Be rude? No way . . ."

"Okay, smartass. I'll be diplomatic but firm. How's that?"

"Thank you. Seriously. I just can't deal with her."

"Feel better after your bath?"

"Much," Kimberly said, taking a pain pill with a swallow of water. "I'm worn out, lady. I think I'm just gonna close my eyes . . ."

Allison stood, switched off the bedside lamp, turned on the ceiling fan, and closed the door behind her. She placed her palm on the door and shut her eyes. Wrapping her other arm around her waist, she bowed her head. Silently, sorrow and grief flowed down her cheeks, her shoulders shaking as she sobbed.

***

Kimberly sat on cool, white-powder sand facing the ocean. Foamy, aqua green waves crashed onto the shore, each one folding in on the last, her body rocking to the rhythm. Salty mist blanketed her face and hair, her curls growing full and wilder by the minute. Seagulls squawked and swooped around her, foraging for shreds of food. The sun dipped lower in the sky, casting a golden glow on her skin. She looked down at her belly seeing movement and feeling the baby kick inside. She smiled, placing her hands on the growing bump, sending love to her baby through her palms. Sunset caught the deep green stone in her ring just right and the twinkle caught her eye. Closing her eyes, she thanked God, the Universe, her ancestors, nature, everything spiritual and holy for choosing her to have this child, this moment, the love of this man, this strong, healthy body, this beautiful beach on which to rest . . .

Suddenly, it grew dark and clouds formed overhead. Wind began to howl, her hair whipping around her face, sand scratching her eyes. She stood in fear, wrapping her arms protectively around her belly. Lightning flashed over the horizon, thunder smashing between the clouds above.

Clear as a bell, she heard the voice of her mother.

"You deserve nothing good, you ridiculous girl. Shame on you for thinking that you ever did. Mark my words, all of this will be taken away from you, and you will die alone. Heartbroken. Just as you deserve."

Kimberly started to cry. "But why, Mother? Why do you hate me? What did I ever do to you?"

"Don't act like you don't know, missy," the voice said. "He always loved you more than he loved me. He was the only thing that was ever good in my life and you stole him from me."

"Who?"

"Your father."

"My father? What the hell? Don't you know how much he loved you? He stuck with you through everything, even forsaking us kids. You know that's true!"

"I was never good enough. Not for my mother and not for my husband, the only two people who ever mattered to me. You will suffer like I suffered, young lady. Mark. My. Words!"

With a crack of lightning and thunder, the voice was gone.

Kimberly looked down. Her belly was flat. No ring on her finger. Her hands flew to her head, feeling only the skin of her scalp. She fell to her knees, sobbing, her body wracked with pain.

"You win, Mother!" she screamed. "This is what you wanted all along! For me to be miserable and alone—well, you WIN!"

Kimberly gasped awake, heart and breath racing, her body bathed in perspiration, tears streaming over her cheekbones. Her arm flailed toward the bedside lamp, colliding with prescription bottles.

"*Allison!*" she cried out.

Her best friend threw open the door and raced to her bed.

"What happened?!" She wrapped her arms around the sweat-laden woman, rocking her back and forth, rubbing her back.

Kimberly panted. "I. Do. NOT. Want. My. Mother. Here." She struggled to slow her breathing, her body screaming in pain. "Promise me. Please."

"Oh, lady, I already did. No worries. I promise you. It'll all be okay."

Soaking the shoulder of Allison's pajama top with her tears, Kimberly choked, "I hate her for ruining me."

***

"Narcotic dreams sprinkled with PTSD," Regina, the hospice nurse, said. She and Allison drank cups of strong black tea at the kitchen table, dawn just beginning to break. The motherly Black nurse's pastel patterned scrubs were cheerful in the early morning hours, her tiny braids twisted into a thick bun. Blessedly, Kimberly was sleeping soundly—no further nightmares. "It's not abnormal for end-of-life patients to have night terrors triggered by stress and fueled by pain meds. You said her family is coming to see her today after being long-estranged?"

Allison nodded. "Kimberly is the reason for the estrangement. She left them all, including her young daughter, and came down here sixteen years ago. They'd all assumed she'd ended her life, due to notes she'd left them. And, honestly, that'd been her plan, but I talked her out of it."

"Well, thank heavens for that."

"Now they're on the island and want to see her. The daughter just turned eighteen. She texted me last night wanting to know what time they should plan to arrive, but I haven't responded yet. I don't know . . . after that episode last night, I'm hesitant to introduce anymore stress. She's more fragile than I thought."

"I appreciate that you summoned me so we could talk about this. First, I don't think she's fragile, I think she's human. She's at the end of her life and knows it. The thought of being faced with people she abandoned probably terrifies her, at least on some level. Coupled with the shame, humiliation, all of the negative emotions associated with guilt . . . it'd be hard for anyone, much less someone whose body is being ravaged by an insidious disease. Kim is extremely strong, considering all she's facing.

"Second, letting her call the shots is important. Don't protect her from things unless she requests it. She'll wind up resenting you and I'm sure you don't want a wedge driven between you in her last days. And finally, she's so fortunate to have a best friend like you, Allison. You've taken remarkable care of her, which has contributed to her longevity. I love that you had a little field trip last night. It was good for you to honor her wishes and not smother her with concern. Too many people make that mistake with hospice patients. You never know when it's going to be the last time they have the desire to get out and do things—their energy levels wax and wane. So *brava* for letting her take the lead. Remember, she knows best what she's capable of."

Allison put her hand over the nurse's and squeezed. "Thank you, Regina. Your words are so comforting. Exactly what I needed to hear."

Regina patted Allison's hand. "My dear, it's quite all right. Remember, you're human, too. Your concerns are absolutely warranted. I'm gonna peek in on her and see how she's doing."

Allison picked up her phone and opened Julie's text from the night before.

Hi Allison—what time is good for tomorrow?

Allison responded:

Hi Julie. She's not awake yet. I'll let you know
Are you staying close to here?
Please let me know how many

of you and who will be coming

She hesitated due to the early hour, but went ahead and tapped send. Immediately, she saw the ghost bubbles of Julie responding

We're at Almond Tree a few blocks away

5 of us: me, Sabrina, Jesse, Taylor, and Grandpa

Allison felt her shoulders relax. She hadn't even realized she'd been tense. No mention of Marjorie. Or Grey, which was a little odd. She wasn't sure who Taylor was, either. Maybe a spouse? Either way, it was a relief that Kim's mother wasn't coming. Hopefully, she wasn't on the island, either.

Thx for letting me know

5 at once might be a bit much

Maybe you can see her in shifts?

Remembering what Regina had just said, she added:

I'll let Kim make the call on that

Thx for your patience

I'll be in touch

Julie's text arrived:

We appreciate it so much

See you soon

It was difficult to gauge emotion in texts, but Julie didn't appear to be angry, as Kimberly had feared. Time would tell.

Chapter Forty-Six — Jack

Taking a healthy swig of coffee, Jack rubbed his eyes. Sleep eluded him last night. Jet lag didn't help. At times like these, he thought about asking his doctor for a sleep aid. But then he remembered his wife's tragic overdose and immediately shoved that thought from his mind.

Soon you'll have the chance to make it up to our daughter, Marjie. Take care of her when she crosses over.

He looked up to see his granddaughter peeking around the wall separating their patios. He grinned, motioning for her to join him.

"Hey nuggarino, it's early. Can't sleep either, huh?" he asked, his voice soft in the morning hour.

Julie shook her head. "Nope. Too nervous." She twisted her long curls into a pile on top of her head and secured them with a hair tie. Kicking off her flip-flops, she tucked her tan legs under her in the chair.

"You get a response from her friend?"

"Yeah, my mom's still sleeping. She'll let us know what time is good later. Also, she asked me how many and who was coming, so I told her. We might have to see her in shifts. She's gonna let my mom make that decision."

"Reasonable. You hungry?"

"A little."

"Let's go ask the front desk where they would recommend for breakfast. Maybe we should leave a note for the others."

"I'll just text them."

"Oh, yeah, right. That's my old age showing."

Julie leaned over and kissed Jack on the cheek. "You'll never be old, Grandpa."

***

Looking over the menu at Banana Café, Jack was pleased with the concierge's suggestion. He settled on lobster benedict and home fries, while Julie ordered pancakes and bacon. Sipping coffee, Jack tried to relax. Images of his daughter floated through his mind. He wondered if he would even recognize her.

"Penny for your thoughts, dude."

"Just a penny? Ain't worth it. I'm holding out for a better offer." Jack winked.

"Okay, a dollar then."

"Now you're talkin, kiddo." He paused. "I was just wondering if I would recognize your mom after all this time, and because she's so sick."

"Yeah. I know. I only know her from photos, but somehow, I think we would know her if we saw her in a crowd."

"Most likely. Hey, what's going on with your college applications? Hear anything yet?"

"Not yet, but it's only February. I'll probably start hearing back before spring break. At least I hope so."

"Got a first choice?"

"I think Wellesley. But I'd be happy to go anywhere in Boston."

"Great city."

"Agreed. Hey, Grandpa, are you familiar with Doctors Without Borders?"

Jack lowered his coffee mug. "Yeah, I've heard of it, sure. Why?"

"Well, you know I was planning on going into medicine. I thought I might apply for an internship with them this summer. I would have to move to New York . . ."

"Wow! That sounds really exciting, nugget. What have Brie and Grey said about it?"

Julie squinched her face. "I haven't told them yet."

Jack was surprised. "Oh?"

"I have until April to apply. I'm kinda nervous because I know they have the 'academic momentum' argument on their side. I would only put off school for a year."

"A year? I thought you said a summer internship."

"I did. But I can apply for more than one term. If I really like it, I want to keep my options open for the year."

"What about college acceptance? Do you think you'll still be accepted if you take a gap year?"

Julie ran a finger around the top of her orange juice glass in slow circles. "Yeah, I don't know. That's one thing I hadn't considered. I have another option, too. I've been in dual enrollment since last year, taking college courses along with my regular high school classes. So I'll graduate with a high school diploma and an Associates degree in general studies. If I stay in Florida for college, I'm guaranteed to start as a junior."

Jack raised his eyebrows. "I knew you were a hard charger, but that's really impressive, nugget." He took a sip of coffee. "Maybe make a list of pros and cons before you apply anywhere and get all your ducks in a row before you approach Brie and Grey. You know how he is about a good argument."

Julie rolled her eyes. "That's for sure. Thanks for your help, Grandpa. I knew you'd be supportive."

"You're a smart cookie. You'll figure it all out. I have no doubt. And you look so much like your mom when you do that."

"Do what?"

"The smartass eye-roll."

Julie giggled, dramatically rolling her eyes again.

As the server placed their breakfast on the table, Julie said, "Hey—looks like the gang's all here." Sabrina, Jesse, and Taylor came through the entrance of the café.

Jack asked the server, "Is it possible to slide a table over to ours? We have three more."

"Certainly. Just give us a minute."

Once accommodated, the latecomers took their seats.

"Good morning. How did everyone sleep?" Sabrina asked.

Speaking all at once, the consensus was that nobody had slept well.

Sabrina said, "Your text said Allison will let us know the time?"

"Yeah. Hopefully soon. I can't stop checking my phone."

Sabrina rubbed Julie's shoulder. "Breathe, sweet pea."

"Oh, hey! It's that guy again." Julie motioned toward the entrance. A bearded man in Ray-Bans, a ball cap, and shorts, with very pale legs in contrast to his tan arms, entered the restaurant and was led to the bar for a seat. "He was at that Italian restaurant last night, too. He saluted me. I thought it was funny."

"Key West is a pretty small town. I wouldn't be surprised if we see a lot of the same tourists over and over," Jesse said.

"Yeah, I'm sure you're right."

Breakfast dishes cleared and the check paid, the Stevens family stood to leave. Julie turned, her eyes meeting the mirrored sunglasses of the bearded man. She grinned and gave him a version of his two-finger salute. He returned her grin and salute, raising his coffee cup. Her phone buzzed in her back pocket.

"You guys, it's the text from Allison. She says eleven o'clock is a good time to come over and see my mom."

Sabrina grasped Jack's hand and looked skyward. "Here we come, Kimberly. Hang in there, sister."

Chapter Forty-Seven — JT

Did they say Allison and Kimberly? No . . . it had to be his imagination. That was just too much of a coincidence. *Knock it off, Allen. You're just conjuring ghosts.*

He shook the thought from his head and drank his coffee. The server behind the bar took his order: three eggs over medium, bacon, home fries, and toast. He stared at the newspaper in front of him without really seeing it. Absentmindedly tapping the ring against the dog tags on his chest, his eyes far away behind his sunglasses.

***

With Kimberly gone and her parents of no help, JT knew the best thing he could do would be to put this chapter of his life behind him and move on. He had three months left in his current enlistment. Having received a meritorious promotion due to his exceptional work in Special Ops, JT was now a first class petty officer. Word had it that he would be named LPO of the line shack of plane captains that launched and recovered the squadron's aircraft, but he wasn't quite sure he wanted the job. It meant a lot of admin, sitting around filling out paperwork, keeping track of all his shop's personnel, and not a lot of being on the flight line, turning and burning. The lead position didn't interest him much, although it might look good on his record.

Nursing a cold draft at the E-Club on base, JT sat alone at the far end of a long bar, keeping to himself. Lost in thought, he barely registered the heated words coming from behind him near the pool tables.

"Hey, watch where you're going, dickhead."

"What? I didn't even touch you, asshole!"

"Uh, yeah, you did. Bumped my cue and made me miss my shot."

"Oh, waaaaah. Cry about it, why dontcha?"

"Look, you prick, if you don't know pool table etiquette, you need to get the hell outta here."

"You don't even know how to *spell* etiquette, dumbass."

The next things JT heard were the splinter of a pool cue and billiard balls rolling around on the floor, along with a couple of sailors attempting to knock each other out, the thud of punches landing. Without hesitation or thought, JT left his stool, strode quickly to the pool tables, grabbed a full pitcher of beer from a nearby table, and proceeded to douse the scuffling men on their heads.

Sputtering, the men struggled to their feet.

"Hey, what the fuck—"

"Get the hell outta here, you fuckin' babies. Folks are just trying to have a quiet beer and some down time. You don't know how to behave. Go home," JT said.

"Who the hell do you think you are, asswipe?"

JT stood extremely close to the beer soaked sailor, sneering into his face. "Your worst nightmare. Go home."

"Oh, wait a minute . . . I know who you are. You're that plane captain that dated Kim Stevens. Best thing she ever did was get out of the Nav. I heard while you were on det, she was giving it away for free in her roo—"

JT's fist slammed into the lager-soaked sailor's nose and mouth. Blood sprayed the man's face, dripping onto his shirt. Red oozed between the man's fingers as he tried to stop the flow, pressing on his shattered face.

"Jethuth, man, what the—"

"Don't you *ever* shut up, asshole? Give me your ID."

"Hell naw!"

One of the bystanders spoke up. "It's Andy Coleman. Second class AME from HSL-60."

The name sounded very familiar.

Two large MP's made their way through the gathered crowd of onlookers. "What happened to this man's face?"

"My fist," JT said.

"ID," the MP closest to him said. JT pulled out his wallet, handing over the green DOD identification card.

"Petty Officer Allen, you're gonna be spending a little time with us tonight." JT turned around to allow himself to be placed in handcuffs. More bystanders shouted in his defense.

"It wasn't his fault."

"He didn't start this."

"You got the wrong guy."

"Yeah, you need to arrest the one that's bleeding. He started it."

One of the MP's addressed the crowd. "We'll be taking statements from each of you, so don't go anywhere. Meanwhile, *both* of these fellas have a cell to call home tonight."

The next morning, JT was released into the custody of the squadron CPO on duty, who drove him to the barracks.

"Allen, you just got meritoriously promoted. Haven't you ever heard the saying, 'One *aw shit* wipes out a whole string of atta boys?' What got into you last night? Were you drunk?"

"No, Chief. Hadn't even finished one beer. The guy needed to be silenced. That's all."

"After all the statements the MP's got last night, it was clear who started everything. But you finished it. You'll probably stand before the XO for this. Maybe even the Skipper. I guess you can kiss the LPO billet goodbye."

"Wasn't really meant for me anyway, Chief."

"Want me to take you by sick call first so they can x-ray that paw?" JT's hand was swollen and bruised purplish red.

"Nah, I'm fine. Just a nick."

"Well, put some ice on that thing and press a uniform this weekend. You'll be standing before one of the bigs on Monday morning. Clean up and tell the truth."

JT exited the duty truck and stood on the sidewalk next to the barracks.

"Will do. Thanks for the ride."

"Allen—did this have anything to do with Stevens?"

"Thanks again, Chief," JT said, not answering, as he turned and walked to the barracks.

***

JT tucked his white Dixie cup cover under his arm and strode purposefully to the hangar quarterdeck. ATCS Foose, the head of Maintenance Control, stood by the doors, waiting for him.

"Petty Officer Allen—let's chat for a minute, yeah?"

JT followed the senior chief back onto the hangar deck and into the coffee mess. They took a seat in a small, aquamarine formica booth.

"How'd it go?"

"Fine. XO gave me time served and told me to put in for some leave."

"Three years in special ops is a long time. Wouldn't surprise me at all if you're struggling to assimilate back into squadron life."

"I'm fine."

"Not too long ago, I was in a similar situation, only it was the Cold War. I think some leave time is a good idea. Also, maybe you should speak to somebody. Get some of the pressure out of your brain." The senior chief slid a business card across the table to JT.

"A shrink?"

"A counselor. He's a no-bullshit, former Navy SEAL. He really helped me get my shit together before I could actually do some harm if my pent up feelings got triggered."

JT slid the card into his wallet. "Thanks, Senior Chief, I'll think about it."

"Turn in that leave chit. Take some time away. Cool off a little bit. You have somewhere you can go?"

"Yeah, I'm good."

"Glad to hear it. When you get back, give that guy a call." JT stood to shake his superior's hand, then headed across the hangar deck to his shop to fill out the paperwork required to approve his leave. He really could use some time away from this place.

***

Opting for a quiet night before his flight to Texas the next morning,

JT drove off base and around the corner to the Fleet Reserve Association. Sitting at the bar in dim light, surrounded by dingy wood paneling, he ticked off a mental checklist. His leave chit was signed and approved all the way up the chain of command, he had a confirmation number for his flight purchased over the phone—he would need to get the boarding passes at the airport—he'd been to the bank and had plenty of cash. He just needed to drive to Jacksonville International at zero-dark-thirty and find a spot in long term parking.

He was going back to Texas for a month. He'd called his parents the previous night to tell them he was coming home for a while. His mom was thrilled—his dad was ready to put him to work. The Allens raised livestock near Austin in a small town called Bastrop. His father and brother, Matt, had been running the farm with a half dozen farmhands for years. Beau Allen told his son he hoped he would develop a taste for farm life over the next four weeks.

"It's hard work, JT, but you ain't never been scared of that."

"No, sir, you're right."

"Maybe you'll consider not reenlisting when your time's up and—"

"Slow down, Pop, I ain't even home yet."

The bar was quiet on a Tuesday night. A couple of old-timers sat at a table playing dominoes, trash talk flowing. A few more were scattered at the bar hunched over their drinks. The bartender kept one eye on ESPN on a tv hanging in a far corner of the room, polishing beer glasses from a dishwasher tray.

JT lit a cigarette and looked at his watch. In about twelve hours, he'd be on his way back home for the first time in six years. It would be really good to see his mother again. A registered nurse in labor and delivery at the local hospital, Ella always boasted she'd probably helped deliver the entire population of Bastrop under the age of twenty-five. She was a curvy, no-nonsense woman with kind eyes and a sharp tongue. She and Beau raised their sons to be respectful, work hard, and not to take life too seriously.

And, man, could she cook.

JT's mouth began to water just thinking about his mama's fried chicken and mashed potatoes. While the Allen family worked hard all week, Sundays were the day Ella could be found in the kitchen, Beau and the boys usually watching some sort of game on tv. They would try to sneak bits of Sunday supper and she'd send them out of her domain with a smack on the hand. Ella would have adored Kimberly. He could imagine those two being fast friends. She would have loved having another woman in the house, especially one her son loved so much. He could have kicked himself for not having taken her home to meet his family. And now, she was gone.

He took a big swig of beer to flush the lump from his throat, draining his glass.

"Another one?"

"Nah, I'm good. Thanks," JT told the bartender, leaving a ten on the bar.

Outside, he lit another cigarette and opened his truck door.

"Thought I recognized your piece of shit truck."

JT turned and saw a man in a white t-shirt and faded jeans leaning against the building, with two black eyes and a bandage across his nose, a baseball bat in his hand.

"Coleman, give it a rest."

"You fucked with the wrong guy, Allen."

"Whatever, dude, you've got nothing to prove here. Your mouth is what got you into shit in the first place. I'd advise you to shut it right now."

Coleman smacked the bat against the palm of his hand over and over again, slowly approaching the truck.

"You trying to intimidate me, Andy?"

"This ain't intimidation, asshole, this is a bona fide threat."

Coleman got closer to the truck. Just as he raised the bat over his head, JT flicked his cigarette into Coleman's eyes and slammed the driver door into his already-mangled face, nailing his gut with the door handle. He brought his steel-toed boot up hard between Coleman's legs. The assailant crumpled in a heap on the gravel parking lot, dropping the bat to cup his throbbing groin.

"You motherfucker!" Coleman screamed, blood and saliva spraying his t-shirt as the previously white bandage soaked red with fresh ooze.

"I told you to give it a rest, dipshit. And if I ever hear Kimberly's name out of your mouth again, it'll be the last time you speak with teeth."

JT pulled out of the parking lot, spraying gravel over the writhing pile of flesh, Coleman's bloody shirt glowing red in his taillights.

***

In a large, maroon Dodge Ram 2500 pickup, Matt Allen headed east on Route 71 away from Austin-Bergstrom International, in the direction of the family ranch. He stole a sideways glance at his brother, his eye landing on the swollen and bruised right hand.

"What's the other guy look like?"

"Ugly as a horse's ass, and that was before I touched him."

"You wanna talk about it, bro?"

"Probably. But not tonight."

"Fair enough. Mama and Pop are way too excited you're here."

"I'll bet. It'll be good to see everyone."

"How long you staying?"

"A month. Maybe longer. Don't know yet. I may have some shit to deal with when I get back to base."

"But you don't wanna talk about—"

"Nope. Later."

Matt waited a beat. "A few of the guys're meeting up this weekend. You game?"

"Maybe. Just need to kinda decompress right now."

"I hear ya. I'm bein' a pain in the ass. Guess I just missed you, brother."

JT reached over and ruffled his little brother's wavy brown hair. "Missed you, too, pain in the ass. Now shut up and drive." JT winked, tipping his head against the headrest, and closed his eyes.

Sunday afternoon, Ella kneaded the dough for her dumplings, as a giant pot boiled on her stove, filling the kitchen with the mouthwatering aroma of chicken, carrots, onions, and spices. Strewing flour onto a marble countertop, she began to roll out the dumplings.

"I like 'em better when you just tear off hunks and throw them in the broth."

"Maybe you'd like to take over Sunday dinner, eldest boy of mine?"

JT crossed the room and gave his mom a peck on the cheek. Ella reached up and touched his face. "So glad you're home, scruffy. When's the last time you shaved?"

"A week ago. Right before I had to go before the XO." Ella put down her rolling pin.

"What happened?"

Beau and Matt came into the kitchen for a couple of longnecks before the Houston Astros game.

"What am I missin'?" Beau's booming baritone asked.

"JT was about to tell me what happened on base. I'm assuming it has something to do with that multicolored hand of yours?"

"I was just minding my own business—"

"Famous last words," his dad laughed.

"And I heard these guys going at it by the pool table. I broke it up. Then one of 'em pissed me off."

"What'd he do?" Ella asked, cutting the dough into dumplings.

"Doesn't matter. I got hauled away by the MP's, but everyone's statements corroborated my story, so they let me go. The XO told me to take leave, so here I am."

"XO?" Matt asked.

"Executive Officer. Second to the Commanding Officer."

"Why do I feel like there's a whole lot more to that story than you're lettin' on?" Beau asked.

"Not much more to tell. The guy's an asshole and I shut him up. Twice."

"Twice?" Matt asked.

"He came looking for me the night before I got here. I don't think he'll be bothering me again."

"There you go, bro!" Matt said, slapping his brother a high-five on his way back to the family room.

Beau met his son's eyes. "Should we be expecting a call from your superior?"

"Don't worry about it, Pop. I'm a grown man. I'll deal with it."

Slapping his son on the back on his way out of the kitchen, Beau said, "I have no doubt, JT. Just don't jeopardize your whole career because you can't control your temper. Speaking from experience here. It's in our blood."

Ella lifted the chicken out of the broth to cool before deboning. She split the chicken with a knife and wiped her hands on a towel.

"What's her name, son?"

"What? I don't know what you mean."

"Jason Todd Allen, I'm your mother. I know you. I've only ever seen you lose your temper to the point of fighting twice in your life. Once was when you and Matt fought over a game of Monopoly, and the other time was when Jackson Harper disrespected Darla Cunningham in front of you at the chili cook-off. If I remember correctly, you'd had quite the crush on her for the longest time. And Jackson wound up with a split lip. Since I doubt this had anything to do with Monopoly, I'll ask you again. What's her name?"

"C'mon, Mama, I'm thirty-four years old—"

"JT."

He pulled his dog tags up through the collar of his shirt, showing his mother the emerald and diamond ring. "Her name is Kimberly. She's the love of my life. And she's gone."

***

"I'm sorry, what?" JT asked the server behind the bar at Banana Café.

"I asked if I can get you anything else?"

"No, sorry, the check's good, thanks."

Out on Duval Street, the sun was making a stunning morning entrance over the Atlantic Ocean to his left. JT needed to clear the ghosts and memories from his brain. He took a right, headed toward the Gulf of Mexico. The distance from one end of Duval to the other was just about a mile and a quarter. Plenty of time to knock the cobwebs from his head and get a grip.

Before he knew it, he was back at Louie's Watering Hole near the Gulf. Despite the early hour, they were open and serving numerous patrons. This time, the song piping out onto the street was The J. Geils

Band's "Love Stinks."

JT chuckled to himself, mumbling. "I'm sensing a theme to the music here."

"Boots!" The raspy voice behind the bar was unmistakable. "Looks like you finally took the weatherman seriously." She eyed his legs. "But you desperately need some beach time. Bud Light draft and a shot of Beam?"

"Madam, you're good at what you do. Let's keep it to just the draft right now. A little early yet for the hard stuff."

"Says you," she said, motioning to the barflies around her. She lowered her voice and leaned in conspiratorially. "Between you and me and the fencepost, I don't think some of these folks ever go home."

"I don't blame 'em. Not when they can spend time with a doll like you."

"Why, Boots, you're quite the charmer. Who knew you had it in ya?"

Extending his hand across the bar, he said, "Name's JT."

"Tammi. So nice to formally meet ya. How long you staying on the island?"

"Not sure. Maybe for good."

"Now you're talkin. Found a place yet?"

"Rented a place for a month. I'll start looking for something more permanent soon."

"If you need a realtor, just say the word. I know the best one in town. Been here their whole life, so they know the island inside and out, who's coming, who's going, who's overpriced, whatever. Let me know."

"Sure, never hurts to have a good connection. Thanks. I'll take the info from you before I leave."

Tammi gave him a thumbs up and moved to the other end of the bar to greet new customers. JT turned and faced the Gulf. The warm morning breezes ruffled over his skin. He looked down at his legs. Tammi was right—they looked like two hairy light sabers. He made a mental note to go back to the hotel and spend some time at the pool this afternoon. It felt luxurious to have nowhere to be, no responsibilities.

His beer drained, JT ventured into the interior of the bar in search of a men's room. Finding it locked, he waited outside the door for the occupant to finish. Dollar bills were tacked all over the walls, scrawled with "so and so was here," or Key West Trip 2000, alongside photographs of celebrities who'd been to Louie's and gotten coerced into taking photos with the bar staff, or with a short, rotund man sporting an enormous grin and squinty eyes, one would assume was Louie himself. Something seemed familiar about one of the girls who appeared in numerous shots, but he couldn't place it.

Back at the bar, he asked Tammi for another draft.

"Last one," he said. "I'm headed back to the pool to get some color on these legs."

"Sounds like a plan. Don't skimp on the SPF, either, Snow White."

"Advice taken. Hey, that guy in a lot of the wall photos back there. Would that be the Louie of Watering Hole fame?"

Tammi grinned and pulled the tap. "Indeed it would be, Sherlock. Yeah, he bought this place almost thirty years ago when it was a dive. Ha! Who'm I kidding? It's still a dive. Sadly, he's no longer with us. Left the whole kit and caboodle to his kid. They have grand ideas for improvements around here once they have a chance to get involved. Got some personal things going on right now, so we'll see. Somehow, island time is different from mainland time. Tends to slow way down here. Could be six months, could be a year, before they're ready to be hands-on." She placed his draft in front of him and crossed to the other end of the bar to pour brightly colored frozen drinks in ridiculously long, skinny plastic cups with tops and straws in neon shades.

Business was picking up. JT finished his beer and left a twenty under his cup on the bar, making his way back down Duval Street. He told himself he had plenty of time to get the realtor information from Tammi. That certainly wouldn't be the last time he'd be seeing her.

With a few blocks to go before the hotel, a group stepped off the crosswalk to his left and proceeded down Catherine Street.

I think that's the group I keep running into.

Faces grim, they didn't appear to be having much fun on their vacation. Out of curiosity, he watched as they stopped in front of a pastel colored bungalow with a white picket fence. They looked at one another, and, something apparently decided between them, they allowed the young girl in their group to open the gate.

Odd, he thought, wondering what was so serious.

Chapter Forty-Eight — Julie

Monday, February 14, 2012

I got a text back from Allison saying 11:00 would be a good time to come over. We were just leaving from breakfast when the text came through and all of us got really excited. We raced back to the hotel to freshen up and find something distracting to do for a couple of hours while we waited.

Aunt Brie called Uncle Grey to keep him posted. Uncle Jesse and Uncle Taylor decided to walk down to the ocean. Grandpa bought a newspaper and is sitting by the pool. I'm too nervous to do any of that. So, I'm writing in my journal and hoping the time flies by.

Where do I even begin? I've always known that Aunt Brie and Uncle Grey weren't my parents. First of all, I call them aunt and uncle, duh. Secondly, I look nothing like them. But the biggest reason is because they've always told me about my mom. They never said that she took her own life, only that they weren't sure what had happened to her. In my little kid mind, that meant she had to be out there somewhere. Maybe she had no idea where I was and was looking for me. They didn't have many, but the few photos they had of my mom were framed and put in my room. When I was little, I memorized her face in those pictures. Whether we were walking on South Beach, or shopping in Midtown, or eating at a restaurant, I would look into the faces of all the ladies around me, hoping to see a glimpse of the woman in those photos, or myself, in them. It wasn't until I was much older that I realized she probably was nowhere near Miami, if she was alive at all, because surely she would have found me by now.

So, every year on my birthday, I would make a wish on my candles to please let me see her again. But it never worked . . . until my 18th birthday a few days ago. Uncle Jesse gave me boxes of my mom's he'd had since I was two years old. I was finally able to see dozens of photos of her.

It was crazy how happy it made me . . . and how sad at the same time. If only she could have seen me growing up. Even if she wasn't the best mom, she was my mom. I often wonder how things would have been different if she'd stayed with me and raised me as her own.

That's why I was pretty stunned when I read her note and realized that she'd probably committed suicide. My family never mentioned it, I guess to protect me, but that had been their conclusion all those years ago, too.

So, imagine how incredibly shocked I was to get a phone call from her! I still can't believe that was only two days ago. Sadly, as sick as she is, we may not have much time with her. I know how deeply her family loves her. I know they're just as excited as I am to see her and hug her and find out what she's been up to all this time.

Selfishly, I just want to spend time alone with her. Maybe I'll remember what it was like to have her all to myself when I was little. Maybe I'll feel some sense of completeness, fulfillment, even closure. I don't know what I expect. I guess I'm hoping for all of it. But we don't even know how much time is left. It feels like every minute that goes by is another whole day I'm missing with her.

As I mentioned before, I know my family is worried about me. They probably think I'm so fragile that I'll shatter at any moment. Truthfully, that's not how I feel . . . anymore. When I was little, I would get really upset wondering how in the world she could ever leave me. Was I a bad kid? Was I too much for her to handle? Did she go away to start a different family? I mean, all kinds of awful thoughts and weird questions plagued my brain constantly.

I would get angry and lash out at the people around me— especially Aunt Brie and Uncle Grey. They took me to see a counselor when I was in kindergarten and I've been going ever since. Not to the same doctor, I mean, I've seen different ones as I've grown up. But my favorite therapist was probably Dr. Whitcomb. She had the most beautiful smile, crazy curly hair, and spoke to me like I was an adult, even though I was still in middle school. She told me straight up what was wrong with me: that I was carrying around giant cases of abandonment and guilt, because I blamed myself. With abandonment comes feelings of unworthiness, low self-esteem, and an inability to trust. And guilt produces all the other ugly things: humiliation, shame, depression. What really woke me up from feeling all the bad stuff was during a recorded session with Dr. Whitcomb that I have played over and over until it was burned into my brain.

Julie, none of the feelings you're having are wrong—they're all valid. But they have absolutely nothing to do with you personally. You're owning them, almost clinging to them, like they belong to you, but they don't. Look at it this way—remember the last time you got sick? Had a cough, fever, runny nose? You felt pretty horrible, right? Well, how in the world did you allow yourself to get sick like that? How naughty of you, right? Wrong. All the things you were feeling were symptoms of an illness that found its way inside your body. But you fought back with vitamins and fluids and rest, and look at you now. You're not sick at all. And you left all of that illness behind, right?

Well, all of the feelings you're having now are not your fault, either. They rest at the feet of those who came before you, and those who came before them. It's the result of an all-too common cycle of generational trauma. But here's the best part: just like fighting back with vitamins and fluids and rest, you can fight back against these ugly feelings you're having. First, you have to recognize that these feelings aren't your fault—they're merely symptoms. Next, you fight back with forgiveness and gratitude and love. And last, you sprinkle all the good stuff from inside you, all around you—share it with others. The only way to fight darkness is with light—no matter how dark it seems, the sunshine is always waiting just above the clouds. The only way to wash away dirt is with clean water. The only way to combat fear is with love. The way to break the cycle is to realize that none of it belongs to you, that you are good enough, smart enough, kind enough, all of the enoughs, just exactly the way you are. There are no mistakes in nature. You're a miracle. And now you have all the tools you need to remember that every single day.

So, from now on, try to do these things each day—forgive those who have hurt you, be grateful for all of your many blessings, even down to your matching socks every day, and love yourself first, then those around you. Do this in the morning when you wake up. Do it in the moments when you are so *mad* you think you might very well be able to spit steel nails out of your mouth. Do it when you feel sad. And before too long, it becomes second nature.

Now, I'm not saying that you'll never have ugly feelings again. That you won't feel darkness sometimes. I'm just saying that knowledge is power, and now you have the power to be the young woman you were always created to be. Because now, my dear, you are whole.

Yeah. She's a pretty incredible therapist. A genius, actually. I don't know if I'll continue seeing her now that I'm an adult, because she's a child psychologist, but I sure would like to speak to her after I meet my mom. I want to tell her everything that happens because I'm sure that this is gonna be one of the most enormous moments of my life. And I'm also sure the tools she gave me so many years ago, that have served me for so long, will help me today.

I told my aunt last year that I wanted to get a tattoo when I turned eighteen. After she rolled her eyes and laughed, she asked me what I wanted. I said I'd like a brilliant sun above a cloud that is showering tiny, pure white hearts—light, water, love—with one word underneath . . . enough.

Chapter Forty-Nine — Kimberly & Allison

Regina sat forward in her chair as Kimberly opened and closed her groggy eyes, yawning, and rubbing scratchy sleep from her eyelids.

"Well, good morning, sunshine. How're you feeling today?"

Kimberly smiled from behind closed eyes. "Hello, Miss Regina. I'm a bit groggy." She opened one eye. "Any chance you've got tea?"

"I do indeed. Let's take some vitals real quick and do our once-over, then you may have all the hot, strong tea your little heart desires."

Kimberly lay still as Regina went through her morning routine—temperature, blood pressure, heart and lung sounds, checking skin, feet, eyes, belly. Kimberly winced as the nurse palpated her tummy, which was no cause for alarm—typical at her stage of illness.

"How's your appetite? Have you been eating?"

"Oh, yes. Alli feeds me well."

"Heard you had a little adventure to Grand Vin last night."

Kimberly grinned. "We did. And I walked by myself—well, walker walked. Don't know what got into me, but it was so nice to be out of the house for a little bit."

"I also heard about the nightmare."

For a moment, Kimberly had forgotten. But now it all came rushing back. A cloud of memory passing over her face.

"It was very unpleasant."

"I'll bet. I'm sorry you experienced that. It's not unusual, however, when you're on pain meds and going through a little stress, good or bad. I understand your long-lost family is coming to see you today. How do you feel about that?"

Kimberly reached out and took Regina's hand. "So happy. So

anxious. So excited. I'm a ball of nerves." Regina smiled, squeezing her patient's hand.

"Of course you are! Well, your exam looks good this morning. Your med chart looks fine. I see you went without meds until bedtime last night. How was that for you?"

"It was okay. Manageable. I didn't need it until bed." Kimberly sat up. "And I don't think I need it now. I want to be clearheaded when I see my daughter."

Regina touched Kimberly's face. "A daughter. My guess is she's gorgeous. Okay, well, that's about it for me today. If y'all need me later, you know where to find me."

"Thank you, Miss Regina. You're an angel."

"Girl, tell that to my momma," she chuckled. "I wish you the very best reunion today, Kim. And remember, you call the shots. If it gets to be too much, you tell Allison to kick their butts out, you hear?"

"I hear."

Regina spoke to Allison in the kitchen while she packed her bag to leave for the next patient.

"Miss Kimberly would like some hot tea this morning. She looks good, Allison. Better than even a couple of days ago. I've seen it many times. When people have a reason to live, a strong will kicks in. I'd say she has weeks, not days."

Allison closed her eyes, placing her hand over her heart. "Thank you. I really needed to hear that."

"Just remember, let her have control. Don't deny her anything, unless, of course, she talks about going sky diving or jet skiing. And good job on keeping her fed and hydrated. Keep it up. You're doing all the right things. Just breathe."

Allison wrapped the nurse in a warm hug. "Thanks for being so awesome, Regina. See you tomorrow."

Carrying a tray of Earl Grey tea and ruby red grapefruit juice into Kimberly's room, Allison smiled at the heart-shaped strawberry tarts and scones she'd purchased from Croissants de France.

"Morning, grandma. How goes it?" She held the tray in front of Kimberly. "Happy Valentine's Day!"

"Oh wow, I'd totally forgotten. Here's hoping today is filled with whole hearts, not broken ones."

Allison set the tray down on the dresser by a window. "I have a feeling it might be a little bit of both. You gonna be okay with that?"

Kimberly nodded. She sat up at her rolling bedside table. Allison brought a cup of steaming tea and a scone.

"Like I said, I've got you. No worries. You need them to leave, you say the word. I have good news, though." Kimberly met her eyes. "Marjorie is *not* coming."

Kimberly sighed heavily and bowed her head.

Looking up, she said, "It's probably bad karma for me to say this, but I'm so very relieved."

"Bad karma? That woman was a monster to you. She doesn't deserve your kindness."

"Who *is* coming, by the way?"

Allison sat in a chair by the window, munching a scone, a glass of orange juice beside her on an accent table.

"Julie, Sabrina, Jesse, Taylor, and your dad."

"Oh! Jesse and Taylor are still together. That makes me so happy to hear."

"Ohhh, Jesse's husband! I couldn't place who it was."

"It's nine o'clock now. What time should I tell them to come over?"

"I need some time to get ready," Kimberly said, absentmindedly rubbing her hand across the wispy hair that remained.

"You got it. I'll send the text now. Finish your breakfast and we'll get ready." Allison smiled.

Kimberly smiled back, emotion brimming in her eyes. "Happy Valentine's Day, lady."

Chapter Fifty — Jack

Jack turned the pages of *USA Today,* unable to concentrate. He read and reread headlines two or three times. Nothing was sinking in. He flipped through page after page, his mind wandering.

Kimberly.

In a very short while, he was going to be hugging his daughter again for the first time in over seventeen years. He kept going over in his mind what he would say to her first. Should he explain about Marjorie right off the bat? Or was that too heavy a piece of news? Certainly not what he wanted to open with. Should he ask what she's been doing all this time? Or should he focus on himself so as not to make her feel uncomfortable or guilty?

Maybe he should just tell her he's sorry. So very sorry. He'd failed her again and again as a father. Maybe he should just say how much he loves her and let her take the lead in the conversation. Maybe she's not well enough for a long talk . . . or any talk at all.

None of them had any idea what sort of shape Kim was in. Allison never said much. Just that maybe they should see her in shifts because all five of them at once could be daunting. He could understand that.

Sabrina approached his chair beside the pool carrying a cup of coffee in both hands, as though warming them, even in the eighty degree morning. She sat next to her dad and touched his knee, getting his attention.

"Just got off the phone with Grey. He was surprised we haven't seen her yet, but wished us a good visit. Something's off with him. I know he and Charlotte are working hard on this case, but he handles difficult cases all the time. I've never known him to seem so twitchy on the phone with me."

"Maybe you're projecting, Brie. He's probably fine. It's you that's a bundle of nerves."

Sabrina sighed. "I'm sure you're right." She ran a hand through her short, silken hair and glanced at the two-tone Rolex on her slender wrist. "Another hour."

Jack folded the newspaper and tossed it on the table between them. "I can't concentrate. I'm reading the same words over and over and retaining nothing. Maybe we should go for a walk."

"Or maybe we could just talk?"

"Sure, peanut. What's on your mind?"

A grin split Sabrina's face. "You haven't called me that in years."

"You'll always be my peanut."

Sabrina touched her father's arm. "Have you thought about what you're gonna say to her?"

"A little bit, yeah. But I keep thinking maybe I should just let her do the talking, if she's able to. That's the thing. We don't even know how sick she is or what she's capable of right now." Sadness creased his face around his eyes. "It's times like these I wish I still smoked."

Sabrina made a face. "Ugh, Dad, I'm so glad you quit those things. I'm sure you added years to your life. Plus, you don't stink anymore."

"Yeah, well, there is that. Have you thought about what you want to say?"

"I have. I vacillate between wanting to rip her head off and wanting to hug her so hard it hurts. I have a million questions. Starting with 'what the hell have you been doing for the past sixteen years?'"

"The million dollar question," Jack said.

"And how about 'why the hell did you run away again, Kimberly?'" Jesse said. He and Taylor had returned from their walk, joining the family at the poolside table.

"And the biggest one—how could you leave your baby girl?" Taylor said.

"Yeah, I think that's the one I want to know the answer to," Julie said. She walked around the pool, dragging an empty chair to the table.

"Oh my word, I'm sorry, Jules," Taylor said. "Me and my big mouth."

"No, no, it's okay. I've had a really long time to wonder about that. The good news is we're even closer to knowing the answer. The bad news is I'm not sure I'm ready to hear it."

Sabrina opened her arms wide. "Come here, baby girl. Scooch in beside me." Julie allowed her aunt's arms to wrap around her. No one spoke for a moment or two.

"Forty-five more minutes," Jesse said. "Favorite memory?"

Jack spoke first. "The day she came home with the keys to Blueberry, the little blue truck. Remember that?"

"That was in Texas. I didn't move out there with you guys," Jesse said.

Sabrina looked uncomfortable.

"Oh, that's right, I'd forgotten that for a minute, son. It was just a lawn ornament in our neighbor's yard. She worked so hard on getting it up and running again. Just the look of pride on her face, like, 'See? I showed you guys.' She never really believed in herself. That was quite an accomplishment for her."

"And then I had to go and wreck it," Sabrina said.

"That was an accident, Brie. It wasn't deliberate."

"Wasn't it, Dad? I was a brat. Nothing mattered to me. Certainly not my sister's truck. It was my choice to drink and drive on grad night. I knew better."

"We all have regrets, honey," Jack said.

"Did she ever even find out?" Jesse asked.

"Does it matter?" Brie asked, visibly upset. "The point is that she cherished that truck and trusted me with it when she went into the Navy, and what did I do? Completely totaled it."

"Brie, don't be so hard—"

"And you know what else? You wanna know what the very last thing was that I said to her? She called asking for help for herself and Jules and I told her no. Implied she would have been a horrible houseguest. Told her she needed to figure shit out on her own and grow up. I've had to live with that guilt for all of these years. I was a horrible fucking sister to the one person who loved me unconditionally."

Julie leaned back and looked up into her aunt's face, locking on Sabrina's eyes.

"And you know what, Aunt Brie? Today, the universe is giving you the chance to apologize. What a gift." Julie kissed Sabrina's cheek and stood up. "We see her in half an hour. I'm gonna go to our room and make sure I look extra nice for my mom. Meet you guys back out here in a flash." Julie walked toward their hotel room, pulling a card key from her back pocket.

Jesse shook his head. "From the mouths of babes. She's right, Brie. It's time to stop beating yourself up. Let's get ready to go see our sister."

Chapter Fifty-One — JT

Lying by the pool, smothered in sunscreen, JT brought an ice cold bottle of water to his lips and took a long swallow. Daisy, the front desk clerk, had been right. The view of the Atlantic from here was spectacular. He took in a deep, cleansing breath, closing his eyes behind his shades. Ocean waves crashed and he was instantly transported to Jacksonville. He and Kimberly stretched out on a blanket, eyes closed, holding hands, lost in the moment. He could smell the tangy air, the sunscreen, hear the seagulls. Jacksonville seemed like another lifetime ago.

***

After his trip to Texas, JT returned to base with trepidation. He hadn't been contacted regarding the assault on Coleman that night at the Fleet Reserve. Although he'd been defending himself, there had been no witnesses. It would be his word against whatever the jackass could dream up. The case could get ugly, bringing Kimberly into the mix, dragging her good name through the mud again. He was unwilling to go there.

Fortunately, he'd heard nothing from his command the entire month he was on leave.

As he paid the exorbitant, long term parking fee at the airport, his thoughts were on Kimberly yet again. Where could she be? How could he possibly begin trying to find her? Her parents were a dead end. She'd mentioned other family—a brother and a sister—but he couldn't recall their names, only that they were also in Florida. Considering there were likely to be thousands of Stevens listings in the phone book, and the fact that the sister most likely had a married name, he was at another dead end. He could try to contact Allison up in Maryland, but he was pretty sure she was either at a new duty station or completely out of the Navy by now. Due to the Privacy Act, he had no way to find her, either.

Not that Allison would be a good source of information, anyway.

When he'd contacted her the first time he'd lost Kimberly, she'd been a tightly closed vault. She'd offered no information whatsoever and had essentially told him to get lost.

Back to square one.

It was making his head hurt. He was getting closer and closer to accepting the fact that she was truly gone. And he didn't like it one bit.

JT turned on his blinker to make the turn into the Naval Station Mayport main gate, when a thought occurred to him.

"I think I'm hungry for a grand slam breakfast. And maybe some information." He smiled to himself as he made a u-turn and sped away toward Denny's.

***

"Just one?" asked the hostess.

"Yep. The counter is fine."

"Follow me."

JT sat at the counter and looked at the menu, though he knew what he wanted. And food wasn't his top priority.

"How ya doin, sir? Coffee?" The server was a middle-aged woman wearing too much make-up, her gum chewing unnerving.

"Yeah, sure. Thanks."

As she poured a cup of black coffee, JT looked around the restaurant. He knew it was probably ridiculous to think she still worked there, but maybe someone here knew her—and maybe they knew what had happened to her.

"You work here long?" he asked.

"About six months. Why?"

JT pulled out his wallet and removed the only photo he had of Kimberly—one of two Polaroids they'd paid five bucks to have taken on The Landings the night he proposed. She had her left hand on his chest, the flash catching the glint of the emerald ring, and the sparkle in her eyes. The photo was pretty beaten up from all the years he'd carried it, all the countries he'd been in, all the nights he'd pulled it out to stare and reminisce. Kimberly had kept the other one.

The server lifted a pair of rhinestone, cat-eye glasses on a chain around her neck and, resting them on the end of her nose, peering at the photo.

"Pretty. I don't recognize her. She worked here?"

"Yeah. Not sure when she might have gone, but she was working here three years ago."

"Hm. I can ask my manager. Meanwhile, you hungry?"

JT placed his order and sipped the strong coffee. After a few minutes, a man emerged from the kitchen, a stack of receipts in his hand, wearing a look of annoyance.

"Help you?"

JT extended his hand. "Hello, sir, I'm Petty Officer Allen from HSL-60 here in Mayport. I'm looking for someone who used to work here around three years ago. Any information you may have would be much appreciated." He handed the slightly crumpled Polaroid to the manager, who kept his eyes focused on JT's.

"You're not a cop?"

"No, sir. Just a friend."

"If you don't have a warrant, I'm afraid I don't have any information for you."

"I completely understand, but, sir, you didn't even look at the photograph yet. If you recognize her at all, can you tell me?"

The manager, whose name tag read Jim Reynolds, pursed his lips. He pulled reading glasses from his shirt pocket and looked at the photo. He looked back at JT.

"Yeah, I know her, and yeah, she used to work here, but not in a long time."

"It's Kimberly Stevens, right, sir?"

"Yes. Now, what—" Jim began, then gasped. He looked like he'd seen a ghost. "Wait. What was your squadron again?"

"HSL-60. I was gone for a very long—"

"You didn't die?" "What? No, of course not, I'm right here, aren't I? Kim was—is—my fiancée. We were engaged before I left on deployment. I was gone much, much longer than expected, but no, I didn't die."

Jim covered his mouth with his hand. "Oh, my dear heavens . . ."

"Sir, can you tell me what happened?"

"You had no contact with her after you left? None at all?"

"No, sir. I was taken from my squadron on a classified assignment and was unable to have any outside contact whatsoever. I know it sounds ridiculous now, but I guess I thought our relationship was strong enough that she'd be here waiting when I got home. I had no idea I was going to be gone for so many years. There was absolutely nothing I could do. As soon as I got back, I went to her place, but she was gone."

Jim laid his hand on JT's shoulder. "Son, I haven't seen Kim in a long time. She left the restaurant because she couldn't handle the hours anymore with the—" He stopped speaking.

"With the what, sir?"

Jim came around the counter and sat on the barstool next to JT's, motioning for him to sit, too.

"One morning, not long after your deployment left, Kim read in the newspaper that a helicopter from your squadron crashed in Bosnia. Everyone onboard had been killed. She fainted right here in the lobby." He pointed to the rug beyond the hostess stand.

"Oh, no. Oh, god. She thought I'd been killed."

Jim nodded, sorrow creasing his face. "Yes. It came as an enormous shock to her. We called an ambulance and everything."

"But she was okay?"

"Yes, I mean, she was absolutely devastated. Brokenhearted, but she recovered. She was convinced you were gone and she somehow found it in herself to carry on. She worked until things got too hard to juggle with the—" Again, Jim stopped himself.

"With the what? What aren't you telling me, sir?"

"What I'm trying to say is…" Jim swallowed. He drew in a long breath. He looked intently at JT. "Kimberly was pregnant when she read that tragic news. She gave birth to a daughter—Juliana."

The bottom dropped out of JT's gravity. He felt as though his brain was hurtling through space.

"I have . . . a daughter?"

"It appears so. I'm being honest when I say I have no idea how you would reach her. I take it you tried calling her?"

"Yes, from Italy. Number was disconnected."

"And her apartment?"

"Yeah, she's been gone for weeks. The super had no information." JT's face was as white as snow. The middle-aged server brought him a glass of water.

Jim handed him a pen and a blank order ticket. "Give me your contact information. If I hear anything at all, I promise to pass it along. This is actually really good news—you're alive! I do hope you and Kim can find each other again."

With numb fingers, JT had trouble writing down his information. Shaking Jim's hand, he left the restaurant in a fugue state. He was a father.

***

As the end of his enlistment was only weeks away, ATCS Foose approached JT about his intentions.

"Twelve years, three enlistments under your belt, Allen. Think you'll re-up?"

"I'm not sure, Senior Chief. I haven't given it the thought it deserves since I got back from leave."

"Have you called BUPERS? Maybe they have some good billets to offer. Or you could request to stay here?"

"I know I have quite a few options. I'll contact them and see what's available. Can I get back to you next week?"

"Of course. Let me know if there's anything I can do to help."

As the senior chief walked away, JT realized the last thing he wanted to do was stay in this squadron. With the memories and the ghost of Kimberly all around him, he'd much prefer a new start. The biggest decision was going to be staying in or getting out. And where would he go that would increase his chances of finding his fiancée and their daughter? Without any leads, he'd all but given up. He touched the lump under his coveralls and t-shirt, feeling the ring against his dog tags.

If it's meant to be, I'll find you, Kim. You and our daughter, Juliana. Don't give up on me.

Back in his barracks room, JT poured a shot of Jim Beam, slung the liquor down his throat, and twisted the top off of a bottle of Budweiser. He sat heavily on his bed, took a deep breath, exhaled. He lifted the cordless phone from its cradle, punched in the familiar number, and waited for the connection to be made.

"Hey, Mama, it's me. Can you get Pop to pick up, too? . . . Yeah, I'm fine, just need to talk to you both. . . . Hey, Pop." He took in another breath, blowing it out audibly. "I'm calling to let you know . . . you have a granddaughter."

That's when the tears flowed.

The conversation had been emotional and difficult. His parents were elated until he'd shared he was unable to find his fiancée and daughter. They'd gone back and forth, offering ideas to him as to where to start looking, had he tried her apartment (yes, that was the first place he'd looked), what about friends (Kim was a loner after she'd gotten out of the Navy), what about her family (he'd tried her parents to no avail). In the end, they'd become just as frustrated as he was. Aside from hiring a private detective, they'd run out of ideas, too. He was not going to hire a detective. Something about that felt slimy and intrusive to him. If he was going to find her, it was going to happen organically or not at all. The hard truth was that Kimberly was just really good at disappearing when she wanted to.

Although emotionally wrung out, he'd felt better after speaking to his parents. It had unburdened him to share his pain with the two people who'd always been pillars in his life. And he'd gained clarity of thought. He'd known what he wanted to do about his Navy career.

***

JT spent the next four enlistments in various commands. He became a rolling stone, making no friends, taking on no attachments—a loner, just like the love of his life. He volunteered for as many detachments and deployments as he could, traveling the world, seeing places he wished he could have taken Kimberly and Juliana to—the Mediterranean, the Caribbean, Japan, Australia—staying one step ahead of his feelings until he was simply able to bury them deeply, insides becoming granite. He took a month of leave every year, spending it in Bastrop on the family farm. Aside from upgrading his truck once, and earning the hard-fought promotion to Chief Petty Officer, nothing much changed in his life.

Once, on deployment in the Caribbean, he struck up a conversation with a master chief at a Tiki hut in Antigua during an evening of down time. The old salt had given forty years to the Navy and was approaching retirement.

"Whew . . . four decades is a long time, Master Chief."

"Call me Dan, JT. You're a chief now, we're peers."

"Okay, but forgive me if it's a little awkward."

Dan chuckled. "I remember the feeling, although it's been many moons."

"Where's home when you retire?"

"Whidbey Island, Washington, son. It was always my favorite duty station. I was married and two of my kids were born there. Bought a place a few years back. Fishing is about to be my primary responsibility."

"Ahh, that sounds nice."

"What about you? Where's home?"

"My folks have a farm near Austin, Texas. That's home of record. But the Navy's my home. I've thought about retirement. Where I might want to go. I don't know if farm life is for me, honestly. I admire my dad and brother for doing it for so many years, but it's just not what I see myself doing."

"Well, what *do* you see yourself doing?"

JT took a tangy sip of the margarita on the bar in front of him. "To be honest? I'd just like to find a place to disappear. Live out my days on a beach or a boat."

"Key West," Dan said.

"What's that?"

"If you want a place where you can disappear, you can't beat Key West, in the contiguous forty-eight. People go there and are never heard from again. The way of life is slow. Nobody gets in your business. If I didn't hate humidity and mosquitoes so much, I'd have bought a place there years ago."

JT stroked his mustache. "Key West, huh? I'll have to check it out sometime."

"Do that. If you get a chance, stay at the Southernmost House near the Atlantic. It's beautiful and quiet, and you can't beat the view."

"Thanks, Master Ch—Dan. Sounds like heaven."

***

JT took another long, cool drink of water and looked around at the heaven that was Key West. He'd made the right decision to come here. He needed to remember to get that realtor information from Tammi at Louie's, but there was plenty of time. He had a month of nothing spread out before him. If only his parents could be here enjoying the island with him. JT frowned and closed his eyes again, a stone forming in his throat.

Chapter Fifty-Two — Julie

I'm almost 100% positive that JT Allen is my father. I forgot to mention that before. In the box of things my mom left me to be opened on my birthday were a bunch of letters from another sailor named Jason Todd Allen who went by JT. According to my mom's journal and the newsy, sappy, drippy, wonderful letters he wrote to her, they were engaged right before he went on deployment. My mom was still in the Navy then.

I'm not sure what happened because a whole bunch of pages after that are ripped out. But, apparently, she got out of the Navy and started working at a restaurant. JT came back from sea and they got back together until he left again. He always seemed to be leaving. Anyway, I'm guessing that's when my mom got pregnant with me because the entries are in May of 1993.

She doesn't write much in the diary at all after that. A few entries during her pregnancy and after I'm born, but I'm thinking that's when life got really hard for her. No more mentions of JT except to say she wished he could see me, and things like that, but I guess they broke up.

I used to wonder if maybe I looked like my dad, but after seeing the photos of my mom at my age, I can see I look almost exactly like her. I'm a little taller than she is, my hair is a little lighter, and my eyes are more of an aqua blue, but I have her face, her curls, and her curves. If we stood side by side at 18, we'd look like sisters.

Which makes me wonder what JT looks like. There weren't any pictures of him in that box. And I wonder what in the world happened to him. I'm trying to decide if I even want to bring him up to my mom. It might be a conversation for another time.

When I get back to the hotel tonight, I'm gonna try to remember to Google him and see if I can dig anything up.

Anyway, it's nice to know that I'm the daughter of Kimberly Marie Stevens and Jason Todd Allen. Kinda romantic, right?

An hour to go before we go see my mom. I'm gonna go join the family by the pool. I'm so excited . . .

Chapter Fifty-Three — Kimberly & Allison

At 10:45 am, Kimberly was seated on the lanai at a table beside the pool. Clouds had begun to gather overhead in swirls of pearly gunmetal gray. A glass of lemonade sat before her that she nervously touched, wiping the condensation on her khaki capris, then touched again. Her lavender blouse complemented the green of her eyes, around which she'd applied a little eyeliner and mascara. Wrapped atop her head, she wore a deep purple silk scarf that matched her sandals. She'd decided against jewelry altogether when her hands shook too much to hook her earrings. She touched the glass, wiped the condensation.

"Hungry?" Allison called, walking from the kitchen through the French doors.

"Oh, hell, no. I'm a wreck. I can't even drink this lemonade."

"I'm making soup, salad, and French bread for everyone."

"That's really nice of you, Alli."

Allison sat in the chair opposite Kimberly.

"Shot of Jameson?"

"Ha! You're funny."

"What? Go big or go home, right, grandma?"

"Maybe a hundred years ago."

"Want me to leave you alone?"

"*No*! Please don't leave. You can hear the doorbell from here."

Allison took her friend's hand and squeezed, then let it go.

"Okay, lady, take a breath. I'm not going anywhere."

Kimberly looked at Allison with gratitude. "Thank you."

She touched the glass, wiped the condensation.

"You look beautiful."

Kimberly touched her scarf. "Do I?"

"Purple is so you. I'm gonna go get a few more glasses and ice. Be right back."

Kimberly touched the glass, wiped the condensation. Touched the glass, wiped the condensation. She swallowed, whispering, "Please let them not hate me."

Then she heard the doorbell.

Her heart jumped into her throat. She could hear pounding in her ears.

"Oh, god, oh, god, oh . . ."

Kimberly looked up to see a version of her younger self walking tentatively out onto the lanai. With a strength that surprised even her, she leapt to her feet and opened her arms wide.

Her voice failed her, as she choked through tears, "Ju . . . lie . . ."

Julie rushed across the pavers toward Kimberly. Seeing her frail figure, she slowed in front her mother, gently wrapping her arms around her tiny waist, careful not to disturb the cannula and oxygen tube on Kimberly's face.

Julie rested her head on her mother's shoulder and whispered, "Momma . . ."

In the kitchen, Allison passed Kleenex out to the group gathered impatiently at the door, keeping one for herself. Not a word was spoken in the room. Everyone held their breath.

"Look at you." Kimberly touched Julie's cheek, finding it soft as down, her eyes brilliant in the sun. "My word, you're gorgeous."

Julie smiled. "I look like you."

"Where's everyone else?"

"They're waiting in the kitchen. They thought I should come out by myself first."

"It's okay if they come out. I promise you and I will have time alone later."

Julie spoke up. "You guys? Come see my mother."

One by one, she watched her family members emerge. Kimberly

held onto the back of her chair for support, heart pounding.

Sabrina—her silken black hair, cropped short and stunning, blue eyes glistening. Jesse—her muscular, tall, big brother, his sandy hair stylishly buzzed with those familiar curls on top. Jack—oh, her dad never aged, his salt and pepper hair wavy, same mustache, same dimples, same mischievous eyes. And this must be her brother-in-law, Taylor—a strikingly handsome man with kindness all over his face, rivulets flowing from his warm eyes.

Kimberly took the oxygen tube from her face and threw it on the chair.

"Come here, you," she said to Sabrina, holding her close.

"Oh, sister, I've missed you. So. Damn. Much," Sabrina said.

Wrapping her arms around her brother's middle, she said, "Jess."

"Kimmy," he sputtered through tears.

Kimberly allowed herself to be folded up in her father's strong embrace. So familiar, as though no time had passed. "Hey, Dad." She thought her heart would burst.

"Hey, my favorite smartass. I love you so much."

"I love you, too. So much."

Kimberly waved Taylor over. "Come on in here, brother," she said, hugging him for the first time. "Thank you for taking care of Jess."

"Oh, honey, I think he does more of the caretaking. But I do love the hell out of him."

"I can see that. Thank you."

Kimberly grabbed her daughter's hand and held it to her lips. "My sweet Juliana. Please sit next to me, okay?"

Once they were seated around the table, Allison closed the kitchen doors and joined them on Kimberly's other side. The energy around them crackled with electricity. Emotions ran high—love and anticipation to be sure, but there was an undercurrent of something else—a thrumming, sizzling feeling. It felt like one spark would cause an explosion. Kimberly took a deep breath and proceeded with caution.

"You guys, this is Allison. My best friend and savior. Literally. I know you all have a million questions, but let me just start with this: I'm so deeply sorry," she said, her voice quavering. She placed her trembling hands in her lap.

"I'll tell you anything you want to know, and no question is off limits, but I need you to know that this was never personal against anyone. It was not a rational decision on my part, but the only one I could make at the time. I was in a very bad place back then. We don't have much time left with each other, but I promise I'll spend all of it listening to each one of you. I owe you that and so much more. But for a moment, I'd just like to speak, if that's okay."

Kimberly took a sip of lemonade and mopped perspiration from her brow and lip, dabbing her eyes and nose. She squeezed her daughter's hand. "Jules—my baby girl. Look at you. You're so beautiful, so grown up. I can see your heart in your eyes. Your pure soul shines in your face. Your aunt and uncle deserve infinite credit for raising you so well. I can't wait to get to know you, love." She squeezed Julie's hand again, but this time saw a shadow pass across her daughter's face. Kimberly blinked and furrowed her brow, but continued on.

"Brie—how can I ever possibly thank you for raising my daughter? You've done an incredible job. You were meant to have her, not me."

"Oh, Kim, that's not—" Brie began. Kimberly raised one finger and shook her head slightly. She was afraid if she didn't finish immediately, she was going to lose all nerve.

"Jess—I'm so proud of you. I've kept up with your success on the internet. You and Taylor look so happy, I could burst. Nobody deserves it more than you." Tears began to work their way loose and slide in slow rivulets down her cheeks.

"Dad—you look fantastic," she said with a smile. "I don't know how you do it, but you look exactly the same as you did when Julie was a baby. Thank you for trying where Mom and I were concerned. It meant more to me than I can say. Where is she, by the way?"

Her family members looked at one another, an awkward silence hanging between them.

Jack cleared his throat. "Kimmy, your mother passed twelve years ago."

Kimberly looked at Allison, each registering the other's shock.

"What happened?"

"She took her own life. Pills. She really spiraled after you disappeared and we all thought you'd died. Don't blame yourself, though, you know she was so tortured her entire life. Counseling, intensive therapy, medication, love—nothing ever helped for long. I don't mean this in a bad way, either, but it was for the best. She's finally at peace."

Kimberly lowered her head and closed her eyes, taking in the news. *Yes*, she silently agreed, *she's at peace. And I can finally let the demons of her go.* She felt something break free inside her shoulders and her entire body relaxed.

"Could I speak next?" Sabrina asked.

"Of course, sister. Please," Kimberly said.

"I wanted to start by telling you . . . I'm so very sorry, Kimmy," her voice breaking. "The last phone conversation we had has haunted me all these years. I was horrible to you. It was inexcusable. I don't deserve this chance to apologize for my behavior, but I'm so damn grateful to have it." Sabrina reached across the table and took one of Kimberly's hands. "I hope you can forgive me. I feel like I'm the reason all of this happened. That you felt you were left with no choice but to take off."

Kimberly held her sister's hand tightly for a moment, looking deep into her icy blue eyes.

"Hear me, Brie. I'm only gonna say this once. None of this was your fault. Not one bit. You did what you thought was best for me at the time. That was love, Brie. How could you have possibly known how sick I was mentally and physically? I had a habit of hermiting anytime things got uncomfortable for me. I deliberately kept my distance from everyone. Somewhere in my sick brain, I told myself this was the only way I could protect myself from pain. I was so wrong, and I know that now. But can you imagine me teaching Jules by my example? Oh my word, she would have been so screwed up. Just look at her now. Look at her! She's amazing. You had a giant hand in that, Brie."

Sabrina let go and placed her hand on her niece's shoulder. Julie squirmed a bit and stared at her lap, her face a jumble of emotions.

"No, this little one, who I keep reminding myself is officially an adult," Sabrina smiled. "This is all Julie. We may have provided her with a comfortable home and life, but this all came from within her. Being a terrific person cannot be nurtured into someone—it has to be there all along. She's a good one, Kim."

Jesse spoke up. "Looks like she broke the damage cycle in the Stevens clan. You ever hear the saying, 'It ran in the family, until it ran into me'?"

Julie stood so fast, her chair fell behind her. "No!" she yelled. "Stop it. All of you. I cannot just sit here and listen to all of this. Mom, I appreciate what you're saying, I really do. Who knew we would ever have the opportunity to hear your own words out of your own mouth ever again, right? But that's the real issue here, isn't it?" She gestured around the table at all of them. No one spoke—they barely breathed.

"We have all been so *angry* all these years. Wait, let me just speak for myself. *I* have been so damn angry my whole life because of you. You left me. Not just that, you *chose* to leave me. You have absolutely no idea how it feels to be abandoned. To know that you were unwanted."

Allison began to rise from her chair, but Kimberly placed a hand on her arm and shook her head.

Hot tears began to pour from Julie's eyes as she clenched her fists at her side.

"I had to switch schools because of my anger. I saw therapist after therapist. I tried sports and working out and whatever else to try to channel this negative energy for My. Entire. Life. Eighteen years. I have worked *so hard* to forgive you, *Mom.*" Her last word was said like an accusation. "And now I'm standing here babbling about I don't know what because my heart is bursting because I'm so happy you're alive but my head is buzzing like bees because I just want to scream and I'm a giant fucking mess!"

Julie collapsed to the ground, sobbing into her hands. Sabrina jumped up from her seat and crouched next to her niece, arms around her shoulders, whispering soothing words into her ear. Allison passed her a linen napkin and attempted to comfort Kimberly, who shook off her embrace.

"I'm fine, I'm fine," Kimberly said. "This is what I needed to hear. Let her finish."

After several minutes, Sabrina helped Julie back into her seat and handed her a glass of lemonade. She took a long sip and a shuddering breath and gave her mother a watery smile.

"I had no idea how badly I needed to say that," Julie said. "I'm sorry I made a scene. We just need some time, I guess."

Her family muttered words of understanding, shaking their heads.

"My daughter," Kimberly said. "You have every right to say and do and feel whatever the hell you need to. You are safe here. You are understood. You are so loved. And I deserve every bit of it. I hope we can all be open and honest with each other from here on out. Don't let my fragile appearance stop any of you. Let me have it." She reached out a tentative hand. Julie clasped it in both of hers.

"Mom, I forgive you. I really do. But I need to say honestly that I would never have had the life and love and opportunities I've had without Aunt Brie and Uncle Grey. I hate that you ran away, but I'm so grateful you gave me to them." Sabrina squeezed Julie's shoulder and smiled.

"That reminds me," Kimberly said. "Where is Grey anyway?"

"He has an intricate case he's working on with Charlotte and their staff this weekend. After he got over the initial shock like the rest of us, he told me to send his love to you. He hopes to be able to see you before . . ." Sabrina stopped, swallowing the rest of her words.

"I hope I can see him, too. I would love to tell him in person how much I appreciate him."

Visibly uncomfortable, Allison jumped up a little too quickly from the table. "Anyone need anything? I'm heading to the kitchen." *Oh dear god, they have no idea.*

"She okay?" Jack asked.

Kimberly stared after Allison as she speed-walked to the house. "I don't know," she said, a touch of concern to her voice. "She does seem a little fidgety. I'm sure this is very surreal for her, too. After all, she's the only person in my life who's known I've been alive all this time. If it wasn't for her insisting that I stay with her and get therapy and treatment, I would have ended things just as I'd planned sixteen years ago. Her generosity knows no bounds."

"I wanted to ask, what treatment did you receive? According to the papers in the box you left for Julie, you had stage II cervical cancer. It can sometimes be aggressive, right?" Jesse asked.

"It can be once it begins to metastasize. The cancer wasn't too advanced back then, but I didn't know it at the time. Allison did a lot of research and discovered a trial for stem cell therapy with the NIH . . ."

"NIH?" Taylor asked

"National Institute of Health. First, I had to be given the all-clear by my therapist. My mental health was pretty fragile. Once she felt I was strong enough to handle the trial—I had to be mentally prepared for success *or* failure—we applied for the opportunity."

"You didn't have health insurance," Jesse said. "The bills must have been astronomical."

"Not for the actual trial. It was covered by the NIH and donors. But I'm pretty sure therapy and my local oncologist were costly. Allison handled all of it. I gave her my wallet, ID, cash, everything I had when I got here and told her I didn't want to deal with anything. She's never said a word about medical bills to me. She's such a godsend."

"What does she do for a living?" Sabrina asked.

"She's a realtor. A very good and sought after realtor. The past few weeks, though, she's been completely devoted to my care, along with my hospice nurse, Regina. You guys'll love her."

"I know properties down here can command quite an asking price," Sabrina said. "Grey and I looked years back when we thought we might want to own a vacation place. A lot of them were outside of our budget range back then. She must make a good living."

"I think she does, yeah, but I've never asked her about her finances. Also, her father recently passed away and left everything to her—she was his only surviving relative."

"Oh, I'm sorry to hear that," Jack said.

"Thanks, Dad. She's okay. He'd been sick for some time. Wasn't known for a healthy lifestyle. He had quite a few irons in the fire, not all of them on the up and up, you know? But he owned a fun little dive bar down near the Gulf—Louie's Watering Hole. He left it to Alli. She's waiting until I'm gone to devote any time to the place. She's even considered selling it. But it does hold fond memories for her of her dad."

"I have to ask, honey," Jack said. "When you had success with the treatment and it looked like your prognosis was good, why didn't you come back? To get Julie or just to see us—let us know you were alive and okay?"

Julie nodded intently, adding, "Yes, the big ask...why did you stay away?"

Kim bowed her head and exhaled a long, choppy breath.

"This is gonna be difficult for me to explain and for all of you to understand, but I'll try if you all will."

The family nodded, preparing for her answer.

"It took about two years for me to actually show progress and start feeling better. I mean, the cancer didn't get any *worse*, but I was still sick. During that time, I never knew when it was gonna rear its ugly head and begin to spread, eventually killing me. I was convinced it could happen at any time, and the doctors just couldn't tell me any differently. The treatment was very new at the time. Nowadays, you hear about stem cells all the time. Back then, not so much. So, I was always in fear of getting horribly sick.

"I left because I didn't want to subject Julie to watching her mother waste away and die. I also knew I was a terrible mother and an even worse sister and daughter. Mom didn't want me around, neither did Brie—sorry, sister, but it's true—and the only person who seemed to give a shit about me one way or the other was that spunky little blonde in the kitchen. To be honest, I wanted nothing more to do with Mom ever again. Our relationship ended the day she snubbed me and refused to meet her baby granddaughter."

Jack rubbed his hands over his face and shook his head.

"I'm so very sorry about all of that, Kim. I've wished for all of these years that I could have gotten a re-do. I made so many mistakes that day."

"Don't blame yourself, Dad. We all know at whose feet this one lays."

Jack nodded, not entirely convinced.

"Anyway, as time went on and my health improved, I decided it was time to embrace my new life on the island. I made peace with letting all of you go. I had to. I absolutely believed it was for the best for all of us. I began working as an advocate for abused women, which turned out to be my life's work. I finally felt like I'd found my purpose. I've been there for ten years now. I really miss it.

"However, I do need to admit something to you guys and I hope you don't totally hate me for it."

The group leaned in, shaking their heads, encouraging her to go on.

"A couple of times over the years, Alli and I made the trip to Miami so I could see Julie."

"Wait—what?" Julie said.

"I know, I know, pretty selfish of me, isn't it? As soon as I realized how easy it was to find people on the internet, I started Googling you. When an article came up that you were playing softball, I begged Alli to take me to see you. We could blend into the crowd and nobody would know. The last time we were there was when you lost the tournament about six years ago."

"Oh my god, I can't believe this!" Julie said, her mouth agape. "You were right there on that field and didn't come talk to me?" She clenched her fists, fighting another urge to scream.

"Oh, honey, I wanted to run over and hug you, but I knew better. You were twelve years old. It would have been so confusing and so difficult for you. It was enough for me to see what a strong and beautiful girl you were becoming."

"This is crazy, Mom. I wish you had—"

"I know. But now do you understand why I couldn't?"

Julie folded her arms across her chest, shaking her head. "Unbelievable."

"Like I said, I made a ton of mistakes. This one hurt me badly. I was inconsolable after that. We never made the trip again. It was just too much. And Alli would argue with me and tell me that my daughter deserved to know her mother was still alive and then we wouldn't speak for days afterward. It just wasn't worth the pain all the way around."

"What made you call on my birthday? How'd you get my number?"

"Alli had your number in her phone. She handed it to me and I called. She said you were eighteen now and it was time. As sick as I am, we knew if I didn't reach out now, I would never have the opportunity again."

"So, how in the world did Allison get my number?"

"Hm. I guess I never thought about it. She's very resourceful. I guess I thought she'd done some research and found it somehow. We'll have to ask her when she comes back out. She sure is taking a long time in there, huh?"

Sabrina pushed her chair back from the table and stood. "I wanted to talk to her about something anyway. I'll go check on her. Be right back you guys. Please don't tell anymore secrets while I'm gone." She winked.

Sabrina found Allison at one of the kitchen counters chopping fresh vegetables for a salad in a large wooden bowl.

"Hey, Allison, need any help?"

Allison startled and looked behind her to see Sabrina approaching, looking stylish in creamy, wide-leg slacks, a navy pinstriped tank top, an ivory cashmere sweater draped around her shoulders.

"Oh, hey, Sabrina. I think I'm all set here, but thanks for the offer."

"I wanted to discuss something with you, and I hope you won't find it awkward or inappropriate. If you do, please tell me. I won't be offended."

Allison put down the vegetable knife, wiping her hands on a kitchen towel. She closed her eyes and took a breath before turning to face Sabrina.

"Sure, what's up?"

"Kim was very candid about the fact that you've taken care of her medical expenses all of these years and never troubled her with any of it. I'm so grateful to you for handling what had to be an enormous burden."

Allison waved a hand in front of her face. "Oh, no, please don't think a thing about it. I was happy to do it. She didn't need the added stress."

"You're probably right. Still, that was extremely generous of you." Sabrina opened her navy Chanel bag, removing a checkbook and an ivory Cross pen. "I'd like to reimburse you for some of your expenses. It's the very least I can do." Sabrina leaned on the counter and began writing a check.
"Sabrina, no, please. Seriously, it's okay. It was no trouble at all. Please, keep your money. I must insist."

Sabrina stopped writing and looked up at Allison.

"Okay, okay. I can see you're adamant about this. I'm sorry—is my offer inappropriate or awkward somehow? I truly meant no—"

"It's not that at all. I appreciate your generosity more than I can say. It's just . . ."

"Go ahead, please."

The moment weighed heavily on Allison. The next words she

said had the potential of being extremely combustible. She could cause irreparable damage. But she didn't want to hide anything any further. She had to tell the truth. Let the chips fall where they may. No more lies.

Please forgive me for this, Grey.

"Sabrina, many years ago when Kim came to me in the middle of the night, desperately ill, just plain desperate, I hadn't been living here long. The house was a gift from my father. I never could have afforded this beautiful place on my own. I was pretty fresh out of the Navy. I worked for him part time at his bar and scratched out a meager living while I studied for my real estate license. I barely had two nickels to rub together and was too proud to accept any further charity from my dad."

"So, your dad paid Kim's medical bills?"

"No. It wasn't my dad."

"Well, then, who? I'd really like to thank this incredibly selfless person."

Allison twisted the dish towel in her hands. She swallowed hard.

"It was Grey."

"I'm sorry . . . Grey? My *husband* Grey?"

"Yes, I called him. I found the number in Kim's—"

"Wait just a goddamn minute. You're saying my husband *knew all along* that Kimberly was still *alive*?"

"*No*, that's not what I'm saying. I mean, partially. Please let me explain."

"I think you've explained enough. I'll assume you received Julie's phone number from him?"

"Yes," Allison said. "It's not what you might be thinking, Sabrina, he didn't know—"

"Didn't know *what* exactly?"

Allison sighed, then spoke frantically. "In the early days of Kim's treatment, I sent bills to him at a PO Box and he took care of them. We never spoke again until he called me on Julie's birthday. I swear to you, he only knew she got the initial therapy and treatment for her cancer. He had no idea she was still alive. He called on Julie's birthday to ask me if she was because he hadn't heard from me in many years. He thought with Julie now an adult, it was time for her to know her mother, if that was still a possibility."

"But *he knew* she didn't kill herself. And he said *nothing* to me or the rest of the family. Wait, maybe they knew . . ." Sabrina stormed out of the kitchen, her eyes burning. She approached the table, her arms waving.

"Hey! Did any of you guys know that Kimberly was still alive? At all? Did anyone have a clue?"

The family looked at each other and at Sabrina as though she'd come unhinged. Jesse stood and went to Sabrina.

"Brie, calm—"

Sabrina shoved his hands away from her.

"I will most certainly *not* calm down. Do you know what Allison just told me? What I found out about Kimberly's medical bills? That *Grey* had been paying them. He was the magnificent benefactor that took care of my sister and he *knew* she was still alive. *He* is the source of Julie's phone number." Sabrina fumbled in her bag for her phone.

All of them were standing now, except for Kimberly, who remained very still in her seat. The sky growled in a low rumble overhead.

"Wait, I don't understand," Jesse began.

"I'll kill him," Jack said.

"He *knew*?" Julie cried.

"Whoa, that's messed up," Taylor said.

"Everyone, please hold on! *Please* let me explain," Allison said.

"Yes, I would really like to hear what she has to say," Kimberly said, her eyes ablaze. "Please, Allison, tell us what's going on."

Sabrina yelled into the phone. "Grey? Yeah, it's me. Listen, I'm about to put you on speaker so you and Allison can explain to all of us what the fuck is going on!" She tapped the speaker button, laying the phone on the table. "Go ahead, we can all hear you."

"Uh, I'd like to know what's going on, too," Grey said through the phone speaker.

"Grey, this is Allison. I just explained to Sabrina that you were the benefactor who paid Kim's medical bills in the beginning."

Silence from the phone.

"Grey, I want you to be very careful right now and explain to all of us how you knew my sister was still alive and you never saw fit to tell *any* of us. Especially *me!* Your *wife!*" Sabrina screeched at the phone.

"Please, if you would just let me explain. This is all my fault," Allison said.

"Go ahead, Allison," Kimberly said, her face a stone.

Allison went over the story again, about how she called Grey in the early days of Kimberly being in Key West and how he generously offered to help with her medical costs.

"It's true, I did help out many years ago. It was shortly after Kim disappeared. I only received about a dozen invoices and paid them immediately. I never heard another word from Allison until I called her on Julie's birthday to see if Kim was still alive," Grey said through the phone.

"Greyson Hanover, I do *not* understand this one bit. How could you keep a secret this huge from me? We have always been so completely honest with each other. You knew how devastated my entire family was at the realization of Kimberly's death. How *could* you?" Hot tears blazed down Sabrina's face.

"I know this isn't going to make up for the decision I made so many years ago, but I'm very sorry. Listen to me for a minute. Julie had just stopped crying every night for her mother."Kimberly placed a hand on her forehead and looked down at her lap.

"When Allison called and said Kim was very sick and needed help, all I could think was that a) I wanted to help in any way I could, and b) that I wanted to protect Julie at all costs. We'd made a commitment to raise her as our own. I was not going to put her through that kind of pain."

"But what about me, Grey? You didn't think you could trust *me* with this information?"

"Brie, I thought about telling you over and over again. And every time I did, I came to the same conclusion. That it was better to protect the two of you from this than to reopen raw, deep wounds that had recently begun to heal. I love you too much. I just couldn't bear to do that to either of you."

"Yeah, well you know what? You didn't have the right to keep something this huge from me. And if you could keep *this* from me, what the hell *else* are you keeping from me?"

Kimberly pumped the palms of her hands in a "slow down" motion. "Hold up just for a goddamn minute. Everybody please sit down. Right now."

Everyone took their seats and looked at the frail woman before them. Nobody said a word.

"Alli, please give Brie that kitchen towel so she can dry her face. Now, before anyone says anything they're gonna regret, let's all remember whose fault all of this is in the first place. Mine." Kimberly pointed at her chest. "Me. I'm the bad guy here. So, before you start misplacing your anger at anyone else, it all starts with me. Okay?"

Sabrina nodded, dabbing her cheeks.

Kimberly placed her hand over her heart. "Grey, from the bottom of my heart, thank you for your generous gift of medical treatment and therapy. I knew I could rely on you to take care of my baby, but then you opened your heart even wider and took care of me. I'll never be able to thank you enough. Because of you, I was able to participate in a stem cell trial that prolonged my life, and for that I'm eternally grateful."

"Thanks are unnecessary, Kim. I was happy to help."

"I wish I had the ability to pay you back, but—"

"Absolutely not, Kim. I wouldn't accept your money. Just knowing you have this time with your family is enough."

Kimberly looked at her best friend. "Allison, I don't appreciate you going behind my back and making this arrangement when you knew the last thing I wanted was for anyone in my family to be aware of my existence. You swore to me our secret was safe and I trusted you to protect it."

"I know, lady, I know. I have absolutely no excuse for breaking your trust. I'm so sorry."

"Apology accepted. That being said, thank you, you hardheaded, fiercely devoted woman. I know you never would have called my brother-in-law for help if you hadn't been between a rock and a hard place."

Allison nodded. "That's exactly true. You know me."

"And, Brie, please don't hate your husband right now. Life is too short. Look at me." She met her sister's red-rimmed eyes. "He did exactly what he needed to do to protect you and Julie. That is the amazing man you married. This is not his fault. It's mine."

"We're still having a talk when I get home," Sabrina said.

"That's fair," Grey said.

"Oh, don't you talk to me about fair—" Sabrina began.

Kimberly raised her hand. "Brie, finish your conversation with Grey later, please. I'm getting tired and I have a few more things I'd like to talk about. Sorry, not sorry, for being a bossy bitch at the moment."

Brie disconnected the call.

Jesse looked at Kimberly. "You okay to go on, Kimmy? Is it too warm out here? We can go inside."

"No, I'm okay. That was a bomb I didn't expect. It's thrown me for a loop, so I can imagine how you guys are feeling."

Allison gave Kimberly a sheepish look, stood from the table, and walked back toward the house. "I'm gonna finish the salad. Lunch in a few minutes, if anyone's still hungry."

"The hospice nurse told Alli that I probably have weeks instead of days left, so that's encouraging. I wanted to ask, if you guys are okay with it, and I know I don't really have the right to request anything of any of you right now, but . . ."

"Go ahead, Mom." Julie took her mother's hand.

"Would you all be willing to spend some one on one time with me? Especially you, Julie. I wanted to ask you if you'd be willing to stay here with us. Spend a few days with me?"

"Oh, yes. I would love that. Only I didn't really pack enough—"

"Don't worry about anything, Jules. Whatever you need, we can get for you," Sabrina said. "Being with Kim is the most important thing right now."

"Agreed," Jack said. "Anything you need."

Kimberly was visibly relieved. "Thank you guys so much. It means the world to me. After lunch, I'm gonna lie down. Jules, maybe you can go gather your things then?"

"Yes, she will," Sabrina said. "I'll take her shopping while you rest."

"Dad, do you mind sticking around? I'd like to hang out with you today, if that's okay?"

Jack stood, circling the table to stand behind Kimberly. He placed his hands on her shoulders and kissed her cheek. "Absolutely. I wouldn't miss it for the world."

Thunder cracked overhead and fat raindrops pelted the table, the bushes, their skin. A pungent aroma of ozone filled the air. Everyone rose to move indoors.

"Oh, jeez, let me get you inside, Kimmy." He reached for her hand. She took it but remained seated.

"Stay with me, Dad. I love the rain."

Chapter Fifty-Four — Jack

Curled up with Kimberly on the leather sofa in her living room, Jack wrapped his arms around a towel draped over the tiny frame of his daughter, her head resting on his shoulder as she folded the damp scarf. He was reminded of tiny Kimmy, damp from a bath in the cooler months, swathed in terry cloth from head to toe, snuggling with her Daddy to keep warm. Knowing this may be the last time he held her in this way, Jack pulled his middle child a little closer, tenderly rubbing her arms.

"I think the last time you cuddled with your old man you were maybe six years old."

Kimberly smiled. "Probably. Now I'm nearly forty-six. Time flies, right?"

Jack closed his eyes and pressed his lips to her forehead.

"Oh, little girl, I have so much I want to say."

Gently pushing away from her father, Kimberly nestled into the opposite corner of the buttery yellow sofa. "Now's the time, Dad. I'm a completely captive and eager audience. Let's put all of our imaginary cards on the proverbial table." She smiled, her eyes still twinkling, still mischievous.

Jack sighed. "When you were small, I knew there was something wrong with your mother. I guess I just thought it was something that would pass—something she would mature out of. There were long stretches of time when she would be doing so well, and I would think, 'This is it. She's finally okay.' And then, there would be another episode."

"Call it what is was, Dad. Abuse."

With a solemn face, Jack nodded. "I never wanted to call it that. Makes her sound like a monster. Like some kind of psychopath."

"But she *was* a monster at times. Especially to me. Not sure why she singled me out. Maybe, in her mind, I represented something she abhorred. Or maybe she hated my 'what you see is what you get' attitude."

"Smart ass brattiness," Jack chuckled.

Kimberly grinned. "Yeah, okay, I'll give you that. Or maybe she was jealous of you and me—of how close we were. Maybe you showed faith in me you didn't show in her. I don't know. How could I love someone who was so damn mean to me? How many times did I run scared of the belt or the hairbrush or the palm of her hand? Until I finally stopped running and she finally stopped making the effort. I think when she was angry with me, at least it showed she cared."

"That's twisted, Kim."

"If the shoe fits."

"Your mother was misunderstood. She was horribly abused as a child. Nobody ever protected her. She developed a stone shell around her heart at a very young age."

"You're still defending her, Dad. She's gone. It's okay to be honest with yourself and everyone else. She was severely mentally ill and needed intense therapy from the time she was a child. But that never happened and her husband and children suffered for it."

"You're not wrong, honey. But what can we do about it now?"

"My pattern was always to run and hide. My entire life. Years ago, I had to forgive her in order to stop poisoning my own mind with anger and hate. I'm at peace with it finally."

"That's so good to hear."

"It wasn't easy and took years of therapy, because of the abuse from Mom and in other areas of my life. But you asked what we can do about it now. Dad, I would ask you to promise me that as long as you live, you'll make sure that Jesse, Brie, and Julie are okay. That if they start to show signs of depression or substance abuse or anything else that you'll step in and get them the help they need. Can you do that?"

"Of course, honey. They're my family. I love them."

"You loved me and Mom, too . . ."

Jack nodded. "I deserved that."

"It wasn't meant to be a dig, it's just the truth. There's no stigma any longer in getting help for mental illness, no matter the severity. We also need to remember to love each other and speak it out loud every chance we get."

"You've gotten very wise in your middle age, little one."

"Impending death will do that to you. Not to mention, having the chance to start completely over. As much as I know it was a crazy decision, I'm grateful every day for having had the chance to hit the reset button. I just wish Mom had been given that opportunity, too."

Jack scooped Kimberly's hands in both of his. "Me, too, Kimmy. Me, too."

"So, tell me about now. What have you been up to? Are you retired yet?"

Jack picked up a coffee mug from the table and handed one to Kimberly. "As a matter of fact, I finally did retire. I know it's hard to believe. A couple of years ago, I turned in my keys and they wished me well. From Eckerd to Rite Aid to CVS. Quite a journey in the world of drugstores. But in the end it was just a job. It kept my mind occupied after losing you and your mother. Then after I retired, I fell in love again."

Kimberly grabbed the couch armrest, a huge grin splitting her face. "Dad! You did?"

"With my guitar."

Kimberly waved her hand in his direction. "Ha. Very funny. Had me going there for a second."

"I started picking it up again after so many years. It was hard at first. I was really rusty, pipes and all. But then things smoothed out. I started gaining a little confidence. I played at a couple of small places around Clearwater on weeknights just trying to get my feet wet. See if the old man could still hold his own after forty some-odd years. A few months ago, I decided I was gonna do something I've wanted to do my entire life. I stayed in various towns all over the Ireland, performing in local pubs for a pint and a meal, then moving on. It's been fantastic. A dream come true."

"Wow, Dad, that's terrific. I'm really happy for you. Please tell me you brought a guitar down here so I can hear you play again."

Jack pulled his phone from his back pocket. "I have the next best thing. Here's a video from my last gig in Dublin. I asked a couple of the local young'uns to record me."

Kimberly took the phone from Jack's hand, turned it horizontally, and pressed play. Tears filled her eyes as she saw her father, looking much younger than his years with a guitar in his lap, living in his gift. Her voice broke as she sang along to The Mamas & the Papas' "California Dreamin'," her harmonies soft but pure.

***

Jack quietly closed the bedroom door, leaving Kimberly sleeping soundly on her down pillows, ceiling fan whirring overhead. Sending a quick text to Julie that her mom was resting, he went looking for Allison. He approached her as she wiped down the granite countertops in the sunny kitchen.

Touching Allison's arm, he said, "Thank you so much. For everything. For the last sixteen years. For saving her life. For facilitating this reunion. Everything."

"Mr. Stevens—"

"Jack."

"Okay, Jack. Believe me when I say it's my pleasure. She's been my best friend for nearly our whole lives. I'd do anything for her. Especially now."

"I know I can speak for all of us. We're very grateful to you."

"Well, you're all very welcome. I just wish I could have convinced her before now."

"Trust me, we all know how stubborn our Kimmy is. I'm sure you tried."

"So many times."

"My granddaughter'll be back here soon. I'll just clear out for now, but I hope it's okay to come again?"

"Any time, Jack. I'll be home every day, until . . ."

Jack nodded, understanding. "Thanks again, Allison. See you soon."

He headed toward the front door, then turned around. "Do you have any idea where I can borrow a guitar?"

Chapter Fifty-Five — JT

After a long, hot shower, JT toweled off, hanging the dog tags and ring around his neck. He wrapped a fist around them for a moment and sat down on the plush hotel bed.

Had it really only been five months? It felt like a year. His memory locked on the day he'd received the phone call that changed everything.

***

The morning of Labor Day the previous year, JT sat at his desk in the line shack of VX-1. He sipped a cup of coffee, reading the morning briefing from the CO regarding the upcoming ceremony commemorating the ten-year anniversary of September 11th, 2001.

After so many years, he'd come back to the squadron that had started it all for him. Airtevron One at NAS Patuxent (Pax) River, Maryland was the Navy's test and evaluation squadron for anti-submarine warfare aircraft. It's where JT had cut his teeth on the Sikorsky SH-60, where he'd learned the bird backward and forward, and where he'd met an adorable, sassy life-support technician named Kimberly Stevens.

Given the choice between multiple duty stations by BUPERS, he'd chosen to come back to Pax. It was nice to be part of a shore duty squadron again—to be able to stay in one place for a bit of time. His parents weren't getting any younger and he needed to spend as much time with them as he could. Deploying to points unknown all over the globe was fine when he was a green, newbie sailor, but nowadays the continental US of A suited him just fine.

The flight line door to the shack opened and the shop LPO, AT1 Jody Drake blew in on a gust of wind, the door slamming behind him. Drake removed his cranial headgear, fastening it to the belt loop of his coveralls by the chin strap.

"Jesus, the wind!"

"The name's Chief, not Jesus. Mornin."

"Good one, Chief. Mornin." Drake poured a cup of coffee and sat in a chair facing JT's desk. He made a face. "Who made the coffee? Tastes like mud."

"Yeah, that would be me. If it's not to your liking, I'll call the butler to bring in a fresh pot."

"Mud it is."

"Briefing from the Skipper is about the 9/11 ceremony next week. Hard to believe it's been ten years already."

"No shit. Well, at least that fucker bin Laden was taken out. Maybe now we can start pulling our troops out of the sand and back to US soil where they belong."

"That'd be good news. CINCNAV is coming down from DC for the ceremony. VX-1 has been chosen to host him and his staff. It'll be dress whites that day, so you need to tell the crew to start working on their uniforms now. Just ribbons, no medals, pressed and shined. Got it?"

"Will do. I have a few pigpens I'll need to hover over."

"You do that, mama hen. We don't need the line being the embarrassment of the command. And it's a Sunday, so the whole squadron's gonna love coming in on a day off."

JT's smartphone in his pocket began to ring. Drake stood to leave. JT saw the familiar number on his screen.

"Speaking of mamas. Anyway, make it a good day out there, Drake."

"Roger that," he said, forcing the door open against the blustery morning.

"Hey, Mama. Ain't it a little early? Thought you had the night shift this month."

His mother choked back a sob. "JT. I need you to come home. It's Pop. And Matt. They're gone, son."

***

On Thursday, September 1, 2011, Tropical Storm Lee formed in the Gulf of Mexico. Texas had been experiencing the worst single-year drought since the 1950's. Grasses were dry, topsoil dust stirring up with every breeze. When the storm formed, farmers all over the state were grateful for what would surely be soaking rains. As with any tropical disturbance, residents in its projected path prepared for every possibility. Homes were stocked with drinking water, canned foods, batteries for flashlights, and gasoline for generators.

By late afternoon Sunday, September 4th, powerful winds preceded the coveted rains, felling trees and knocking down power lines. The parched, crispy loblolly pines caught like tinder at the electric sparks from downed cables.

And the winds kept blowing.

The wildfire spread with unprecedented speed in Bastrop, Texas. The power company rerouted the power grid, shutting down electricity to the localized area to aid firefighters, but the blaze raged on. Multiple areas were evacuated. Folks began to pray harder than ever for the blessed, much needed rain. All medical personnel were called in to local hospitals for emergency duty.

After sending home the crew to check on their own homes, Beau and Matt Allen spent frantic hours spraying their family home and barns with water from multiple hoses, herding the cattle as far away from the structures as possible. They soaked the animals and the grass upon which they grazed.

"Radio says the state park is ablaze!" Matt shouted to his father. He pointed to the orange glow beginning to get brighter, smoke hazing the air.

"Matt, make sure you soak that shed behind the barn real good. Get going now!"

"It's coming in fast, Pop!"

Less than ten miles away, Ella Allen was assisting in the delivery of twins. Both newborn boys were strong and healthy, if a little small. Ella smiled as she handed one baby each to the eager, tearful new parents.

She would later say, that as she'd left that happy room, she could have sworn she felt a head rush and a tremor right at the moment of explosion, when the wildfire wrapped around the gas cans in the Allen Family Farm shed.

***

Removing his dress white cover, JT lay it on the bureau of the Austin hotel suite, and sat next to his mother on a small sofa. He took her hand with tender care. Silent tears flowed from the corners of her eyes as she slowly breathed. In, out.

"Come stay with me in Maryland. We can find a place together. You can find work at a hospital near the base."

Ella shook her weary head. "No, son. My work is here. My community is here. I've lived here my whole life. I love you, darlin, but I'm not moving to Maryland."

"Where will you go?"

"I have friends, honey, and my sister isn't too far away. I'll be okay."

"Mama, I can't just leave you out here."

Meeting her son's eyes, she said, "JT, your life is in the Navy with those helicopters. It's all you've ever known. You just take care of you, okay? You know your mama comes from strong stock. I'll be just fine. Look, if I need you, I promise to call you." She patted his hand.

"I'm not going back for a while. I'll stay as long as I need to so I can help you get your affairs in order."

"My affairs. Listen to you. Your daddy and I have always had our affairs in order. When you own a farm, you have to plan for every eventuality. We're insured to the sky and we had very little debt. My affairs *are* in order, honey." Ella placed a hand on her son's cheek. "I appreciate that you're worried about me. I promise you I'm gonna be okay. I somehow always knew I would outlive your father. But, Matthew . . ."

JT wrapped his arms around his mother's shoulders and closed his eyes, placing his chin on the top of her head.

"Did he tell you he and Leigh Anne had finally picked a wedding date?" she asked.

"No, he didn't."

Ella dabbed her eyes, nodding. "Longest engagement in the history of Texas. First, she wanted to finish school, then he went to business school, then she decided she was going to grad school." She chuckled softly. "So much education and never any time for anything else. Matt worked that farm just as hard, or harder than, your daddy. Said he wouldn't marry her until they were able to live together in the family house, and he wasn't about to do that until Pop and I retired. As soon as we told him we were ready to live out of the RV on the road next year, he couldn't get her on the phone fast enough. She's a patient girl, Leigh

Anne. I love her like my own." She looked up into JT's eyes. "Now what's she gonna do? The house is gone. The farm is gone. It's all gone." Fresh tears welled in her eyes, spilling as she closed them.

JT held his mother close, letting her lean on him for a long moment as she cycled through emotions. After a few minutes, she looked at her watch, steeled her spine, and said, "Folks'll be waiting for us down in the conference room. The labor and delivery center set up a private dinner. Let's go show our gratitude, son." She stood at the mirror, reapplying lipstick.

"Mama. I love you."

She crossed the room and patted the smooth cheek of her middle aged son.

"And I love you, Jason Todd. I promise you, I'm gonna be okay. Let's go downstairs."

Later that night, exhausted from shaking hands, hugging so many people he knew, and quite a few he didn't, JT carefully hung his dress uniform in the hotel closet. In a white undershirt and boxer briefs, he tossed a finger of Jim Beam "down his gullet," as Beau used to say, and crossed the room to the neatly made bed. He picked up a pillow, held it to his face, and with all of the strength he had left in his body, opened his mouth and screamed grief until his throat was raw.

***

"Chief Allen, you're sure about this?"

"I am, Skipper. Twenty-eight years is a long time. I'm ready to call it a day."

"Very well." The captain stood and circled his desk, extending his hand. "I appreciate you coming to see me personally. We've crossed paths a few times during our time in this man's Navy. I've always had nothing but the utmost respect for you, Chief. You'll be missed."

"Thank you, sir. The feeling is mutual."

"Be sure to see Master Chief on your way out so his staff can get started on your out processing. Fair winds and following seas, sailor."

"Aye, sir.

***

Donning board shorts and a tropical print shirt, JT felt as though he was finally beginning to assimilate to island life. Forgoing a ball cap, he ran his fingers through his hair and put on aviator glasses. He'd passed a walk-up on Duval that served some great smelling fried food. He was thinking a lobster roll and fries were on tap tonight.

The tables and standing bars were all filled at the tiny restaurant, so he took his food to-go.

What the hell. I'm halfway to Louie's anyway. I'll grub there.

He passed a number of souvenir shops, a posh gallery featuring blown glass ocean waves, and a real estate office. That reminded him to get the realtor information from Tammi, if she was behind the bar tonight.

Arriving at Louie's, he noticed the song coming from the pipes this time was Cheap Trick's "If You Want My Love." He laughed out loud. "What is it with this place and love songs?"

Instead of standing at the bar, he chose a high top table inside to sit and eat. Not the kind of place to have servers waiting tables, he left his food and went to the bar to place an order. A slender Black man with long dreadlocks and a bright, white smile greeted him.

"What can I get you?"

"Bud Light draft and a shot of Beam."

"Coming up, bro."

"Tammi off already?"

The man pulled the tap and tipped the cup underneath. "You just missed her. Her shift ended a few minutes ago. You a friend of hers?"

"Nope, just a fan."

The bartender laughed and grabbed the Jim Beam from the rows of bottles. "She has lots of fans, our Tammi. She's quite the ambassador of the island."

"Indeed."

Placing the drinks in front of JT, the man said, "That's eight fifty."

"Start a tab?"

"You got it, bro." The man took the receipt and placed it vertically in a cup next to the register.

"Much obliged." JT took the drinks back to his table to tuck in to the food that had made his mouth water the whole way down Duval.

"Boots!"

With a giant lobster roll held in both hands, his mouth happily full, JT looked up to see the petite, tanned figure of Tammi walking over to his table.

"Forgot my cigarettes in the back room so I came back for a minute. Nice surprise seeing you here. How's your stay going?"

JT wiped his mouth. "Pretty well so far. It's only been a couple of days and I feel like I'm finally starting to blend in."

Tammi nodded, checking out his surfer boy attire. "Nice threads." Her laugh was muddy gravel. "Hair's still a little short to be a true islander, but the beard's a good start."

"Appreciate the compliment, ma'am. I think. When I was here earlier, you mentioned a realtor?"

"Oh, right! I forgot to give you her info. Hang on, I'm pretty sure we have a business card." She went behind the bar to look, dipped her hand into a bag under the bar, and came back to his table. Placing the card in front of him, she said, "Here you go. Allison Johnson. Best realtor on the island. She also owns this joint. Her dad was the infamous Louie. She's in the middle of some personal stuff, so I wouldn't bother her right away, but you said you had time, right? Maybe give it a couple weeks before you call her."

She placed some Hershey's Kisses on the table by his beer.

"And Happy Valentine's Day, Boots."

Chapter Fifty-Six — Julie

Back at the hotel, I was filled with energy. Usually crying leaves me so drained, but it's like new life has opened up inside me. And even though we only have a few days to be together, I'm relishing every moment I can spend with my mom. The last thing I want to do is spend time shopping for clothes.

I don't care what I wear as long as I'm comfortable. I live in t-shirts, cut-offs, and flip-flops at home. Which is why when Aunt Brie suggested going to Lily Pulitzer to 'pick me up a few things.' I said, "Isn't there a Target around here?" To that, I received the Stevens Family patented eye roll.

Shopping sucks. But I know Grandpa is spending vital time with my mom, so I allow Aunt Brie to treat me like her paper doll for an hour or so, and I just keep smiling. Like I said, new life!

It was a fascinating afternoon. After my meltdown (yikes), I tried to just stay as quiet as possible and listen—something my therapist taught me. She says it's so much more important to hear what people are saying than to always have to interject my thoughts. Especially at my age. I'll admit, this is very, very hard to do at times, because I tend to get really fired up about certain things, like human rights, the climate crisis, and something as big as your mom coming back from the "dead." Today, though, I just listened and absorbed what everyone else had to say.

Let me say that in the entirety of my life, I have never *seen my aunt Brie so fired up. I mean, the words flying out of her mouth were like something I'd hear on the softball field. She was* pissed. *And I get it, I really do. It blew my mind that my uncle knew my mom hadn't died. While I understand why he kept that from us, especially me—I was just a tiny kid—I think he should have told Aunt Brie. I really hate to say this because I love them both so so so much, but I hope their marriage can make it through this. It's a pretty big speed bump.*

Oh, and Mom coming to Miami to see me play ball?? I mean, what the actual . . ? That spun my brain, dude, I'm not gonna lie. I mean, she actually saw me. In person. And she didn't run up and hug me. I don't know, man . . . if I ever have kids, I'm just saying, they're gonna be the top priority of my life. Seriously not trying to judge or belittle my mom. She told us all about her mental and physical health, and I do get it. But wasn't she in a much better place then? I guess seeing me in person must have hit her really hard. Like the gravity of the decision she'd made probably left her totally shook in that moment. Still . . .

So, even though I spent much of today saying nothing, I'm gonna have plenty to say when I go back over there tonight. I got a text from Grandpa that she's resting, so I'll head that way once he's back at the hotel. My bag is packed for about a week. That's me being hopeful. Who knows how long I'll have, or whether she'll want me there the whole time, but I don't intend to leave unless I'm asked.

My first thoughts when I saw her were that she's so pretty, even though she's very sick, and that she has a very powerful command of a room. I wonder if she was always that way. According to her journal, she was pretty much of a loner and not super assertive, so maybe it's just something that's developed as she's gotten older. Maybe fulfilling her life's purpose working at the shelter brought that out in her. All I know is she's fierce!

Some questions I'm gonna ask:

1) Who is my dad and why wasn't he ever in my life? (Pretty sure I'm right, but I gotta know for sure)

2) Why are there no photos of him in the box?

3) Why are so many pages torn out of the journal?

4) Where's the ring that was in that velvet box?

5) I know it might be morbid, but how do you want to be remembered?

With so much going on in my life lately, I'm a little overwhelmed. Okay, a lot overwhelmed. Not only did I get to meet the mother I thought was dead, I have decisions to make about my future that need to happen in just weeks, and I feel like I've been so sheltered and protected my whole life, I'm a little terrified to cross these unfamiliar streets without holding the hand of a grown-up, figuratively. So, after spending some time with my mom, putting all of this craziness into perspective, maybe then I'll feel ready to tackle the world.

I've been thinking about sandhill cranes lately. I was fascinated with them when I was in middle school. Not just because they're beautiful and have a really cool walk and their babies are adorable. I mean, that's what attracted me at first—oh my word, those babies have butterscotch fur! Anyway, what really amazes me about those creatures is that although they're pack animals, usually traveling in groups of 4, the babies become completely independent at 10-12 months! They leave the parents and cleave to another group entirely, of other young ones or of non-breeding adults. It's a pattern they repeat over and over, and they do just fine on their own at less than a year old! It's crazy to me. I don't know what sandhill crane years are in human years, but their lifespan is approximately 20 years. Considering healthy humans live to be approximately 80, that means they go off on their own at 4 years old! I mean, holy crap. Humans are way less independent and self-sufficient. Carlee's oldest brother is still living at home and that boy is nearly 30! But they remind me of my mom and her siblings. How they went off on their own at young ages and never looked back.

No matter what happens next, no matter what decisions I come to, no matter how much time I have left with my mom. I know one thing for sure: I want to be as fierce and independent as a sandhill crane.

Chapter Fifty-Seven — Kimberly & Allison

The rich, mouth-watering aroma of baking banana bread awoke Kimberly. She opened her eyes and breathed deeply through her nose. Even with the oxygen line in place, the smell of the fruity, nutty bread was enough to make her stomach rumble. She wondered what time it was. The thought hit her. Was this afternoon just a dream? Or did I really see my entire family and hold my daughter today? She turned her face, lifted the shoulder of her blouse, and sniffed. Her father's cologne.

It was real. It had actually happened. She wrapped her arms around herself and squeezed, shaking her head in disbelief.

"They were really here," Kimberly whispered to herself. She sat up to take a drink of water and pain bolted through her torso. She sucked in a sharp breath through gritted teeth and gripped the bedside table. On casters, the table rolled on the tile out of her grasp, causing Kimberly to fall from the bed, landing hard on her right side.

"Oh! Agghhh!" she cried out. They'd removed her throw rug to facilitate the table and walker, and now, lying on the cold Spanish tile, she regretted that decision.

Allison burst through the door, panic in her voice. "Oh my god, Kim, what the hell happened?"

"I tried to . . . reach the . . .ughhh."

"Are you hurt? I don't want to touch you yet if you're hurt. Can you take stock real quick?" Allison scanned her body for signs of blood, but saw none.

Lying on her side on the floor, Kimberly wiggled and twisted toes, feet, hands, wrists.

"All good, I think."

"Okay, honey, I'm gonna get behind you and lift under your arms. Here we go."

Allison eased her friend from the floor, careful not to jostle her too much. She turned her slowly, setting her down on the bed. "Okay, Evel Knievel, just sit still and let me get the oxygen back where it belongs." She sat on the bed next to Kimberly, placing the cannula under her nose. "Breathe deeply, lady."

Kimberly closed her eyes, resting her head on Allison's shoulder.

"Well, that was graceful," Kimberly said.

"Ten out of ten from the Russian judge."

"I should get high scores for the degree of difficulty. I guess the brakes weren't applied on the table wheels."

"My fault entirely," Allison said.

"Oh, stop, you've been so busy preparing for my family and everything—"

"No excuse. I know better. It won't happen again. Cross my heart. How're you feeling?"

The look on Kimberly's face told the story. She was in pain. Her belly, her muscles, her bones, everything inside her ached. Her stomach threatened to rebel.

"That good, huh? Let me give Regina a call. I'll—"

"No, it's okay. Just let me rest." Kimberly lay back on the pillow and closed her eyes.

On the phone, Regina said, "I'm on my way to check on her. Just got held up at a previous appointment. Walking your way as we speak."

"I know I'm probably overreacting, but I don't want to overdose her or anything."

"Allison, she's end-of-life. Everything probably hurts like hell. Try to stay ahead of the pain with her meds schedule and don't worry about a thing. She'll be counting on you to keep her comfortable."

"You're the professional." Allison looked at the floor. "Hearing 'end-of-life' out loud feels awful."

"I know, honey. Let's keep her still and comfortable for now. Let me hear from you in a few hours, deal?"

"Sounds like a plan. Thanks as always, Regina. We appreciate you so much."

"Just doing my job, girl. I'm almost to your place," she said and ended the call.

And that's when Allison heard the scream.

Chapter Fifty-Eight — Jack

As Jack ascended the stairs leading to the vast porch of Grand Vin, he noticed all the tables were filled with folks sipping wine, noshing on cheese and fruit, and savoring the quiet Monday evening on Duval Street. He stepped through the open door and to his right, at Allison's instructions, into the small bar area.

"And how are you this evening, sir? Is there a wine we can interest you in or did you come to sample?" The man behind the bar had a spray of honey curls on top of his head and deep brown eyes as warm as his smile.

"Hi . . . are you Dustin?"

"The one and only. Pray tell, who sendeth you, my lad?"

Jack extended his hand. "Name's Jack Stevens. Allison Johnson told me I'd find you here. I'm Kimberly's dad."

Dustin gasped, placing a hand over his mouth, before grasping Jack's and shaking effusively.

"Oh my goddess, I didn't know a father of Kimberly existed. Please, please, come in and have a seat at the bar. Tell me what I can do for you. How *is* our girl this evening?"

"She seems to be having a good day. It's the first time I've seen her in about seventeen years."

Again, Dustin gasped. "Well, that would explain why we never knew you existed. Let me pour you a glass of wine and you can tell me your sad tale, kind sir. Cab, Pinot, Sancerre?"

Jack shook his head. "A glass of sparkling water would be great, thanks."

"You got it. Be right back." Dustin swiveled around the short bar, heading toward the back room for a chilled bottle of San Pellegrino. "Sugar!" he whispered to Geno. "That man at the bar is *Kimberly's father.*"

He locked eyes with his husband. "Father! I thought maybe the girl had been hatched, for Pete's sake. No mention *ever* of a family."

Geno peered around Dustin's shoulder. "Hmm. Interesting. Let's go have a chat with Kimberly's father."

The men took their places behind the bar. Dustin poured the fizzy liquid into a high ball glass, studding it with a lime wedge.

"One sparkling water for the stranger. This is my husband, Geno, by the way. Geno, meet Jack Stevens."

"Pleased to meet you, Geno." Jack held out his hand.

"Likewise, Mr. Stevens."

"Jack, please."

"Jack it is. You say you're Kim's dad? We've known that sweet woman for many years and never heard any mention of family."

Jack sipped the water, the bubbles tickling his mustache. He wiped a hand across his mouth and placed the glass on the bar. "Allison said I could trust you guys—that you're very close to her and Kim. Our family was never what you would call close. In fact, you could probably say we wrote the book on aloof. Many years ago, we were all led to believe Kim had ended her life. My other daughter and her husband raised Kim's daughter—"

"Daughter!" Dustin and Geno said in unison.

"Yes, Julie. She turned eighteen a few days ago, and that's when we got the call from Kim that shocked us all. We raced down to Key West as soon as we could." Jack looked at his water glass, lifting it again to his lips.

Dustin and Geno exchanged glances, mouths agape. "Well, this certainly sheds new light on our angel. She has a family and she's a mama, too!" Dustin said.

Geno spoke up. "So, if you don't mind me asking, why are you here talking to us when you should be spending time with your prodigal daughter who's in her last days?"

"I just left her house. Allison sent me here. I'm a musician," Jack said, pulling out his wallet to hand them his business card. "When we got word that Kim was still alive, I was in Dublin, Ireland. I left almost everything and flew here immediately. Kim was always soothed by my music, but I don't have my guitar. Allison said I could possibly borrow a guitar from Geno . . .?"

Geno examined the business card. The resemblance between Jack and Kimberly was undeniable. Geno smiled. He patted Jack's shoulder. "Kind sir, I would be delighted to loan you a guitar. Acoustic or electric?"

As Jack headed back down Duval Street toward the hotel, guitar case in hand, he realized he hadn't borrowed any picks for the guitar from Geno.

In his room, Jack opened the case, searching the pockets on the crushed velvet interior to no avail. Jack sighed. Then a thought occurred to him.

He removed his wallet from his back pocket, opened it, and digging into a barely used chamber, discovered what he knew had been transferred from billfold to wallet for fifty years. An ivory pick faded to a yellowish hue, emblazoned with *Cabana Lounge, St. Petersburg, Florida.* He'd known the pick would come in handy someday.

Chapter Fifty-Nine — JT

JT's jaw dropped. His hand trembled slightly as he read the information on the business card.

Allison Johnson
Real Estate Agent
619 Duval Street
Key West, Florida 33040
786-555-9100 x101
ajpioneer@kwrealtor.com

But what floored him—what he couldn't peel his eyes from—was the photo on the card. There she was. Kimberly's best friend from the Navy. From VX-1. The squadron nickname was "The Pioneers." It had to be her. She had barely changed in thirty years.

Puzzle pieces began to fit together in JT's mind.

The familiar blonde in the photos on the back wall in the bar.

The family he kept running into in town had mentioned Allison and Kimberly.

He'd seen them all approaching a bungalow on Catherine Street.

Kimberly had thought JT had perished in a helo crash. She'd been despondent with a little baby. She was never close to her family. Of course, she'd run to Allison. They were best friends—the only friend Kimberly ever really had, besides himself. *Of course!* It all made sense.

"Ha ha!" JT laughed out loud. Tears burned his eyes. He held the card tightly in his fist.

Allison's office. He would go there right now.

He tossed out the rest of his dinner, slapped a twenty on the bar, and ran out onto the sidewalk.

Slow down, idiot. You look crazy.

JT slowed to a more reasonable pace. He compared the street numbers on each of the storefronts with the number on Allison's business card. He was getting closer.

The door to 619 had *Key West Real Estate* in white lettering. He grabbed the door knob and turned. Locked. He knocked on the glass of the door, but there was nobody inside. He looked at his watch. Shit. After 5:00 pm.

JT pulled out his cell phone and dialed the number on the card.

"Thank you for calling Key West Real Estate. Our office is now closed. If you know your party's extension, please dial it now—"

He punched in 101.

"Hi, you've reached Allison Johnson. Your call is very important to me, so please leave your name and number and I'll call you back as soon as possible. Please note, I'll be on a leave of absence until March. I look forward to helping you find your dream home at that time. Have a beautiful island day!"

He tapped the red 'end' button on his phone. Dammit. Now what?

He thought about the house on Catherine Street. It was probably completely inappropriate, but . . .

JT's mind was on overdrive as he speed-walked, dodging window shoppers on the sidewalk, toward the bungalow. What if Kim was at that house? What if that's where she's been *all this time,* just three minutes from his hotel? What if he was just conjuring ghosts again, trying to make things fit his desperate narrative?

He slowed his pace again. This was just crazy.

Get a grip, Allen, you're losing what marbles you have left.

He stopped at the corner of Truman and Duval at the red light. Waiting for the walk sign to change, he noticed the same pretty, young woman again walking up Truman and turning left onto Duval. The same direction he was headed. She had her curls swept up in a high ponytail and a backpack slung on her shoulders.

Come on, light, change already!

The numbers counted down to zero and the walk sign changed. He crossed Truman and stayed a safe distance behind the girl, leaving a few other people between them. As they neared the corner of Duval and Catherine, he saw her look both ways and step out into the street to cross Duval.

He waited until she crossed, then he followed.

In a moment, she was at the gate of the bungalow.

He approached her, his breath coming in fast bursts, heart thudding in his ears.

She reached for the handle of the gate.

Without even thinking, he reached out, grabbing her wrist.

"Juliana . . .?"

The girl jerked her head in his direction, eyes wide with fear.

Her mouth dropped open and she screamed.

Chapter Sixty — Julie

Seems like it's taking forever for Grandpa to get back from Mom's. I've packed my bag with all my old junk and the new junk, too, read some more of Mom's journal (I love all the stuff she wrote about fixing up the little blue truck), brushed my teeth, had some crackers, brushed my teeth again, and now I'm sipping on a bottle of water just waiting.

After we got back to the room, Aunt Brie dumped my shopping bags on the bed and said she was going for a long walk. She's really, <u>really</u> upset. I've never seen her like that before. I can't blame her. I just hope she can work it all out in her head and calm down before we go back home. I have never seen my aunt and uncle fight, and I really don't want to see it now. They are the epitome of the perfect couple. I hope they can stay that way.

My uncles went down to Mallory Square. They want to watch the sunset and have cocktails. I'm sure Uncle Jesse is processing a lot of stuff, too. The whole world changed today for all of us. I can't even imagine how he must be feeling. I mean, as far as I've been able to tell, he was closer to my mom than anyone. He's such a tenderhearted man. I know this has to be really weird and hard for him.

I can't wait till Grandpa gets to the hotel so I can go back and see her. I've waited my whole life to spend time alone with my mom. Of course, a few days ago, I thought that meant looking at her photos and reading her journal. It's nutty how life takes twists and turns you'd never expect.

I'm really looking forward to asking her all the questions I have, and talking to her about my future plans. I wonder how she'll feel about me possibly joining Doctors Without Borders. Maybe she won't think it's so crazy to take a gap year before college. Maybe she'll even have some good arguments for me to use when I approach Uncle Grey about it.

Oh, wait, I think I hear Grandpa in his room next door. I'm gonna tuck my journal in my bag and write more tonight at Mom's. Holy cow . . . I still can't believe it.

Chapter Sixty-One — Kimberly & Allison

As Regina came around the corner of Allison's street, an ear-piercing scream came barreling through the air like a siren.

Inside the house, Allison raced for the door. "What the hell . . . ?"

Regina bounded down the sidewalk hollering, "Get your hands *off* of her this instant!" The nurse reached him in no time and swung her medical bag at the head of the bearded man, smacking the mirrored Ray-Bans to the ground. He dropped the girl's wrist and raised his hands in surrender, shielding his face as the heavy leather satchel came at him again.

Julie continued to scream as she ran toward the house, colliding with Allison, who held Julie's frightened face in her hands, and yelled over her screaming, "Are you okay?!"

Julie stopped screaming, her head bobbing up and down, her breathing erratic.

"Get inside, *now*," Allison commanded, as she marched out to the street.

"Ma'am, stop! Please stop hitting me! This is all a misunderstanding!" the bearded man pleaded with the nurse.

Allison grabbed the bag as Regina swung it behind her, ready to strike again, her eyes wild.

"Regina! She's okay. She's in the house. It's okay, my friend."

Regina panted, her shoulders heaving up and down as she snatched her phone from the pocket of her scrubs.

"Don't you go *anywhere,* you pervert. You stay right there. Allison, hold him, I'ma call the police right now!"

"No worries. I got this," Allison said, sliding a 9mm pistol from the waistband of her shorts.

The man, keeping one hand raised, slowly bent down to retrieve his glasses from the road. As he stood up, his eyes met Allison's. Then he saw the gun. She didn't look away. Recognition registered. Then shock. With her free hand, she pulled the phone from Regina and thumbed the 'end' button.

"What the . . . Allison, what are you doing?" Regina cried, eyes wide.

Still locked on the face of the man, she said, "It's okay, Regina. I know him."

"What? You do?"

Allison handed the phone back to Regina and slipped the handgun back into place.

"I do." Her face a cloud of confusion and disbelief, she said, "Way to come back from the dead, Lazarus. You've got a *shitload* of explaining to do."

Chapter Sixty-Two — Jack

Tuning a guitar felt like a little like riding a bike. From the time he was in grade school, Jack had never lost the ability to hear the right pitch with each twist of a tuning peg. Sitting in a chair on his hotel lanai, he held the borrowed Taylor acoustic guitar on his lap, the pick between his teeth, twisting and twanging as each string finally hit the right note. He strummed softly, making adjustments until the chords he played hit that magic sweet spot in his ear. He smiled to himself, recalling the last time he'd tuned his own guitar, just a week ago.

***

Jack sat on a barstool by a wood stove in the corner of a dimly lit pub in Oranmore, Ireland called MacDonaghs, or more affectionately known by the locals as The Thatch, due to its old world-style thatched roof. He'd landed in Galway earlier in the day. While renting a car, he'd asked the young man behind the counter what pub he would recommend that wasn't touristy and allowed live music. The rental agent immediately mentioned The Thatch, giving him quick directions from the airport.

"Take a right turn out of the car park, hang a right at Carnmore Cross, three roundabouts, then left onto Main Street in Oranmore. You can't miss it."

Jack held up his cell phone. "Thank the techies for GPS, huh?" He pulled up the pub on Google and away he went.

After the pull of a Smithwick's Blonde and a quick word with management, assuring them he wanted no money for his time, Jack set up in the corner, tuning his Gibson, tip jar on the floor next to him, in case anyone was feeling generous. Some of the older gents eyed him suspiciously, raising eyebrows and tipping their heads. The bartender just shrugged and pulled a tap of Guinness.

Having no microphone, Jack simply spoke to the patrons around him—the same words he used before each of his pop-up performances.

"Not your typical entertainment, I know. I'm just a retired Yank living out a dream. So, please bear with me. If you have any requests, I promise to do my best. My name's Jack, and this is 'Something' by the Beatles."

A typical night had Jack playing for an hour. Most of the songs in his repertoire were from the '60's, with a smattering of '50's and '70's thrown in for good measure. He might get one or two requests, and usually ended the night with enough tips for a pint and, sometimes, a meal.

The Thatch, however, proved to be better than typical. After playing a number of ballads, Jack stood and ripped into "Walk Don't Run" by the Ventures. He noticed toes starting to tap, fingers drumming on the bar. Keeping up the energy, he launched into "Help Me Rhonda" by the Beach Boys. Before he knew it, folks stood up and started dancing. The bartender tipped an imaginary hat to him. Jack winked and kept the night rolling with "Sweet Caroline" by Neil Diamond. When he reached the chorus, the entire pub shouted "bah bah bah" in place of the horns. Drinks were flowing, his tip jar filling. Requests were coming from young and old and, for the most part, he was able to fulfill them.

After two hours, his hands began to get sore and he desperately needed a bathroom break. He thanked the crowd and began to pack up the Gibson. A chorus of disappointment came from the pub patrons. They wanted more. He chuckled and agreed to one last song. As he played the familiar introduction, the happily drunken revelers lifted their pints, gin and tonics, and whiskeys to sing along.

When Irish eyes are smilin', sure tis like a morn in spring
In the lilt of Irish laughter, you can hear the angels sing
When Irish hearts are happy, all the world seems bright and gay
And when Irish eyes are smilin', sure they steal your heart away . .

.

The love that flowed over Jack in the applause and claps on the back from a local weeknight crowd in the little town of Oranmore, County Galway, Ireland, lifted his heart and spirits like they hadn't been in many years. He wiped a tear with the back of his hand as he bent to load the Gibson back into its case. If only his family had been there to see it. He made a mental note to ask someone to record him on his phone at the next pub. But this night had been special—sprinkled with faerie dust. If he never had another crowd like this one, it wouldn't matter a bit. He'd always have this night.

***

Softly, Jack strummed the Taylor and hummed the Celtic tune, grinning at the memory.

Jesse burst through the small lanai gate.

"Dad, pack up the guitar and come with me. Something really fucking weird has just happened. You're *not* gonna believe this shit."

Chapter Sixty-Three — JT

The last time JT had seen Allison in the 1990's, she was a feisty sailor with a saucy mouth that made up for her short stature. Now, he realized, the only thing that changed was the fire in her eyes aimed directly at him.

"Allison, let me explain."

"Oh, you're damn sure gonna explain. No question about that. Regina, would you please go inside and check on—"

"On it," Regina called over her shoulder.

"What the hell are you doing alive? And at my house? Do you have any idea the pain you've caused for Kim and her entire family? I want to know the whole story and you'd better hurry it up because I'm completely out of patience today."

"If we could just sit down—"

Allison crossed her arms over her chest. "We will not be sitting down. We will stand right here in front of my house. You talk now and talk fast. And *truth*, Allen. I want the truth."

"Is Kim here?"

"That is *none* of your goddamn business. Speak. Now."

JT sighed, his shoulders heavy. "I didn't die in that helo crash in Bosnia."

"Thank you, Captain Obvious."

"I'd only been over there a short time on deployment with my squadron when I was ordered to report to a SEAL unit."

"Classified, top secret, yadda, yadda."

"Correct. Believe what you want to believe, but this outfit was involved with conflicts in three separate nations. It was so deep cover, I didn't even know the true names of any of the SEALS, only their call signs."

"Mm hmm. Go on."

JT ran a hand through his hair and down his face. "We weren't allowed any communication, in or out, with anyone outside the command, especially civilians. I told myself that Kim understood things like this, that she'd been a sailor long enough to realize what was happening. Of course, hindsight makes me sick, realizing not only would she have been privy to zero intel, all she knew was a helo from my squadron had crashed and naturally assumed I was onboard. Mind you, I knew none of this at the time."

"Uh huh. Keep going."

"The first opportunity I had to call her was in the Med on the way home in 1996. I tried calling five times. The number had been disconnected. When I arrived back at Mayport, I raced over to her place, but the super told me she was gone. I tried her parents, but they never called me back. I couldn't remember the names of her siblings or where they lived. And I had no idea how to reach you. I went to her former job—"

"Denny's?"

"Yes. The manager looked at me like he'd seen a ghost. I guess Kim had seen the newspaper article in the restaurant and fainted. He said they'd called an ambulance. He also said she'd been pregnant at the time. Apparently with my daughter. Juliana."

Allison blinked and shifted her weight from one foot to the other. JT could see she was starting to soften, to believe him.

"You've known you had a daughter since 1996 and you never made any attempt to find her?"

"I told you I tried to find Kim to no avail. How was I going to be able to find her daughter? My parents mentioned a private detective, but that felt slimy to me. If I was going to find them, it was going to be organic. Of course this was long before Google and Facebook."

"And when technology advanced, why didn't you?"

"I threw myself into my career. Made chief, traveled the world on deployments, put everything behind me. I was considering re-upping one more time, but then the wildfires last September in Texas took out my family farm."

Allison's arms dropped to her sides. "I'd heard about those. There were fatalities."

"Our farm was destroyed. My father and brother along with it."

Closing her eyes, Allison put a hand on JT's arm. "I'm really sorry to hear that, JT."

"Thank you. It hasn't been easy. My mom's still in Texas and refuses to leave. She's stubbornly independent. I couldn't stay there. I retired from the Navy and came here in the hopes of disappearing from life, from pain, from everything. I'd been told a long time ago that this was the place to do it. I don't think I ever knew you were from here."

"Then how did you happen to be standing in the middle of my street grabbing my guest by the arm?"

"Louie's Watering Hole."

"What does the bar have anything to do with—"

"I became friendly with a very talkative bartender on my first day here."

"Tammi."

"Yeah, she's the one. She asked if I was temporary or staying. I said I was thinking of staying. So, she gave me your business card. I saw the old photos on the back wall. I put two and two together. And here I am."

"Well, Agatha Christie, that's quite a story. I commend you on your deduction skills. Yes, I'm a realtor. I'm happy to help you find a listing on the island next month. I'm on leave."

"I called the number on your card and heard your outgoing message, so I knew that."

"Then, I'll ask you again. Why are you here?"

"Because in the past couple of days, I've continued to run into a family on the street and in restaurants. I overheard one of them say 'Allison' and one of them say 'Kimberly,' and I thought it was a complete coincidence. Until I realized that if Kim went anywhere to disappear, she would have come to you."

Allison opened the gate behind her. "JT, there are chairs here in my front yard. Have a seat. I'll be back in a few minutes. But if you move, if you leave, or if you try to approach my house, I'll shoot you, do you understand?"

"Are you holding me hostage?"

"Yes. Sit. Don't move. I'll be back." Allison turned on her heel. At the top of her porch, she turned to look at JT. She pointed two fingers at her eyes, then at him. *I'm watching you.* He nodded and sat back in the chair.

She's just as bossy as she ever was. Some things never change.

Chapter Sixty-Four — Julie

"Pick up, pick up, pick up, Aunt Brie." Julie paced the floor in Allison's living room, the cell phone in her ear ringing and ringing. Hopefully her aunt hadn't turned off her ringer when she went for her long walk. "Come on! Pick up, please!"

"Hey, Jules, I'm almost back to the hotel, I—"

"Aunt Brie! That man tried to grab me! I was almost to Allison's house and he came from behind and grabbed my wrist!"

"What man? Oh my god, are you okay, honey? I'm coming right over."

"That man I kept seeing all over the place. Ugh, he's just a skeeve! I'm fine. Mom's nurse clocked him in the head with her bag and Allison's out there talking to him now. I think she has a gun. You don't need to rush over here. I'm okay. Mom's nurse is with me."

"A gun?! Can you please put the nurse on the phone?"

"Hang on. Ma'am, my aunt would like to speak to you." Julie handed Regina the phone.

"Hello?"

"Yes, hi, this is Sabrina Hanover, I'm Julie's aunt, Kimberly's sister."

Regina looked at Julie and smiled.

"Ah. Her daughter. Yes, she's lovely, just like her mama."

"Thank you. Listen, can you tell me what just happened in the street?"

"It's like Julie said, a man grabbed her wrist. But Allison seems to know him. She called him Lazarus. Like the one Jesus raised from the dead?"

"I think I've heard the story, yes . . ."

"Well, Miss Firecracker is out there giving him the who's and the what for's right now and he don't seem to be going nowhere, so I'm guessing it's all okay."

"Thank you for explaining everything, ma'am."

"Regina Stockwell. Please call me Regina."

"Regina, thanks so much for staying with my niece."

"It's my pleasure, Sabrina. I'll stay as long as she needs me." Regina handed the phone back to Julie.

"I'm sorry I called all weirded out."

"No! You did exactly the right thing."

"Oh my gosh, that dude is sitting in a chair in the front yard and Allison's coming back inside. I'm putting you on speaker. Hang on." She tapped the icon on the phone. "Can you hear me?"

"Yep, I'm with you."

Entering the living room, Allison closed the door behind her.

"Was Kim able to sleep through all this?"

Regina turned toward the bedroom. "Oh my stars, I completely forgot to check on her." She silently opened the bedroom door a crack and peeked in, then closed the door, tiptoeing away. "She's asleep. Thank heavens. She doesn't need to be upset."

Allison held up a hand. "Later. We'll talk about that in a minute. I need everyone to sit down." Regina and Julie sat on opposite ends of the sofa. Allison removed the gun from her waistband and placed it on the fireplace mantle.

"My aunt's on the phone with us." Julie held up her cell phone showing it on speaker.

"Jesse and Taylor are here, too," Sabrina said from the phone. "Got you guys on speaker, too. Where's Lazarus? Are you calling the cops?"

"Who's Lazarus?" Allison asked, confused.

"That guy out there," Julie indicated, jerking her thumb over her shoulder. "Regina said you called him Lazarus."

Allison put her hand to her forehead and let out a soft chuckle. "I was being a smart ass. Because he's reappeared after we thought he was dead."

"What?" Sabrina asked.

"That seems to be going around," Taylor said.

Allison sat in a wingback chair. She clasped her hands together and rested her elbows on her knees.

"Julie, I have something really important to tell you. I need you to know this before we tell your mother, because she's going to need all of our support when this bomb drops on her."

Julie gasped and covered her mouth. "He called me Juliana . . ."

Allison nodded.

A tear squeaked out of the corner of Julie's eye, slowly traveling down her cheek. She met Allison's eyes, as the realization dawned on her.

Nearly inaudibly, Julie whispered, "Oh. My. God. That man outside? Is he my father?"

Allison took in a deep breath. She nodded. "Yes. That's your father outside. Jason Todd Allen. He goes by JT."

"But I thought he—"

"We all thought he died in a helicopter crash in Bosnia. Turns out he was never anywhere near that aircraft."

Julie dropped her head into her hands, rocking back and forth. "This is too much. This is too much."

"Jules, we are running over there right now. Don't move. Don't do a thing till we get there, okay?" Sabrina shouted through the phone's speaker. "Jess, go get Dad. Julie, honey, we'll be right there!" She disconnected the call.

Allison crossed the room and wrapped her arms around Julie, stroking her back.

"I know. It's a lot. Just take deep breaths. Try to relax."

Regina came back from the kitchen with a glass of water, placing it in front of Julie on the coffee table. She peered out the window. The man was still in the Adirondack chair, leaning forward, his hands clasped, elbows on his knees, looking very uncomfortable.

"I'm gonna peek in on Kimberly one more time, then I'll leave y'all to it. This has been a hell of a day for this family. I'll pray for each of you. Please keep Kimberly as calm as you can. Lord have mercy . . ."

Julie looked up at Allison, who handed her a tissue. "I don't think anyone understands. I've never felt so happy in my entire life." Her face broke out into a giant, watery grin as she stood and headed toward the door.

As Julie emerged onto the front porch, JT stood. He put his hands on his hips, then dropped them, ran a hand through his hair, over his beard. He pulled off the Ray-Bans, placing them in the pocket of his tropical shirt.

"Sorry," he said. "I'm, uh, pretty nervous right now and have no idea what to say."

Julie came down the steps and walked tentatively toward JT, taking him in. Thick, wavy brown hair with a light sprinkle of silver, mustache and beard mostly silver with a little brown left, not super tall like her uncle, but a lot taller than her mom, slender, his formerly white legs now quite sunburned.

"I don't know what to call you."

"We could start with JT, if that's all right with you?"

Julie nodded. "I'm Julie."

"I'm so incredibly pleased to meet you, Julie." His voice broke. He placed a fist in front of his mouth, struggling to keep his emotions in check.

"Maybe we should sit?" Julie motioned toward the chairs behind him.

Sitting down, they faced each other.

"This is awkward," she said.

JT nodded. "You're so beautiful. I'm sorry. That's probably creepy of me to say."

Julie shook her head. "No. From anyone else but you, probably. But, no. It's nice."

"I deeply regret not finding you sooner."

"We can go forward from here."

"I'd like that very much."

"Me, too." Julie looked at her hands in her lap. "My mom's really sick. Cancer. She's on hospice."

JT closed his eyes. Pain creased his face.

"So she is here. How much longer?" he asked.

Julie shrugged. "At first we heard days, then weeks, either way, it's not long enough. Her energy comes and goes. She's sleeping right now."

JT nodded.

"We can go see her together when she wakes up. Her nurse said we need to keep her calm."

"I'll do my best."

"Can I ask you something?"

"Anything."

"Did you ever fall in love again?"

JT's dark brown eyes pierced Julie's blue-greens. "Never. Kim was the absolute love of my life. I never even looked at another woman."

"That's kinda sad."

"It's just how it is," he said. He looked into her face. "I hate that the first time you laid eyes on me, it was in fear."

Julie frowned. She reached over, taking JT's hand. She heard his breath catch.

"I think I'd rather call you Dad."

JT swallowed. "I think I'd like that."

"Can I hug you?"

JT stood, opening his arms. "I would be honored."

Julie folded herself into his body, wrapping her arms around his waist. His arms encircled her back, pulling her close, trickling tears resting in his beard. She placed her cheek on his chest and then pulled back.

"What's that?" She pointed to his chest.

JT pulled the chain outside of his shirt. His dog tags tinkled against an emerald ring, glistening in the sun.

"This is your mother's engagement ring."

Julie stepped back, her smile enormous. "The empty ring box! How do you have that ring if it was Mom's?"

"She sold it to a pawn shop near her old apartment in Jacksonville. I bought it back. I've been wearing it around my neck for sixteen years hoping I would have the chance to put it back on her finger."

"Can I touch it?"

"Of course." JT slipped the chain from around his neck, handing it to Julie. She held the tags in the palm of her hand, reading his identification. She picked up the ring between two fingers, turning it in the sunlight, admiring its beauty.

"Jason Todd. Nobody ever called you by your real name?"

"Just my mom and dad. And only when I was in trouble."

"Oh . . . I have other grandparents!"

JT looked solemn. "You have a grandma, yes. She is going to be so excited to meet you. But my Pop passed last year. And my brother. Together."

Julie's hand flew to her gaping mouth. "Oh no! Oh my god—what happened?

"Wildfires in Texas. Wiped out our family farm and a gas explosion killed them."

"That's so terrible." Julie covered her eyes, woozy from all of this information coming at her all at once.

The gate in the white picket fence swung wide open. Sabrina, Jesse, Taylor, and Jack stormed into the front yard, approaching Julie protectively.

"Maybe you should introduce us, Julie," Sabrina said, arms folded across her chest.

Pointing from left to right, Julie said, "Sabrina, Jesse, Taylor, and Grandpa, meet . . . JT Allen. My dad."

Jack stepped forward. Hands on hips, he examined the man standing next to his granddaughter.

"It's really him, Grandpa. I looked at his dog tags." She offered the dog tags to Jack who peered at them quickly, then looked back at JT.

"And just where the hell have *you* been all this time?" he snarled.

JT opened his mouth to speak. Allison called from the porch. "Hey, everybody. Let's give JT a break for a second. Trust me, I already grilled the man. Can all of you come inside, please? Kimberly's awake. And I think it's time her little family was finally reunited."

Chapter Sixty-Five — Kimberly & Allison

Kimberly sat up in bed, propped up on her pillows, sipping a glass of water.

"How'd you sleep?" Regina asked.

"Pretty well, although I may have made a few mistakes," she grinned.

"Ha ha, very funny, Miss Thang," Regina chuckled. "Seriously, I hear you took quite a spill. You got lucky this time, Kim."

"Thanks for taking care of me, ladies. My guardian angels."

"My pleasure, honey. Now, you take it easy the rest of the day. I understand you have some family visiting to do."

"Yes, my daughter is coming to stay for a few days. I'm so excited to get to know her. She's an adult now, Regina."

"I've seen her, and I must say I was right. She's absolutely lovely. I'm really outta here now. Duty calls. You rest, ya hear? Allison, call me if you need me."

Regina and Allison exchanged looks.

"Aye aye, captain." Allison gave a quick salute. Regina closed the door behind her.

"Is Julie here?" Kim asked.

"Yes, ma'am. Before she comes in, I have some things I need to tell you."

Allison sat at the foot of the bed, holding onto the lump of Kim's feet under the covers. She took a deep breath and let it out slowly.

"You okay? You look like you could use a stiff drink. Has something happened?"

Allison chuckled. "Oh, you could say that every day and twice on

Sunday, and you wouldn't be wrong."

"Spill it."

"Well . . . I'm not sure how I'm supposed to tell you this so I'm just gonna rip off the band aid and hope for the best."

"You're scaring me."

"JT Allen is standing outside that door." She motioned to the bedroom door.

"Allison, what the fuck is wrong with you? Why would you say something so terrible to me? Today of all days. What are you trying to do to me?"

"Kimberly. Look at me. Look in my eyes. I am telling you the truth."

"Stop it. Just stop it. You know as well as I do that he died in—"

Allison shook her head. "He didn't. That's what I'm trying to tell you. He was not on that helo that crashed. He was attached to a top secret SEAL command that wound up being gone three years. He had no way to reach you."

Kimberly set down her water glass, pulling her feet away from Allison's grasp and crisscrossed her legs beneath the covers. "This. Is. Not. Funny. Knock it off now," she said, her eyes blazing.

"Okay. I'll let him speak for himself. JT, come on in."

The door opened and a slender, bearded man entered. Kimberly drew in a sharp breath, covering her mouth with her good hand.

"Ho. Ly. Shit. No way. It can't. You can't. I don't understand what the actual fuck is happening right now." Kimberly's face contorted, hot tears burning rivers down her face. "You can't be here," she blubbered. "You *died!*"

JT knelt beside her bed, taking Kimberly's hand away from her face and holding it in both of his.

Softly he said, "I didn't. I'm here. It's really me. And I love you so goddamn much."

Kimberly choked on her words. "I'm losing it. I'm crazy. That's what it is. I thought I saw you on the street and now I've conjured you in my bedroom. I'm looney tunes. It's the cancer. It's the drugs. This is not *happening*!"

From across the room, Allison said, "Lady, I assure you it is. It's really JT. He and Julie have met. I'm gonna send her in now and leave the three of you alone." Allison opened the door and motioned for Julie. She entered the room and closed the door behind her.

"Mom, it's really him. It's my dad. And look!" Julie opened her hand. Lying between two military dog tags was an emerald ring. *Her* emerald ring. This could not be real.

"But how did you—"

"I bought it back from the pawn shop near your old place in Jax," he said.

"It was still there?"

"I got there just weeks after you left."

Kimberly took her hand from between JT's. With uncertainty, she touched his face with her fingertips. He closed his eyes. Like a blind woman reading braille, she felt his beard, his skin, his eyelids. Tenderly, she opened her hand, cupping his cheek as he leaned into her palm.

"Is it really you?" she whispered.

"It's really me, girlie," he said, opening his eyes. "I love you."

"I love that you love me." JT stood, gently pulled Kimberly up into his arms, and kissed her lips, feathery, soft, slowly.

Behind them, Julie cleared her throat, tapping JT on the shoulder. He touched Kimberly's face, then turned back to his daughter. She held up the ring, then placed it in his hand.

He held Kimberly's left hand in his own.

"Kimberly Marie, love of my life, my heart, my soul, my everything, will you marry me?"

Fresh tears flowed from her smiling eyes as she nodded, watching him slide the ring on her finger for the second and last time.

Julie threw open the door to her nervously awaiting family in the living room.

"You guys! My parents are getting married!"

PART THREE
Wednesday

Chapter Sixty-Six — Key West

"You ready?" Jack placed his left hand over the petite fingers wrapped around his right bicep and squeezed. "It's showtime."

***

Following Julie's announcement to the family of Kimberly and JT's reengagement, everything kicked into high gear. Allison's little house became a flurry of activity—the phone never leaving her ear as she called a florist, caterer, baker, photographer, and her favorite notary public. Her urgency was made crystal clear to each vendor, as well as promised bonuses if they could pull this off. Allison barked orders and commands into her cell phone for the next three hours. Everyone took to calling her "The Little Admiral," and not always behind her back.

But she'd pulled it off. She'd arranged an elegant, cozy wedding on her lanai in less than twenty-four hours.

JT had a few jobs—something to wear, rings, license, and convince his mother to fly to Key West immediately. The guys agreed to go together to pick out their clothing. So, he took a quiet moment to call his mother and explain the entire, incredible story. Ella had been overcome with emotion. She'd agreed to hurry to the airport and get on the late night flight her granddaughter had found for her on the internet. Her granddaughter!

As far as attire, Allison had merely one rule: no shoes.

Jesse and Taylor took Jack and JT to Assortment, Inc., just off of Duval, to buy upscale island attire. Each of them emerged with assorted cream, gray, and khaki linen island shirts and Bermuda shorts. JT had one more errand to run before he arranged a cab to get to the airport. He spied a jeweler on the other side of Duval. Just outside the door, he hesitated. Pulling the pack of cigarettes and lighter from his pocket, he took one last look, tossed them into a trash can, opened the door, and entered under the ding dong of the door alarm.

Sabrina convinced Grey to drive down from Miami in the morning for the evening ceremony. She asked him to stop by J. Del Olmo Bridal to scoop up an off the rack creation Sabrina purchased over the phone. All it took were Kimberly's measurements, texted photos from the boutique, and a credit card. She and Julie actually did go to Lily Pulitzer for their outfits this time, choosing a little something for Allison, as well. Sabrina found a jewelry store and purchased matching ankle bracelets for the four ladies—delicate white gold chains adorned with tiny starfish.

Jack tapped on the front door of Allison's bungalow for the third time before opening the door.

"Hello? Anybody home?"

"I'm in here, Dad," Kimberly said.

Jack found her sitting on the side of her bed, oxygen cannula under her nose, the bedside table rolled up close, painting her fingernails a pale pink.

"Nobody answered, so I just—"

"It's okay. Allison's in the shower and everyone else went shopping."

Jack smirked at his daughter, face hard in concentration, tip of her tongue pressed to the outer corner of her mouth, dipping the nail brush and drawing careful strokes of the lacquer across her nails.

She looked up. "What?"

"I just don't think I can ever recall you painting your nails. That's such a Brie thing."

"Yeah, I know. One and done. This shit sucks."

Jack chuckled. "You know, it's not really necessary. I think that boy would marry you covered in dirt in a burlap sack."

Kimberly's grin was broad. "Yeah. Yeah, he would. Is this really happening? My head is still spinning."

Jack sat in a chair by the window. "Well, if it's not, tell me now, so I can take back the frou frou linen duds I just bought."

"Never. Even if it wasn't happening. I'd pay big money to see you dolled up in linen." Her manicure complete, she twisted the bottle top and began to blow across the sticky nails.

"How are you feeling, kiddo?"

"Like I'm on cloud nine."

"Physically."

"A bit lower cloud."

"If this is too much, you say the word. I'll pump the brakes on all this pomp and circumstance."

"Nah. Did you see how transformed Alli became? She's in her glory. I'd never dream of taking this away from her. I mean, honestly, I'd be happy with just me, JT, and Julie on the beach. Nothing official. Just us, sand, surf, and sunset." She swept her hand in front of her. "But this is cool, too."

"Well, I heard Allison and JT giving information to the county, and given your . . . situation . . . they've issued the license with no waiting period. So, it's definitely official."

Kimberly's eyes twinkled. "I'm getting married tomorrow, Dad."

"Yes, you are, little one."

"Will you walk with me?"

"I can't think of one other thing in the universe I'd rather do."

***

The following afternoon, the lanai became a paradise of color. Allison's deep pink bougainvillea bushes tangoed with hibiscus in gold, orange, and fuchsia, deep purple and blush pink clivia, and fragrant white jasmine, white faerie lights woven throughout. Lily pad candles floated lazily in the pool. Sunset painted the wispy clouds with periwinkle and flame. Magic sparkled in the sky.

Guests scattered comfortably around the lanai, feet bare in the warm evening. Sabrina and Grey sat together on a garden bench. Julie's legs dangled in the warm water of the pool, her sundress pulled up over her knees. Taylor reclined on a chaise lounge pressed against Jesse, his arms wrapped around Taylor's chest, their hands clasped. Dustin sat cross-legged on a patio chair, Kat and Luci next to him, hands entwined. Ella chose one of a pair of high-backed rattan chairs, illuminated by jasmine and twinkling lights. Regina sat in the other, a deep red hibiscus tucked into her hair. Allison stood at the open French doors, gave a thumbs up toward the far end of the garden, where Geno stood under a pergola draped in bougainvillea, next to a slightly jittery JT.

Ethereal string quartet music flowed around them. Breezes fluttered through the air, rustling plants and flowers, silky on their skin.

Jack appeared in the doorway, his daughter holding on to his arm.

He whispered, "Sure you're okay without the oxygen?"

"I'm fine for just this one night. I feel like a teenager again."

Allison placed her hands on either side of her best friend's face, kissing the tip of her nose, then scooted across the pavers to get cozy in the chair next to Dustin.

In the glow of the evening, Kimberly was luminescent. She appeared to float on air, as Jack led her slowly toward her groom. Her gauzy, white halter dress defined exquisite—delicate layers of gossamer chiffon, shimmering with dainty crystals, brushed the floor as she moved. A halo of white lobelia and baby's breath encircled her head, cascades of wisteria flowing to her shoulders.

Jack kissed her cheek and winked, taking his place next to Julie, plunging his feet into the pool next to hers.

Geno whispered, "Ready?"

Kimberly nodded.

JT whispered, "Never more." He held her hands tenderly in his.

"Loved ones, we're here to complete the joining of hearts that began decades ago—the miraculous ending of a journey, culminating in, not two, but three lives blended together from here forward.

"Kimberly Marie and Jason Todd, the Universe is mysterious. It is not ours to question how or why things happen the way they do, only to appreciate and be grateful for each moment, as they are truly gifts. Many stars and energies aligned to bring us to where we are in this moment.

"One look at the sheer bliss in the eyes of these beautiful humans restores our faith in humanity—that love truly will find a way.

"Words are tangible things. Words carry power—the power to uplift and tear down, the power to clear paths and send hearts soaring. Ladies and gentlemen, I'm going to step back and allow Kim and JT to speak their words to each other's souls."

JT cleared his throat, emotion filling his eyes. "My love. I've spent many long nights, in lonely places all over the globe, looking up at the moon and wondering if you were seeing the same one—if you were thinking of me, too. I've spent my life merely going through the motions, never knowing what would be waiting for me at the end of the day. Now I know. I'm the most fortunate man on earth to be able to take you as my wife tonight. And to accept the highest honor of being a father to our daughter. I love you."

Kimberly's smile shone brighter than the rising moon. "My heart. Here you stand before me when just yesterday, I didn't even know you were alive. My world shattered without you—without Julie. Piece by piece, I began to put it back together. Little did I know the final pieces would be placed by you and our daughter, tonight in front of everyone we cherish. I've spent countless hours writing and speaking words—in journals, in letters, shouting them across the sky. But none of them mattered until now. I'm so honored to spend all of my final days with you as my husband. I only wish there were more. I love that you love me."

JT removed a small box from his pocket, emptying the contents into his hand. He slid the smaller band onto Kimberly's finger. "With all that I have, and all that I am, I marry you."

Kimberly took the larger band, sliding it onto JT's finger, repeating his words.

JT then looked toward the pool. "Julie, can you come join us?"

Surprise filling her face, Julie pulled her dripping legs from the pool and padded toward the pergola. JT held up a fine, white gold chain, upon which dangled a tiny emerald pendant.

As he joined the clasp at the back of her neck, he said, "Our daughter—the living proof of our love so many years ago. We love you, now and always." All misty eyes were on them as the couple hugged their emotional girl.

Geno said, "What a gift to have been able to witness this organic, authentic love between such a sweet family. My husband's gonna have to save me a tissue back there. The only thing left to do is pronounce the two of you married. Please seal your vows with a kiss."

JT gently lifted Kimberly's face to his. His lips lightly brushed, then pressed into hers. Their guests tossed rose petals into the air, cheering and applauding the lifelong loves, finally bound.

***

"If you'll bear with me, folks, I'd like to show my love to the happy couple the best way I know how." Jack sat on a barstool near the garden, the borrowed Taylor acoustic in his lap. He began the intro to Eric Clapton's "Wonderful Tonight," and JT held Kimberly close, gracefully spinning her slowly across the lanai.

"Dad sounds great," Jesse said, beer in hand, arm around the waist of his husband.

"Right? I was just thinking how long it had been since we sat around the campfire listening to him play for hours," Sabrina said, sipping champagne from a flute.

"Weddings are so romantic. We should have another one, Jess," Taylor said.

Jesse pulled him closer. "Handsome, every day is like a wedding day with you."

"Ugh, go back to the room, you too," Sabrina said, winking as she walked toward the kitchen. Grey caught her by the elbow as she moved past."Hey, hon, I wanted to—"

"Not now. Not here," she said. "I appreciate you getting the dress for Kim. She looks like an angel."

"Doesn't she?" Allison asked, walking past with a tray of bacon wrapped dates. "Want any before I take these outside?"

"Mmm, yes," Sabrina said, nabbing a few of the delectable morsels. Grey looked at her, surprised.

"What?" she said. "I'm hungry."

He grinned. "Nothing. It's just good to see you eating something besides rabbit food. Can I get you a slice of cake while you're at it?" He wrapped his arm around her slender waist, kissing her temple.

"Ooooh, cake."

Grey laughed, shaking his head. "You're sexy when you eat."

"Hey, let's go tell the lovebirds what we did for their honeymoon." Grey followed Sabrina out to the lanai.

Jack played the last chords of "Can't Help Falling in Love," by Elvis Presley, and the dancers applauded, returning to their seats.

Sabrina and Grey approached JT and Kimberly as they sat in the illuminated rattan chairs, like royalty on thrones. Sabrina knelt in front of her sister, taking her hand.

"Hey, you. How're you feeling?"

"I'm positively floating. Really tired, but floating."

"Listen, I know it's not realistic to send you guys on a honeymoon, but we wanted to do something for the two of you."

"Aw, Brie, you didn't have—"

"Yes, we did. Now, it's not much, but we rented a yacht for you guys for a few days. It's fully staffed, all the bells and whistles. It launches down by Mallory Square tomorrow, whenever you arrive. Just go, be together, have some fun. Make some memories." Sabrina squeezed Kimberly's hand, her eyes welling.

"Thank you, brat. I love you."

"I love you back. Now, quit being sweet or I'll cry. Again."

JT extended a hand to his new brother-in-law. "Thanks, Grey. We really do appreciate it."

"The least we could do. Welcome to the family, JT."

Taylor came up from behind Sabrina, bearing a tray with multiple glasses of champagne.

"We'd like to do a toast, so take one, if you please."

Jesse lifted his glass and called out, "Good evening, everyone. I'm the brother of the bride, and my husband, Taylor, and I would like to say a few words."

A hush fell around the lanai, as people lifted their glasses in anticipation.

Taylor spoke first. "What a glorious evening. Weddings are amazing. When Jesse and I fell in love, marriage for us was illegal. The world has come a long way, and still has a long way to go."

"Yes, my love, all true. What's amazing is seeing these two come together when none of us even knew they were still with us. But time is precious and moments are few," Jesse said.

"We'd like to raise a glass to Kim and JT. May every single moment they have together be filled with love."

"May they live out their days in truth and happiness. And may they know they are so loved by all of us here."

A resounding chorus of "Hear, hear!" accompanied by the clink of glasses filled the night.

"That's quite a family you've got there." Jack turned to see to whom the unfamiliar voice with the soft, southern twang belonged. A woman stood to his left, admiring the bride and groom on the other side of the pool and the siblings surrounding them. She wore a cornflower blue sundress, her silvery hair twisted into a loose bun, brown eyes sparkling like the diamond studs in her ears, and the wedding band on her finger. She lifted a champagne flute to her lips.

"Thanks, I think so, too. I don't think we've met." He extended his hand. "Jack Stevens, father of the bride."

"Ella Allen, mother of the groom."

Laughing, Jack said, "Oh, of course! You got in late last night, right? Well, I guess we're all family now. Is your husband here? I'd love to meet him, too."

"I lost him last year. He'd have been over the moon to see JT so happy."

"I'm so sorry to hear that, Ella. I completely understand the feeling." Motioning toward the table, Jack said, "Please, let's have a seat."

Kimberly tapped JT on the arm. "Hey, husband. Look over there. My dad. Your mom." She raised her eyebrows.

"Hey, wife. They're just *talking*. I think the romance of the day has gotten to your pretty little head."

"What's gotten to my head is this champagne. I think I need to lie down. Can you take me to my room?"

JT looked around the lanai, filled with their guests, drinks and food flowing out of the kitchen, beautiful music and laughter dancing in the air.

"I think I have a better idea."

***

JT wrapped Kimberly's arms around his neck and scooped up his bride across his arms. He carried her through the door to his private bungalow, the moon shining bright on the Atlantic Ocean behind them.

Gently, he placed her on the bed, lifting the crown of fragrant white flowers from her head. Like a whisper, he softly brushed her face with his fingertips.

"I can't believe I'm looking at your face. Your adorable, button-nosed, bright green-eyed face. And you're my *wife.*"

"It's too much, isn't it? Completely surreal. I don't know how this happened and I don't care. All I know is, I've been in love with you since the day I saw you shooting pool at the bar on base, and now you're my husband. It's like nothing else in between ever mattered."

"Except Julie."

"Yes, except Julie."

"She's incredible, Kim."

"She is. No credit to me."

JT cupped Kimberly's cheek. "I have another idea."

"You're just full of ideas tonight."

"Let's take her with us on the yacht. I'm sure it's way too much boat for just you and me. And you really need to spend time with your daughter."

"*Our* daughter."

JT smoothed her feathery hair back, kissing her forehead. "Our daughter."

Kimberly locked eyes with her husband's, falling, falling into the deep brown velvet. One by one, she began to undo the buttons on his shirt, never leaving his gaze. She reached to slip the open shirt free of his shoulders.

Sliding his shirt to the floor, he held both sides of her face in his hands. "How are you feeling? Are you . . . I mean, can you . . .?"

Kimberly nodded and smiled, leaning in to place her lips on his, softly, the tip of her tongue teasing his, more deeply, taking his bottom lip into her mouth, sweeping her tongue over and over.

JT moaned, a long-buried rumbling aching to pour forth. He stood, sliding his thumbs under the hem of her filmy gown, pushing it upward, over her thighs, up her torso, lifting it past her raised arms, and depositing it on a bench at the foot of the bed. He drew in a deep breath and drank in the beauty of his wife with his hands, his eyes, his mouth—her bare, silken breasts, the curve of her smooth belly, her hips. He tucked his hands under her bottom, slipping her tiny white silk panties free. Unbuttoning his shorts, he dropped them to the plush rug.

Lying beside one another, they became familiar again, with shoulders, arms, chest, hips, thighs, JT slowly and deliberately traversing every inch of Kimberly's body with restrained hunger, drawing out the moment into long, luxurious minutes of touch and taste. Kimberly moved under his fingers in a dreamy rhythm, her body responding to every clasp, every exploration with mounting desire, her need for him boundless.

JT wrapped one arm under Kimberly's back, sliding her up to the pillows. He breathed into her ear, "I'll be so gentle. I promise."

"God, I hope not," she groaned. He chuckled.

Grinning at one another, he entered her slowly, tentatively, moving in response, following her guidance, gradually filling her. She dug her fingers into his back, gasping, grabbing his glutes, pulling him in tighter.

In a moment of explosion, they cried out, holding onto each other as they glided back down to earth. She laughed, smoothing his hair with her palm, a tear falling from his cheek, dropping onto hers.

"My wife," he said.

"My husband," she said. "Favor?"

"Anything."

"Never leave me again."

"That," he kissed her eyelids, her nose, her lips, "is a bona fide promise."

Chapter Sixty-Seven — Atlantic Ocean / Gulf of Mexico

Julie waved down the pier at her waiting parents, running forward to greet them, her backpack bouncing against her shoulder blades. Her long curls were swept up into a pile on top of her head, black Converse slapping the boards as she made her way to the slip with the awaiting boat.

"Sheesh! Holy cow. This one is ours?" Julie said, shielding her eyes from the sun to take in the majestic boat.

The Aqua Luna stretched one hundred twenty seven feet from bow to stern. Her daunting profile astounded as they approached to board.

JT rolled a shared suitcase and pushed Kimberly's wheelchair. The new bride looked particularly festive in a bright red, lemon yellow, and cobalt blue floral sundress, a floppy, yellow sunhat shielding her face.

"Tiny vessel, don't you think?" JT said with a wink.

"So generous of Brie and Grey. I can't believe it," Kimberly said, mouth agape, hand pressed to the crown of the hat as it fought against her in the ocean wind.

"A wheelchair, Mom? Are you feeling up to this?"

"Just a precaution, Jules. *Dad* thought it might be best after all the activity yesterday." She winked.

"Well, *Dad* is probably correct," JT grinned.

"Welcome aboard the Aqua Luna," came a voice at the top of the gangway. The family turned to see a trim, deeply tanned man just a few inches taller than Julie, wearing a crisp, white polo shirt, navy shorts and a beaming smile, beckoning them aboard. "Captain Buck Steehler. Happy to meet you folks. Please watch your step as you embark."

Two crew members took their luggage and assisted them aboard, deftly maneuvering Kimberly's chair. One of them, an extremely fit, Black twenty-something with a sleek ponytail and striking green eyes, introduced herself as Vedette.

"I'm your chief stewardess. Please don't hesitate to ask for anything you may need to make your voyage more comfortable. Allow me to show you to your cabins."

They entered through the main salon, rich with cherry African makore wood and Italian leather furniture. Kimberly removed the oxygen line and stood up from the chair.

"We can leave these in here for now."

Vedette led JT and Kimberly up to the VIP suite, while her fellow steward, a blonde, college-aged man called Randy, escorted Julie to the main cabin. Every surface sparkled and gleamed inside the ship. The passengers hesitated to touch anything for fear of leaving a smudge or smear. Vedette showed Kimberly the discreet onboard elevator.

"This will take you to the upper deck and sky lounge, in case the ladders are too much, madam."

"I can't thank you enough, Vedette."

"My pleasure. Once you're settled, we'll have refreshments for you on the aft deck before lunch. Please let me know if there's anything else I can do." As she took her leave, Kimberly reached for JT's hand.

"Is it me, or is this bonkers?"

He laughed, wrapping her up in his arms. "Uh, yeah, girlie. You could say these past couple of days have been nothing *but* bonkers. But the best kind of bonkers." He looked down into Kimberly's face with concern. "You okay, love? You're perspiring."

Kimberly nodded. "Just a little overwhelmed. It's been a lot."

"It has. You wanna lie down before lunch?"

"No way, man. I'm not missing a moment of this."

"It's only Wednesday. We have the boat till Saturday. It's okay if you need to rest."

"Race you to the aft deck." Kimberly grinned, a twinkle in her eye.

"You're on!"

***

The sun began to disappear in a blaze of rich amber over the Gulf of Mexico as the newly minted family sipped beverages on the uppermost sun deck, ocean wind like so many fingers running through their hair. Captain Buck guided them through the deep aqua sea in a lazy pattern through the Atlantic, into the Gulf, and back again. Rather than sailing to any other ports, they'd asked if they could dock in Key West each night. Kimberly felt better having Regina nearby, just in case.

They sat in comfortable silence, JT and Kimberly holding hands, Julie snapping copious photos on her iPhone—her parents' silhouettes against the sunset, the incredible views of the open ocean, a few indulgent selfies. The photos would later show the couple unable to take their eyes off one another.

Vedette appeared at the top of the ladder. "Dinner is served in the dining room. Please follow me."

Once the family was seated, Vedette and Randy served a gourmet meal prepared by the chef in the galley. A roasted beet and walnut salad, followed by grilled snapper, truffled mashed potatoes, and green beans almondine. By the time creamy slices of raspberry cheesecake were placed before them, Kimberly raised her hand in decline.

"Oh, no, I don't think I can fit another morsel."

"Come on, Mom, you only live once—" she began, then flushed a deep crimson. "Oh, jeez, I'm so sorry. I don't know what the hell I was thinking."

Kimberly covered Julie's hand with her own. "Honey, look at me." Julie met her eyes, shame on her face. "Let's please not tiptoe around each other. Every second we have is precious. I'll be damned if I'm gonna waste any of them being sensitive or angry or any other thing but grateful. Don't censor yourself around me. Ever." She reached up and smoothed a tendril of Julie's curls back behind her ear. "You look beautiful tonight."

The afternoon sun had kissed Julie's face, spraying tiny freckles across her cheeks and nose. Silver and turquoise earrings dangled over her tanned shoulders, complementing a ruffled white sundress and sandals.

"Thanks," she said, wiggling her toes. "I even put on shoes."

JT lifted a bottle of beer to his lips and laughed. "You're my daughter all right. Barefoot is always best when you can get away with it."

Julie reached across the table to fist bump JT.

"See? That's what I'm talking about."

Julie polished off her cheesecake and gulped down half of her ice water.

"When you guys are done, I'll meet you in the salon. I have something to show you."

Kimberly and JT took their seats on a leather sofa, rolling the oxygen tank alongside. Kimberly curled her legs under her and leaned against JT's chest. Julie entered carrying a thick book.

"Whatcha got there?" JT asked.

Kimberly gasped. "I know what that is." She looked up at JT. "It's my journal. I started it when I was a little girl. I left it for Jesse to give to Julie for her birthday. I wanted her to know my story."

Julie sat on an adjacent couch and handed the book to her mother. "It's such an incredible gift, Mom. I loved reading it. Especially pages like this one." She opened the journal to a page she'd tabbed and began to read:

Tonight, Allison dragged me to the Cellar Door and two things happened. First—I turned 22. And second—I just met the cutest guy on the planet. He's clever—bummed a light from me like every 20 mins and I totally fell for it. But it looks like he doesn't know how to tie his shoes. Might not be the brightest bulb in the pack.

JT tipped his head back and laughed. "I still hate tying my shoes."

"Or this one."

I can't stop staring at this gorgeous ring! Oh my god, I have no idea what I did to deserve this man, but I would do it over and over and over again if it meant winding up with him forever. I can't believe he's leaving for the Med. This sucks so bad. Why is it every time I'm happy, the Universe conspires to make me miserable? I'm just not going to let it bring me down tonight. Nothing can. Not after my fiancé made love to me down at The Landings. I've never felt so complete in my entire life. I've never felt like I was ever good enough for anyone until now.

Julie looked up from the journal to see her mom's tearful smile, her dad's mischievous grin.

"That was one helluva night," he said.

Kimberly tipped her hand back and forth under the overhead lights watching the jewel twinkle. "You could say that again."

"But, Mom? I noticed a number of pages torn out of the journal. What's that about?"

Kimberly frowned. "Jules, there are some things I just didn't want you to see. Ugly, painful things I'd rather protect you from."

"I can totally understand you feeling that way when I was two, Mom. But what did you just say at dinner? That I shouldn't ever censor myself with you? I feel the same way. Our time is short. We need to be completely open with each other. Don't you think?"

"She's got you there, girlie."

Kimberly nodded. "You're right. I did say that. You can ask me anything, kiddo."

"Okay," Julie said, flipping through the pages. "What happened here? There's kind of a whole section missing."

Kimberly sighed and sat up, away from her husband. Leaning forward, she rested her elbows on her knees and looked at her daughter.

"As many times as I've shared this story with the women I've tried to help over the years, it never gets any easier to tell."

JT ran a comforting hand up and down her back. "Take your time, Kim."

"I'm okay. Julie, there's no reason to sugarcoat it. When we were in the Navy and your dad was on deployment, I was raped."

The journal slipped from Julie's hands to the floor.

"Oh, Mom . . ."

Kimberly told her daughter the abbreviated version of her story, sparing her the most cringeworthy details.

"So, when I saw the photo tacked up on the bulletin board in our squadron concession shop, I knew two things—that it would be my word against his and that I would never be able to work with dignity in that squadron again. I also knew deep inside that your dad would never want me after that. I was soiled."

"And that's where your mother was wrong, Julie. She'd been so psychologically and emotionally damaged, she couldn't even wrap her head around the fact that someone could love and support her unconditionally. I'll admit, I was just a young, good ol' boy from Texas, and when I first saw the photo, I was pissed and disgusted. But then I remembered all Kim had told me about the guys who harassed her over and over in her shop at the squadron. I put two and two together." JT wrapped his arm around Kimberly's shoulders and pulled her close, kissing her temple. "Unfortunately, by the time I got back to the States, she was gone. Out of the Navy. No way for me to reach her."

"Mom, what happened?"

"I took some leave time while they did a preliminary investigation, but without any witnesses, it became a he said/she said, and he denied everything. I was unwilling to undergo the torture of a court martial. I didn't file charges. My enlistment was nearly up anyway, so it was either reenlist, or take an early out, which I did. If I'd had it to do over again, I probably would have handled it differently.

"But listen, honey, that wasn't the first time I was sexually harassed or abused. It was just the last."

JT sat back and looked at Kimberly.

"What are you saying, Kim?" JT's jaw muscles flexed.

"I'm saying that it was a completely common occurrence for women to be mistreated as objects of sexual desire, and not just in the Navy, but in civilian life, too. I can't count the number of times my ass was grabbed, or some guy hugged me just a little too long, pressed against my chest. I would walk down the street and hear wolf whistles and cat calls. Men, especially older men, would just lean over and kiss you without your permission in all sorts of social situations.

"In the Navy, I was subjected to locker room talk on a daily basis because I was the only woman with scores of men on numerous occasions. The expected response in order to be part of the boys' club was to laugh along and shrug it off, no matter how raunchy or abrasive their jokes became. I even found out at one point in my first squadron that about a dozen sailors started what they called a 'flow chart.' It was kind of like a spreadsheet on poster board. The guys' names across the top, all the females in the squadron listed down the side. They earned points and stars for each sex act they committed against these women, consensual or not. Probably half of the shit on there was fabricated by boys not wanting to have their macho egos bruised. But the point is that women were treated as nothing but animals. In fact, I'm sure these assholes were kinder to their own dogs that they were to the women in our squadron. It was insecurity fed by jealousy—they were threatened by our existence. I have yet to speak to even one female veteran or active duty member who doesn't have a story of some kind of harassment or abuse.

"But the worst part about all of it? Men were, and some still are, conditioned to believe that women *loved* this. That we took it as a compliment. That it was harmless flirting, heavy petting, boys being boys, whatever other 'innocent' terms society concocted back in the day to excuse the perpetrators from accountability. And for decades, when women tried to have a voice, to say *no*, this is *not* how I deserve to be treated, we were ignored, shunned, demoted, fired, or, in the most extreme cases, beaten and even killed. All to prop up the fragile male ego.

"So, you see why I was drawn to the work I've done for the past ten years. I've tried to give women a voice. To lift them up when they've been kicked into the proverbial gutter. To help remove their boots from our necks."

"Ruth Bader Ginsburg," Julie said, reaching to take her mother's hand. "I was never taught that quote from her in high school. I read it in a meme on the internet."

"That doesn't surprise me. Sadly, school curriculum and textbook content is mostly written and approved by folks who don't believe, or want our children to know, the truth. It threatens their position at the top of the hierarchy. Whether it's about women's rights or the rights of Black folks, People of Color, the LGBTQ community, or any other marginalized group, the truth is being withheld and literally whitewashed in our schools. Which is why the more things change, the more they stay the same. Until and unless we raise our children to know the absolute truth, as ugly and horrifying as it is, people will always be marginalized and we will never be able to fully evolve and grow as a species. Nothing makes me more angry or more sad." Kimberly squeezed her daughter's hand and leaned back against the sofa. "But I digress. I tend to get on a soapbox."

"You're a passionate woman, Kim. It's one of the things I've always loved and admired about you." Turning to Julie, JT said, "You should have seen your mother hold her own against the old boys' club back in the day."

"I'm not surprised," Julie said. "Mom, you're my hero."

"Oh, honey, you're sweet. I'm just one woman trying to right the wrongs one day at a time. Well, I used to be. Unfortunately, my body isn't able to keep up with my spirit any longer." Kimberly stood. "In fact, I think that's about it for me tonight. You two, please stay and enjoy each other. Have a little dad and daughter time." A broad smile spread across her face. "I never, ever dreamed this moment would happen. If I died tonight, I would be absolutely complete."

The looks on their faces gave her pause. "I mean, I don't plan on it or anything," she teased. "Good night, loves."

Up in the main suite, Kimberly undressed and pulled a nightgown over her head. Reflecting on the words she had spoken to her daughter, she thought, "*Mom, if only I could have known you from this place in my life. If only we could have understood each other as abused women, as kindred spirits. If only…*"

"I forgive you, Mom. I forgive all of it," she said.

Unable to conceal it any longer, she grimaced, hands gripping her belly, the electric zings more frequent. Hands trembling, she tapped a pain pill and sleep aid into her palm, barely getting the tablets into her mouth fast enough. She swallowed them with half a bottle of water, holding a clammy fist to her pursed lips, fighting her body's urge to send them right back up. Splashing cool water over her face, she startled at her reflection—ghostly pale, dark circles, sunken cheeks. Makeup and pain meds were only going to mask the truth for so long. She didn't have much time left.

***

Above on the sun deck, Julie tipped her head back marveling at the plethora of stars. Miles from shore without light pollution, it looked as though the Milky Way was close enough to reach up and touch. Billions of twinkling lights against the blackness of space had a way of making one feel infinitesimal.

Vedette handed Julie an icy bottle of water and a thick napkin. She turned to see JT ascend the ladder holding a bottle of Heineken. "Can get you a frosty mug for your beer, sir?"

JT lifted the green glass in salute. "Thank you, Vedette, but that's okay. No sense in me being all highfalutin just because I'm on this fancy barge." He winked, taking a long pull of lager.

Vedette's smile was warm. "In about half an hour, we'll be pulling into port for the night. Is there anything else I can bring the two of you before we dock?"

"I'm good. You good, Jules?"

"I'm good."

"Looks like we're good, Vedette." He said. "Thanks so much for everything today."

"My pleasure, sir. There's a full bar and stocked refrigerator in the salon if you'd like anything further. Have a peaceful evening." She descended the ladder.

Julie watched her go. "She's really beautiful."

"She is. And extremely professional. I like Randy, too. What'd you think of him?"

"Huh? Oh, I mean, he seems nice, yeah."

JT tipped the bottle toward his lips again, hiding his grin.

"Your mom's sound asleep. Bless her. So, tell me all about yourself, daughter. Your hopes, your dreams, your aspirations."

Julie sipped her water, thoughtful. "I don't even know where to start. Haven't you been a little bit blown away by the past couple of days? My mind is all over the place."

"Oh, girlie, I'm right there with you. It's like life was just black and white up until two days ago, and then, all of a sudden, it burst into technicolor fireworks. I'm still trying to process all this. At the same time, trying to live each moment like it's the last because of your mom. If I could have one wish, it would be to slow down time."

Julie nodded. "Same. Or, better yet, rewind it."

"I hear ya. I regret so much." JT took a swig of beer, exhaling loudly. "Eighteen years of regrets."

"I understand, but I really wish you didn't feel that way. I mean, nothing was within our control. Everything happens the way it's supposed to, right? So, shouldn't we just be grateful for now?"

"Are you sure you're only eighteen?"

Julie stretched her arms above her head and yawned. "I'm sure I'm exhausted. Can we pick this up tomorrow?"

"Of course. Whatever you want, kiddo."

Julie crossed the deck, placing a hand on JT's shoulder. "Thank you for bringing me along on your honeymoon. It means so much to have this time with my parents. Oh my word—my parents. Mind-boggling."

JT stood and opened his arms. Julie stepped in, wrapping around him. He kissed the top of her head.

"Your granddad woulda loved you so much. And your uncle Matt." He breathed deeply. "Someday, whenever you're ready, I'll take you to Texas. The farm's gone, but the land they worked so hard is still there and it's still ours. It's a part of you, too, Julie."

"I'd like to see it. And I can't wait to hear all about them." She pulled away, looking up into his face. "Sleep well, Dad."

"You, too, girlie."

Once alone, JT drained his beer and looked up into the sparkling night sky.

"Pop, if you can hear me, please watch over them. Ain't a damn thing in this world that matters as much as those two."

The lights of Key West came into view as JT descended the ladder. He stepped onto the plush carpet of the salon closing the door behind him. At the bar, he poured two fingers of gold whiskey from a decanter and turned to watch their approach to the pier through the windows. After so many years at sea, the lights of a night approach never got old. He sipped his night cap, warmth spreading through his belly. If he'd been asked to come up with one word for this moment, it would have been contentment.

***

Breakfast was served on the covered aft deck on a perfect, breezy Thursday morning. Sunshine glistened on the waves as the Aqua Luna eased out to sea.

Julie sipped grapefruit juice and glanced up as JT joined her, looking extremely comfortable in a Guy Harvey tank top and board shorts, sporting his aviator Ray-Bans.

"Mornin', sunshine. How'd you sleep?"

"Like an infant. Where's Mom?"

"She's a little slow moving this morning. I waited for her but she asked me to just go ahead on. She'll be with us shortly."

Julie's brow furrowed. She began to push back her chair. "I should go down there and—"

JT held up one hand. "She's okay, kiddo, I promise. Just let her take her time. She doesn't want anyone making a fuss over her. Well, this all looks great!"

The morning spread in the center of the table contained scrambled eggs, bacon, sausage, biscuits, melon, assorted jellies, and whipped butter. JT poured a cup of steaming coffee and snagged a biscuit. Julie picked at her eggs.

He bit into his biscuit with gusto and chewed. "Not quite as good as my mama's, but not too bad. What'd you wanna do today? They have a couple jet skis down below. Challenge ya to a race."

"Oh, you're on. Only . . . I don't know. I'm worried about Mom."

"I get it. I do. But I have a feeling I know what she'll tell you."

"She'll tell you to get on a jet ski and have fun, if that's what you want to do," Kimberly said as she approached the table, oxygen caddy in tow. JT jumped up and pulled out a chair for her.

"Here's my beautiful bride. Have a seat, missus."

Despite the vivid coral and turquoise of her sundress, Kimberly appeared pale. Her hands shook as she placed her napkin in her lap.

Julie leapt from her seat and took Kimberly's plate from its placemat. "What can I serve you, Mom?"

"Oh, I'm afraid I don't have much of an appetite, Jules. I'd love a cup of tea, though."

"Coming right up." Julie disappeared into the salon.

JT lifted Kimberly's hand to his lips and kissed. "You're trembling."

"It takes a little bit for the morning meds to kick in. I'll be okay."

"Are you in pain?"

"Today's not a good day so far."

"Kim, let's go back. Let's get you home."

"I *am* home, JT. Wherever you and Julie are, that's home. I'll let you know if we need to go back to shore."

JT's eyes fastened on Kimberly's. "Promise." It was not a question.

"Promise."

Julie returned and took her seat. "Vedette's bringing your tea as soon as it's ready. You sure I can't get you something to eat?"

"Okay, sure, honey. How about a small bite of everything? It all looks lovely."

Julie dished up a little of everything on her mother's plate, relief in her smile. "Make sure you put on sunscreen before we go out, old man. You got some burnt ass legs."

"So I've been told."

"Good, that's settled. You two have a blast. I can watch you from right here," Kimberly said.

Vedette and Randy emerged from the salon. Randy served Kimberly a cup of tea, placing a small pitcher of hot water and a basket of tea bags by her plate.

"Good morning, folks. Did I hear a mention of jet skis?" Vedette asked.

"Yes ma'am," JT said. "This little girl of mine thinks she can beat her old man in a race. Care to weigh in on this?"

Vedette chuckled. "I think you have your work cut out for you, sir. She looks pretty fierce." She winked at Julie.

"You got that right. He's going down," Julie said.

Randy said, "I'll let the first mate know you'll be wanting to take them out, sir. Give us about twenty minutes?"

"Sounds perfect, Randy, thanks. Can you guys stop with the 'sir' stuff, though? I'm just JT. I wasn't even called 'sir' in the Navy."

"It's not protocol for us to use your first name, sir."

Kimberly looked at JT. "I never even asked you. At what rank did you retire?"

"E-7."

Kimberly grinned. "Vedette, is it okay for you guys to call him Chief?"

***

Her phone buzzed in the pocket of her sundress. Kimberly pulled it out to see a text from Regina:

Hey Miss Kim
Just your friendly neighborhood hospice nurse
Checking to see how you're feeling today
Did you take your vitals?

Kimberly smiled and responded:

Vitals are good, bp a little low
I've had better days w/pain
Other than that, wonderful time on the ocean

Regina's response came quickly:

How low is your bp?
What's your pain level 1-10?

Kimberly typed:

90/60 — pain 7-8 in waves but manageable

As soon as Kimberly hit send, her phone rang.

"Hey, Miss Regina. I didn't think I had cell service out here."

"It's FaceTime Audio, honey, it works over wifi. I know it's your honeymoon but I really need you to consider coming back home. I don't like the idea of you being out on the open water without me or a medical facility close by."

"My friend, I know you're concerned and I really do appreciate it. But I have a DNR, as you know. If it's my time, it's my time. I'll rest if I need to, but I'm absolutely not missing out on these hours with my husband and daughter. I've waited my entire life for this moment."

Regina sighed. "I know, I know." She paused. "Okay, listen. Stay on top of the pain with morphine. Don't hesitate to double your dose if you need to. If you get lightheaded, nauseous, severe pain, anything, I want you to take your little self to bed. Don't be a hero. Everybody'll understand. They love you. Just take care of you, okay? And if you need me, *please* don't hesitate to call. And don't be afraid to ask the captain to come back to port, ya hear?"

"Regina, I know it's your job, but please don't worry about me. I'm in good hands out here and I'm having the time of my life. I promise I'll take care of me."

"That's all I needed to hear, Kim. Just rest and love up your family. I'll see you Saturday afternoon as soon as you get home."

"It's a date. Thank you, Regina. I appreciate you, my friend."

Kimberly slipped her phone back into her pocket, pulled out a small, blue tablet, and popped it into her mouth, swallowing it down with lukewarm Earl Gray. She mopped her brow with a navy linen napkin, hands shaking.

Randy appeared and began clearing the breakfast dishes. "Is there anything I can bring you, ma'am?"

Kimberly said, "My wheelchair and a ride in that elevator, Randy. I think I need to rest for a few minutes."

"Absolutely. Back in a moment." Randy closed the salon door behind him. A minute later, Vedette emerged. She knelt beside Kimberly's chair.

"Mrs. Allen, is there anything I can do? Would you like a cold compress for your head?"

"That would be nice, Vedette, thank you. I just really need to lie down. And, please. Not a word to the Chief or Julie, okay? I don't need them worrying about me at all. I'll be fine."

"Yes, ma'am. Consider it between us."

"And please be sure to wake me when they get back. I'd like to have time to freshen up."

"Done."

***

Lunch in the salon was grilled shrimp wedge salads and iced tea. Kimberly cut the iceberg lettuce and moved it around the plate, but not a lot of it made it into her mouth. She beamed as Julie babbled all about their morning of racing on the jet skis.

"Mom, it was so badass! Those things are like motorcycles on the water. I've ridden on the back with Uncle Grey before, but this was my first time driving my own. Now I totally want one. Maybe I'll trade in my car for a motorcycle. What a rush!"

"Whoa, slow down there, filly," JT said. "Motorcycles are pretty dangerous. Nothing between you and the asphalt besides a layer of clothing and a helmet. I'm pretty sure your aunt and uncle would have a word or two to say about it, too."

"Yeah, yeah, but it would be so awesome! Plus, I'm eighteen now, so . . ."

"Which doesn't mean your parents and your guardians don't have the right to offer advice, honey," Kimberly said. "Well, maybe I don't, but I don't care. I love you. We just want you to be safe. There's nothing wrong with taking motorcycle safety classes and seeing if you still like it. Should I mention it to Brie?"

Julie put down her fork, wiping her lips with her napkin. "That's kind of something I wanted to bring up."

"What's that, kiddo?"

"Now that I'm an adult, and I've found my parents, maybe it's time I moved out of my aunt and uncle's place."

Kimberly and JT exchanged a look.

"I mean, I know I have to finish my senior year and I still don't know where, or if, I'll be going off to college in the fall—"

"If?" Kimberly asked.

"Well, I've been thinking of applying for an internship with Doctors Without Borders, and possibly taking a gap year. But finding you guys has kind of changed things."

"Go on," JT said.

"I was thinking. Maybe I could stay here in Key West. With you guys. I mean, now that you're married, you're not planning to stay at Allison's, are you? Won't you and Dad want to get a place of your own?"

Kimberly reached out and took Julie's hand. "Oh, sweetheart. I'm on hospice. You do understand what that means?"

"Yeah, I know. But what if you still have weeks left? Or even months? Don't you think we should spend all the time we have left together? I can switch to online classes just until I graduate. I don't need many credits anyway. What do you guys think?" She looked back and forth between the faces of her parents.

"Jules, your mom might not have—"

"Wait," Kimberly interrupted. "I think she's right."

"I am?" Julie's smile was enormous.

"Nobody knows how much time we have left together. I think we should make the most of it. Terrific idea, Jules. I'll text the best realtor on the island, who happens to be my best friend, and see if she can find us a place for rent that—"

"Well, to be honest," JT said, "I was already planning to buy a place on the island before I discovered you were here. We can just step up the process. And our home can always be Julie's home base no matter where she is on her journey."

Julie's fist punched the air. "Awesome! Oh my god, I'm so *happy*!" She leapt from the table wrapping her arms around each of her parents in a tight hug. "These are literally the best days of my entire life. I love you guys so much."

"Love you back, young'un," JT said.

Kimberly was too overcome with emotion to speak.

***

Julie and Kimberly were alone in the salon. Julie sat cross-legged on the floor in front of Kimberly, her mother braiding her long hair into a herringbone.

"Where did you learn to braid like this, Mom?"

"Oh, honey, your aunt Sabrina had the longest, silkiest black hair when we were kids. She used to beg me to braid it constantly. Most of the time, I was that mean older sister that told her to get lost." She laughed softly. "But I was secretly jealous of that spectacular hair of hers. Eventually, she would get me to brush and braid it, although she never could return the favor with my curls."

"My hair is curly and you seem to be doing okay."

"You have luxurious loose curls, Jules, not like the thick, tight ones I had. Your hair is gorgeous." She kissed the top of Julie's head.

"Thanks, Mom." She paused. "Tell me about when I was little."

"Oh, my goodness. Where to even start?"

"How about the beginning?"

"You mean labor?"

"Yep."

Kimberly tipped her head back and laughed. "Okay then. It was a long labor, fourteen hours, but a pretty quick birth once you finally got going. You were a big baby. Nine pounds."

"I saw that on my birth announcement. Yeesh."

"Yeesh is right. You were always hungry. I was constantly feeding you. But you slept beautifully. Only five days old the first time you slept through the night. Nobody believes me, but it's true. It's like you somehow knew it was just the two of us, so you took it easy on me."

"How very considerate of baby me."

"Yes, indeed." Kimberly patted the top of Julie's head, continuing to pull quarter-inch strands and tuck them across and behind. "Your favorite cereal was Honey Nut Cheerios, your favorite juice was apple, and you loved *Barney and Friends*."

"I did? Yikes."

"It was adorable. You knew all the songs. And you loved when I sang you a lullaby at night."

"Which lullaby?"

"'All the Pretty Little Ponies.' The version by Kenny Loggins and Crosby, Stills, and Nash."

"I don't even know who those people are."

Kimberly chuckled. "I'll bet if I played the song for you, you'd recognize it, though."

Julie slipped her iPhone from her back pocket and spoke to it. "Siri, find 'All the Pretty Little Ponies' by Kenny Loggins."

The song came up and Julie tapped play. When the flute and

acoustic guitar intro began, Julie turned to look at her mother, eyes welling.

"I remember," she whispered, as a lone tear rolled down her cheek.

***

The ocean seemed particularly calm that evening, the water shimmering in gleaming moonlight. Captain Buck expertly steered the Aqua Luna through the two oceans as they blended, swirling around the island of Key West and the surrounding dots of land off the Florida peninsula.

The Allen family reclined on the sun deck, or, as they'd taken to referring to it at night, the moon deck. Vedette arrived with after dinner drinks on a tray—bourbon for JT, Diet Coke for Julie, and hot chamomile tea with lemon for Kimberly.

As she turned to take her leave, Vedette said to Julie, "Would you like to come see the bridge? It's kinda cool. And Captain Buck is super nice."

"I'd love to." Julie followed Vedette down the ladder.

Kimberly wrapped her hands around her mug and leaned into JT's chest. He wrapped his forearm around the tops of her arms, cupping her shoulder in his warm hand, and kissed the crown of her head.

"Love to know what's going on in this beautiful head right now."

"Mm. Honestly, just gratitude. For this tea, this boat, this night." She tipped her head to the side to look into his face. His eyes were even darker in the moonlight. "Mostly for you and our daughter. That you never held a grudge. That you never gave up on me. That you found your way back to me. I did a terrible thing so many years ago."

"Stop right there," JT chastised gently. "We've already been over this. The events of the past have only shaped us, not defined us. We've all made mistakes, some bigger than others. You did the only thing you knew to do. I thank all that's holy that Allison saved you from yourself that night. Just to have the chance to hold you in my arms again has made everything worth it. Every last day and night of all these years without you."

"You never found anyone else?"

JT raised the glass to his lips and shook his head. "Nope. Didn't interest me. I mean, I wasn't celibate, if that's what you're asking, but I never fell in love again. My work and my family back in Texas was all that mattered. I kept you close to my heart." He tapped the emerald ring on Kimberly's finger.

"I still can't believe you were able to buy this back. It was meant to be, huh?"

"Yes, ma'am, it was. Have you been thinking about where you'd like to live on the island? You know it way better than I do."

"I texted Allison. She knows what we're looking for. I'm sure we'll hear back from her by tomorrow with a few ideas. She also says she has some news for us when we get back. I tried to pry but she said to focus on nothing but one another while we're out here. That it'll keep until Saturday."

"Interesting. Sure hope it's good news. So, what about you, girlie? Ever find anyone to share your time through the years?"

"Nope, just Allison."

"Oh, really?"

Kimberly laughed. "No, not like *that*, silly. Short of a sexual partner, she's been everything in the world to me. My best friend, confidante, partner-in-crime, roommate, and now caregiver. I love her with my whole heart."

"She's a good woman. Even though she scares me half to death."

Kimberly laughed. "Yeah, I get that. She's a feisty little thing. And I wouldn't put it past her to cut someone if they threaten anyone she loves. Or shoot 'em."

"I'll keep that in mind."

Kimberly reached up and stroked JT's beard. "I don't think you have anything to worry about, big guy."

"How're you feeling tonight, my bride?"

"Wiped out, honestly. I think I need to get myself into bed."

"Allow me to do the honors, Mrs. Allen."

"It would be my pleasure, Mr. Allen."

***

Julie and Vedette descended the ladder from the bridge to the main deck and entered the galley.

"Another Diet Coke?"

"Nah, thanks, I'm good. Maybe a popsicle or something though?"

"Hm, I think there are fruit bars in the freezer. I'll check." Vedette opened the freezer and began searching through the compartments, sliding aside packages of fish and meat.

"The view from the bridge is amazing, Vedette. Thanks for taking me in there. What a nice guy Captain Buck is, too."

"Agreed. He's a great guy to work for." Locating a frozen strawberry bar, she pulled it out of the freezer, unwrapped it and handed it to Julie.

Julie tasted the top of the popsicle. "How long have you been a yacht stewardess?"

"Let's see, what's today?" She looked at her watch, then looked at Julie, one eyebrow raised. They laughed. "I'm kidding. No, I've been on boats since I was a kid. My father and grandfather are commercial fishermen. I started stewarding during summers in college at The U. I needed money and I love the boat life. This is my first season on the Aqua Luna, though. How do you like her?"

"The boat? Oh, I love it. Her." Julie flushed. "It's a gorgeous vessel."

"It is indeed. Majestic."

"Perfect word. So, you've graduated?"

"Yep, in December. Bachelor of Science in Marine Biology. I plan to go back and eventually earn a doctorate, but I'm taking a gap year. Building up my bank account. Scholarships are hard fought. Especially for immigrants."

"You weren't born here, then?"

"Martinique. I've been here since I was two. My whole family is here. Well, across the other keys, not in Key West." Vedette checked the contents of the refrigerator against a checklist for breakfast and closed the door.

"That's awesome. Have you ever been back?" Julie bit into her frozen treat.

"A couple of times. My mom and dad go every year to catch up with cousins and stuff, but I've been too busy with school and work. Someday I'll go back when I have time. Just to relax. It's beautiful. But I love Florida, too. It's my home."

"Mine, too. I live in Miami now, but we're moving to Key West. I'd love to see some Caribbean Islands, though. I'll bet it's a whole different world."

"Oh, it is, for sure. I have to check the aft decks. Do you want to come with?"

Julie licked the empty stick and threw it in the trash beneath the counter. "Absolutely. Lead the way."

Closing the salon door behind them, the girls stepped across the main level aft deck. Julie walked to the railing over the fan tail. She slipped the elastic band from the end of her braid and pulled her fingers through her curls to loosen them as they cascaded down her back. The froth trailing behind the boat was mesmerizing.

Vedette placed a couple of towels in a cabinet hamper and joined Julie at the railing.

"When I was a little girl, my grandfather used to tell me if I stared long enough at the wake, I'd get to see a mermaid."

Julie laughed. "And did you ever see one?"

Vedette shook her head, her long, sleek ponytail whispering over her shoulders. "Sadly, no. But not for lack of trying. Every single time I went out with my dad and granpé, I stared and stared, but she never showed up for me." She grinned, her eyes twinkling.

"Well, her loss." Julie leveled her gaze on the smooth skin of Vedette's high cheekbones. "What does your name mean? It's French, right?"

Vedette nodded and pointed up, her smile as brilliant as the night sky. "Star."

"That's beautiful. It's perfect."

"Your lips are red."

Julie's fingertips grazed her bottom lip. "What?" she asked.

"Your lips. From the popsicle. They're very red."

"Oh. Yeah. I'll bet they—" Vedette leaned close and softly

feathered her lips across Julie's. Julie closed her eyes, her breath a quiet gasp. Vedette moved back and shook her head.

"I'm so sorry. I'm, god, I'm—"

"No," Julie whispered. "It's okay. You're not wrong." She took Vedette's warm hand in hers. "You're not wrong."

Vedette squeezed Julie's hand. "I'll get fired. We can't. I'm so sorry." Vedette touched Julie's cheek, brushing a loose, long tendril of curls. Then she turned swiftly and made her way down the starboard side of the deck and out of sight.

Julie drew in a deep breath and exhaled slowly, grazing fingertips across her lips. She closed her eyes, seeing Vedette's magnificent, almond-shaped eyes, her striking cheekbones, her perfect mouth. She opened her eyes and leaned on the railing, looking into the foamy wake for the tails of mermaids.

***

Dawn was barely breaking across the horizon when Julie opened her eyes Friday morning. A faint tinge of pink and gold painted the sky. She sat up and smiled.

"A new dawn, indeed," she whispered to herself.

The boat was quiet as Julie made her way up to the kitchen. Chef Marie was preparing breakfast, humming along to the song playing in her earbuds. Julie tiptoed toward the warm, roasted aroma coming from the coffee pot. Seeing her out of the corner of her eye, the chef jumped.

"Oh! You scared me half out of my skin!" Marie laughed, hand covering her heart.

"Sorry," Julie whispered, pointing to the Bunn machine. "I'm just sneaking a cup and I'll get out of your way."

Marie waved a hand and continued to chop peppers and onions for the morning's frittata. "No worries, miss. Take your time."

Julie took her coffee up to the sky lounge outside her parent's suite. On a sofa under a window, she curled her legs underneath her and stared out at the dawning morning in Key West. Glancing at her phone, she saw it was 7:00 am. They weren't due to head out for another hour yet. She was looking around for a throw blanket when the door to the suite opened and her father emerged looking distressed.

"Dad?"

"What? Oh, Julie. You're up here. Good. Listen, your mom's not doing very well this morning. I'm going to find the captain and ask him not to go anywhere yet."

Julie bolted from her seat and raced into the suite. She knelt beside the bed where her mother lay with her eyes closed, bathed in sweat, her breathing shallow. Julie felt her forehead. Clammy and cold.

"Momma? It's me. Are you awake? Can you open your eyes?"

Kimberly's eyes fluttered open, unfocused. She slurred as she spoke. "Jules. Climb up here next to me, honey."

Julie circled around the bed and curled up next to her mother. She took her hand, wrapping it in both of hers. "I'm here. Please tell me what you need."

"This. Right here. All I need."

***

JT approached Captain Buck on the bridge, his Navy Chief Petty Officer demeanor taking over.

"Skipper, it looks like we have an issue."

"How can I help, Mr. Allen?"

"My wife has terminal cancer and has taken a turn for the worse. I think we'll need to call the trip short. Could you call for an ambulance?"

"Of course," said Buck, lifting the mic on his radio. "What hospital?"

"She's on hospice. They just need to take her home. She has a DNR."

Buck's face was solemn. "I'm so very sorry to hear this, sir."

"Thank you. My daughter and I will get packed up. Please let us know when the ambulance arrives."

"You got it. We'll take care of it."

JT raced back to the suite.

"Jules, go down to your cabin and pack up. Bring your stuff back here asap." He pulled out his cell phone and tapped.

"Hey there, JT. It's a little early. I was gonna send you guys listings later—"

"It's an emergency. Kim's taken a turn for the worse. We have an ambulance coming. Can you call Regina and have her meet us at the house? We're bringing her home, Allison."

Chapter Sixty-Seven — Catherine Street

Regina closed Kimberly's bedroom door behind her and joined the eager, anxious faces in the living room of Allison's bungalow.

"JT, you did the right thing getting her back home so quickly. I've given her a sedative and she's resting. I'd advise all of you to stay nearby and spend time with her. It's not time to call the doctor just yet, but it's close." She reached for Allison's hand. "I'm so very sorry."

"Thank you for everything. Are you leaving?"

"I need to go speak with the doctor and file some paperwork. I'll be back in under an hour. Call me immediately if there's any further deterioration."

"Will do. Thank you, Regina."

Regina nodded. She patted JT on the shoulder and opened the front door. "Be there when she wakes up. She'll want to see all of you."

Jesse, Taylor, and Jack nodded from the sofa.

"We're not going anywhere," Sabrina said. She pulled her phone from her clutch bag and walked toward the kitchen. "Grey, you may want to come back to the Key. It's not good news. Kimmy doesn't have long now."

Julie burst into tears, pushing past her aunt to get outside to the lanai.

JT met Sabrina's eyes. "I'll go." He stepped through the French doors. Kicking off his flip-flops, he stepped onto the top step of the pool and sat next to his daughter, putting an arm around her shoulders.

"It's not fair."

"I know, kiddo."

"We *just* got her back."

"I know."

"This hurts so fucking much."

"Yeah, it does."

"Nobody better tell me to be strong."

"You don't have to be, Jules. Just feel it. Let it out."

Julie tilted her head back and screamed at the cloudy sky. 'THIS SUCKS!!" She collapsed in tears on her father's chest. He held her close, rubbing her back.

"Yeah. It sure does," he said, emotion choking his words.

***

Allison entered the bedroom like a whisper, quietly closing the door behind her. Kimberly lay sleeping, hair plastered to her head with perspiration, her mouth dropped open, cannula under her nose. Her face was a sickly gray pallor, her breath rattled in her lungs. Death was coming quickly for her best friend. It was time for her family to say goodbye.

As she turned to leave the room, she heard a sound coming from the bed. She turned to see Kimberly's eyes open, her fingers beckoning.

"Well, hey there, grandma. What's shakin'?" Allison's bright grin didn't make it all the way to her eyes.

"Hey."

"Are you up for a little company? There's a bunch of Stevens and Allens out there."

"Yeah."

"Thirsty?"

"Yeah."

Allison poured a glass of water and held the bent straw to Kimberly's lips. She managed a little. Allison set the glass on the nightstand.

"I'll go tell them you're awake."

The room full of solemn faces was like a punch in Allison's gut.

"You guys, she's awake, but very weak. Anything you've been waiting to say, needs to be said now. Be gentle with her, okay?"

Jesse stood. "Is it okay with you guys if we go in first?" Sabrina and Jack nodded.

Taylor pulled two chairs next to the bed and the men sat close. Jesse took Kimberly's hand.

"Hey, Kimmy."

"Jess."

"Are you in pain? Need anything?"

"I'm okay. Tired."

"We're not gonna keep you, sister. Just wanted to let you know that I've always loved you so very much. Even when you were a moody brat. Even when we didn't speak for years. You're my little sister and nothing will ever change that."

Kimberly's face moved into a wan smile.

Taylor patted the blanket over her leg. "Kim, honey, I don't want you to worry about a thing. Jess and I will always take care of Jules. We'll make sure she needs for nothing. And we'll always keep your memory alive for her. You rest, sweet one. Just take it easy. We got you."

"Thank you, Taylor."

Taylor stood and kissed Kimberly's forehead. He left the room to give Jesse a private moment.

"Listen, I know life wasn't always good to you. And I'll always regret the missing years. I could have helped. I could have taken care of you. But I know you did what you had to do. I understand. Just know I'll always take care of our family. I promise. And if I talk to you now and then, let me know if you hear me, okay?"

"I'll try."

Jesse kissed both of her cheeks. "I love you, brat."

"Love you, Jess."

Back in the living room, Jesse said, "Brie, you may not want to wait for Grey. It'll be hours before he gets here."

Sabrina nodded and walked to the bedroom.

"Hey, sissy." She sat next to the bed and reached for Kimberly's hand.

"Hey."

"Remember that time when we'd first moved to Texas and you

took me clothes shopping?"

"Yeah."

"And then you bought me ice cream."

"Mhmm."

"I didn't understand why you were all of a sudden so nice to me. I mean, we hadn't ever really gotten along our whole lives.

"Sorry bout that."

"Here's the thing. That one time reassured me that no matter how you may have acted toward me on the outside, that inside you were just a teddy bear. And you always loved me. I knew that from that day on."

"I wasn't a good sister."

"Neither was I, Kimmy. And I'm so sorry."

"We're good, Brie."

"Please don't worry at all about Julie. She's a fantastic young woman. She'll always do you proud. Keep an eye on her, though, will ya? She's about to soar out into the great big world and we won't be able to be with her all the time."

"Do my best."

Sabrina tenderly wrapped her arms under her sister's back and pressed close.

"I love you so much, Kimmy. I don't want you to hurt anymore." Tears flowed from Sabrina's eyes onto Kimberly's blanket.

"Love you. I'm okay. Tired."

Sabrina kissed her sister's cheek. "You rest. Be at peace, Kimmy. All is well."

Closing the door behind her, Sabrina blew her nose into a tissue and said, "Dad?"

Jack stood and crossed the room. He wrapped his arms around Sabrina and began to choke up.

"I don't know if I can do this, Brie." He sputtered as he sobbed.

Sabrina rubbed her father's back. "I know. I know."

Jack squeezed his youngest daughter tight, then opened the door.

Kimberly looked as though she'd drifted off to sleep.

"Kimmy?" Jack whispered.

Her eyes fluttered open. "Daddy."

Jack took a seat and held his daughter's hand. "This is terrible, honey. I just don't know what to say."

"Just sit with me."

"You got it. I'm right here, little girl. My favorite smart ass."

"Proud of that."

Jack chuckled. "I've missed you so much. Everything about you. Your laugh, your sarcasm, even your eye-rolling. A dad's not supposed to play favorites, but you always had a special place in my heart, Kimmy."

"I used to be scared."

"Of what, honey?"

"Of dying."

"And now?"

"Not scared. Just tired."

Jack stroked his daughter's forehead.

"You can rest, honey. Just close your eyes. It's okay."

"Dad?"

"Yes?"

"I hope there's no heaven."

"Why would you say that, Kim?"

"Cause I never wanna be far that away from you guys again."

***

In the kitchen, JT slid his phone into his back pocket and stood next to Julie at the counter.

"That was your Grandma Ella. She's still on the island at the hotel. I've asked her to join us." Julie nodded.

Allison set a plate of blueberry and cranberry muffins on the kitchen table. "In case anyone's hungry," she said, and stepped onto the lanai, taking in a long breath.

Jack came into the kitchen, wiped his eyes with a handkerchief and tucked it into his pocket.

"I think maybe it's time the two of you were with Kim. Probably Allison, too."

Julie gestured toward the lanai. "Can you let her know, Grandpa?"

Jack nodded. "Go be with your mom, nugget."

***

JT held Kimberly's hand and stroked her cheek. Julie lay next to her. Allison sat on the foot of the bed, her hand on the blanket covering Kimberly's leg.

"Thank you for marrying me, girlie. I love you so much."

"Love that you love me."

"Mom, you'll be out of pain soon. It's okay to go to sleep. Just let go. I hope I'll always make you proud."

"Make yourself proud, baby."

"Grandma, my world has been infinitely better with you at my side. I'll miss your spunky ass."

"Me, too, lady. Thank you…everything." Her words became more labored, more slurred.

Julie pulled her iPhone from her back pocket and tapped. The last words Kimberly heard as she slipped from their world into the next were *"Hush a bye, don't you cry, go to sleep, my little baby . . ."*

Chapter Sixty-Eight — Julie

We scattered my mother's ashes at sunset on a warm, humid evening.

Aunt Brie and Uncle Grey arranged for all of the family to board the Aqua Luna for one last cruise around the island. Vedette was not part of the onboard crew. I was grateful. Too many emotions as it was.

In our hands, each of us held a tiny rice paper box housing a bit of Mom's remains. One at a time, we said a few words in her honor and flung the boxes into the sea. We watched as the paper melted away into the choppy water, the contents slipping beneath the surface.

Although we've heard it's the dry season in Key West, for the second time this week, the skies opened up and a drenching rain fell over us. Nobody ran for cover.

"She loved the rain," Grandpa said.

I couldn't be sure if it was raindrops or tears streaming down his face.

I looked up at the sky, the pieces of my shattered heart falling all around me into the puddles forming at my bare feet.

I'd had my mother back for less than a week.

PART FOUR
Beyond

Chapter Sixty-Nine — Jesse

As he unlocked and rolled up the hurricane shutters posing as doors, Jesse felt the morning sun on the back of his neck. For a moment, as he always did, he closed his eyes, took a deep breath, and grinned.

"I feel you with me, sister. It's gonna be a good island day. And it's your day after all." A glance at his watch reassured him he still had half an hour before the first patrons seeking hair-of-the-dog morning nips or hot morning coffee before hitting the ocean would be arriving. And at least two more hours before the ferry pulled in from the Gulf Coast bearing holiday travelers.

Clipping the shutters securely open, he slid the buzzing phone from the back pocket of his cargo shorts.

"Jesse Stevens."

"Mornin', sir. It's Pete at Pirate Woodworks. Just letting you know we'll be by in about an hour to hang the new sign."

"That's great, Pete. Crowd should still be relatively thin. You guys have sawhorses to block off the sidewalk while you work? I saw the sign in the shop last week and that sucker's pretty heavy."

"We're all set for precautions, sir. Would you rather we wait until you're closed just to be on the safe side?"

"Pete, my friend, we're rarely closed. This morning will work just fine. If I'm not here, my general manager, Tammi, can handle anything you need. How long to do you think it'll take?"

"Brackets and base were hung last week, so I'm guessing an hour, give or take."

"Perfect. Thanks, Pete. Can't wait to see your awesome work hanging over the bar."

Tammi approached from across the street as Jesse slipped the phone back in his shorts.

"Mornin', boss. How goes it?"

"It goes, little lady. How about yourself? All ready for the big season, I see."

"December first through January second, I embrace my true lineage." Tammi bobbled her head, jingling the shiny bells at the end of her red and green elf cap. "And check these out," she said, swirling her tiny feet bedecked in green pointy elf shoes covered in red bells and silver garland.

Amused, Jesse said, "We're gonna hear you coming a mile away."

"That's kinda the point. I'm so short, I tend to be overlooked in a throng of tourists. Especially the big Christmas crowd."

"Well, not this year," Jesse said, smiling.

"Have you seen our handiwork from last night?"

Jesse shook his head. "Haven't been inside yet. You get any sleep last night?"

Tammi waved her hand dismissively. "Enough. I'm off after lunch anyway. Plenty of time to sleep before the big reveal tonight." The bodiless jingle of bells in the dark recesses of the bar made Jesse chuckle in spite of himself.

"Ready, boss? Three, two, one . . ." The thunk of the breaker switch gave way to a winter wonderland of bright lights, multi-colored metallic garland and silvery icicles everywhere the eye could see. Large, sparkly ornaments hung at different intervals from the ceiling. Even in the morning light, the effect was magical. Tonight was going to be astounding.

"I've always loved Christmas," Jesse said.

"I do now," Tammi said from behind the bar. The rich aroma of freshly brewed coffee began to fill Jesse's nose as Tammi readied the bar for the morning crowd.

Raj arrived, his smile beaming like a lighthouse, braids swinging with each step.

"Merry Christmas, mi bredren. How ya stay this fine day?"

"Fine as a frog's fart, Raj," Tammi said. "How come you look like the cat with the canary this mornin'?

Raj waved his cell phone in the air. "Ah, Christmas playlist, people! Time to get in the spirit!

"Excellent, Raj. Go ahead and bluetooth it to the sound system," Jesse waved toward the back office. Let's get the blood flowing this beautiful morning."

"True dat, boss. I'm on it."

While Tammi stacked clean Solo cups in holiday colors, Jesse backed into the street and looked up at the facade of the long-established bar. The hand carved, custom teak and walnut sign would look perfect in the length above the doors. What better time than the holidays to usher in a new era? It had been nearly three years. It was time.

"Boss, handsome dude at three o'clock. Just sayin'."

Jesse looked to his right to see Taylor approaching from the south end of the street, two lattes in hand.

"Well, aren't you a sight for sore eyes?" Jesse took his coffee and leaned in for a kiss from his husband.

Taylor patted Jesse's behind and grinned. "Those eyes of yours wouldn't be so sore if you'd close 'em every now and then. What'd you get, four hours last night?"

"Closer to five. I'm fine, honey. Just excited."

Taylor ran his hands through Jesse's hair, stopping at the back of his head to grab a handful. He leaned in to meet Jesse's freckled forehead and kissed the tip of his nose.

"I know, love. This is very special. Can't wait to see the new sign, too."

"In about an hour. Stick around if you don't have any client meetings."

"Nope, I'm all yours this morning. Allison's taking the early one up in Islamorada. She promises to be back for the unveiling."

"She'd better. None of this would be possible without her."

Taylor walked into the bar and gasped. "It's like a Christmas faerie land in here! Tammi, you do this yourself?"

"With a little bit of elf dust, dimples." Tammi's gravelly giggle blended with the tinkling of the bells on her jaunty hat.

"You, my dear," Taylor said, kissing her hand, "are precious."

"Flattery will get you everywhere, mister. Come check out the wall of shame. I don't think you've seen it since it's been updated."

Taylor followed Tammi past the brand new barstools pushed under weathered teak bars scattered throughout the space to the back hallway where dozens of yellowing photos and hundreds of dollar bills were stapled to the pocked wood paneling. They'd promised Allison never to change the wall. Passing many old photos of Louie Johnson and his scantily clad servers with various celebrities and interesting island characters from back in the day, they reached a newer section on the back wall. There in summer wedding garb were assorted photos of Kimberly, JT, and everyone they loved from the week they'd found each other again and joined their lives. Taylor reached up and touched a profile shot of Kimberly, a sunset behind her surrounded by nothing but waves, a candid from their honeymoon boat trip.

"Even at the end of her life, love shined from within that woman. She's sorely missed," Taylor said.

Tammi looked up into his eyes. "She would have been so proud of all of y'all." He squeezed the petite woman's leathered hand. A reggae version of "Oh Holy Night" rang out through the speakers. Taylor bounced to the syncopated rhythm, twirling Tammi as they made their way back to the bar at the front of the club.

"Nice choice, Raj, my man."

The ebullient bartender grinned, his shoulders grooving. "Told ya, right? Got hundreds of jams on this playlist. Jammin' for all da people today!"

Taylor approached Jesse at the bar as he returned his phone to his pocket and began unloading a box filled with custom coasters and napkins. He held them aloft.

"Whadda ya think?"

The image on the coaster was a caricature from a photo of Kim and Allison in their Navy days wearing flight suits, arms around each other's shoulders, holding bottles of beer, bent over in a tearful belly laugh.

"Dude, full on grin every time I see that."

"I know, right?"

The new name of the third location owned by business partners

Tom Harding and Jesse Stevens, the one that would be revealed tonight on the new sign, the staff's new tank tops, and all the paraphernalia and merchandise throughout the bar would surely have made Kimberly smile every time she saw it, too.

Jesse's phone rang a third time.

"Hey, Brie, what's up? You on your way down?" He listened to his sister, nodding along as she filled him in. "Okay, cool. See you then." He rang off. "Sabrina and Grey'll be here in a couple of hours. She says she hasn't been able to reach Dad. I haven't been able to either."

"You focus on your big reveal. I'll see if I can locate Jack." Taylor stepped outside and around the corner away from the thumping reggae. He tapped his father-in-law's phone number but it transferred immediately to voicemail. "Hmm," Taylor said, pocketing his phone.

"Hey, bro. Beautiful mornin' ain't it?"

Taylor looked up to see backward ball cap wearing JT ambling down the sidewalk in aviators and board shorts, a box of donuts in one hand, his long legs in full stride.

"Indeed it is." Taylor hooked thumbs with JT, grasped his hand and leaned in for a one-armed hug. "Gotta love the end of hurricane season."

"Amen to that one, sir. Brought breakfast. Jess inside?"

"He is. He'll appreciate the grub and an extra pair of hands. Wait till you see the new gear."

"Oh yeah, I can't wait. He wouldn't let me see or know anything in advance."

"I'll come with you. Can't wait to see your face."

JT and Taylor entered the bar, hearing "Little Drummer Boy" with an island beat. Placing the box of pastries on the bar, JT took off his aviators, looking all around at the shimmery splendor.

"Wow. Wasn't it just summer like yesterday? Tammi, it's like Disney World Christmas in here. Nicely done, girl."

"Why, thank you, Boots. Bang up job, if I do say so myself."

Jesse approached carrying a small paper gift bag and handed it to JT. "A little something to commemorate the unveiling tonight."

Reaching inside the bag, JT lifted out a longneck beer koozie, a black tank top, a black hoodie, and a framed image all emblazoned with the new logo. Kimberly and Allison's laughing caricatures over the bar's new name.

JT laughed out loud at the image. "Aw, man, this is perfect, Jess. She would have loved this."

Jesse clapped a hand on JT's shoulder and squeezed. "Happy to hear you say that, bro. And I hope you and Julie come here often. Consider it home."

JT looked at Tammi. "It's felt like home since the day I got here so long ago. Thanks, man. It means a lot."

Raj approached with chilled mudslide shots for the group, a lone shot of Jim Beam neat for JT. "It's a bit early, but it be island time, mon. To the two ladies."

"And those of us who love them," Jesse said. Shots were tossed and a hush fell over the group for a moment.

A couple of older gents in fishing gear approached eyeballing the decorations. "This place open? Holy hell, this ain't Louie's Watering Hole anymore."

Jesse clapped his hands and rubbed them together. "Good morning and welcome, gentlemen!"

"Yeah, I got these old salts, Boss," Tammi said. "Hector. Luis. Catch anything?" She nabbed a bottle of Jameson and a steaming pot of fresh brew. "It's past noon on the Emerald Isle—let's make those coffees Irish."

"Well, top o'the mornin' to ya, Tammi," said Hector, grinning.

"Aren't you just the cutest lil leprechaun?" Luis laughed. "I'm an *elf*, dumbass. Get your holidays straight."

"Annnnd, we're off to a rousing start," Jesse said.

Chapter Seventy — Allison

The morning sun shone in from the east as Allison headed north on US-1 for the hour and forty-five minute drive to Islamorada. She'd told Taylor, her new real estate partner, she'd be happy to take this morning's meeting with their client. One local brewery was attempting to buy the much larger facility of another brewery that was sadly going defunct. It was simply a matter of some contracts and a good faith deposit and they were done for today. Closing would take place in a couple of weeks.

To be honest, Allison loved time alone on the road. She'd gone from being somewhat of a loner to being surrounded by Kimberly's family and friends on a constant basis. While their concern and genuine care was very sweet, at times it got to be too much. Allison sought refuge in quiet nights on the beach or, her newly discovered passion—a long sail in the Gulf on her new Catalina 30 she'd christened Go Big, Grandma.

She'd also made some big decisions since Kimberly died. One was to sell the home she'd shared with her best friend for sixteen years. The value of her property had improved greatly and she was able to find an adorable two-bedroom cottage on the water with a dock for her boat.

Another was to sell Louie's Watering Hole to MTH Ventures, Inc. and Two Dudes Bar & Grill LLC. She knew she just didn't have the heart to invest the resources needed to bring the old pub up to code and freshen up the space. The old salty fishermen and local bar flies loved the dark, dank interior and the friendly, no-nonsense staff she had in place, but it was time to keep up with the times and attract new clientele while not alienating the regulars. Tom, Jesse, Taylor and Allison had multiple meetings and brainstorming sessions, and tonight she would see, like the rest of the island, what the incredible team had come up with for a fresh new look.

She just had to get this business meeting over with, maybe have a light lunch on the boat, then head to the west end for the unveiling. A wave of melancholy crashed into her heart.

"I wish you were here to see all of this, grandma. It's not gonna be the same christening the new bar without you. Miss you so much." She wiped a lone tear from the corner of her eye, cleared her throat, and steeled herself for the meeting as she swung into the parking lot, her tires crunching on shells.

Chapter Seventy-One — Jack

Lifting his buzzing phone from the nightstand, Jack opened one eye and saw that it was Sabrina. He laid it back down unanswered. If it was an emergency, she would follow the rejected call with a "911" text, as had been the family agreement ever since Kimberly had been found alive a few years ago. Was it only a few years? Sometimes it felt like a decade since her passing. Sometimes it felt like only yesterday. He frequently found himself wanting to call his eldest daughter to share news with her or just to see how she was feeling. The realization that she was gone was going to be like a stone in his chest for some time to come.

He could talk to Sabrina later at the bar. He didn't intend to miss the unveiling of what Jesse and Tom had done to revamp Allison's father's old bar. In fact, he might be persuaded to pull out his guitar and play a thing or two to keep the celebration going.

Jack buried his face in the fluffy white pillow and curled up under the blanket. Being retired had its perks, like no alarm clock and not having to answer your damn phone if you didn't feel like it.

He lifted his phone once more to check the weather app. Nothing but sunshine in the forecast on this first day of December. The Gulf waters were still fairly warm. Maybe a ride on the jet ski after lunch would be fun. He caught sight of the new, white gold band on his ring finger. Smiling, he wondered how long it would take to get used to the feeling of jewelry on his hand again after so much time. And how long it would take for the family to come around to the idea. Life with Marjorie had been far from a picnic and he knew his kids genuinely did want him to be happy. He only hoped the kids wouldn't resent their decision to keep their wedding intimate and private. Not that they didn't love their families, but at their age, it just felt right to do their own thing. They could always have a party later.

What was it Sabrina had said when she was younger? "It's easier to ask for forgiveness than permission." Yep, that was their adopted mantra. It would be put to use when they showed up a little late to the unveiling tonight, too.

Jack peeked under the covers to see his bride snoozing with most of her hair covering her face. He reached over and gently slid the silvery dark curtain away from her sleeping face. She opened her deep brown eyes and grinned.

"That tickles."

"Oh does it? Here, let me kiss it and make it better."

"Mmm, that sounds like heaven." She slid closer as Jack softly caressed her face, placing tender kisses all along her silky skin.

"Has it really only been three days?" Jack asked.

"Three whole days as your missus. Hopefully three more decades to come."

Jack kissed her forehead, her nose, her lips. "I can't imagine any days without you in them, my love."

She wrapped a strong, tanned arm around Jack's waist and raised up on one elbow, silk chemise sliding down her shoulder.

"As long as you feed me. I need nourishment. I'm starving."

Jack kissed her neck, her shoulder, her collarbone, her breast. "Just a few more minutes, okay? My heart can't take all this beauty before me."

She tipped back her head and laughed, a deep throaty sound Jack had come to crave—a sound that made his entire body respond in ways he hadn't cared about in many years.

Encircling her tightly in his arms, he whispered through her hair, "I'm so in love with you, Mrs. Stevens."

"What a coincidence. I'm absolutely crazy about you, Mr. Stevens."

It would be a bit longer till breakfast.

Chapter Seventy-Two — JT

JT frowned, depositing his phone into the pocket of his board shorts.

"Penny for your thoughts, Boots." Tammi handed him a chilled bottle of water. "I thought you were heading home before the grand reopening tonight?"

JT opened the bottle, taking a long, thirst-quenching drag. He lifted the bottle in salute. "Thanks for this. Yeah, I'm leaving. Just having trouble reaching anyone, that's all."

"Julie's at school, right? Isn't it finals week at The U?"

JT nodded. "It is. But she's usually johnny-on-the-spot with that phone of hers. Wears a dang Apple watch that buzzes so she never misses a notification." He shook his head. "Can't imagine being *that* attached to your phone."

"No way, Jose. They can keep all that mess. Everybody who knows me knows where to find me. If I ain't here at the bar, I'm on the beach or sleeping. Or a little bit of both." She winked. "Don't worry. That kid'll call you when she gets a minute. Talk about busy, though. Double major, fast track to her degree—I've never seen anyone hit school like a freight train before. That girl's got drive."

"She's on a mission, all right. Her mom would be so proud. Speaking of moms, I haven't been able to reach mine since last week. I think she went to my aunt's place in Dallas, but I thought that wasn't supposed to be until closer to Christmas. I also have a hunch she's been seeing some guy in Austin, too, but I can't prove it. Oh, what the hell. I'll reach 'em when I reach 'em. Thanks again for the water, Tammi."

"Anytime, dude. See you tonight."

JT made his way to the open, rolled-up doors. He lifted a hand toward Jesse and Taylor.

"Great job in here, fellas. See you at sundown."

As he made his way toward Blue Heaven for brunch, his mind was troubled. It wasn't like his daughter or his mother not to take his calls. Since losing his wife to cancer, JT found himself worrying about the other loves in his life. More than was reasonable, he supposed. They were grown women who didn't need him breathing down their necks.

He paused to allow one of the wild roosters to cross the sidewalk in front of him.

"Hey, why did the chicken cross the road?" he asked the rooster, laughing to himself. "Sorry, sir, I'm sure you've heard that one a million times. Shit, I'm losing it," he said, shaking his head.

Seated in the restaurant with his order placed and a steaming cup of joe in front of him, he was scrolling through the news on his phone when a call rang through from Julie.

"Well, there you are, book worm. How're finals going?"

"Great! I have so much to talk to you about, Dad. What time is the reveal tonight?"

"The plan is at sundown, so around 5:30."

"Cool. I'll meet you there."

"Your uncles are planning to have it catered with island favorites, so don't eat ahead of time."

"Food? At the bar? That's a first."

"Yeah, and probably a last, unless they decide to go all out and put in a commercial kitchen. I don't know. I think Jesse likes just having a watering hole down here as opposed to the full service places in Daytona and Fort Lauderdale."

"Okay, so I won't eat and I'll meet you there at sundown."

"Jules, it's a long drive. I know everyone will love seeing you, but don't you have to get back for finals? I'm sure they'll understand if you skip it."

"Don't worry about me, old man. I got this."

JT grinned. "Yeah, I'm sure you do. Okay, kiddo, see you tonight." Sipping his coffee, he wondered what he'd ever done to deserve her. He raised his mug in a solemn salute to the woman who should be by his side enjoying this life.

Chapter Seventy-Three — Julie

I can't wait to share all my news with my family tonight. I know it's my uncle's night and I don't want to steal his thunder, but I really don't know when we'll all be together again for a while.

So much has changed since my mom died. I've been so busy I haven't had a moment to sit and write. Here goes:

Jesse and Taylor bought a beautiful home in Jupiter near Carlin Park. I've only been there a couple of times, but the best was last year when they hosted Thanksgiving for the entire family. We all had breakfast every morning on the lanai to an amazing sunrise over the ocean. They really are living the dream. Their decision to buy Louie's from Auntie Allison was a win/win for everyone. Nobody knows better than my uncle Jesse how to run a bar. Allison can focus on her real estate business with Taylor, and she'll probably be able to retire soon and just sail that pretty boat she bought. She deserves it. After taking care of my mother for so long, that woman is a saint in my eyes.

My dad's been hired on as a contractor for Sikorsky and his biggest client is the US Navy. He travels all over the place instructing pilots and mechanics on every aspect of the H-60 helicopters. I don't see him all that much, but when I come down to his little place in Key West, we have a blast together. He bought us jet skis and he's teaching me how to ride his new motorcycle. He seems happiest when he's busy. During quiet times on the island, I catch him drifting off somewhere in his mind, miles away. I know he misses Mom. Someday he'll be ready to move on. Meanwhile, I just squeeze his hand and respect the silence. I think it's enough.

Aunt Brie and Uncle Grey are finally in a good place again. Things were super rocky after my mom resurfaced and we found out Uncle Grey had sorta been in on her disappearance all along. I say sorta because he legit didn't know if she was still alive until my birthday.

But anyway, those two nearly split up. You don't want to cross my aunt Sabrina. She's a no-bullshit kind of woman. I kinda think that runs in the family. Anyway, when I moved out of the condo to go to school, they rescued a litter of three kittens! It was only supposed to be one little girl, but they met her brother and sister and fell in love. You should see Grey with the girls, and the little boy follows Brie around like a shadow. So, now they are the crazy cat people in a bougie high rise condo. Cracks me up. As long as they're happy.

Grandpa is really enjoying his retirement. He sold the house in Clearwater and bought an enormous RV. He loves the fact that he can take his house on wheels anywhere in the continental US. He's been traveling all over the country performing in little bars, visiting state parks, and checking all kinds of things off his bucket list. When the bug hits him to leave the country, he parks the behemoth at Uncle Jesse's and hops a flight out of the Fort Lauderdale airport. A couple years ago, he got a wild idea to go to SXSW in Austin and he's been going back annually ever since. I told him there are other festivals across the country, but he seems really drawn to this one. He's definitely enjoying himself. Such a cool dude.

And as for me? Well, my focus completely shifted. Let's just say the time spent on the Aqua Luna totally changed my life.

Chapter Seventy-Four — Two Sailors

A golden glow filled the sky as the sun set over the Gulf of Mexico. Signs on the closed hurricane doors and a sandwich board on the sidewalk read:

CLOSED FOR PRIVATE PARTY - REOPENING TO THE PUBLIC AT 8:00 PM

A cloth tarp covered the custom wooden sign above the doors with ropes hanging down either side. Jesse and Tom stood by the ropes, glasses of champagne in hand. The folks in the crowd before them each held a plastic flute of bubbly, wearing excited grins. A crowd of curious tourists began to gather across the street.

Julie's Apple watch buzzed.
Running late. Be there asap. Promise!

She smiled and sipped her champagne.

"Friends and family, welcome to the unveiling of the reimagined, best little watering hole on Key West," Jesse said. "I know a lot of you have fond memories of Louie and his beloved bar. From what I understand, he was quite a character."

"You can say that again!" Allison said, raising her flute. Dustin and Geno wrapped arms around her shoulders, hugging their pal.

"His incredible daughter has graciously allowed us to usher in the new age of the bar. We hope all of you will appreciate our vision. It's still your favorite little pub with a splash of pizzazz and a lot of spunk . .

. just like the women it's named for. Ladies and gentlemen, please give a rousing island welcome to Two Sailors—Key West!"

The ropes were tugged and the cloth fell to the ground, revealing the caricature and name carved into the long wooden sign illuminated from above and below. The crowd whooped and applauded.

Allison's hand flew to her mouth, tears welling in her eyes. "You guys…it's…I can't even. It's perfect." Jesse and Taylor gathered her in a warm embrace.

"So happy you approve, Alli."

Taylor kissed the top of her head. "There was no way we weren't naming this place after the most badass broads we know!"

"She would have loved it," Allison said. "And on her birthday, too!"

"That was the idea," Jesse said. "Tammi, Raj, let's open her up and have a party!"

The bartenders rolled up the middle door and locked it in place. The crowd gasped as they laid eyes on the sparkling holiday splendor inside.

"Holy Christmas, Batman!" Julie said.

"We plan on being *that* bar," Jesse said. "The one that goes nuts for each holiday. Themed drinks for the whole month, decorations and lights everywhere. Yeah, it's gonna be a blast."

Sabrina fist bumped her brother. "Nicely done, Jess! It's just marvelous in here. Kimmy would have gotten such a kick out of it."

"I wish she could have seen it, sister. Maybe her energy will grace us with her presence now and then."

"Oh, I think she's always here, brother."

"Speaking of being here, where the hell is Dad?"

Sabrina sighed and rolled her eyes. "Beats the hell outta me. I know he planned to bring the RV down here but I haven't been able to reach him in days."

"I hope nothing has happened . . ."

"No, no, I'm sure he's fine. He's not chained to his phone, that's for sure. And I didn't text 911, so he knows it's nothing urgent. I also know he wouldn't miss this. He'll be here."

***

After filling a plate with mini lobster rolls and conch fritters, JT wrapped an arm around his daughter's shoulders and hugged her to him. "Hey, cutie. It's good to lay eyes on my ridiculously busy daughter."

"You're one to talk, mister. Pensacola last week, DC before that, where are you off to next?" They stood at one of the new bars nibbling their food.

JT raised his palms. "Nowhere, I swear. I'm here for the holiday season. No more work until January. So, what should we plan? A sail to the Caribbean? A jaunt to jolly olde England?"

Julie grinned. "You wanna take a trip for Christmas this year?"

"I was thinking about it. It'd be fun. Just the two of us on a well-deserved rest. What do you think?"

"I think—Oh, Grandpa, there you are! And . . . Nana?" Confusion crossed Julie's face as Jack approached them with JT's mother, Ella, close behind.

"Mama?" JT said. "What are you—" As Jack and Ella drew closer, they could see the two of them were holding hands. Jack swirled Ella around to his side, beaming.

Seeing their father enter the bar, Sabrina and Jesse made their way over to their family.

"Hey, Dad, where've you been?"

"Yeah, I've been trying to call—"

Jack cleared his throat. "Kids, meet my new bride."

"Wait . . . what?" JT said.

Julie squealed and threw her arms around her grandparents. "Eeeee, you guys! So perfect! But how did this? I mean, how did you—"

Ella looked at Jack, then spoke in her rich, deep voice. "Well, it just kind of happened. We exchanged information when you and Kimberly got married, son. Jack came out to South by Southwest in Austin a couple of years ago and looked me up. We met up for dinner, got to talking, and we realized we really enjoyed each other's company."

"I've been scooping Ella up whenever I'm in Texas and taking her on gigs with me when she can get away from the hospital. We've been dating for over two years now and, well, we decided it was time to make the commitment."

Ella placed a hand on JT's shoulder. "Now, Jason, before you get upset with me for keeping secrets, let me tell you I wrestled with telling you over and over. I just decided that until Jack and I made it official and legal, I didn't feel it was right to say anything to anyone. It was a very private courtship. I hope you understand."

"Mama, I just—"

"JT, I want you to know that we did not come to this decision lightly. I love your mother very deeply. She is exactly what I've been missing in my life. She's incredible and warm and intelligent and kind . . . I can see why you're such a terrific man, having been raised by someone like Ella. And I promise you, I'll take such good care of her for the rest of our lives." Jack extended his hand.

The family stood still as though holding a collective breath. Sabrina's hands were clasped at her face, hiding a grin. Jesse and Taylor stood, arms at each other's waists.

JT took Jack's hand, squeezing just a bit too hard. "Sir, it's an honor. I'd say welcome to the family, but . . . ." Jack's face split into a wide smile as he threw his arm around JT's neck. The family shouted for joy and embraced the brand new couple.

Tom approached from behind. "Are congratulations in order over here?"

Jesse turned to meet his business partner. "Indeed, Tom. Our widowed parents have gotten hitched."

"Tammi?" Tom called out. "Another bottle of champagne over here, please."

"You got it, Big Boss."

***

Julie checked her watch again. 6:30 pm. No new messages. She swept her hair up into a high ponytail and crossed the room to where JT was chatting with Kat and Luci about his new Harley Davidson.

"Hey there, pretty lady," Kat said. "How's school going?"

"Hey, Kat," Julie said, leaning in for a hug. "Everything's great. Thanks for asking. Mind if I steal my dad away for a minute?"

JT and Julie stepped toward a quiet area of the bar, taking seats at a high top table.

"What's on your mind, girlie?"

"Dad, I've been waiting all night to tell you my news." She took a swig from a bottle of water and grasped his hands."I earned my Bachelor's early—at the end of May."

"Already? Why didn't you tell me?"

"I didn't tell anybody. I didn't take part in the ceremony so nobody got announcements. Because I had a plan."

"Oh yeah? But you mentioned you were taking classes this summer, didn't you? Or have I completely lost it?"

"Sort of. I'd been studying and I took the LSAT. Dad, I passed my first try. I got accepted into the School of Law at The U. I started in September and just finished the first half of year one toward my JD."

"Law? Really? Congratulations, kiddo, I'm so happy for you!" He squeezed her hand. "But why the pivot from medicine?"

Julie fidgeted with nervous excitement. "Do you remember the conversation we had that night with Mom on the boat? When she told us about military sexual assault?"

"Yes, of course, sadly."

"I've decided I'm going to pick up the fight where she left off. But I'm going to do it from the inside."

"Meaning...?"

"As soon as I graduate law school, I'm applying to OCS. In the Navy. I'm going to make it my mission to defend the women who have been voiceless. I'm going to bust my ass to change the way things are handled. Nobody should have to suffer in silence. I want victims to know that they are heard. And I want to do everything in my power to get them justice until, hopefully one day, my services are no longer needed. That's my goal, Dad."

JT sat back in his chair. He blew out a deep breath and smiled.

"Well, my word. I am sitting here in awe of my daughter. Girl, I'm ... speechless. No wonder you've been so 'busy' every time I try to call. You literally were." He stood and wrapped his arms tightly around his daughter. "Your mother would be so proud. I have absolutely no doubt that you'll make a difference. Good on ya, Juliana."

As they pulled away from each other, a voice came from near the bar.

"Julie! Jules! I'm here!"

Julie turned to see Vedette running toward them, her long black hair flying. Julie grinned and opened her arms. Breathless, Vedette hugged her tightly and said, "So sorry I'm late!"

"No worries at all. Dad, you remember my—"

"Your roommate, yes. Hi, Vedette, it's so good to see you again." As they sat back down at the table, JT asked, "Are you still working on the yacht?"

"Oh, the yacht! No, I only did that for a short time."

"Dad, Vedette is back in school. She was accepted into the PhD program at the Rosenstiel School at The U. She's gonna be a doctor of marine biology."

"Well, color me impressed. Look at the two of you bootstrappers, holy hell."

"What can I say, Dad? It's in my blood," Julie said with a wink. Vedette clasped Julie's hands on top of the table. Matching antique bands with deep star moonstone gems glinted under the twinkling lights.

A dawning grin spread across JT's face. "Any other secrets you want to share?" He chuckled.

The young women looked at each other and smiled. Julie said, "She's my rock, Dad. She's been with me through everything these past three years and motivated me beyond what I thought was possible."

"We motivated each other, Mr. Allen. She's my partner and best friend. I love her," Vedette said, beaming.

"No wedding bells yet, though, old man. We have a lot left to accomplish. But we'll do it at each other's sides."

JT stood and squeezed his daughter's shoulders. "Little girl, there's nothing you *can't* accomplish with real love in your corner." He winked at Vedette. "I think this calls for some champagne. Be right back."

As he walked away from the table, emotion overwhelmed him. The news from both his mother and daughter washed over him like a wave, smoothing all the rough edges. Any worry or concern he'd had for them melted away.

Bypassing the bar, JT stepped outside and ran his hands through his hair. The sun had nearly set over the choppy winter waters of the Gulf of Mexico. Feeling for the emerald ring resting against his chest once again, he closed his eyes and lifted his face to the sky.

"Happy Birthday, girlie," he said, and a soft rain began to fall.

The End

Resources for survivors of military sexual trauma:

- NSVRC - National Sexual Violence Resource Center - www.nsvrc.org
- VA's Healthcare Services for MST - www.mentalhealth.va.gov/mst
- RAINN's National Sexual Assault Hotline - www.rainn.org (DOD Safe Helpline 877-995-5247—call 24/7 from anywhere in the world
- Protect Our Defenders - www.protectourdefenders.com

THANKS TO:

Kelly Harms, Julie Cantrell, and Kerry Lonsdale for handing me the keys to the queendom

Megan McKeever—the maven of continuity and clarity who made the book infinitely better

Johnny Shaw—my favorite smartass novelist with the most giant heart

Suzanne Guillette for holding the heart of a long distance (not so) stranger, and invaluable guidance

Jodi Picoult for decades of inspiration, a feisty spirit of truth, and genuine kindness and support—thank you for *always* answering texts, emails, dm's—you walk the walk, Wonder Woman

Donel for beaches, wine, belly laughs, honesty, perspective, and all the love always

Dana for bursts of energy at always the right time, amazing dinners, and the biggest smiles ever

Monalisa for being my final (and favorite) reader—and Phil—part two was born at your secret hideaway

Cindy for steadfast faith in the real me especially when I was empty— you're the epitome of authenticity

Trace for just about everything—so, so, so glad you were born

Kath for music, motivation, the lifelong vault, and all the fun stuff ever

Bethany for honest love, the truest heart, and the brightest, light-up-a-room smile

Kristie for being a role model in confidence and truth

Bobby for your devotion and brattiness—don't ever change

Candi—my muse, my inspiration—I still hear you belly laughing

Liz for giving a shit and having the right words at the right time, always

Vince for being the brother I would choose—your support buoyed me

Pat & Shell for selfless and absolutely hilarious love

Lloyd for honesty and friendship, and the bonus of sharing DNA

Lisita for love, truth, sisterhood and so many uses for eff words

DJ for renting headspace and showing up now and then to air out the curtains

Heidi for the non-bullshit, tough love, and super fun, random visits — we're long overdue

The Ohio & PA Knakes for unwavering support

Mom for living and loving and always knowing, your friendship was my cornerstone

Momma for life and roses, the brightest blue eyes and the best giggles

Dad for making each one of us feel like your favorite (even though I know it was me)—miss you so much it hurts

Ashley, Bella, Celena, Tally, Landry, Diana, Leia, and Winterfell—Best. Furballs. Ever.

All my nieces and nephews—I'll may not be the coolest aunt, but I'll always love you most (okay, I might be the coolest)

To my Navy brothers and sisters—You have no idea what you gave and continue to give to this woman, this country, our humanity. With gratitude, I honor you

Austin for loving and giving and caring with your whole heart—and for being my son

Jacqui for feeties, ringlets, lullabies, road trips, laughter, tears, and oh so many snuggles—I gave you my heart, you gave it wings

Jim, my partner—for listening—for being MH, my granite, my galaxy, my breath — it was always you.

www.ingramcontent.com/pod-product-compliance
Lightning Source LLC
Chambersburg PA
CBHW021843010726
47493CB00005B/1527